'The Reward of Time'

A Third Novel by David Lawrence

The Continuation from 'The Dawn of Togetherness'

authors
On Line

Visit us online at www.authorsonline.co.uk

An Authors OnLine Book

Copyright © Authors OnLine Ltd 2007

Text Copyright © David Lawrence 2007

Cover design by David Lawrence and James Fitt ©

All rights reserved. No part of this publication may be reproduced, stored in a retrieval system, or transmitted in any form or by any means, electronic, mechanical, photocopy, recording or otherwise, without prior written permission of the copyright owner. Nor can it be circulated in any form of binding or cover other than that in which it is published and without similar condition including this condition being imposed on a subsequent purchaser.

ISBN 0 7552 0272 4
ISBN 978-0-755202-72-0

Authors OnLine Ltd
19 The Cinques
Gamlingay, Sandy
Bedfordshire SG19 3NU
England

This book is also available in e-book format, details of which are available at
www.authorsonline.co.uk

To Mike and Janice

'The Reward of Time'

'Sometimes the lessons are harder to teach rather than learn'

Best Wishes

David

'The Reward of Time'

Contents

Beginnings	1
A day in court	2
Evening and news	23
Christmas at the mansion	35
A new start	39
A visit from Stavros	59
A new day	67
A visit to the past	112
A question from the law	123
Morning and a fresh start	135
A meeting with Alex	143
The garage	156
Time and people, closing in!	170
A house and its captives!	184
Louise's doubt	202
The Reward of Time	206

'The Reward of Time'

Sometimes

Sometimes, when we love someone, they do not hear
Sometimes, that love is not requited
But, even unrequited love
Deserves a reward, Sometimes

Chapter One

Beginnings

"Now Andrew, I want you to tell me more about yourself, well let's say Louise and the past few months, you know, what you had both been doing!"

"But what good is it going to do?" I started, and I went on "I can't remember a bloody thing that's happened in the past two weeks, so what good is the last six months or so going to do?" I questioned the person who had asked me to recall my past, that person being a therapist called Stuart Thomas, the consultant at the hospital had recommended that I see him. I'd been suffering from some form of amnesia since I'd been found wandering in Chillingston Woods a few days ago.

"Well, Andrew. Yesterday we covered the meeting you and Louise had in Smiths some time ago, and right up to the attempted kidnap of you..." he began only for me to cut him short.

"And what bloody good did that do?" I angrily asked banging my fist on the coffee table in front of me at the same time.

"You must try to relax yourself Andrew, it won't help matters if you're over excited," Stuart said, his voice controlled and composed. He continued, "If you can talk me through the most recent past, say the months after the court case, then it may well trigger something in these preceding weeks, some thought that we may be able to expand upon, that in turn may help you to recall what has happened to you," the mild mannered Stuart said, his voice firm, but not condescending.

I held my head in my hands, at the same time I closed my eyes as if I were gazing at the back of my eyelids, would this help me recall the recent past?

"Can you cast your mind back to the day of the court case, you know in Bristol?" Stuart again asked.

"Yes I think I can, but that's not the problem, it's what has happened in these last few weeks that is bothering me," I once again began to reply, almost in a protesting form.

"Try and explain it as you did yesterday, as if you'd written it down in your diary." he paused, I lifted my head and looked across at Stuart, he had an astute memory, recalling from the day before that I kept a daily record of events, then he continued "you did tell me that you keep a diary, didn't you?" he finished with a question.

"Yes," I started to say, and then something else occurred to me, I hadn't done any writing for a little while, but this prompt gave me the impetus I needed to gather my thoughts, so I continued.

Chapter Two

A day in court

Well, it was late November and that found Louise and myself sat in the corridor of Bristol Crown Court, the Number One Court to be precise, and the reason for this visit to one of the highest of judicial establishments in the land was the trial of Louise's former father-in-law, Len Shaw and his nephew, Mark Shaw.

I have to confess to feeling very nervous, this was to be the first time I had faced either of these men since my abduction by the two bungling fools back in August, but I still feared the anger that Len was able to project across a room, all the same I was expected to give evidence, after all it was a case the crown had brought against them regarding my failed kidnap. My mind was running over the past, it still seemed as clear as the day it had taken place, from being forced into the back of Len's dirty, smelly van to the moment I was given the opportunity to escape.

"Come along darling, they've called your name!" It was the voice of Louise that snapped me out of my reminiscent state, and instantly taking my hand also giving it a gentle squeeze.

"Yes of course," I immediately replied, at the same time attempting to stand, as I did, so did Louise, I looked directly into her eyes, they were full of that confidence, a gentle kiss on the side of my face and I was ready to go into the court, and she was to give me more words, words of reassurance spoken softly and calmly as only she could.

"Now just remember to stay focussed, think of what Mr Robin-Palmer told you!" I just returned her look. Mr Robin-Palmer was the barrister in charge of the prosecution, and he had briefed the both of us fully on what we were to say, 'answer the questions precisely, giving as much detail as possible, and don't be drawn into lengthy conversations'.

Advice easily taken in when sat in his chambers in the company of our solicitor, I say our solicitor because Louise was also expected to give evidence, and she too would be required to relay her account of the morning in August, when I set off for my run from the Cornish residence we owned. She was also expected to travel to London later in the week, that need was to give evidence at the trial of Delphine Jarman, the sister of Daphne Belington, for it was Delphine who was the mastermind behind the drug running operation, also the former lover of Gary, Louise's ex-husband. But all the advice in the world doesn't really prepare you to go into court and face your accused.

"Are you ready Mr Jackson?" a voice asked by the side of me. I turned to my left and standing with his black cape flapping just slightly was one of the court ushers, his left hand on the door handle of the court doors, his right hand came offering some guidance, then he spoke again. "I'll lead you to the witness stand."

Louise leant forward and kissed me on the cheek, then her own words of reassurance, "it will soon be over and done with…" she paused and with one more kiss finally said, "good luck."

As I walked in through the doors I felt as if the eyes of the entire courtroom were on me, and to be truthful they were, I felt extremely nervous, this wasn't the first time I'd been in a court of law, no, I had spent several months in and out of court rooms at the time I was having my inheritance proved, both in this country and of course America, but they were civil courts, and the difference now being that this was a criminal case, brought by the crown on my behalf against the two men who had abducted me in the Cornish lane.

The usher escorted me to the witness stand, once stood behind the oak surrounds of this almost pulpit feature he passed me the Bible along with a copy of the oath. Before reciting the words on the card I was now holding in my left hand, the Bible being firmly gripped in my right, I cleared my throat, at the same time lifted my head up so my voice would be projected fully into what seemed like a packed courtroom.

Once the task of swearing my oath was out of the way, the usher took the Bible and card from me, this gave me the opportunity to look around the room, instantly my eyes came into contact with Len, his stare was as menacing as on the other occasions we'd met, but today he looked clean and tidy, his hair was as short as normal, but he'd had a shave and was wearing a light blue suit, he looked well, prison life must be good for him I began to think to myself, sitting next to him was Mark, his nephew and accomplice in my kidnap, his appearance was much the same as his uncle's, I scanned my way around the rest of the room, I didn't spot any one that I instantly recognised, one more sweep with my eyes, it was then that I caught Len mouth the words 'you bastard'.

Quickly I focused in front of myself, there, getting up from his seated position was the barrister acting for the crown, the prosecution, as Mr Robin-Palmer approached the witness stand he smiled, and then when he was about six feet away he greeted me in his customary manner.

"Good morning Mr Jackson," his words eloquently spoken.

"Good morning," I replied, all the time maintaining eye contact with him.

"Mr Jackson, for the benefit of the court would you please confirm your personal details," he paused then added, "your name and occupation."

"Indeed," I started to reply, continuing "I am Andrew Jackson of Chillingston Manor, Chillingston in the county of Wiltshire." I finished, but I'd forgotten something that I was later to be picked up on.

"And your occupation Mr Jackson!" Mr Robin-Palmer asked, very firmly.

"I am joint owner of Jackson and Shaw Enterprises," I said in reply to the question.

"Would you please explain to the court what line of business you are involved in Mr Jackson," the barrister asked again looking directly into my eyes.

"Yes, I jointly own a chain of hotels in Scotland, and I am also part owner of a garage in Bristol," I told the court.

"Thank you Mr Jackson," was the barrister's response and he continued, "would you please describe to the court and members of the jury what took place on the morning of Monday 24th August this year," he paused cleared his own throat, apologised and went on, "in your own time Mr Jackson."

I went on to explain about the sporting challenge between my sons and myself, a run of the country lanes in Cornwall, the fact that I had set off on the run having been given a ten minute head start, and that after half an hour I had encountered the wrath of Len Shaw, not naming him, or his nephew Mark, on account of having been advised not to, just to say that two individuals had abducted me, before I had chance to continue Mr Robin-Palmer interrupted me with a question.

"Mr Jackson, do you recognise the individuals in question?"

"I do sir." I nervously replied still maintaining that look into his eyes, then he unnerved me a little with his next question, and forcing me to look again at the occupants sat in the dock.

"And can you point them out…" he paused at the same time spun round to look at the members of the jury, whist standing still he continued, his manner forceful and very firm, I wasn't in for an easy ride even from this man who was on my side. "Mr Jackson, please address you reply to his Lordship, the judge!"

I looked in the direction of the judge, a man in his late sixties, a pair of half rimmed wire glasses perched on the end of his nose, his black and crimson robes looked fresh and clean, his wig white, a new look to it.

"Continue Mr Jackson!" the judge said, his tone firm and forceful.

"The two men sat in the dock are responsible for my abduction!" I replied equally as firmly as I had been spoken to, at the same time looking in the direction of Len and Mark, then turning to look at his lordship again.

"Thank you Mr Jackson," the judge retorted, again looking at me over his glasses, he then seemed to scribble frantically on a piece of paper, or it may have been a notepad.

"And am I correct Mr Jackson in saying that these two individuals, namely, Leonard Shaw and his nephew Mark Shaw bundled you into the back of their blue transit van?" Mr Robin-Palmer asked.

"That is correct sir," I replied again looking in the direction of the judge.

"Right," Mr Robin-Palmer began and turning to look at the jury again he continued, "once you were in the back of the vehicle did either of the accused tell you why they had abducted you...?" he paused and looked back in my direction adding, "did either of them mention a ransom?"

"No sir!" was my sharp reply looking in the direction of the jury this time.

"Did they speak of anyone else, Mr Jackson?" he asked.

"We had very little conversation, but Len Shaw did mention someone by the name of Dee!" I replied.

"Now Mr Jackson, did you at the time of your abduction know of anyone by the name of Dee?" Mr Robin-Palmer asked looking at Len and Mark as he delivered the question.

"No sir, at the time I was unaware of anyone by the name of Dee!" I replied.

"But you do now know that individual in question?" he asked, that firmness back in his voice. Then he took a change of tack, relaxing his look upon myself he began to address the jury and from time to time looking in the direction of the judge. "Ladies and gentlemen of the jury, your Lordship, for legal reasons we are not allowed to name the individual in question, the reason being that this person has just started a court appearance in connection with another matter, so for the time being I will..." he paused and looked in the direction of the defence team sat a few yards away from my solicitor, then he continued, "my learned friend will be keeping to the same legal undertakings, we will be referring to this person by the name of Dee!" He was once again looking at myself awaiting a reply to his earlier question, the defence team had nodded their approval to his statement.

"I do know the person in question now sir," I said resting my hands on the oak top of the surround in front of me.

"Forgive me Mr Jackson," the barrister began, and his next question was to catch me unawares slightly, "if I might just take you back to your occupation, what was it you said you did for a living?"

"Well," I began trying to recall what I had said only a few minutes ago, as it came back to me I continued, "I'm joint owner of a hotel chain in Scotland, I also have some financial interests in a garage in Bristol that my sons manage."

"And just to refresh the memories of the members of the jury, could you tell us the name of your company?"

"Yes," I began unsure of where this line of questioning was going, I hadn't been briefed about this style, all the same I continued, "the name of the company is Jackson and Shaw Enterprises."

"Thank you Mr Jackson," Mr Robin-Palmer began, then looking once again at the jury he continued, "now ladies and gentlemen of the jury, you may well have noticed a connection between the name Shaw," he looked in the direction of Len and Mark, then carried on, "between the Shaw in Mr

Jackson's company name and the two gentlemen sat in the dock," turning to look at myself again he asked, "Mr Jackson would you be kind enough to elaborate upon the connection?"

"Yes sir," I started to reply only to be cut short by Len, all of this must have been too much for him and despite his clean and tidy appearance he soon reverted to type.

"He don't have to tell you nothing..." Len angrily shouted across the court room to me, and he continued, "she was my daughter in law..." his words died away as the judge brought his gavel down with considerable force.

"Mr Shaw!" the judge began. his tone unwavering, I looked in his direction, now he'd removed his glasses and was almost glaring at Len, then he spoke again, "I will not tolerate any sudden and unnecessary outbursts in my court!" and the judge finished with a question, "do I make myself clear Mr Shaw?"

"Yes sir," was the mumbled reply from Len, now covering his mouth with his right hand, but he was still glaring in my direction.

"Please continue Mr Jackson," the judge instructed, now looking at myself.

"Well," I began, unsure if I should mention Len by name, but then he had in his own way enlightened the jury to the connection between himself and Louise, so I continued, "as you have just heard, Mr Shaw was related to my business partner, Mrs Louise Shaw through marriage, Louise was married to Mr Shaw's son, Gary."

"And now he's dead, and that bitch and him had something to do with Gary being killed!" Len screamed across the court from the dock, now he was on his feet, his hands waving in front of him in my direction.

"Mr Shaw!" the judge's voice pounded across the courtroom, looking straight at Len he continued, "I obviously didn't make myself clear a few moments ago, if you refuse to do as I have instructed then I shall have you removed from the court, do I now make myself clear?" with those words the judge looked in the direction of the defence team, and he spoke again, "I suggest Mr Parkinson that you have a word with your client with regard to the correct way to behave in a court of law."

"I will indeed your Lordship," the Council for the Defence replied, at the same time looking towards Len and Mark, but in fairness to Mark he was completely innocent of any wrong doings in the court.

"Mr Jackson," the judge began, looking at me again he continued, "how long have you known Mrs Shaw?"

"Over ten years your Lordship," I nervously replied, and the judge had another question for me.

"Have you been in a relationship for that period of time, I mean with Mrs Shaw?"

"No sir, we have been business partners for just over a year now," I told the judge.

"But Mr Jackson, you do have a more intimate relationship with this lady, don't you?" he asked.

"I do now sir," was my instant answer.

"How long have you been in this relationship?" Just a touch of frustration in his words now.

"Well we renewed our friendship approximately two and a half years ago," I said now looking towards the members of the jury.

"Thank you Mr Jackson," was the judge's reply and he continued, "do carry on Mr Robin-Palmer.

"Thank you your Lordship," the barrister said at the same time he stood in readiness to address myself, and he continued, "now Mr Jackson, going back to the day that you were abducted by these two men, I clearly remember you telling the members of the jury in graphic detail what happened, can you recall either of them saying what they were to do with you?" He finished and was awaiting my reply.

"The only comment I recall with regard to what was to happen to me was that this individual by the name of Dee would give them instructions as to what they had to do with me," I told him.

"So we've established that it was Len and Mark Shaw who bundled you into the back of their Transit van, and that they awaited instructions from a third party as to what had to be done with you," the barrister turned and again looked in the direction of the members of the jury, then spoke again, "Mr Jackson, could you please enlighten the members of the jury, and of course his Lordship as to how you managed to escape from your captors?"

I went on to explain in as much detail as I could the awful night I had spent in the back of Len's filthy van, how the rain had pounded on the roof for most of the night, the cramped conditions I was kept in, without any food and the way I had managed to escape the following morning, more by luck and Len's stupidity, but not using that word precisely, and how I managed to make it to the river, I was about to continue with details of the time I had spent in the disused plate-layers hut when Mr Robin-Palmer requested me to stop, with just a nod of his head.

"Thank you Mr Jackson," he said, at the same time indicating for me to sit down, I did as he suggested and he continued, "that your Lordship is the case for the prosecution, I have no further questions," he paused looked in the direction of the defence team and finished with a few more words, "no doubt my learned colleague will have some questions to ask."

"Mr Parkinson, would you like to start your cross examination now, or adjourn for lunch?" the judge asked, the question prompted me to look at my own watch, it was fast approaching mid-day.

"I will continue, if I may your Lordship," was the reply from the man I only knew as Mr Parkinson, he made his way around the dividing barrier and stood directly in front of me, I was by now standing again. He looked up at me before continuing, "good morning Mr Jackson," his tone light and his words spoken clearly, the greeting again prompted me to look at my watch, it was now eleven fifty five, still morning, I returned the greeting and as I did so I noticed his eye contact with me change, I should have guessed then that I was in for a hard time.

"Mr Jackson, would please be kind enough to repeat your name," Mr Parkinson asked, his glare now making me feel very uncomfortable, I glanced across at the prosecution team, Mr Robin-Palmer nodded his approval for me to continue.

"My name is Andrew Jackson," I said after clearing my throat, a little surprised by the question.

"Haven't you forgotten something Mr Jackson?" Mr Parkinson asked as he shuffled some paperwork in his hands, his eyes probing. Yes I'd forgotten something alright, my middle name.

"Of course, my second Christian name," I began to reply only for his stare to intensify so I continued, "I am Andrew David Jackson."

"Thank you Mr Jackson...," he paused so as to unnerve me a little more, and then he continued, "is it possible that you may have forgotten anything else?"

"No, everything is quite clear in my mind," I said just pausing to add, "it's not often I use my middle name."

"That's fine Mr Jackson, and now with my own mind reassured I will continue," he said, as I watched him look down at the paperwork he was holding in his left hand, he turned it over as he began to address the jury only turning his head to look at myself, he went on, "now I notice Mr Jackson that you are wearing glasses, something you seemed to have remembered to bring with you today..." his words drifted away as the barrister for the prosecution jumped to his feet.

"My lordship I don't see whether Mr Jackson has his spectacles or not has anything to do with the case!" Mr Robin-Palmer protested, Mr Parkinson returned to his seat.

"Mr Parkinson has this line of questioning any relevance?" the judge asked, again looking over his own half rimmed glasses.

"Indeed your Lordship, it has a great deal of importance to the case," the defence barrister replied having stood to answer the judge's question.

"Then please continue Mr Parkinson," was his Lordship's reply.

"Mr Jackson..." Mr Parkinson began again looking directly at me; he went on, "you say that on the morning of the 24th August the two accused bundled you into the back of their van, is that correct?"

"It is sir," I confidently replied to the question.

"Oh, by the way Mr Jackson, are you long-sighted, or short-sighted?" Mr Parkinson asked again catching me by surprise with the change of subject.

"I suffer from long-sightedness," I replied still somewhat puzzled by the question itself, but Mr Parkinson's reply was quite straight-forward.

"Thank you Mr Jackson, now can you tell me if you had your glasses on when you went for that run?" he asked, now a demanding look in his eyes.

"No, I didn't," I replied, a little frustration in my voice and in doing so falling into the trap that he had laid for me.

"Had you forgotten them?" Mr Parkinson sharply asked, and he sarcastically added, "like your name?"

"No sir, they were in my back-pack," I quickly retorted, remembering in my mind that Louise had placed them in one of the side pockets for safe keeping.

"But you are sure that it was the accused who abducted you?" the barrister asked.

"Yes sir I am sure!" I confidently replied.

"But you didn't have your glasses on, how can you be so sure?"

"Because after a little while Len, I mean Mr Shaw let me put them on," I said thinking that it may bring matters to an end.

"OK, now Mr Jackson, can you remember exactly what time it was when the alleged abduction took place?" Mr Parkinson asked.

"Well not exactly, as I have already stated, I didn't have my glasses on, but it was approximately half an hour after setting off from my Cornish home," I replied, still puzzled by the style of questioning.

"And what time did you set off for that run?" was the question in reply to my answer.

"About eight fifteen," I told the man now stood a few feet away from me and looking directly up at me.

"Thank you Mr Jackson," Mr Parkinson started to reply, and after looking in the direction of the jury continued, "but of course you can't remember exactly, as you didn't have your glasses on, or more likely you've forgotten!" He finished and once again was looking at me.

"No I haven't forgotten," I sharply replied falling into his trap.

"But, by your own admission Mr Jackson you've already said you can't be exact, come to that you seem to suffer from some form of amnesia; you'd forgotten your middle name this morning!" he paused, and could sense I was beginning to become a little rattled by his style of questioning, so as to unnerve me a little more he changed the subject and went on. "Right Mr Jackson, let's go back to that run, or was it a jog in that country lane," his words had a slightly sarcastic tone to them, and he continued, "can you remember seeing anyone else?"

I wasn't sure how I should answer this question, it had been agreed by both parties that Delphine's name wasn't to be mentioned in court, so I glanced at the prosecution team before attempting to reply, Mr Robin-Palmer nodded his head in approval of a reply, but would the defence barrister try and force the woman's name from me? I would have to pick my words very carefully in response to the question.

"Yes I did see someone else," I replied keeping it as brief as I could.

"And is that person in this court today Mr Jackson?" came the response to my answer.

"No sir!" I said, just a touch of frustration in my voice.

"But you weren't wearing your glasses, on the day in question, how can you be so sure?" Mr Parkinson asked sensing my irritation.

"My Lordship," Mr Robin-Palmer quickly said rising from his seat at the same time, he continued, "we did agree upon a point of law regarding the disclosure of the individual that Mr Jackson met in the lane."

"Indeed you are correct Mr Robin-Palmer," the judge began to reply, and having gained Mr Parkinson's attention he continued, "I do hope this line of questioning is leading in a positive direction and you're not trying to catch Mr Jackson out."

"I'm not your Lordship, I am still trying to establish the facts for the jury, your Lordship," was Mr Parkinson's reply.

"Then please continue Mr Parkinson," was the judge's somewhat frustrated response.

"Thank you your Lordship," Mr Parkinson said, as the prosecution barrister returned to his seat, he then continued, "Mr Jackson I put it to you that you didn't see anyone in the lane on that morning, other than Len and Mark, and I suggest Mr Jackson," he paused and looked in the direction of the jury indicating that he wanted their full attention, convinced he had it he continued, "that you wrote to Leonard Shaw, purporting to be this character 'Dee', indicating that Len should abduct you, and it was your sole intention to get them out of the way…"

"That's absolute rubbish!" I immediately replied, at the same time as I spoke I noticed some movement at the back of the court in the public gallery, as I focussed on the suddenness of the upheaval I saw Alex, his fawn Macintosh draped over his arm, his look was one of reassurance, but looking at Len I could see a smug grin on his face, this was his suggestion, that I had arranged everything.

"My Lordship, I must protest, this is the most preposterous allegation to make!" Mr Robin-Palmer proclaimed almost at the top of his voice, standing at the same time, he continued in a slightly more sombre manner, "to suggest that Mr Jackson organised the attempted abduction is outrageous, when we know full well that there was a third party involved in the entire affair!"

"Your objection is upheld Mr Robin-Palmer," his Lordship replied, then addressing the Defence Council he continued, "Mr Parkinson, please do not try to mislead and confuse the members of the jury, just try and ascertain the facts, after all it is The Crown which has brought the case against the accused on behalf of the victim!" His words were spoken with a considerable amount of authority leaving the defence team with no option but to change their style of questioning, or so I thought.

Suddenly one of the double doors below the public gallery opened and a man dressed in a dark grey suit entered, he looked in the direction of the judge, bowed his head slightly, I looked at his Lordship and noticed him nod his head, a sign of approval for the man to continue, he made his way in the direction of the defence team and passed one of the solicitors a piece of folded paper, just as Mr Parkinson was about to resume his questioning, a hush fell around the courtroom as the defence solicitor studied the note, then he passed it to Mr Parkinson.

"My Lord," Mr Parkinson began, now looking at the judge, still holding the paper in his hands he continued, his tone low and very respectful, "if it pleases your Lordship, may my learned friend and I consult you in the privacy of your chambers?"

I looked at the prosecution team their faces reflected my own bewilderment, what was going on? I asked myself.

"I think Mr Parkinson, Mr Robin-Palmer and ladies and gentlemen of the jury, that now would be an appropriate time for an adjournment," the judge paused to look at his watch, I did the same, it was twelve thirty, he continued, "I will see both parties in my chambers at one thirty..." he paused again and his attention was upon both teams, he continued with more words "I trust both of you will consult during the luncheon adjournment!" His closing statement, then he stood.

"All rise!" was heard to ring around the court room, then the shuffling of seats and feet on the wooden floor.

I looked in the direction of where Alex had been standing, he was still there, an open and expressionless look to his features, I would say he was as bemused as myself, that was along with the prosecution team, and it wasn't until I had made my way back out into the corridor and the waiting Louise that I was to find out what the note had contained, by then Alex was long gone.

"What's happened?" were the words that greeted me as I returned to the corridor and the waiting Louise, her smile as big as ever and as I approached her she put her arms out to embrace me, she continued to speak very softly in my ear as she held me, "is it lunch time?"

"Yes..." I paused for I didn't know what was going on and would have to wait for Mr Robin-Palmer to join us so as to enlighten the both of us, but I did continue, "the judge did call for a recess, not so much the judge more like that defence team, I'm very confused by it all Louise." I confided. I had no sooner said the words and Mr Robin-Palmer was at our side.

"Andrew, Louise," he began and taking us to one side he continued, "to be honest with the both of you I'm not sure where the case is going, I'll know more once Mr Parkinson and I have met in the judge's chambers after lunch, all I know at present is that the note had something to do with the trial of Delphine that also started this morning," He stopped then added, "I'll see the both of you back here in about an hour or so."

"Yes, OK." we both replied, Louise now as confused as myself.

We made our way out of the courts and in the direction of Corn Street, and the regular French market that takes place at least once a week at this time of the year, the smell of fresh garlic and onions hung in the air, there seemed to be every variety of cheese on display along with fresh fish and fine vegetables. The hour luncheon adjournment seemed like the longest hour of our lives, we casually wandered around the market stands, both of us repeatedly looking at our watches. By now we were standing outside of the Corn Exchange, and I was resting against one of the 'nails' that stand in front of the Corn Exchange, so called because of the dealings that took place here many years ago, hence the very old expression 'on the nail'.

"What do you think could have happened?" Louise asked at the same time squeezing my arm slightly.

"I don't know," I replied still very puzzled and somewhat despondent by the events of the morning in the court, I continued, "I do know that both of them gave me a very hard time," I paused, looking around for somewhere to go and rest our feet I continued, "let's see if we can get a coffee and a sandwich before we have to go back," I finished and as I did began to lead Louise towards a coffee shop that was tucked away down an alley to the side of the Corn Exchange.

Once inside we made ourselves comfortable at a small round table, I ordered some sandwiches and a pot of coffee for the two of us, then I went on to explain in every detail what I had been asked in the court, along with my reply to the questions.

"I'm sure it will soon be over," Louise told me in the most reassuring of ways, her eyes oozing that confidence, but I still felt unnerved by the style of questioning from both Mr Robin-Palmer along with that of Mr Parkinson, and to accuse me of instigating the whole affair was so outrageous it was almost beyond belief, the way things had been brought to a sudden halt had taken my mind off the unexpected sighting of Alex, so that was the question I put to Louise as she finished her second cup of coffee.

"Did you see Alex while you were waiting in the corridor?" I enquired as I picked up my own coffee cup; her expression instantly told me she hadn't.

"No Andrew I didn't!" her tone as astonished as her look and she continued, "when did you see him?"

"Just before we broke for lunch, he was standing at the back of the public gallery," I replied recalling Alex with his Macintosh draped over his right arm.

"He must have left the court via a different exit, are you sure it was Alex?" Louise said as she replaced her cup on the saucer and she continued with another question, "I wonder what he was doing in court?"

"I'm positive it was him, we made eye contact as I was being accused of instigating the whole affair," I began to reply to Louise, and I went on, "it was as if he was trying to tell me to keep calm." My words drifted away as I remembered that it was shortly after that exchange of eye contact that the morning's events were brought to a halt, but I still didn't connect the event of the note being handed to the defence team and Alex appearing in the court.

"Well perhaps we'll see him this afternoon," Louise said as she glanced at her watch and she added "I think we need to be making a move, just so we aren't late getting back."

"Yes I think we should," I replied taking Louise's coat off the back of her chair and holding it so she could slip her arms into the sleeves.

"Tell you what!" Louise began taking me by surprise, not only with her next statement but also her action as she came close after doing the buttons up on her coat and kissing me on the cheek she continued, "let's spend Christmas in Scotland, you know at the mansion, as we did last year..." she paused looked long and hard into my eyes, but I couldn't pick up any tell-tale signs of what was to come next, I was still recoiling from the sudden change of subject but this was one of her traits and she continued, "perhaps this year we can invite Jackie and the rest of the family, it's time you met her!"

My mouth had fallen open, we still had the afternoon to get through but Louise was making plans for Christmas. "Don't you think we need to get this hearing, and of course Delphine's trial out of the way before we start planning Christmas?" I enquired.

"Of course you're right darling," Louise started to reply as we headed towards the door of the café and once outside and stood in the flagstone lane she continued in her positive and forthright manner, "but we will need to plan for Christmas whatever happens..."she paused again looking down the road she continued to speak, "lets get a magazine so I have something to read this afternoon, I've finished reading the paper."

"OK," I replied and went on as we headed towards a newsagent's, "I'm sure you are right about Christmas, it just seems we have so many things going on in our lives, we hardly have time for a rest," I said as we walked back towards the courts, once Louise had picked up a copy of the *Country Life* magazine and paid for it. Back on Corn Street I continued, "Perhaps it's time we arranged to have some assistance, you know maybe a secretary."

"Andrew, that's the best idea you've had for a long time," Louise told me as we approached the steps to the court and as we entered through the large doors she went on, "I'm sure I know just the place to find the right person."

"I'm sure you do," I said recalling Louise's astute knowledge of these types of things, I was to be cut short by Mr Robin-Palmer greeting us as we approached the Number One Court.

"Mrs Shaw, Mr Jackson!" he began as he ushered us to a quiet corner, and then he continued, "stay here Andrew and Louise, I think I'll have some good news for the both of you when I return from the judge's chambers."

"But..." I started to ask desperately wondering what good news he could possible have for us, only for him to say that he would see us in a few minutes and for the time being he couldn't say any more, then with his black robe flapping as he spun round, a wedge of paperwork under his arm he was off down the corridor. I looked at my Louise; for once she was as taken aback as I was, a bemused and puzzled look upon her face. But she wasn't going to let the actions of Mr Robin-Palmer play upon her mind.

"Now where were we?" Louise asked as she sat down after unbuttoning her coat.

"Aren't you concerned about what's happening here?" I asked somewhat anxious by her casualness towards the situation we now found ourselves in.

"Andrew, as I've told you on other occasions, things will sort themselves out," she paused to gather her thoughts, and then continued, "now about this secretary, I'll start by looking in this *Country Life* magazine, sometimes they have people looking for work, you know advertising their services, if I don't have any luck there then I'll try some of the agencies."

I sat down beside Louise, there was no point in arguing with her, she had the organisational bit well and truly between her teeth, I wouldn't be able to dissuade her from these mental plans she was making. I glanced at the magazine she was holding, studying as best I could the advertisements, time was very slow to pass, so I got up and made my way to the window that looked out over a small courtyard, much to my amazement I saw Alex walking across it shaking his head in a manner of disagreement. I stood speechless for a few moments, unsure of what I should say, I glanced back at Louise, she was engrossed in making notes in her diary, but she did look up and caught my mesmerised state.

"What is it?" she asked as she got up from the seat and came towards me a concerned look upon her own face now.

"Alex is down in the courtyard," I replied as once again I looked out of the window, by now Alex was putting his coat on, his head still going from side to side, Louise was at my side and she looked down into the cobbled area.

"So it is. Do you think he could be a witness?" she asked after taking my arm, adding, "he doesn't appear to be very happy Andrew."

"I don't think so, it looks as if he's on his way," I said as we both watched Alex make his way out of the courtyard through some wrought iron gates that led into a narrow high walled lane.

I was about to remind Louise that I had seen Alex in the public gallery before lunch when I sensed the presence of another person close to us, turning I could see it was Mr Robin-Palmer, a very cheerful and a somewhat satisfied look etched upon his face.

"The good news Andrew is..." he paused and looked at Louise then added, "and it's good news for you as well Mrs Shaw, neither of you will have to appear in the witness stand any longer."

"Why?" we jointly asked, both of us completely surprised by his statement.

"Well, it seems that Delphine has changed her plea," he stood looking at our very puzzled expressions before continuing just holding the moment a little longer, then taking our arms and leading us towards the court doors he continued, "for some reason she has admitted the entire affair was her doing, that was at about ten thirty this morning, she changed her plea to guilty, and has also admitted organising your attempted kidnap Andrew," his words hung in the air, I'd spent nearly two hours in the witness stand giving evidence and I needn't have, now that brought a question from me.

"But how does it change this case?" I asked unsure if I should feel relieved or not.

"Mr Parkinson has persuaded Leonard and Mark Shaw to change their pleas to guilty, there's little point in them denying that they weren't involved, Delphine has named them saying that she hired them to kidnap you Andrew," Mr Robin-Palmer said, his words had a sincerity to them, but at the same time it made both Louise and myself question Delphine's motive for changing her plea.

"It seems a little strange that her case has come this far before she decided to admit her guilt," I said looking directly into Mr Robin-Palmer's eyes, they moved slightly in the direction of Louise before he replied.

"Well it would appear that she was told what sort of sentence she was likely to receive if she were to be found guilty by the jury," he paused and lowered his tone somewhat as he continued to speak, "she has offered to give information that will apprehend the rest of the network, and of course the local dealers…"

"And in return?" I began to ask, as I did I felt Louise grip my arm knowing what I was getting at I continued, "what's in it for her?" my eye contact firm and unwavering.

"There's every possibility Andrew, Louise that she'll receive a reduced sentence…" his words drifted away as he started to look in the opposite direction trying to avoid my intense glare, instantly I knew there was something Mr Robin-Palmer wasn't telling Louise and me.

"No there's more!" Louise promptly interjected.

"It seems…" Mr Robin-Palmer started to reply then leading us towards the corner he continued, "you must understand she will have put herself in a very vulnerable position by giving evidence against so many people, she may have to be protected for the rest of her life."

"She's done a deal, hasn't she?" Louise almost snapped back at Mr Robin-Palmer taking him by complete surprise.

"We don't like to refer to it in quite such terms," he sheepishly replied and he went on, "professionally it is called plea bargaining, Delphine will supply the prosecution team with information that the authorities can act upon, and in return, she kind of maintains her freedom."

"You mean to say that she will walk free from the court?" I angrily asked adding, "after what Louise went through to bring Delphine to justice, she gets away with it!"

"It won't be easy for her Andrew," was the start of Mr Robin-Palmer's reply pausing I noticed his expression change along with his words, "she will be monitored for the rest of her life, firstly so she doesn't have any threats made upon her life, she will have to have a new identity..." he was now cut short by Louise.

"But what's to stop her getting involved in the same business again, once the attention has died down, in a few years she could easily be operating the same style of enterprise," her words had their own forcefulness to them and that look was back in her eyes, peering, questioning right into Mr Robin-Palmer's soul, and the look was to make him think very carefully about his reply.

"As I have just said, she will be under surveillance for many years, everything she does will be carefully scrutinized, the people she meets, telephone calls and where she travels, I can assure you she won't be able to conduct any form of business without the authorities knowing about it," his own tone had now changed to one of forcefulness, but I'm afraid it was no match for Louise's manner, and I don't think he was prepared for her next question.

"And what if she should try another stunt like she did with Andrew, but maybe next time it won't be an adult; she might try something with my children!" Louise asked and now there was anger in her voice along with a touch of frustration.

"I can assure you that she will never be allowed to do any such thing, you must trust me!" he replied his own voice slightly raised.

"Excuse me Mr Robin-Palmer, but what about the two clowns standing in the dock at the moment? What sort of sentence will they receive for admitting their guilt?" I asked, feeling just as angry as Louise.

"They may well have changed their pleas, but let me assure you, Len and Mark will still receive heavy custodial sentences," he paused and trying to reassure us continued, "this judge is very firm on matters of this sort, and don't forget Len has a history of being in trouble with the law," he stopped again still wanting to restore confidence he went on, "I should think we're looking at ten years for Len, and I should think Mark will be in the region of five to six years."

Suddenly a feeling of sympathy came over me forcing me to ask a question but it wasn't Mr Robin-Palmer that replied to my enquiry.

"But what will happen to Mark when he comes out of prison?" my tone had changed as well as my facial expression.

"Andrew, don't start having any feelings of remorse or sorrow for Mark, he may not be that bright, but he knew full well what his uncle was getting into!" was Louise's prompt reply, a small amount of irritation in her voice, she continued and her words explained her frustration, "he was capable of stopping his uncle, or at least helping you, but he did nothing," she paused again to add just a few words, said with true feeling and a look that said as much as her words, "he deserves to go to jail!"

"It's just that..." I started to say in an attempt to explain my thoughts that Mark wouldn't have anyone to look after him when he came out of prison, but it was as if Louise was once again reading my thoughts for she interrupted me mid-flow.

"Mark has some other cousins on the other side of the country who will take care of him when he has served his time in prison!" she told me looking directly into my eyes, that firmness in her gaze and her words telling me that part of the conversation was over.

"You will both need to come back in to the court to hear the change of plea that is going to be offered to the judge and of course to hear what his Lordship has to say," Mr Robin-Palmer told us his tone now a little more relaxed maybe due to Louise's astute nature and understanding of her late husband's cousin.

"Mr Robin-Palmer," Louise began looking at the barrister she continued, "do you think Andrew and I could have a few minutes together alone before we go into the court?"

"Yes of course, it will take a few minutes for the judge to dismiss the jury now that there has been a change of plea," Mr Robin-Palmer replied unaware of Louise's reason for requesting some privacy and he finished with, "you will be called when we need you." With his closing words he was on his way into the court.

"What is it Louise?" I started to ask sensing that there was something on her mind, and it was a matter of urgency that she speak to me, I went on, "I can see that you have something on your mind."

"I have, I think it's not only time we arranged to have a secretary, but we also need to look into the security issue," she paused and took my arm, I knew from her words and now her actions what she was referring to, I was to share her concern as she continued to talk to me, her tone very quiet but at the same time very firm, "I'm not very happy about Delphine walking out of court a free woman, remember Andrew I was the one who confronted her face to face."

"Yes," I began recalling the words both Stavros and later Alex had said to me, but whilst Len and Mark had been in custody as well as Delphine I again hadn't felt a need to pursue the issue any further, but now it was Louise who had brought the subject up and it would need some careful consideration, so I went on, "perhaps we could have a word with Duncan, he seems well briefed when it comes to matters of security, after all we did appoint him as head of hotel security."

"I think we're part way to solving the concern we both have," she paused and came very close to me, I could feel her body heat as she stood in front, and she went on looking into my eyes her words had real feeling to them, "I don't trust Delphine, she told me that she had plans to start her business again, next time using British Telecom..." her words drifted away as she kissed me tenderly on my lips, pulling away she added, "I lost you once, I don't want to lose you again."

By now I'd slipped my arms around Louise's body and I was in the process of pulling her tighter to me when the doors of the courtroom opened.

"Mr Jackson, Mrs Shaw the court is waiting," it was the usher who had escorted me earlier in the morning, he was stood holding the door open with his left hand and indicating with his right that we should be going in.

Together we made our way into the court as directed by the usher, the jury had been dismissed and the public gallery was also empty, just the respective legal teams sat in their places, the judge sat at his bench, now he had removed his glasses, he nodded as we entered and made our way towards the prosecution team, we sat next to Mr Robin-Palmer, it was once we were seated that I looked in the direction of the accused, Len and Mark, as I looked I sensed Louise doing the same, Len looked even more irritated than before, his stare was most intense, his jaw was moving like he was grinding his teeth with anger, I glanced sideways at Louise, she was maintaining her own piercing look. Both Len and Mark were still seated, it seemed like an age before the judge spoke, but his voice was clear and full of authority.

"Would the two accused please stand!" The Clerk to the Court's voice echoed around the now sparsely occupied courtroom, I looked again at Louise, her stare was just as intense, Len was still grinding his teeth, or so I thought, then as I looked in his direction I noticed his mouth open and he mouthed the word 'bastards' Louise maintained her look, then the judge began to speak.

"Leonard and Mark Shaw, you were brought before this court accused of the unlawful abduction of Andrew David Jackson on the 24th August this year, now it seems to myself and the learned council acting both for the crown, and your own defence team that you have both changed you plea to guilty, this I can take as a sign of your joint remorse for this, the most despicable of acts, and in light of this change of plea I shall be sentencing you accordingly," the judge paused and moved some paperwork on the desk in front of him before continuing, looking up he went on, "Mark Shaw, as you weren't the instigator of the abduction, and this is your first appearance before a Crown Court I feel that a more lenient jail term is in order, you may not have been in charge of the operation, but it seems to me that you did not make any attempt to stop your uncle carrying out this vengeful act, I therefore sentence you to five years in prison, with a review to take place after two years, with the possibility of parole after that date if your behaviour has been of a good nature." He stopped and I together with Louise looked at Mark, the colour drained from his features and it looked as if he was about to fall to the ground, I felt Louise's left hand take my right hand and give it a hard squeeze.

"That ain't fair..." Len began to bellow and after looking at the now distressed Mark he went on, "he was only doing what I told him." He stopped, but it was the judge who brought him to a halt.

"Mr Shaw please remember where you are, this is still my court and I shall be grateful if you would conduct yourself accordingly, and in reply to your outburst perhaps Mark's separation from you will teach him to think for himself." the judge stopped again and moved more paperwork then addressing Len with full eye contact after removing his spectacles he went on.

"Leonard Shaw you were the mastermind behind this failed kidnap and fortunately for you and Andrew Jackson it was bungled, for if the consequences of your action had ended in the serious injury, or worse the death of Mr Jackson then you may not have found yourself in this court facing abduction charges," he paused and placed his glasses on the end of his nose then continued, "I have read the notes pertaining to your history and have taken into account that you are no stranger when it comes to matters of the judicial system in this country, I am therefore sentencing you to spend…" again the judge paused intentionally or not we weren't sure, but he did glance down at his paperwork before resuming his address to Len, "I recommend that you serve ten years in prison and that your date for parole review be set at six years." He finished and as he did so Louise's hand gripped mine much harder and I'm sure I heard her say 'yes' through her clenched teeth.

"Take them away!" the judge ordered. Louise and I looked again at the two shocked individuals in the dock, as the warders came to lead them away Len shouted at the two of us.

"This ain't over yet Jackson…" his words drifted away as they were forcefully taken out of the dock. The judge let this outburst pass, I glanced up at him and he was gathering his paperwork together.

"All rise," the Clerk to the Court said, and as instructed we did, once the judge had left the court Louise put her arms around me and pulled me tight to her body.

"I love you," she softly whispered in my ear, I replied by telling her that I too loved her. We were interrupted from our embrace by a heavy hand on my shoulder, it was Mr Robin-Palmer's, there then followed a great deal of hand shaking and back slapping, even from the defence team, and I was sure I heard one of them say it was 'a fair outcome'. Louise and I were invited to go for a celebratory drink by Mr Robin-Palmer we agreed and met the other members of the prosecution team in the local pub for a swift one.

And a quick drink it was, both Louise and I found the atmosphere somewhat over-powering, sure we shared everybody's elation at what seemed like a successful outcome, but I sensed that there was something still playing upon Louise's mind, glancing at my watch I could see it was now three thirty, looking out of the windows I could see the early evening darkness was beginning to descend, by the time we would get back to Chillingston Manor it would be dark, we said our farewells and made our way out onto the pavement on this cold November afternoon, after buttoning my coat I took out my mobile phone from the pocket, Louise removed hers from her handbag, almost in unison we switched them on, and after initialising simultaneously they began to ring, surprised we looked at each other before answering.

These calls were from the voice bank, informing each of us that we had at least one new message, we looked at each other, and I then gestured for Louise to take her call first.

"No, you go on, it's probably something to do with the business," she paused then added, "or one of the boys."

Of course she was right, the hotels had been very busy in the last few weeks, due to the publicity with regard to my abduction, the garage had also had a massive upturn in business and I remember Peter saying, and I quote 'more work than we can handle'. Carefully I dialled the number to retrieve my messages and was greeted with the response that I had one new message, and it certainly wasn't a voice I was expecting to hear. It was Alex, and his communication went as follows, 'Andrew I need to see Louise and yourself as soon as possible, please call me when you receive this message.'

"It was Alex!" I started to tell Louise only to find her with her own phone held to her right ear she nodded in response to my comment then went on.

"I've got a message from him as well," she said as she lowered her phone, she went on, "he sounded as if it was urgent!" her face showing her own concern as well as my own and she continued, "I think you'd better call him Andrew."

I looked at my phone went into the directory and found his number, as I pressed the button to call Alex I looked at Louise, my mind began to race, what could be so important that he needed to see us? I asked myself, as I put the phone to my ear it began to ring out, Louise drew close to me and pressed herself against me, her left ear next to the phone, this wasn't the first time she had done this, in fact many times she had listened to calls in this way, and as before her arm wrapped itself around me pulling me closer to her on this cold autumn evening, I in turn slipped my arm around her waist just as Alex answered his phone.

"Collins!" his tone the same as his answer short and to the point.

"Alex," I started to say, then feeling Louise squeeze me a little tighter I went on, "it's Andrew." And that was enough.

"Ah, Andrew, my boy, I hope you and Louise are well?" was his reply, now just the slightest sound of relaxation in his voice.

"We are indeed Alex, Louise is at my side," I said now looking into her eyes, I saw her say 'go on' so I continued, "Alex you said you needed to see us, is there something we need to know?" I asked not quite expecting the reply I was about to receive.

"Well I need to see you both very soon," he replied softly but more importantly there seemed urgency in his voice, this Louise picked up on after my return comment.

"Shall we say we get together at the weekend?" I enquired naively, still not sensing his need to see us, it was then that Louise took control of the situation along with the conversation, for suddenly she removed the phone from my hand and as I spun round placed it next to her ear.

"Dinner tonight Alex!" not in a questioning manner more of an understanding of Alex's requirements, I couldn't hear his response but Louise went on "Andrew is having one of his cautious moments Alex." I moved myself closer so I could hear what was being said.

"Yes that would be nice Louise," he replied, and he went on with a question of his own, "what time?"

"Let's say eight o'clock Alex, will you be on your own, or will your wife Sonia be accompanying you?" Louise asked and then looked at me.

"Oh, it will only be me," Alex told her as once again I pressed my ear to the phone.

"We look forward to seeing you at eight Alex, take care," Louise said as she handed me the phone, I could just make out his closing good-bye, and he was gone, but Louise continued to speak to me, "well that's it darling, Alex is coming to dinner and I'm sure we'll know more by the end of the evening!" By now she was looking directly into my eyes, her own slightly closed, I sensed she was trying to once again read my thoughts, I was unable to hide my anxiety, it was concern as to the need Alex had in seeing us, but Louise had indeed read my thoughts along with the tone and manner of Alex's words, in her mind, she had the situation completely under control.

"Andrew," she began after slipping her own mobile phone back into her handbag and taking my arm in readiness to make our way to the multi-storey car park she went on, "I'm sure there is a perfectly rational explanation for why Alex needs to see us," she paused talking along with her steps, looked me in the eyes once again and went on, "I can tell you're worried, but things will be much clearer after we've seen Alex." Her words had that confident ring to them of old, showing she had a much better understanding of the situation than I had.

"Of course you are right," I began to reply to Louise as we made our way along the already festively lit High Street in the direction of the car park, I continued thinking to myself that Christmas had once again started far too early, "I am worried, there's no point in me saying otherwise, it was just the way Alex seemed when he left the courtyard, he was shaking his head," I paused trying to recall his actions I had viewed from the window, I went on once they were clear in my mind, "it was as if he'd had a shock."

"Well Andrew as I've already said, we'll find out once we've seen him," Louise replied firmness in her voice indicating that was the close of that subject.

"Don't you think that Christmas seems to start earlier and earlier every year," Louise said as we neared the entrance to the galleries car park, this comment brought back my own thoughts of an instant ago.

"Yes, that's just what I was thinking a few seconds ago," I replied at the same time looking up at a star-shaped light-festooned thing hanging from a street light, we both stopped and looked down Union Street, the shop lights were white and very bright, people seemed to be everywhere, and now the office workers were pouring onto the streets, traffic was at a standstill, some people had bags in their hands, others just scurried along perhaps making their way home, from some of the lights in Union Street hung Father Christmases, others had snowmen, more of those obscure star-shaped things, further down the street were some reindeer, all too much for the two of us to take in.

"Come along Andrew, let's get back home to the children," Louise said as she tugged at my arm.

"And what are we going to have for dinner?" I asked as we approached the car, today we'd brought Louise's BMW, it's easier to drive in town, plus it doesn't draw so much attention to ourselves as does the Porsche, the lights flashed as I pressed the key-fob, but the doors didn't unlock with the same thud as the Porsche.

"I think I'll cook a nice chicken casserole," Louise replied as I opened the passenger door for her to get into the car adding "thank you." as she slipped into the car.

As we made our way through the busy city centre Louise phoned Chillingston Manor, explaining to Susan that we may be an hour or longer before we arrived home, I heard Susan say that she would give the children their tea, she also asked if there was anything she could do for us in readiness for our supper, Louise did ask her if she could get some chicken out of the freezer, and perhaps give the children a bath, the reply was positive.

Chapter Three

Evening and news

It was gone six by the time we had negotiated the hectic Bristol rush hour traffic and then driven the thirty or so miles to Chillingston Manor, Louise instantly set about fixing supper for the three of us, Susan had not only given the children their tea but had also bathed them in readiness for bed, for both of the children were in their nightclothes, all that was needed was the nightly ritual of the bedtime story.

"Andrew, mummy!" were the words that greeted us as we entered through the double oak doors of Chillingston Manor, they were issued jointly from James and Sarah as they ran to meet us, Susan the nanny not more than a step behind them. Louise instantly bent down to pick up James as she did so Sarah sprang into my waiting arms her own firmly around my neck.

"We missed you," Sarah began, at the same time looking in the direction of James she continued, "didn't we James?"

"Yes we did," he replied as he tightened his grip around his mother's neck.

"Well, Andrew and I missed the both of you," Louise replied as she gave her son a kiss on his cheek, this action was to prompt Sarah to plant her lips on the side of my face, then more words from Sarah directed towards James, "and now a kiss for Andrew."

So Louise and I had to have a separate kiss from each of the children, this was now the most natural of things to happen, whenever Louise and I had been away, whether it be on business or for social reasons both of us had a great deal of fuss bestowed upon us by the children.

"Well I see that you are both ready for bed," Louise said as she lowered James to the ground.

"We are, but will you come up and tuck us into bed please mummy..." Sarah began to reply to her mother only for James to interrupt her.

"And will you come and read a story to us?" he asked, as he made his way in my direction, taking my hand he continued, "please Andrew!" his childlike tone almost begging me.

I looked down at this little boy, his own eyes peering into mine, his right hand firmly gripping my left hand, he had his mother's deep blue eyes, but still had his blond infantile hair, I glanced across at Sarah, she was now standing next to Louise, back I looked at James, he had all the features of his sister, a kindness to his look, he was a big boy for his age, as yet he didn't possess Sarah's astute manner, his size was the only feature he had inherited from his father, whether he possessed Gary's temper was something that would only manifest itself in time, if it was going to at all.

"Of course I will," I began to reply to the children, stopping when I heard another voice.

"I trust everything went well, Louise, Andrew?" it was Susan the nanny asking the question and in doing so diverted my thoughts away from the question James had asked me.

"Yes quite satisfactorily, thank you, Susan," Louise replied but not revealing any details, and then continued with a question of her own, "and have these two scamps behaved themselves today?"

"They have, but I do think they are ready for their beds," Susan replied, her words firmly spoken in a motherly fashion, for if we hadn't got back then she would have taken care of the nightly arrangements.

"In that case it's time you both went on up, I shall be up in a little while to tuck you in, and Andrew will be up before me," she paused with her reply looked into my eyes and I instantly knew a request was on its way, "Andrew will be up in a few minutes, but I need him to do a little job for mummy first."

With her words still hanging in the air the children began to skip their way up the wide staircase towards their bedrooms, Susan following behind them.

"I'll be up in a few minutes," I said, as she neared the top of the staircase, she looked back down in my direction.

"OK," was her reply along with the children's.

"And what little job would you like me to do for you?" I asked as I moved closer to Louise, who by now had started to remove her coat, I took it and draped it over my right arm.

"I'd like you to fix me one of my mother's favourite drinks," she said as I made my way towards the cloakroom to the side of the staircase, momentarily I had to think, what was her mother's favourite drink, then as I was removing my own coat it came to me.

"Would that be a nice gin and tonic?" I asked as I hung my overcoat on the rail.

"Yes please darling, I'll be in the kitchen," was Louise's reply as she headed in that direction.

I made my way into the study, there I fixed Louise a gin and tonic, for myself a small malt whisky, I took the glasses into the kitchen and placed Louise's on the work surface next to the fridge, after putting some ice in the glass, together we toasted the day, and the success of at least having Len and Mark behind bars.

"This won't take long to cook," Louise said as she placed her glass back on the work top.

"I see you have everything under control," I began to reply and I went on with a request, "is there anything you would like me to do?"

"Well, I did think you would change before Alex arrives!" was Louise's somewhat forceful response.

"But of course," I said realising that I needed to get out of my formal business suit at the same time I glanced at my watch, it was now nearly seven o'clock, I'd need to get a move on I thought to myself, Alex was due at eight.

"I'm going to have a quick shower and change myself," Louise told me after she finished her drink and she continued, "don't forget you are going to read to the children, everything here is sorted."

I followed Louise up the wide wooden staircase, but at the top she headed in the direction of our bedroom, I made my way in the direction of the children's bedrooms, I could hear their voices, giggling and laughing together, as I entered Sarah's room I could see both Sarah and James sitting on the edge of Sarah's bed, a storybook firmly in Sarah's hands.

"This one, please Andrew!" they both said as I approached them, the book in Sarah's outstretched hands.

I made myself as comfortable as I could perched on the edge of Sarah's bed, that was after she had installed herself under the covers, James wriggled his body a little closer to my own, the story took no more than ten minutes to read and as always seemed to do the trick, by the time I finished Sarah was on her side and fighting the need for sleep, her hands under her head, she was struggling to stay awake, James by now resting against my body and as I glanced down at him I could see that he had his thumb in his mouth and he was in fact asleep, carefully I put my arm around him to steady his body as I bent over to kiss Sarah goodnight.

"Goodnight Andrew," her words softly spoken as I raised myself up still maintaining my grip on James so he wouldn't fall.

"Goodnight, God bless," I replied as I took James in my arms, I made my way into his own bedroom, carefully I placed him under the covers, he stretched as I kissed him and softly wished him goodnight.

Next was a visit to the bedroom I shared with Louise, she was sat at the dressing table having had her shower and completed dressing she was now applying her make-up.

"You're not going to be long in the shower, are you?" Louise asked as I got closer to her.

"No, ten minutes and I'll be done," I replied as I proceeded to remove my clothing, with my words I looked again at Louise and as I did so she stood, tonight she was wearing a full length evening dress, her shoulders exposed apart from the thin bright blue straps that were holding the dress in place, she moved just sufficiently to allow the dress to fall to its full length, then her words.

"How do I look?" she asked.

Before replying I looked again at the elegant woman stood only a few feet away from me, the make-up applied to perfection, her hair up in that bouffant style I loved so much, just a few ringlets of her auburn hair falling to her shoulders.

"You look..." I paused and as I did Louise turned just slightly at the same time moved her head in an upward direction, I continued, "stunning!"

"Thank you," she said and went on, playfulness in her voice, "now you will have to get a move on, I'll see you downstairs in fifteen minutes," she paused again as she made her way towards the door, there she stood and continued to speak, "I need you to help me get a few things ready, I mean lay the table."

I was in and out of the shower in less than ten minutes, another five and I was in the kitchen, Louise had the dinner well under control, to the point that it was almost ready, I made my way into the dining room and had just completed the task of laying the table when I heard the door bell ring, the sound reverberated around the high ceiling above the hall, I glanced at my watch as I made my way in the direction of the hall, it was seven fifty five.

"I'll get it!" I called as I approached the entrance doors, I faintly heard Louise reply with an 'OK'.

"Andrew my boy!" the usual greeting I received from Alex as I opened the right-hand oak door, his right hand came up to take mine, in his left, a bottle of wine. Alex continued to speak as he released my hand, "it's good to see you my boy."

"And it's good to see you Alex," I replied, in my mind I was going to say that I'd seen him from the window of the courts this afternoon when suddenly we were both distracted by the voice of Louise as she entered the hall. "Alex, you're looking so well."

"Louise," Alex promptly replied as we both looked in the direction of the door that lead from the hall into the kitchen, then his arms opened, Louise approached and took hold of Alex around the waist gently kissing him on both of his cheeks.

"As always Alex, you're right on time," Louise told him as she offered to take his coat, as he slipped out of it he passed me the bottle of wine, I glanced at the label, Louise's favourite, Chardonnay. Louise continued to talk as she took his coat, "dinner will be ready in ten minutes."

"Thank you," Alex started to say, then looking at me he went on after taking the wine from me, "this Louise, is for you," he said as he passed her the bottle of Chardonnay.

"Oh Alex, you shouldn't have bothered," she paused, leant forward and kissed him again on the cheek and went on, "it is my favourite!"

I made my way to the downstairs cloakroom, as Louise and Alex continued with their greetings I had just closed the door when Louise spoke to me again.

"Andrew, take Alex into the lounge and fix each of us a nice drink, I'll join you in a few minutes," her words softly spoken but very precisely.

Alex and I made our way into the lounge, there I fixed him a gin and tonic, the same for Louise, malt whisky for myself, we made ourselves comfortable and awaited Louise, looking across at Alex as he was sat in one of the leather, wing-back chairs prompted me to ask him a question.

"You said that you needed to see us Alex," I paused and took a drink from my glass, then continued, "you sounded as if it was some bad news, urgent I think you said."

"Well I don't think I said urgent," he paused and took a drink from his own glass before continuing, "I do have some very important news for the two of you."

"Is it something to do with Delphine?" I foolishly asked, I say foolishly for I hadn't taken in what Alex had said, and he was to remind me quite sharply.

"Andrew, I said the both of you!" his words spoken firmly at the same time he moved forward in his seat, picked up his glass and emptied it in one swift movement, I was a little taken aback by his sudden change in manner, something I'd never seen before.

"Is everything alright?" Louise asked as she entered the room, looking in my direction she may have been able to detect my slightly disturbed state, she glanced at Alex.

"Yes Louise, everything is fine," Alex began to reply to her question, then looking at me he went on, "I'm sorry Andrew, I didn't mean to be short with you, but it's been a long day, and the news I have effects the both of you."

"Well let's go into the dining room and you can tell us about your day over dinner," Louise said as she picked up her glass toasting the two of us as she took a sip from it.

We made our way into the dining room, I sat at the head of the table, Alex to my right and Louise opposite him, the chicken casserole was excellent, accompanied by roast potatoes, carrots, green beans and fresh broccoli, once Louise was seated I poured the wine, it was then that Alex spoke.

"A toast to the two of you," he paused as he raised his glass, we both looked at him, instantly we could tell there was more to be said, he went on, "a successful day!"

"Yes a successful day," Louise and I said as our glasses came together, then Louise spoke directly to Alex, I looked as she began to speak, her gaze was intense, Alex must have felt as if he was in for a questioning, he shifted slightly on his seat, she continued, "but there is something else on your mind Alex," she paused and looked harder at Alex, then continued, "I sensed a hesitancy in your tone as you toasted us Alex!"

Alex put his glass down, sat back in his chair before he began his reply.

"Of course you're right Louise, there is something else I have to tell the both of you," he paused I was unable to decipher his signals, but not Louise.

"It concerns what has gone on today, doesn't it Alex?" her words precise and accurate.

"Yes it does," he started to reply picking up his glass he took a sip then went on, "it was me you saw in the gallery this morning Andrew, at the time I was unaware that Delphine was going to change her plea..." he stopped, thinking Louise was going to interrupt him but she was only picking up her own glass, as soon as it registered he went on, "I must have found out at about the same time as you two did that she decided to turn queen's evidence." He paused long enough for me to ask a question.

"But her changing her plea doesn't really affect us, does it Alex?" I asked a little concerned, after all I had seen him stood in the courtyard at the back of the courts shaking his head.

"No!" he very firmly replied, taking both Louise and myself by surprise with the suddenness of his response, and he continued, "I'm sorry, I don't mean to be so jumpy, it's just that you both went through so much to bring her to justice, not that Delphine has got away with the crimes, it's just that she has avoided going to prison," he paused again, looking at Louise he went on, "then in return she has agreed to reveal all the names and addresses of her accomplices involved in the trafficking of the drugs, and I mean all of them, including the ones on the street."

"But you now think Alex, that we should be investing in some good security, don't you?" Louise enquired, looking across at me as she asked the question.

"Yes I think you should," Alex began to reply, then continued, changing the subject, at the same time picking up his knife and fork he went on, "let's eat our dinner, Louise has worked so hard it would be a shame for it to get cold," he took a forkful of chicken and after clearing his mouth continued to speak, "I don't think you're in any danger from Delphine, or for that matter from any of her accomplices, but just as a matter of course you need to be vigilant."

"In that case I'll talk to Duncan in the morning," I replied to Alex's statement, Louise nodded her head in approval of my suggestion, Alex looked a little puzzled by my name dropping, I sensed I needed to inform him who Duncan was, so I went on, "Alex, Duncan is head of our hotel chain security, he is well informed when it comes to such matters, he'll be able to point us in the right direction."

"Good, and if there's anything I can do to help then you only need to ask. my boy," Alex replied.

And both Louise and I knew just what he meant when he referred to help, after my attempted kidnap we had been wrapped in a blanket of SAS security, and now I felt as if once again that security was close at hand. We continued to talk as we consumed our meal, the conversation drifted away from the security issue, we discussed the hotels and how well they were doing, and winter can be a very profitable time in the remote highland regions of Scotland. As Louise was returning to the room with our desserts Alex's mobile phone began to ring.

"Excuse me," he said as he rummaged in his inner jacket pocket, once in his hand he studied the display very carefully. I thought it may have been his wife calling him, but as he stood up and asked to be excused again I figured it must be a call to do with work, Alex made his way towards the door before answering the phone and that was with the customary "Collins." He then went out of the dining room and into the hall, Louise and I could make out a few of his words, but none of them fitted into any kind of conversation.

Alex was gone for no more than a few seconds, a minute at the most, his return into the dining- room took Louise and myself a little by surprise, but so did the look on Alex's face, for now he had a smile to his features and it was he who spoke before we had a chance to question him.

"That Louise, Andrew was the Operations Commander," he paused as he made himself comfortable in his seat again, then continued, "it would seem that the authorities have already started to act upon some of the information Delphine has given to them."

Both Louise and I looked at him, each of us unsure of exactly what Alex meant.

"Sorry Alex, you've lost me, I don't know about you darling," I said, looking again at Louise, she winked a reply, and then spoke.

"I think I know what Alex means, darling," her own smile beginning to form.

"It seems that several police forces up and down the country have conducted some high profile and unexpected raids..." he paused and picked up his glass, then went on, "now we have something to toast, several of the big names in the drug dealing circle have been arrested."

"Well that certainly seems to be worth toasting," Louise said a tone of reassurance in her words and a broad smile beginning to form on her lips.

"You must realise Andrew, Delphine will never be a free woman," Alex began to tell me, then looking across at Louise he continued, "not even her sister will know where she is."

That statement had a very cold ring to it, her dealings within the drug smuggling fraternity had only brought her seclusion in the end, in some ways it was a worse sentence than going to prison, at least there she would have been able to see her family, but also she would have had the prospect of being free at some future date, but by turning queen's evidence she had confined herself to a lifetime of isolation, I felt a likeness to my own situation, then reality kicked in, I had the love of a good woman to support me, I may not have my sister Rachel and now was not the time to dwell upon the past, or any feelings of sorrow for Delphine, as Louise was to instantly remind me.

"Andrew, don't start feeling sorry for her!" Louise sharply told me, her gaze equally as firm as her words, for she was indeed reading my inner thoughts, if that is possible, she continued, "Delphine would have had you murdered if you remember correctly, she was in charge of a very large operation, Len and Mark could have easily killed you, now they have got exactly what they deserve, and Delphine has forfeited her family for the business she was running."

Louise's statement was indeed correct, and took no time at all to sink-in, as if her words weren't enough to bring me back to reality then Alex was to add a few more.

"I would much rather Delphine go to prison, at least after ten or fifteen years she would have been free, but now..." he paused and picked up his glass, emptied it in one go then went on, "now she is going to cost the taxpayer a fortune for the rest of her life."

"But hopefully by the time Len and Mark are released they will have learnt how to behave in a more public spirited manner," Louise said as she looked across at Alex.

"Well let's hope so, they do so many things with the prisoners these days, they will both be given the opportunity to improve themselves," Alex started to say only pausing to look at his glass.

"Sorry Alex," I said as I started to refill his glass, it then dawned on me that Alex may well have to drive; I stopped pouring the wine to ask a question, "Alex will you be staying the night?"

"I did think I would be able to drive back to the hotel, but I must say I'm feeling a little light headed, perhaps I can leave my car here and phone for a taxi," Alex started to reply, but Louise was to make a suggestion before I had a chance to say another word.

"Alex, you know you're more than welcome to stay here, I'll go and make up the bed in one of the guest rooms as soon as we've finished dinner," Louise told the two of us, indicating at the same time that she would like her own glass refilled.

"As long as you're sure it's not too much trouble," Alex said, I continued to fill his glass that was after attending to Louise's.

"Of course it's no trouble Alex." Louise promptly replied.

"I hope you won't mind the children running around in the morning," I added light-heartedly. Alex nodded his reply, picked up his glass and took a long sip, then words.

"I do have some more information for the two of you," he paused and looked hard into my eyes, I was unable to read what he was about to say, then as he put his glass down he went on, "well it concerns you Andrew more than Louise," he stopped to look at her, she nodded indicating for him to continue, "well it would seem that Jan Van-Elderman is dead." He stopped as if that was all he had to say on the matter, but I felt a need to know the circumstances under which Jan had met his death, but the fact that Alex had said Jan was dead had come as something of a shock, I momentarily sat back in my chair.

"I can see Andrew that this has taken you a little by surprise," Alex said stealing the moment.

"You're right," I began to reply trying to regain my thoughts and remember my last encounter with the Dutchman. That had been at Stavros's the day after Gary had been killed, I looked at Louise, she had never met the person in question, but knew a great deal about him, due to the information I had been able to relay to her, he was best described as a ruthless thug.

"Louise, you never had the misfortune to meet this man, did you?" Alex asked as I was still digesting the information with regard to him being dead.

"No Alex I didn't, but from what Andrew has told me I haven't missed a great deal," she replied reaching across to take my hand.

"I'm not sure what I feel Alex, shock, or is it surprise," I paused trying to put my feelings into some sort of order, once in my head I continued, "I think it's a mixture of both, I'd only met him the once, but he left a lasting impression, I would like to say relief but that seems a little disrespectful, he was after all a human being."

"Yes Andrew and he was a human being in the most basic of forms," Alex started to reply and he continued, "it was his intention to kill Gary that was before Nana was forced to intervene."

With those words more of the encounter with Jan came back into my mind, his statement at the time was clear, 'he was going to kill Gary,' revenge for the death of his brother at the hands of Gary Shaw, then who knows who he may have turned his violent attention on.

"How did he die Alex?" Louise calmly asked, bringing a sense of normality back to the conversation.

"Well from the information I've been given," Alex began to reply at the same time picking up his wine glass, he took a long drink from it, almost clearing it, then went on, "Jan seemed to settle down quite well in South Africa, I think I mentioned that before, anyway it seems that he got involved in drug dealing, something he had extensive knowledge of, but then he managed to," Alex paused, once more he lifted his glass, it was still in his hand, emptied the contents into his mouth, looked very long and I would say hard at Louise then continued with a change of subject, "if you're sure it's not a problem then I will stay."

"Of course it's not a problem Alex, but please continue," Louise replied sensing that he had something of an unpleasant disclosure to make she added, "Andrew, Alex could do with another drink!"

I looked at the glass that Alex had had the gin and tonic in, his hand now very close to it, a quick glance towards Louise she nodded indicating for me to refill it.

I reached across and picked up the glass, "I wouldn't mind a refill!" Louise promptly requested, I made my way across the room to the drinks cabinet, within seconds I had the glasses filled, gin, tonic and the chink of the ice against the glasses as I sat back in my seat.

"OK, what I have to tell the two of you is somewhat disturbing," Alex began to say, after taking a pull from his fresh gin and tonic he went on, "not only had Jan got himself involved in the distribution of drugs, he seemed to have picked up on his brother's bad habits." He finished and again lifted his glass; Louise did the same and took a long drink from her own glass.

"Alex you still haven't explained how Jan came to die," Louise said with her fresh drink in her right hand.

"Well it would seem from what I've been able to ascertain that he got involved in the sort of enterprise his brother had been dealing in, that was before Gary prematurely ended his life," Alex paused and looked at Louise and myself, our expressions had changed to ones of almost disbelief, Louise took a long drink from her glass, I did the same, Alex continued, "it wasn't just paedophilia he became involved in, the authorities have informed us that he was also selling children, well more so babies." He stopped and took another drink from his glass, giving me the opportunity to ask a question.

"And how long had this been going on Alex?" I enquired at the same time looking at Louise; I could see she had the same feeling of sickness coming over her at the thought of Jan being involved with the abduction of children.

"About a year!" was Alex's reply, then he emptied his glass in one swift movement, after placing it back on the table he resumed the conversation, "anyway it would seem that he crossed paths with some very unscrupulous villains doing much the same as he was, apparently he was out one evening about ten days ago conducting some business when these other individuals caught up with him."

"So he was killed by some other gang members?" I quickly asked, wishing to bring the conversation to a close, for I have to say I was beginning to feel most uncomfortable, firstly that Jan had got involved in the type of filth that had angered Gary, and worse he'd gone one step further, in that he was involved with the smuggling and abduction of children.

"No, it wasn't anyone from the other gang Andrew," Alex started to tell us, and he went on, "what Jan and this other group didn't know was that they were being carefully monitored by an ex-policeman, he was working as a private investigator for someone who had their child stolen, anyway he got rumbled and Jan along with some of the other gang members gave him a beating, then a few days later this 'go it alone cop' went after Jan, he wasn't happy just to kill him, no he blew him up, planted a bomb under Jan's car and bingo he was blown off the face of the earth."

"Bloody hell Alex, that's a bit extreme, if you don't mind me saying so," I said still shocked by what he had just told us.

"And he didn't finish with the killing of Jan," Alex started to say, still looking at our bemused faces, he went on, "next were three members of the other gang, he went round to one of the bars where they frequently went for drinks, there he got involved in a gun battle, as I said shot three dead, but was fatally wounded himself, died on the way to hospital."

I sat trying to digest what Alex had just told Louise and myself, I hadn't liked Jan, but I would never have wished him dead, as far as I was concerned he was out of the way, in South Africa he couldn't bring any harm to any of us, not just Louise and myself, but also Stavros and the rest of our adoptive family and thoughts of Stavros prompted me to ask Alex another question.

"Does Stavros know Jan is dead?" I enquired looking at Louise as I put the question to Alex.

"Yes he does," was Alex's straight reply, and he added, "he was more relieved than you appear to be Andrew."

"Well Andrew," Louise interjected into the conversation, stopping Alex she continued, "morbid it may seem, but now I do think we have some news to celebrate," she paused and picked up her glass and went on raising it in the air, "Len and Mark have both been sent down for a long time, Delphine won't be causing us any more problems, and from what you've told me the world is a safer place without Jan Van-Elderman."

"You are of course right Louise," Alex concurred lifting his own glass as he said the words.

"Excuse me Andrew!" Stuart suddenly said, his voice instantly snapping me out of my trance- like state, the unexpectedness of his interruption made my whole body shake, at the same time I gripped my head with both of my hands in an effort to control my convulsing body.

"I'm sorry," I stammered in response to Stuart's interruption.

"That's OK Andrew," Stuart said and he continued with a question, "this Jan," he paused again, looked me directly in the eyes and went on, "is he Swedish?"

"No, he was Dutch," I paused just recalling the name and wondering why he'd stopped me, "but he's dead!" I added, after a few moments of thought.

"Yes of course, you did say he was dead," was Stuart's somewhat hesitant reply, and then he added, "would you like a glass of water Andrew?"

"Yes please," I replied, at the same time I tried to push myself up from the seat I'd been in for some considerable time, but I felt as if I didn't have enough strength in my arms.

"Its OK Andrew I'll get it for you," Stuart said and as he spoke he was out of his chair and on his way to the kitchen, in what seemed like no time at all he was back with not just a tumbler but a jug of chilled water resting on a tray, together with a fine lead crystal tumbler, the ice in the jug rattled and chinked against the side as he placed the tray on the small coffee table that occupied the space between us.

"I think now would be a good time for you to take your medication, don't you Andrew?" Stuart asked as he resumed his position in the chair opposite me.

"Well I don't see that it's doing any good!" I questioned raising my voice slightly.

"Its early days Andrew, don't expect too much of yourself!" was Stuart's stern reply.

I managed to pour myself a glass of water, took a sip, it was cold and hurt my teeth as it washed over them.

"Now take these," Stuart said as he passed me two tablets, one pink in colour, the other an off shade of white.

They both tasted foul, and as I swallowed the last one I told Stuart that I disliked taking them.

"They'll help you relax, and in turn may encourage you to remember the events of the past." he replied.

As I reclined back into the chair after placing the tumbler back on the tray, Stuart had another question for me.

"Are you ready to continue, or would you like to discuss something else?" Stuart enquired, his expression relaxed, but his eyes were slightly closed.

"Yes, I'll go on," I replied making myself a little more comfortable in my chair, as I did I noticed Stuart cross his long legs and then pick up his notepad and pencil from the table.

"Right Andrew you've just told me that Louise suggested you spend Christmas in Scotland, do you recall if that's what happened?" Stuart asked.

"Yes, I think I can remember that far back." I said.

Chapter Four

Christmas at the Mansion

We made our way to Scotland, that is Louise, myself and the children on the 20th December, it was as always a long drive, we took the BMW, due to the fact that we needed plenty of space for the entire luggage, along with the Christmas presents. Leaving Chillingston Manor at approximately ten o'clock we shared the driving, it was gone seven in the evening by the time we arrived at the mansion, of course that was the preferred name Louise had given to the old Victorian house I owned in the back of beyond in the Scottish Highlands. Nancy and Donald were waiting to greet us, a meal already prepared and that was much appreciated. The house had been elegantly decorated, a large spruce tree in the hall, on top a giant silver star, all that was required to make the picture complete was for someone to turn on the Christmas lights that adorned the tree.

Louise's parents, Diane and Trevor, arrived the following day, they in fact decided to fly to Scotland, well Inverness airport, there they hired a car and completed the journey in just over two hours, a wise move I remember telling Trevor. 'Sound' was his own reply to my comment. Diane commented on the fact that the mountains were covered in snow something neither she nor the children had noticed on their first Christmas visit the year before, and we weren't to be disappointed, for if you're looking for snow then Scotland is probably one of the best places to see it, and the views from the mansion were quite stunning.

We'd had a fresh fall of snow by the time Louise's sister, Jackie her husband Jeremy and their children arrived, the boy, his name Gavin, is twelve years old and a tall lad for his age, taking after his father Jeremy, the girl Lorain, on the other hand took after the Morrisons, well let's say the female line of the family, a very pretty ten year old with long auburn hair similar to Louise's and of course Sarah's. Jackie's hair had been trimmed so that it fell just to collar length but still possessed that curl to it, and of course facial features she had inherited from Diane.

Now the other thing that I remember of Jackie was an expression Sarah had used to describe her aunt, and I quote 'Bossy', and that trait was soon to manifest itself in my own direction and that was on Christmas Eve.

"Andrew, you go and make a start on laying the table," Jackie told me, her tone somewhat domineering, I was somewhat taken aback by her manner, she hardly knew me, yet spoke to me as if we had been acquaintances for years, I glanced in the direction of Sarah and I picked up her mouth the words 'told you she was bossy', I managed to nod a reply and watched as Sarah returned a grin and a wink to me. I carried on with the task that I'd been assigned to not challenging what Jackie had said, even though it was my house, or as Louise named it the mansion, but on Christmas Day, Jackie was to ruffle the feathers of Louise and was to pay the price for what is best described as over-stepping the mark.

We had spent the morning in the large lounge of the mansion, unwrapping gifts and entertaining ourselves, my sons William and Peter had been unable to attend the family get- together due to the inclement weather, Inverness had been closed since Jackie, Jeremy and their children had arrived, this was as a result of the severe snow storm that had swept across the region, closing most of the highland routes in and out of the country.

Twelve thirty and Louise came into the lounge to inform us that dinner was ready; we made our way into the dining room, as always the table was laid to perfection, everything in its rightful place, this Christmas each of us had our own name tabs reminding each individual of where we had to sit, we had taken our respective places and Sarah was sat to my right and was to make the most simple of requests, but it wasn't her mother who responded with a reply.

"Mummy, can I taste the champagne?" Sarah asked after we had finished making ourselves comfortable at the dinner table.

"No you can't young lady!" Jackie replied taking myself and some of the others at the table completely by surprise, Louise included, and it was Louise who was to respond in a very forthright manner to her sister, adding more surprise to the request.

"Jackie, I don't need you to make decisions for me!" Louise instantly said, her tone almost to the point of anger, and after looking at me she continued," Andrew and I will decide what is best for the children." And that ended the conversation, I looked around the table, Jackie looked what would best be described as embarrassed, someone who had suddenly been put in her place, Trevor and Diane both just nodded, Jackie's husband Jeremy tried to look away, the conversation may well have been over but Louise's actions were far from finished, she picked up the champagne bottle and part filled her daughter's glass, to which Sarah responded as I had come to expect.

"Thank you mummy," she said, at the same time looking in my direction.

I just smiled and picked up my glass and suggested a toast, "Merry Christmas," I paused before adding, "and a happy new year."

We all brought our glasses together, then quite to my surprise Trevor had something to add.

"Sound, but I think you're forgetting something Andrew," he said causing me to look in his direction my expression somewhat confused, this was sufficient for Trevor to continue, "I think Diane and I have a toast of our own to add," he paused just long enough to judge whether he had the attention of the rest of the family, and he did, he went on, "to the coming year and the marriage of 'pudding', I mean Louise and Andrew."

I hadn't forgotten our planned wedding; to the contrary our forthcoming marriage had been very much on my mind, but the events of the past few months had meant we hadn't had a lot of time to spend on wedding preparations, but as our glasses came together again I looked into Louise's eyes, they had a new and determined look to them.

"Yes, our wedding and the future darling!" she said, at the same time she leant across to kiss me.

We spent the rest of the day entertaining ourselves, Trevor reminding all of us of some of the awful stories Stavros had told him, they seemed even more amusing told for the second time and Trevor even managed to exaggerate them a little more.

Later, once we had made our way to bed Louise took me aside and told me "I've got something very special on, just for you!" taking me by the hand she lead me to the bed, she was still fully dressed, I for my part had started to remove some of my clothes, I stood with my shirt unbuttoned and pulled out of my trousers, my shoes already removed.

"Come here!" Louise almost demanded at the same time taking my hand she pulled me towards the king-sized that was in the master bedroom, the very bed I'd made love to Louise on upon our reunion here in Scotland. She pulled her skirt aside revealing her stockings, the tops of which were edged with white lace.

"Now you know what you have to do!" her voice full of that authority that I couldn't disobey, and she went on, "I want you, and I mean *want you!*"

I knew exactly what Louise meant and required, she wanted loving as I had on many other occasions, but it was always different under her terms. Our lovemaking went on and on, first me giving myself to her, each and every orgasm she had I received as much pleasure as she did, carefully I explored the intimacies of her body as I had on many other times, and when the time was right Louise gave herself to me completing this most required act with a joint and wonderful climax.

"As soon as we can, that is in the New Year, we will start to organise our wedding." Louise told me as we lay still in the after glow of our lovemaking, our bodies slowly recovering from the exhilarating exercise.

"Did you ever think Louise was just after your money?" Stuart asked inquisitively making me once again come out from my evoking of the past; I looked across at him and his eyes were shifting from side to side.

"It never crossed my mind!" I instinctively and sharply replied, not recalling what Len had said to me when I was in the back of his van after I'd been kidnapped, and not understanding Stuart's reason for interrupting me, and I continued, "why do you ask?"

"Let's say it's a bit of a test," was Stuart's immediate reply calming me somewhat and to add credence to his reply he continued, "I'm trying to help stimulate some of your memory cells, just to see how far back you can remember."

"Well, that was something that Len tried to suggest when I was in the back of his van," I replied.

"That's good Andrew, it's exactly what you told me yesterday," Stuart said as he looked across at me, at the same time he made some notes in the open notepad that was resting on his lap.

"But I don't remember telling you that yesterday!" I swiftly retorted, before Stuart responded he made some more notes and seemed to nod in an approving manner.

"As I've said, things will fall into place soon enough," Stuart replied, and in a way to relax me continued, "now how far did you and Louise get with the arrangements for your wedding?"

"Well it wasn't just into the New Year that things started to fall into place," I told Stuart as I resumed my relaxed position in the chair I finished explaining the time of year when things got underway, "it was April to be precise."

"Carry on Andrew," Stuart almost instructed me.

Chapter Five

A new start

I felt Louise's hand tighten around my left arm and instantly I knew words were on their way, words I wasn't expecting.

"Darling, I can't see anything I like!" she very softly whispered and paused, I looked into her deep blue eyes, they had something of a bemused look to them, then she continued, "I don't mean to sound ungrateful, but nothing really seems to catch my eye."

The words *were* spoken very quietly so as not to alarm the sales assistant who had been dealing with our enquiry. Instantly I understood what she meant, we had travelled to New Bond Street, London's diamond centre; the purpose of the visit was to choose an engagement ring, and so far we had looked at five, or maybe six trays of the most outstanding rings, but nothing struck me either, still it wasn't my place to say so, yet her statement gave me the opportunity to pose a question to Louise.

"But where do you think we can find something you may like?" I enquired, my tone equally as quiet as Louise's, but I was feeling just a little frustrated, we had after all given up a day from our business to come to London for this venture. I felt that my question may have been a little on the empty side, I say empty as I wasn't offering an alternative establishment myself, New Bond Street, had been the suggestion of Louise's mother, Diane.

Then I should have anticipated the reply Louise was going to come back with, but then as I have said in the past, she never gave any indication when she was going to spring a surprise upon me.

"Well I'm sure I know of somewhere far more suitable....." She paused trying to indicate through her eyes what was about to come, but still she caught me out, sensing my lack of observation she continued. "Somewhere *you* and *I* will feel far more at ease in."

"Excuse us!" I said to the young female sales assistant who had by now returned to the other side of the desk we had been escorted to upon our arrival in the shop, in her hands another tray of engagement rings; they sparkled and caught the bright light shining from above in the ceiling. I stood and my left hand went to the back of Louise's chair, I pulled it back slightly as Louise arose from it, she took my arm and together we made our way to a display cabinet on the other side of the room, I glanced back at the young lady and gave a courteous wave of my right hand.

"And this somewhere..." I paused still not understanding the full implications of Louise's statement I continued, "is it somewhere I should know?"

"Well I'm sure I don't have to give you too many clues!" she started to reply, her eyes aglow, those cheeks just the slightest of redness to them, then as if the final indication, her right hand came up to her neck and the tips of her fingers almost danced their way along the edge of the diamond and gold necklace she was wearing.

"You mean...." I started to exclaim only for Louise to place her index finger on my lips, then her words.

"Now you remember!" she said very softly, but at the same time quite forcefully, and she continued, "now you go and make our apologies and I'll see you outside," again she paused, her smile told me what she was about to say, "tell the young lady I'm not feeling well!" again she stopped but it was only momentarily, "don't forget to give her a tip!" her manner full of authority, but at the same time a light-heartedness in her tone.

I made my way back to the desk that only a few minutes ago we had both been sat at and made myself comfortable on the chair again.

"I'm dreadfully sorry..." I began only to be cut a little short by the young lady.

"But you and Mrs Shaw haven't seen our full range yet Mr Jackson." Her words spoken with little concern for our feelings, more I thought for the fact that she was maybe losing a sale.

"As I was about to tell you," I started again, this time with a little more determination in my voice and I continued, "my fiancée, Mrs Shaw has developed something of a headache and is in need of some fresh air, I do apologise for what must seem like a waste of your time, but..." I stopped as by now my right hand had found a note in my trouser pocket, discreetly I removed it and glancing down I could see it was a twenty pound note, what the hell I thought to myself. I turned and looked towards the door as Louise made her way outside and onto the busy pavement, once she was out of the building I continued. "I am dreadfully sorry to have inconvenienced you, but as you can see Mrs Shaw is not at all well," pausing again I passed the twenty pound note across the desk to the young sales assistant. "Please accept this as some form of recompense for wasting your time."

"Mr Jackson I couldn't!" was her instant and somewhat beleaguered reply.

"Well if you won't take it personally then please ensure that it is forwarded to a local charity, you know, one that your firm supports!" I replied firmly, at the same time I stood pushing my chair back as well, again I glanced in the direction of Louise stood outside of the shop, and as I looked I saw someone brush past her, there seemed to be the slightest of contact between them, instantly I started to make my way towards the door.

"Well if you insist Mr Jackson…" I faintly heard the young lady say as I got to the entrance door, at the same time the click of the lock being released held my attention but it drifted away as I got outside and to my Louise's side.

"Are you alright?" I asked at the same time I was scanning up and down the street looking for the person who had come into contact with her.

"Yes, I'm fine darling!" was Louise's strong and determined reply and she continued, "someone just nudged me, I'm OK, some people are very clumsy you know," with those words Louise took my arm and with her right hand she pointed down the street, "look he's bumping into everyone."

And sure enough as I looked I could see a figure almost stumbling along this busy London thoroughfare, his hands stuffed into the pockets of what seemed like a black hooded zipper jacket, the hood firmly up over his head, but this person's stance had a familiarity to it, even viewed from the back I thought I knew this individual, but then as I looked around me I could see many familiar looking people, but as always the capital of this country is full of many similar looking people. But Louise was to pick up on my concern.

"You're in danger of becoming paranoid Andrew," she softly said, at the same time taking my left arm she continued, "do your coat up darling, it's still quite cold."

With her words the wind indeed picked up and forced me to button up my outer jacket, it may well be April but as is often the case the weather can change with a sudden unexpectedness at this time of the year. As for her comment regarding a sense of paranoia, this was of course brought about from my encounter with Louise's former father-in-law, Len and his nephew Mark, last year.

"I'm sorry," I started to reply as we made our way along this busy street in the heart of the capital, but Louise was to interrupt me with words of reassurance before I had chance to continue.

"Now, you know that Len and Mark are safely locked away," she paused and looked into my eyes then continued, "and they will be remaining in prison for a long time."

Her words had a reassuring firmness to them, and of course she was correct, Len and Mark had both received long custodial prison sentences, ten years for Len and five years to be precise for Mark, he would be released before his uncle, but only if he behaved himself whilst in prison, Len on the other hand was informed that he must serve the full ten year term, this being due to his previous criminal record. Louise must have read my thoughts as we momentarily stopped again and looked into each other's eyes, instantly she picked up on my thoughts.

"Although Delphine won't be a guest of Her Majesty, all of her accomplices in the drug running and smuggling organisation that she was in control of will be!" Louise told me, a look of determination in her eyes along with the tone in her voice, and then she continued slightly more light-heartedly, "come along Andrew, let's get back to the station and catch the next train home to Bristol!"

With those words her right arm went up in the air and again she spoke, but this time her voice was high, and the reason was to hail a cab, "taxi!" she called, for as well as having a conversation with me, Louise had spotted an empty black cab coming in our direction, no sooner had she said the words and it was pulling up.

"Where to gov'?" the driver asked through the half opened window.

"Paddington Station please!" was Louise's prompt reply, for my part I opened the door, first for Louise to get into the cab, I followed once she was seated.

Once inside of the taxi it was the cabbie who spoke again. "Up on business, or is it pleasure, love?" his tone jovial, by no means prying, his London accent easy to understand, and it was Louise who replied to the question aimed at herself.

"Actually, you could say it's pleasure," was her straightforward answer, and she continued, "we've been looking for an engagement ring, to be precise."

"You'll need a wedge of money if you're thinking of buying one here in New Bond Street darling!" he replied, laughter in his voice as he emphasised the 'darling'. At the same time we pulled away and joined the stream of quite fast moving traffic.

"Well we have saved up for some considerable time, so we have a bit of cash to spend!" Louise promptly replied, looking across at myself as she said the words a massive smile to her lips, at the same time she shrugged her shoulders slightly, I noticed her eyes sparkling like the diamonds she had around her neck. Her comment was sufficient to bring another question from the driver.

"Didn't see anything you liked then?" I looked into the rear-view mirror as he spoke; his eyes were focused on Louise almost as if he were studying her features as well as interrogating her and before she had chance to answer his question another was on it's way, this time I thought it was the old line every taxi driver comes up with from time to time. "I know you, don't I?"

Louise took my hand in preparation to answer so I thought, but she didn't have to reply at all, the cabbie did it for her, that was after first turning his gaze in my direction.

"You're Mrs Shaw, and you gov' are..." he paused just momentarily "are Mr Andrew Jackson!" he said as he steered the cab along this very busy road, and he continued before we had chance to confirm or deny his assumption, "well I never, fancy having you two in my cab!"

"You are of course right!" Louise said as she made herself a little more comfortable on the seat crossing her legs as she did so, her tone was very much to the point, not condescending, but spoken almost trying to steer the conversation away from ourselves.

"Made the headlines last year didn't the two of you!" he said, it wasn't so much a question more of a statement, and he was extremely correct in his observation, but Louise was going to be quick informing him that it was last year, in the past, and that's where it was going to stay.

"Correct again, I am Louise Shaw, and this is Andrew Jackson, but we don't feel a need to discuss the events of last year." Louise replied to the driver's last comment, her tone now full of authority, for now she was looking up at the rear-view mirror and managed to catch the cabbie's eyes, although they were exchanging looks via a mirror, Louise's look was intense and unwavering, poor man knew exactly what she meant. Her comment brought a change of subject, but back to the first one, that of an engagement ring.

"Have you anywhere else in mind that may have what you're looking for, Mrs Shaw, Mr Jackson?" he asked as he resumed his gaze towards the road.

"Oh I think I know just the right place," I replied giving Louise's hand a squeeze at the same time, it prompted her to once again look in my direction a smile formed on her lips, this was the first time I'd spoken since getting into the cab. By now we had joined Marylebone Road and in fact were nearing the station, Louise reminded me to have some money ready so as to pay the driver, I removed my wallet and took out a twenty pound note, she nodded indicating that it should be sufficient, I think that we both thought that the conversation had dried up between ourselves and the cabbie when quite by surprise he came back with another question along with a statement.

"Have you named the day yet? Haven't seen anything in the papers!" he enquired, as again he glanced in our direction.

"At present we haven't decided, but an announcement will be made shortly," Louise quickly replied, very softly she continued so that the driver wouldn't be able to hear, a confident look to her features. "We can ask Dennis to take care of the announcements perhaps he will be able to find some wedding consultants as well."

It wasn't to say Louise wasn't capable of taking care of these arrangements herself, but we had taken on Dennis as our personal assistant and part of that role included acting as secretary, organising our day-to-day events and taking care of many of our business matters.

Dennis had come to work for us just after the legal case against Len and Mark had come to court, he worked out of the Bristol office we had, and very soon picked up on our every need, organising our business calendar and within no time our social diary as well, the result was to have more time to spend in each other's company and of course more time with the children.

To say we hadn't made plans wasn't really true, tentative arrangements had been made, but nothing was set in stone so to speak. September was the month preferred by Louise for the wedding, it's a milder summer month, the heat not so oppressive, but the date hadn't been set, recalling from the last occasion when I'd got married there always seems to be a hundred and one things to do, and something is always forgotten, when we had discussed the wedding in the presence of Sarah she was quick to ask if she could be a bridesmaid, in fact I remember her almost begging her mother to allow her what must have seemed a simple request to Sarah. With these thoughts going round and round in my head we pulled up at the station concourse.

"Come along darling!" Louise's voice firm and strong snapped me out of my somewhat trance like state.

"I'm sorry, I was miles away," was my slightly slow reply as I recovered my bearings and senses, then I had to rummage in my trouser pocket to find the twenty pound note. Almost as soon as we pulled up I passed the note to the cabbie through the open glass divider, at the same time telling him to keep the change, his reply was as instant as his initial conversation.

"Thanks, Mr Jackson," he paused just momentarily then continued, "Mrs Shaw, and good luck with the wedding!" he finished as I vacated the cab still holding the door for my Louise and offering her my arm as support as she stepped out of the taxi.

"Thank you darling," Louise said, at the same time kissing me on the side of my face, her right hand holding onto my left arm, the driver took the twenty pound note, then she turned and looked into the cab and catching the driver's attention she continued, this time speaking to the cabbie, "and thank you for your kind wishes."

"Thank you." I added as I slammed the cab door.

We both heard the muffled reply of, 'thanks,' and almost instantly he was on his way.

I found the return train tickets securely placed in my wallet as we made our way towards the platforms in Paddington Station, Louise looked at the display and informed me that we had a twenty minute wait for our train to arrive, that together with the ten minute interval required to clean and tidy the carriages meant we had sufficient time to have a coffee before we boarded the train.

At thirteen fifteen we made our way to the first class carriages, our tickets were valid for travel at any time of the day, I made a point of switching off my mobile phone, Louise followed my example after removing her top coat, that was the next thing I did, and then we placed them on the overhead rack. Carefully we opened the copy of *The Times,* and spread it across the table, we hadn't had chance to read it during our journey to the capital, but now we had the perfect opportunity, Louise was sat next to the window, and as the train started to pull out of Paddington at thirteen thirty she leant her head onto my left shoulder.

For my part I scanned the open pages, but as on other occasions nothing really grabbed my attention, I glanced at Louise and noticed that the gentle rocking motion of the train had induced her into sleep, I relaxed myself in the seat and joined her in this most needed of slumber, I'm not sure how long we slept, but as the train trundled over a set of points and the carriage suddenly shook, I awoke, as did Louise. She stretched her body within the confines of the seat, at the same time shaking her hair, I stretched my arms out in front of me, and glancing at my watch I could see we had only been asleep for ten minutes, at the most, I offered to go and get some coffee from the restaurant car, Louise asked if I would bring her a sandwich, and if possible a cake. As I set off I watched her as she took a notepad together with a pen from her handbag, she placed them on the table in front of her, that was after folding the newspaper in half.

"Well go on then!" she forcefully said, indicating with her hand for me to get a move on adding "and don't forget the cake."

So off I went in search of the restaurant car, the motion of the train made me feel something like a sailor on the deck of a big ship as I swayed from side to side, the restaurant car was placed between the first class carriages and the standard, in fact two carriages away, I had to join quite a queue, and the coffee was served in plastic cups with what I thought were poorly fitting lids, the sandwiches wrapped in some plastic cling film, as were the two cakes I purchased, and it was all unceremoniously put into two paper bags, by the time I'd wobbled and swayed my way back to Louise I was sure that the lids would have come off the coffee and I was pleasantly surprised to find they hadn't.

"Oh I thought you'd got lost!" Louise sarcastically quipped as I neared our seat.

"Well there was quite a queue," I replied in my defence, but by now I was looking into her eyes, they were smiling before her lips started to say anything else. I resumed my seated position before asking her what she had been doing.

"Well as you can see I've been making some notes," she paused and moved the notepad closer to the centre of the table, "notes to do with our wedding," she told me pointing with her pen at the page full of text.

"But I thought you said about engaging the services of a wedding consultant," I said, as I studied the page as best I could, for once again we rattled over a set of uneven points, the clatter of metal against metal seemed to fill the carriage, momentarily deafening both of us.

"Yes I did, but there are some things that I will need to take care of," Louise replied, as she took a cup of coffee from one of the bags, then she continued, "oh look you've bought me a nice cake!" surprise back in her voice.

After removing my own cup of coffee and the sandwiches, together with the other cake I took a closer look at the notes Louise had been making, indeed she had thought of all the things that would be left off any list I would make, then one particular line caught my eye that brought a comment from me.

"Wedding dress, I thought you might like to go with Jill and choose something," I said, pointing at the line myself, and recalling Jill's astute sense of clothing.

"But Andrew, look at the next line, I've written that we will need bridesmaids' dresses, and possibly a pageboy's outfit," Louise said as she prepared to take a bite from the sandwich.

"I dare say that you could get them all from the same place," I replied taking the other half of the ham and cucumber sandwich.

"I expect I could, but I remember Susan, our nanny saying that there is a very good dressmaker in Chillingston, I thought I might use her," she paused looked into my eyes and went on, "in fact I've seen some of her work, and of course you are right, I will take Jill with me."

"That's fine with me," I said as I picked up my coffee again, then something took my interest in the paper, just a small headline, it referred to some bad weather that had battered the shoreline of Cornwall for the past few days, reporting that at least six people were feared drowned in the severe storms that had lashed the Cornish coast overnight; a family of four were reported lost at sea, presumed drowned, a man and woman along with their two children, the family were out in their fishing boat when it capsized in heavy seas off the Lizard Peninsula, their bodies still hadn't been found, and that was after an extensive air and sea search, a spokesman for the coastguard pointed out just how hazardous the weather can be at this time of the year, closing his statement he said that due to the high winds and strong tides it was possible that the bodies may never be found. In a completely separate incident, two people, a man and woman out walking their dogs were washed of the quayside at Newquay, their bodies were recovered later the following morning, and the article continued with other details of the storm.

"Have you seen this Louise?" I asked feeling somewhat distressed by the article.

"Darling that's terrible," Louise responded taking my hand, at the same time sensing my concerned state, as she too studied the article in the paper. Then she continued,

"Those poor souls, what an awful thing to happen," she paused again looked at me and went on, "perhaps we could pay our respects when we visit Cornwall, Do you think we should stay at Warmingstow Heights Andrew?"

"Well you did mention about going to Truro, you know to find that jeweller's," I said, in my mind I knew we could stay with Stavros and the rest of the family if we wished, but again my attention was drawn to the newspaper, but it was Louise who spoke as she too had noticed that the article continued with something of an unpleasant twist in the news.

"Andrew, it says that the fishing boat had sent a mayday signal in the early hours of the morning, but the weather conditions were too severe to scramble the helicopter, and it was several more hours before the sea had calmed down sufficiently for the lifeboat to be launched." She finished and I looked closely into her near weeping eyes.

"It just goes to show how treacherous the weather can be at this time of the year," I started to reply, and I went on, "of course we can pay our respects when we visit the Duchy." I finished and at the same time gave her hand a reassuring squeeze.

"Thank you," she replied, just the slightest of a smile to her lips.

We arrived at Bristol Temple Mead station at fifteen hundred and the train seemed to come to a halt quite suddenly. After putting our top coats on we made our way out of the train and onto the platform and as we did a very strong cold wind blew, Louise took my arm and pulled in close to my side.

"Gosh!" she exclaimed and her left hand went up to her collar and pulled it up to offer herself some more protection.

"Come on," I said as we began to make our way towards the exit, the sound of another train coming into the terminus almost drowning my words, as the noisy roar of the engine died away I continued, "we can get a taxi back to Chillingston." Louise glanced at her watch as I said the words and I sensed she had other plans before we returned to the Manor.

"Let's pop into the office and see Dennis," she paused and looked into my eyes, then went on, "you know, to get the ball rolling with regard to organising the wedding consultants."

"OK," I started to reply, knowing that there was little point in me arguing to the contrary, for Louise now had some of the arrangements set in her mind, not only that but time would soon disappear, it may well be April, but September would soon be with us. "Shall we take a taxi to the office?" I asked as we neared the exit that lead into the entrance hall.

"Well, we could walk, it would keep us warm, and it's only a ten minute stroll," she replied, then quite suddenly added, "tickets darling!"

I quickly found my wallet it was in my inner jacket pocket and as we got closer to the ticket inspector I removed the tickets from it.

"Thank you, sir, madam," the inspector said as we made our way through the barrier.

The foyer of the station was full of people, some just stood looking up towards the screens displaying the arrivals and departures, their necks straining, some making their way in the direction of the platforms, their trolley cases clunking a regular beat as they passed over the gaps between the paving slabs, many of the people were carrying additional bags, it appeared to be something of an obstacle course to get to the main doors and avoid bumping into someone, but make it we did.

Momentarily we stood looking in the direction of the main road, the slope of the station incline seemed to have cars everywhere, many of them taxis, and it certainly was a busy afternoon, it crossed my mind to ask Louise again if we should take a taxi, for there seemed to be an abundance of them, a few of them were parked with their engines still running, the clatter of the diesel engines mingled with the many conversations going on around us. But stood here in the late afternoon, the wind outside of the station complex seemed to be colder, as I exhaled I could see my breath, we are in for a cold night I thought to myself.

"Come along Andrew!" Louise said, tugging at my arm as she said the words, taking me out of my previous thoughts.

"Sorry, I was miles away," I replied and now I felt that cold wind again, cutting like a knife, it made me shiver, just a little. We started to make our way down the station approach when suddenly we were stopped; it was a woman calling my name, that made the two of us come to something of an abrupt halt.

"Andrew!" the voice called again, a tone of jolliness to it, but at the same time my name was being called in something of a casual manner making me think it was another man by the same name that was being beckoned, but then I picked up on the style and harmonics of the voice, this was someone I knew of old, and someone Louise had never met, as I was digesting this recollection of the past and trying to put it into some sort of order the woman called my name again. 'Andrew.'

Some of my distant past suddenly started to return to me and in doing so it reminded me of a life prior to Louise coming back into it. I looked round and standing about twenty feet away from Louise and me was another woman I had worked with for a few years after Louise had left the office, her name, Melissa.

I sensed Louise squeeze my right arm a little tighter, as I've said we had stopped walking and now we were both facing this woman who was approaching us, in her right hand a large dark brown handbag, in her left a black laptop case. I studied her as she made her way towards us, she was wearing a full length brown coat, the colour matched the handbag perfectly, and had the appearance of being very expensive.

Now I hadn't seen this woman for what must have been five or maybe six years, and as I've said she came into the office as a replacement some time after Louise had left, she was drafted in until a more permanent member of staff could be appointed, as it turned out the office and members of staff became surplus to requirement and the entire centre was moved across country, Melissa left the company under a much better redundancy package than many of the others who had stayed on hoping to find employment somewhere else in the company, but since her leaving I'd never given her a second thought.

"Hello," I said as this woman stood a few feet from Louise and me.

"Is that all I get?" she replied, I looked into her hazel eyes, they seemed bright and they too matched her hazel hair that was short and cut into her neck, just enough to cover the fawn scarf that was protruding from the collar of her coat, she pulled her head back a little as she spoke, instantly I thought she required an introduction to Louise.

"Oh, I'm so sorry," I began and turning to look at Louise I could see she had already started to smile, "this is Melissa Thorne," pausing again I sensed

Melissa come a little closer but I continued giving Louise's full title, "Melissa, this is Mrs Louise Shaw."

"That wasn't what I meant!" Melissa said, at the same time placing her laptop on the ground and putting her right hand on my shoulder then she kissed me on the left side of my face coming between Louise and me. Her actions took me a little more than by surprise and what she said was to alarm me even more, "Andrew you were never that reluctant when it came to kissing me when we worked together!"

I glanced again in the direction of Louise as this woman pulled away, she looked even more surprised than I felt, but then Melissa was to take our minds off this startling introduction by offering her hand to Louise but as she did so the surprise returned.

"Its so nice to meet you Louise," she said as their right hands came together and she continued directing her comment to Louise, and these words had something of a cutting edge to them, "so you're the woman I replaced in the office," she paused and her eyes flashed in my direction, a slight smile to her lips, then she went on, "and now you're back in his life, you know Louise, he never stopped saying how much he wanted you," again she stopped and now turned to look at me, "isn't that right Andrew?"

"It's nice to meet you Melissa," was Louise's somewhat startled reply but still she held onto her demeanour.

This comment was, I would say, a little unfair, very few in the office knew of my true feelings for Louise, when we worked together or after she'd left, for as is often the case one thing said in jest is often taken out of all context by others, and then it gets interpreted into something of a vulgar nature.

"Well I'm not sure that I spoke that much about you darling after you'd left," I replied directing my words to Louise but still feeling somewhat embarrassed by Melissa's comment. But in truth I had confided in some of my closer work colleagues of my fondness for Louise, but these people were ones I trusted and I have to admit that Melissa wasn't one of them, she had always been a little on the forward side for my liking, sure she was pretty, and well presented but had proved early on that she couldn't be trusted, that was only over a passing comment with regard to someone else's ability to do the job correctly, unknown to myself this comment was repeated and as always exaggerated and blown out of all proportion, the result was a disagreement with the individual in question that lingered on for some considerable time.

"Did you have a relationship with this Lisa?" Suddenly it was the voice of Stuart interrupting my thoughts of the past.

"Sorry Stuart!" I replied again holding my head.

"I didn't mean to startle you Andrew, but," he paused and I watched as he uncrossed his legs placing his notepad on the table he continued, "it's the only way to stop you, you've become so engrossed in recalling the past Andrew, it proves that there isn't that much wrong with your long term memory, well let's say the not so distant past anyway." He finished and was leaning across the table slightly.

"What did you ask me?" I enquired trying to recall Stuart's question.

"I asked you if you had had a relationship with the woman you spoke of, Lisa, wasn't it?" Stuart asked.

"No, and her name was Melissa!" I sharply replied, now this was the second time that Stuart had misplaced something I'd told him, I put it down to his style of therapy, he seemed to be digging but his question prompted me to go back to working with Melissa, "we danced at an office party on one occasion, and she was upset one morning when I came into the office," I paused so as to gather my thoughts of that day so long ago and as I did something Louise had said that evening after our unexpected encounter with Melissa.

"Well let's go back to that meeting at Temple Mead railway station in Bristol, on the station approach I think you said!" Stuart said as he once again reclined in his seat.

"Let me see," I began, at the same time I picked up the glass of water, took a long drink from it, and then went on, "we just parted, Melissa saying it was nice to see us..." I stopped, for something else had been said that lodged in Louise's mind and was to recall itself later that evening, much the same question as Stuart had asked, "no, Melissa said to Louise that I had a good ear for listening to people's problems."

I watched as Melissa climbed into a waiting cab and then went on her way, just a wave of her right hand and she was gone, Louise and I did as planned and walked to the office we have in town.

"Andrew, you said, have in town!" Stuart again interrupted me, and he went on with a question, "do you remember?"

"Yes I do, and as far as I know I still do." I replied, and added, "well, Dennis is still running the business from there, with the help of the management team Louise and I had set up."

"OK, I'm sorry to interrupt you Andrew, please continue," Stuart told me.

Louise and I made our way to the Bristol office, as Louise had said it was only a short walk, and it warmed us up, I didn't give Melissa any more thought, nor did we mention it, we were more concerned with crossing the roads safely.

I remember standing in the foyer of the administrative centre where our office is situated waiting for the lift to arrive.

"That will have to be changed!" Louise told me looking towards the plaque on the wall, our names etched on the brass plate, the title being, 'Jackson and Shaw Enterprises'

Dennis was busy working, but pleased to see us, he informed us that we had messages from Louise's mother Diane and one from William, my son, and strangely a lady making enquires about the hotels, Dennis thought she was rather vague, but didn't pursue the issue, lastly he said he'd had a call from the security firm that had installed the alarm system at Chillingston Manor, some modifications were required to it.

We took care of all the messages that required our immediate attention, and then made our way home to Chillingston Manor, Louise of course asked Dennis if he would make some tentative enquires with wedding consultants, and draw up a list, ready for her to conduct interviews.

It was quite late in the evening by the time we arrived home, we'd taken a taxi, William had offered to run us back to Chillingston but that meant taking him out of the garage and he'd told me that they were extremely busy, in fact the purpose of his call was to tell me that he and Peter were looking for bigger premises, something I didn't have a problem with, after all they were running the business.

By the time we arrived back at the Manor the children were in bed, Susan had taken care of all the necessary requirements with regard to that, all that was needed from me was that nightly bedtime read, as soon as that task was completed Louise and I had the evening to ourselves, I remember now, rather than Louise cook a meal we took a leisurely stroll to our local pub.

"You see Stuart I can remember a lot of the details from some time ago!" I said bringing myself to a halt quite abruptly.

"That's very good Andrew," was the start of Stuart's response to what must have seemed like a flash of inspiration, and he continued, "perhaps we should call it a day for now, you know pick it up again tomorrow." He finished and looked at his watch.

I looked at my own, it was two thirty, it wasn't late and now I felt as if I was beginning to get somewhere, so I went on, "No Stuart. Please let me continue." I almost begged.

"OK, only for another hour or so," he paused and looked at the containers of pills on the table in front of him, then he added," you'll need to take some more of these this evening, just help you relax and sleep." His voice was once again stern and very strong.

I went on. As I've said, that evening we walked from the Manor to the village of Chillingston, this was made all the easier for us by the fact that we had a footpath running through the grounds of Chillingston Manor, it comes out on the edge of the village, there is a concealed gate in the boundary wall, the gate is normally kept locked, but tonight Louise had brought the key for the padlock with her. The sun had just gone down as we headed out and onto the high street, the street lights flicked on almost as if by request as we passed by them; slowly the orange sodium glow was engulfing the whole of the village. The lights were already on in most of the houses we passed, the interior lights projecting out of the tiny leaded windows that were set in the thick Cotswold stone walls and out onto the road ahead of us that was before the occupants drew the curtains for the night. I remember thinking that this was the most picturesque of Cotswold villages even in the fading evening light, the moss-covered roofs shone as the moonlight dodged it's way from behind the light blanket of clouds that were passing over the night sky to give additional illumination, but it was still a cold night, and there was every indication that we would be having a frost, we passed by the first pub in the village, 'The Chillingston Retreat', preferring the hostelry situated opposite the common, where the duck pond is, the name of the establishment is 'The Ox and Plough'. Now it's something of a hazardous route to the pub once you've crossed the main road, as I've said the other side of the common is the duck pond, quite full at this time of the year, due to the natural spring that feeds it with icy cold water, but more importantly was the treacherous driveway that leads to the pub, it's full of potholes that always seem to be full of water, once these were negotiated we were inside this Tudor-style public house, it was typical of this type of building, low beams, small windows and very thick walls, as always we were greeted by the landlord in his place behind the bar, we weren't very regular visitors, but once you've been in two or three times, then he remembers you by name.

We had the most pleasant of evenings and ate in the restaurant attached to the side of the pub, the meal itself was splendid, complemented with a fine bottle of red wine, the walk back to the Manor seemed to take no time at all, but it was very cold and as I'd noticed on our way to the pub we were in for a very hard frost.

When we got home, it was just after ten, Louise had been a little quiet, only with myself, it wasn't unusual for her to be withdrawn, I put it down to her being tired, after all it had been a long day, the trip to London had been something of a wasted journey, but when we made our way to bed the real reason for her quietness was to be revealed to me.

I was lying in bed waiting for Louise to join me, we'd looked in on the children, both were fast asleep, I'd cleaned my teeth and installed myself in bed as Louise took care of her requirements, as she slid under the covers she immediately posed a question to me.

"This Melissa, you never mentioned her before," she said as her head went onto my chest her tone demanding.

"To tell you the truth, I'd forgotten all about her," I replied to this simplest of questions, but Louise wanted to know more.

"What did she mean when she said you were a good listener?" her question had that probing edge to it as she asked she also looked into my eyes.

"Well, one morning when I came into the office I found her in tears..." I began to reply only for Louise to stop me in mid-flow.

"And was that due to husband trouble?" now she had pushed herself up in the bed a little and was looking deep into my eyes.

"She wasn't married, but it was due to partner problems," I said, as I did I sensed where this conversation was going and the next comment reinforced my thinking.

"A little bit like me then, when I used to cry on your shoulder!" her statement made me sit up, just a little.

"You could say that," I began my reply but thinking very quickly I needed to reassure Louise of one thing, "Louise the seeds of my love for you were already sown, there was no way I could have fallen for her."

"But Andrew she is quite pretty," Louise responded, a playful look now in her eyes.

"Louise, I was struggling to come to terms with my marriage falling apart and the ever increasing prospect of loosing my job, the last thing I was thinking about was having a fling with a young woman in the office," I told her, she was now sat up in bed, I was beginning to feel that this conversation could easily get out of hand as Louise had become just a little agitated.

"You haven't said if you fancied her," Louise asked almost as soon as I finished talking, her tone now was one of enquiring, I'd never seen her like this before, it was as if she was looking for something that wasn't there, and she continued, "as you never mentioned her before, are you trying to hide something from me Andrew? Did you have a little box for her?" she finished and could sense I was somewhat upset by her comment.

"No," I angrily began to reply, and went on, "that's not fair, you're reading more into this than there is, she didn't even come close to being a friend, let alone anything else, sure we had a dance at the office party, but nothing else, a peck on the cheek and that was all."

By now Louise was trying to take my hand, clearly she could see I was distressed, I pulled away slightly and was about to get out of bed when she spoke again.

"I'm sorry, I didn't mean to upset you, and obviously I have," she paused and took my hand again, this time I relaxed so she could have it, she continued as I slid back into bed, "well unknown to yourself there were other women in the office at the same time as I was there, that did fancy you," she stopped and the suddenness of her statement made me look into her eyes, "don't look so surprised Andrew, it's not only men that look and fancy the opposite sex, and often we compare notes!"

"Why are you telling me this now, is it just to pacify me because I'm upset?" I asked still feeling a little put out by the initial interrogation.

"No my darling, it's what goes on in so many offices, it's office life I suppose, the place I worked in after I'd left you had several couples who were having affairs." Louise said again pulling me closer to her. And she continued, "I can see by your reaction I have no reason to doubt those words of love you told me in Cornwall all that time ago," she paused to gather her thoughts, then had one more question, "please forgive me, I am sorry."

Her words of asking for forgiveness reminded me of something I'd said to her on another occasion when we'd had a slight difference, that I would forgive her for anything, and at least now she had apologised to me, it also made me think of the past and what had gone on between us, and a question of my own came into my head, so I asked it of Louise after accepting her apology.

"You know that I'd forgive you for anything, and I mean anything," I said as I started to make myself comfortable in bed again, Louise did the same and drew in close to me, then I felt the time was right to ask the question.

"What would you have done if I had died when I was out in the back of beyond, you know if I hadn't been able to get away from Len and make it to the village?" I enquired, but the reply wasn't what I was expecting.

"What would you have wanted me to do?" Louise asked rubbing my chest as she spoke.

"I'd have wanted you to carry on!" I paused for I felt that I needed to be a little more precise, "and if that meant finding someone else to spend your life with then so be it."

"And that's what I'd want for you!" was Louise's emphatic reply her facial expression telling me as much.

Well April moved on, Louise took take care of the arrangements with regard to the wedding plans, I know she interviewed at least four companies before making a decision, and that was after consulting with Jill. Louise and I had a weekend in Cornwall, staying at Warmingstow Heights, it was just the two of us, the purpose of the visit was to choose an engagement ring for Louise, and also buy the wedding rings, the weekend was very successful, but one thing played on my mind for a little while, the man we employ to look after Warmingstow Heights informed us that a yacht had been moored in our bay for a number of days, Louise suggested that it may have been sheltering during a storm, but since our return from London the weather had been fine and as I've said this played on my mind for some time.

I made some tentative plans for a holiday with Stavros and the rest of our adoptive family in his homeland, Greece, that was planned for May and with all the precision I had come to expect of being with Louise and her involvement it took place, one thing that struck me was the bond that seemed to build between Sarah and Nana, it was a little strange, never spoken about, but there was an evident attachment between the two of them. I recall one particular incident.

"Nana," Sarah started politely and very articulately, "could we go for a walk please?"

Her question prompted us grown-ups to stop talking and look in the direction of Stavros's daughter, Sarah's request was direct and very much to the point, at the same time her blue eyes were almost burning into Nana.

"Yes, that would be very nice!" Nana replied, only the slightest hesitation in her voice, but at the same time her reply was direct in its answer.

Louise, Stavros, Marie and I watched as Sarah slipped off the chair, her hands gripping the sides as she did so, at the same time Nana stood and as they came together Sarah's right hand slipped into Nana's left, once again their eyes made contact, something told me that Sarah had a need to be alone with this woman, I glanced at Louise and I'm sure she sensed the same feelings I had.

"Louise," Stavros began, after looking in our direction he went on, "that daughter of yours is very astute!"

"You are correct Stavros," Louise started to reply and after taking my hand she continued, "she's well aware of what her father was involved in." she paused again and was about to reveal something I was well aware of, "she is very good at keeping secrets."

"Andrew, Louise," Stavros began, and continued, "sometimes it is better that you don't know the truth, you understand? Yes. Often lessons are harder to teach, rather than learn!" And I was well aware of what Stavros was referring to and also Sarah's ability to keep secrets, as with regard to Louise's comment and I remembered our own.

"Andrew, you're aware of what your friend was referring too, aren't you?" Stuart again asked, his interruption didn't seem untimely, but all the same brought me out of my mesmerised state, sure I had mentioned Stavros, along with Alex, in previous conversations, but I hadn't gone into any detail as to what that involvement was. Something in Stuart's question, or rather the manner in which he asked the question made me feel slightly uncomfortable. He seemed to be prying, almost digging for information that had no relevance to the present time or the most recent past.

"I am, but they have nothing to do with what has happened to me in the last week," I replied, still just a little perturbed by his question, and he had another he wanted to ask me, not leaving the subject alone.

"Andrew, have you heard from your friends?" Stuart asked as he leant across the table, at the same time pushing the tumbler of water towards me, "have some more water," he added.

"Yes I have," I replied, not giving any more detail to my reply.

"Is that Stavros or Alex?" was his immediate response.

"Well Alex actually," I said as Stuart sat back into his chair his manner now relaxed again, and I continued "Alex phoned this morning," I paused trying to regain my thoughts of earlier in the day, that had become a little difficult, but slowly the events came back to me. "Yes, Alex asked if I'd meet him the day after tomorrow at his golf club."

"And what did you say?" Stuart enquired his eyes as questioning as his response.

"I said it's too soon for me to be out and about!" I told him that was after thinking deeply, I still felt very uncomfortable about going out alone.

"What if I accompany you?" Stuart asked his features relaxed as was his tone as he sat back in the leather easy chair.

"Stuart, I think it's rather a lot to ask of you," I said as I picked up the tumbler of water and I took a sip.

"Andrew," he paused before continuing, looked me in the eyes and went on, "we can have session on memory recovery in the morning and go to the club in the afternoon, what do you say?" was Stuart's reply to my own question and he went on, "I can be on hand if you start to feel uneasy."

"If you're sure you don't mind," I said feeling just a little more confident about the prospect of going out, I went on, "where had we got to?"

"You had just started to explain your relationship with your friend Stavros…" Stuart started to say, but was cut short by the telephone ringing, he finished by adding, "go on you answer it."

I made my way into the study; it was William my eldest son, he as always enquired about my health, mental and physical, the conversation went on for a few minutes and concluded with a question that I needed to share with Stuart before I could make a decision upon his request. I turned the question over and over in my mind as I made my way back to the lounge, as I entered Stuart picked up on my puzzled expression.

"What is it Andrew?" he asked at the same time replacing his notepad on the coffee table.

"That was my eldest son, William," I started to say as I resumed my seated position.

"Has he said something to upset you Andrew?" Stuart enquired.

"Not directly," was all I could manage as a response.

"If not directly then what did he say that has made you so uneasy," Stuart asked.

"He would like me to go to the garage tomorrow, or the day after, well as soon as possible, he says he needs the space in the workshop and would like Louise's BMW moved," I paused trying hard to recall his words, now it seemed as if I couldn't remember things that I'd been told only a few minutes ago, I rested my head in my hands in an effort to help.

"Take your time Andrew," Stuart said very softly repeating, "just take your time."

"He says the police have told him the car can be disposed of!" I replied still trying to put some order into the conversation that was now rapidly fading from my memory.

"It will be another chapter of your past laid to rest," Stuart said, his words spoken with an even more confident tone to them, almost an eagerness in the words, wanting me to have the car disposed of, and he continued, "then you can start to look to the future and rebuild your life," he paused again and looked at his watch, then went on, "that is once next week is out of the way."

There was something about what he'd just said that puzzled me, not so much about next week, more the point of laying the past to rest, I was at this moment having trouble recalling the past, so forgetting it forever wouldn't be that much of a problem, but these thoughts were once again stolen from me by Stuart making an observation.

"Andrew, it's now four thirty," he paused as I looked at my Omega watch, it was indeed four thirty, Stuart went on, "I suggest we call it a day for now, and as I've already said we can continue in the morning, sadly I have an appointment in the afternoon, but the following day we can start early," he paused, moved forward in his seat, then went on, "that is before we go to the golf club and meet your friend Alex." He finished and was now looking directly at me having moved further forward on his seat in readiness to get up.

"OK," I said as I stood, I continued as Stuart reached down to the side of the chair and picked up his briefcase, I watched as he rested it on his lap, with a flick of his thumbs the metal clasps snapped open, as he placed the note book and his pen in the case I asked a question, "what time shall we say?"

"I can be here by eight!" was his very quick response as he stood, he was somewhat taller than me and as he looked down at me, I felt a little insecure along with a wanting to regain my memory.

"That will be fine," I replied, at the same time I started to make my way towards the hall as I got to the door I went on, "I was awake early this morning..." I cut myself short, "I think I was."

"Right Andrew, it's important that you relax this evening, and also very important that you remember to take your medication," Stuart said as we neared the front door, as I held the door open for him he continued, "it's a nice place you have here."

"Yes, I've lived here a long time," I started to reply, but then something else came back into my mind, "but I have a house somewhere else, don't I?"

"You do Andrew, yes you do!" Stuart said as he passed by me in the porchway, standing on the step outside he went on, "you've been telling me about the house you own in Scotland, along with the manor house at Chillingston, also the property in Cornwall."

"Stuart, I'm having trouble remembering anything!" I said now feeling even more confused.

"That's because you're tired Andrew, you've just told me that you were up early," Stuart said, at the same time he patted me on my shoulder, "go and get some rest and I'll see you in the morning," he paused speaking and on the step, then looked me in the eye and continued, "it may not seem obvious Andrew, but there will be a reason for all that has happened." How little did I understand his words, and it was to be some considerable time before their significance was to come to me.

He finished and made his way down the steps of my house in the suburbs of the city and on to his car. As he approached his car his right hand slipped into his inner jacket pocket, I watched as he held his mobile phone in his hand, his thumb danced its way over the keypad, then up to his head it went, I thought I heard him say, 'things are going fine' but I couldn't be sure, he placed his briefcase on the ground next to the driver's door, then removed a small bunch of keys from his trouser pocket, it was then that he turned and looked in my direction, "go on in Andrew, do as I said, get some rest," he called to me, then he continued to speak into his mobile phone, I was unable to make out any more of his conversation due to the traffic on the road and more importantly the fact that Stuart had by now got into his car, but his conversation did continue for several minutes, I gave up waiting for him to leave and made my way back indoors.

I stood in the kitchen and looked around me, now I was wondering what I'd come in here for; I rubbed my forehead with my right hand at the same time I yawned, the day really had caught up with me. I made my way into the lounge, relaxed in one of the winged armchairs, this lack of recollection was now beginning to depress me, and I couldn't even remember why I'd moved back into my house in Bristol.

I must have fallen asleep, I was awoken by the telephone ringing, by the time I'd come to and rubbed the sleep from my eyes it had stopped, investigating to find out who had phoned me only revealed that the caller had withheld their number, I looked at my watch, it was now seven fifteen, Stuart had left at four thirty, I been asleep in the chair much longer than I first thought, it was time for some food.

So I set about the task of making a meal for myself, all the time wondering what had happened to me that could have made me forget the past few days, more like a week so easily, once I had prepared my dinner I made my way back into the lounge, setting the small coffee table I turned the television on, perhaps some item of news would bring my past flooding back to me, but it didn't, I watched the television with as much interest as I had in the meal I'd prepared, then as the program changed so did my curiosity, for some reason I was transfixed, unable to move away from the TV, the program was a semi-documentary into the way prisoners of war have been treated, particular attention was paid to the methods that are used to get information from these individuals, not only was sleep depravation mentioned but also the use of the suggestion process, by repeatedly telling someone that they may have done or been involved in some particular act of violence or illegal operation, that together with the administration of certain drugs often has the required effect of obtaining an admission of guilt.

The problem with this often-used method of interrogation is that many innocent people have been convicted of crimes they haven't committed, as the program came to a close it left my mind in something of a quandary, something had happened to me that I couldn't explain, but my thoughts were stolen from me by the ringing of the front door bell, I wasn't expecting anyone, maybe Stuart had forgotten something and had returned to retrieve it, I thought to myself as I made my way along the hall, but it wasn't Stuart who was stood on the other side of the sliding porch door as I pulled it open.

Chapter Six

A visit from Stavros

"Andrew, my friend!" were the words that greeted me as I slid the frosted glass door to the right on its runner.

"Stavros!" I cried as I almost fell into his waiting arms.

"Come, come my friend, tell me what has been going on!" he said as he lead me back into the lounge, all the time his big strong arms supporting me.

"Stavros, I wish I knew what was going on myself!" I told him after he'd helped me to a seat.

"Andrew if you don't mind me saying you look completely washed out," he said as he sat in the chair next to me, his right hand still resting on my shoulder. I turned and looked him directly in the eyes.

"I feel drained Stavros," I paused once again trying to put the recent past into some form of order, but before I had chance to continue Stavros spoke again, this time with another question.

"Tell me Andrew, why are you back in your old family home, I have been to Chillingston Manor, it is all locked up, I mean the gates are chained together, Andrew you must tell your old friend what has been happening," he paused and had one more question to ask me, and it was going to be the most painful of answers I would have to give, "and where are Louise and the children? I have also been to Trevor and Diane's, there is no sign of them! Have you had some sort of fall out?" he asked.

"Stavros, Trevor and Diane have gone to stay with Jackie, their other daughter for a few days," I began with my reply, I was desperately trying to avoid telling him what I'd been told but he was able to pick up on my concern.

"Andrew, I asked you about Louise, Sarah and James, where are they?" his words hung in the air, and were spoken with a firmness that meant I couldn't avoid answering him, I had no choice but to give him a reply.

"Stavros, I've been told that they are dead!" I said, at the same time I buried my head into my hands, leaning forward I could feel his right hand on the back of my neck. I added, "they were killed in a terrible car accident." I sat in this position for what seemed like an age, all the time Stavros's rugged old fingers gently massaging the back of my neck and the lower part between the shoulder blades, and it was Stavros who broke the silence between us, but now his words were spoken softly and in the most reassuring of ways.

"My friend, I'm at a loss for words to comfort you!" his voice was wavering, emotion in every word he spoke.

"I don't know what has happened to me or anyone else in the week leading up to the accident." Was all I could say in reply to my now shaken friend, I looked up in his direction, he was a strong man, but this dreadful news had all but reduced him to the state I'd been for days, I continued as best I could, "apparently I was found wandering in Chillingston woods, dazed and very confused."

"Surely Andrew someone has been able to tell you what has happened?" Stavros asked, now his voice almost back to its normal level.

"I was told…" I began, for now I was recalling what I'd been told by the police, I couldn't remember a thing that had happened before the accident or after, "the police told me that our car, well Louise's BMW had been involved in a hit and run, as a result it had burst into flames, they didn't have a chance of getting out…" my words drifted away now to be replaced by tears.

"I can clearly see the distressed state you are in Andrew; I shall fix us a strong drink!" Stavros told me, and as he said the words he was up and out of his chair and on his way to the study where the drinks cabinet is.

"Stavros this state is made all the worse because I can't remember anything," I called as I started to follow him into the study, then I added, "I'm not sure I should be having any alcohol due to the medication I'm taking," I paused almost knowing what Stavros's response would be.

"Andrew my child, I am here now and will be staying the night, I am sure if you miss one night, well I don't think it will harm you that much, you understand, yes!" he replied as he opened the drinks cabinet, he went on, with the brandy bottle in one hand and a bottle of malt whisky in the other hand.

"I have been having some help," I said as I watched Stavros pour two very large drinks.

"What sort of help have you been getting?" Stavros asked as he passed me the lead tumbler almost full of malt whisky.

"For the past few days I've had a therapist here with me, you know the sort that deals in memory recollection, before that I stayed with Trevor and Diane, that was after I'd been discharged from hospital," I paused took a pull from the tumbler before continuing, "it was at first thought that I may have had a blow to the head," again I stopped and rubbed the back of my head with my right hand, it felt a little tender, but nothing as if I'd had a knock on it.

"Come, let us go back into the lounge," Stavros said as he guided me in that direction.

"Anyway Stavros what brings you to this part of the country?" I asked as I resumed my position in the armchair.

"Andrew I have been in London on some business," he paused himself and took another drink from his glass, then resting the glass on the arm of the chair he went on, "my cousin has been in the country and has asked me if I will help him set up a new company, but that is of little significance in comparison to what is going on with yourself." He stopped and again took a pull from his glass, then surprisingly said, "I didn't see anything in the papers!"

"No, I felt…" I stopped for now something had come back to me, "well it wasn't just me, Trevor and Diane also thought it would be best if the press didn't get too involved, this coming so soon after Len and Mark were sent down, anyway the press have had far too many stories at mine and Louise's expense, all Trevor, Diane and I want is some privacy," I paused again as I recalled something else from the past that had occurred at the same time, once in my mind I continued, "anyway Stavros, the papers have been full of other issues, the terrorist bombings, along with the chocolate scandal, I think our news only made it onto the back pages."

"I understand, but Andrew is there a possibility that they were involved in whatever has happened? I mean Len and Mark!" Stavros asked stealing my own thoughts.

"No, they're not bright enough to have done this sort of thing," I said as again I began to recall something from only a few days ago, "the police think it was joy-riders, they found the other car, a Range Rover in the woods, that was also burnt-out."

"My friend once again I apologise for not being home when you were kidnapped," Stavros started to say, I put my hand up in the air indicating for him to stop.

"Stavros every time we meet you say how sorry you are that you weren't home," I paused and looked into his eyes, then I continued, "that is in the past, they are safely behind bars now." But in the back of my mind I did wonder if Len could have organised this terrible act.

"My friend, there isn't that much wrong with your memory, if you can recall me apologising every time we are together," he said, it made his statement seem as if it had been a test, a test to see just what I could remember.

"Tell me Andrew, just how is this therapist helping you? And what medication are you taking?" Stavros asked confirming my previous thoughts of him testing me, only his style would be completely different.

"He's given me some drugs to help me relax, then I can start recalling the events from the past, no particular day but they do make me a little more lucid, I've also got something to take when I go to bed, they really do help me go off to sleep." I told Stavros, I looked at him again as he emptied the brandy glass in one swift movement.

"My friend you still haven't told me why you are living here in your old house!" Stavros asked.

"Stavros, even now it's difficult for me to remember," I paused just long enough for Stavros to get a few words in.

"You sit there and get your mind together while I go and fix us another drink, come along Andrew, finish your whisky!" As always his words had that authoritative ring to them, but at the same time a gentleness to them, I did as he instructed me, but as I sat alone a question came into my mind, and as soon as Stavros was back in the room with the refilled glasses I had to ask him.

"How are the rest of the family?" I said as I looked up at him, in his hand an even bigger measured glass of whisky.

"They are all fine, but my friend they will be devastated when they hear of your sad news," he said as he passed me the tumbler of malt, he continued as he made himself comfortable once again in the chair next to me. "Demetri is running the business while I'm away, that is because Andreas is in America, you know Andrew that he was keen to go, so it is a bit of a working holiday, he is looking for some new outlets in the States, as for Marie, well she is helping in the shop with Demetri, I have only been away a few days…" he paused and took hold of my hand then continued, "but now I need to stay with you, it is important that I am here for you, yes!"

"You don't have to Stavros," I began to reply, then something came into my head and I had to ask the question, "Stavros, you didn't mention Nana."

"Well as you are aware of her business then it is safe for you to know," he started to say stopping to take a drink, then resting his glass on his lap but still steadying it with his right hand he continued, "I understand she is on one of those exercises, I think its referred to as a tactical operation but just what it involves I have no idea." He finished.

"It seems like a life-time ago that she saved Louise's and my life…" my words drifted away as I realised what I'd said, for now I was alone, but Stavros wasn't going to let me dwell on what I'd just said, for he was in as quick as a flash with his own words.

"There my friend, as I've said nothing wrong with your memory!" he looked again into my eyes, perhaps reading my inner thoughts as he had done on many occasions in the past, then continued, "tell me Andrew, have the arrangements been made for the funerals?"

Now here was a question, I had been informed of what was going on, but it was now a case of scouring the inner depths of my mind to recall what I'd been told.

"Have you eaten?" I asked avoiding the hard work involved in bringing the past to the fore in my mind.

"Yes I have Andrew, you have no need to worry yourself about that," he replied after taking a sip from his glass, he added, "but you didn't answer my question."

"I've been told that the funerals can't take place until a full and," I paused as the official police statement came back to me, "until a full and proper identification has taken place, that will involve dental checks along with a DNA test, that is if any evidence can be located," I stopped again in an effort to recall what arrangements had been made, more or less clear in my mind I continued, "well I involved Dennis our secretary, he got in touch with the local funeral directors, apparently they have everything in hand."

"OK, that is good, but you say that you've been in hospital!" Stavros questioned me once again.

"Yes I was taken to the hospital after I was found in the woods, apparently I passed out in the ambulance on the way, so I was put on a drip, along with all of the other paraphernalia of tubes and attachments," I told Stavros, and I went on, "but that is about as much as I can remember being told Stavros, that is until I started to recover in the hospital, then slowly, and I mean very slowly things began to fall into place."

"Then carry on Andrew, I won't rush you, in your own time, yes!" the waiting Stavros replied.

I came round, completely unaware of where I was, the first thing I realised was I couldn't breathe, well, not easily, I tried to put my right hand up, as it felt as if something was in my throat, but I couldn't bend my arm, I tried desperately to look at it, but my vision was very blurred, I attempted to lift my left hand, but that had what seemed like wires and tubes attached to it, it was then that I heard a voice, a woman's voice I didn't recognise, and after hearing it once it would be some time before I was to hear the voice again.

"It's alright Mr Jackson, just take it very steady," it was a female, very soft, and gentle, soothing almost.

I looked in the direction the voice had come from, and could just make out the figure of a person dressed in white, then the voice again, but not directed at myself.

"He's coming round, you'd better call for the doctor," I heard this female say.

"Where am I?" I struggled to ask, but the words wouldn't come out, indeed I did have a tube in my throat, it then dawned on me that I must be in a hospital.

I relaxed my fight with the wire and plastic tubes attached to my left arm, I felt exhausted, my eyes stung, and there was a strong smell of antiseptic, I had an awful job to breathe through my mouth and ached in places that I forgotten I had, let alone thought could ache.

I then sensed that there was another person stood by the bed, I could just turn my head a little, and it was this person who spoke to me next.

"Mr Jackson, my name is Doctor Taylor, you've been involved in a car accident, so don't be surprised if you're feeling as if you have pain in every part of you," he told me as he leant forward and stared into my face, I couldn't make out any of his features, but he did seem to have a somewhat darker complexion.

Then his words began to sink in, car accident? I can't remember that, I can't remember anything, I'd been out with Louise and the children, for the evening, I don't remember an accident, but those thoughts were to be taken away with the offer of the removal of the tube stuffed down my throat.

"This might hurt!" the nurse said as she took hold of the plastic protrusion sticking out of my mouth, hurt wasn't the word, one quick pull and it was out, but in the process I felt as if I was about to be sick, my relief at having this dammed thing removed was only to have a soreness to replace it, and I still had equally as much difficulty in breathing, and more when it came to talking.

"Where's Louise?" I managed to ask, it was a simple request, but I recall it being met with a click of the doctor's fingers, and almost in an instant I slipped back into a sleep, without receiving a reply to my question."

"And how long did you have to wait for a reply to your question Andrew?" Stavros asked, not interrupting in the same way as Stuart had, no for Stavros shared my pain and sorrow.

"It was the following morning Stavros, when I came round again Trevor and Diane, along with my children were at my bedside," I said, and now as I sat here telling my friend other parts of this muddled and confused jig-saw, some other parts began to fall into place, along with a recollection of their joint pain of having to tell me that their wonderful daughter was dead, together with the grandchildren that they both adored, both of my sons and respective partners were equally as distressed.

"You said that you had been out with Louise and the children, do you remember where?" he enquired then once again emptied his glass, going on he said, "let's have another."

"Stavros I have to take my medication!" I called to my friend as he was in the other room I was recalling what Stuart had told me before he left.

"Andrew, as I said, it won't harm to miss a night, anyway it might not be safe to mix whisky with drugs," was Stavros's distant response. I was processing his reply when something of the fateful evening came back to me; it was before we left Chillingston Manor.

"Stavros," I started to say as he entered the lounge the refilled glasses in his hands.

"Yes Andrew, what is it?" he said now with something of a smile to his features.

"Something has just come into my mind, I think it was the evening of the accident, Sarah and I were sat in the lounge of Chillingston Manor," I stopped and lowered my head into my hands, these thoughts and recollections were there somewhere but would take some dragging out of my mind, "yes, Sarah and I were waiting for Louise to come down from upstairs when the telephone rang, Sarah begged me to let her answer it, and of course I gave in, I must say it was a pleasure to hear her talk on the phone, she was just like her mother." I stopped, again I'd reminded myself of what I was now missing, I struggled with my emotions, after a few moments I continued, "she answered with 'Chillingston Manor, Sarah Shaw speaking, can I help you?' even though I was sat in the lounge and Sarah was in the hall I could hear her loud and clear, but after answering the phone she didn't say anything else, she just came back into the lounge and sat down next to me, when I enquired who it was, she said it must have been a call centre, and I now remember her saying it was someone with a foreign accent, at the time I thought it was odd, we had a preference service to stop those unwanted calls and not only that, but the residential line to the Manor was ex-directory." I finished and took a pull from my refilled glass.

"Maybe it was one that slipped through the net Andrew, yes!" he replied, at the same time looked at his wristwatch, "Andrew, I had better phone Cathedral View…" he paused and nodded his head, "I won't say anything to Marie about your terrible misfortune, I had better tell her when I get home."

"Help yourself Stavros, you know where everything is," I said as I too looked at my watch, it was now ten o'clock and the day, together with the whisky had caught up with me, I placed my still well filled glass on the small coffee table, removed my spectacles and rubbed my eyes, I could faintly hear Stavros speaking to Marie, his tone quiet but at the same time reassuring.

Whilst sat alone listening to Stavros speaking to Marie part of a conversation came back to me, it was a discussion I'd had with a consultant at the hospital and in fact the very reason that Stuart was visiting me on a daily basis, as these thoughts were fresh in my mind I had to share them with Stavros as soon as he'd returned to his seat, but before I had chance to say anything he had words to share with me.

"My friend, Marie sends her love," he paused before continuing holding his glass he went on, "I have said that you haven't been too well, I didn't go into any details, and even more fortunately she didn't enquire as to what has been wrong, I will explain things when I am home, you understand, yes!"

"I do indeed Stavros, I may well find myself staying with you, would that be alright?" I asked, as if I had to, and I promptly reminded myself of my connection and allegiance with this family.

"Andrew, you know that you don't have to ask, as soon as the funeral is out of the way I will expect you to be staying at our home!" he told me and at the same time patted me on my shoulder, his action reminded me that I had some thoughts I wanted to share with him.

"Stavros," I began looking directly into his eyes.

"Yes my friend what is it? I can see something is on your mind," he replied.

"Well, when I was in hospital the doctor said," I paused for I needed to be sure of what I was going to say, "the doctor said I was suffering from traumatic amnesia, I could take weeks, or maybe months to recover the past, or I could find that overnight I might have my memory back." I stopped as I sensed Stavros wanted to ask a question.

"And the worst case scenario my friend?" his eyes as enquiring as the question.

"I think he said that there is a possibility I may never regain my true thoughts of the past," I replied to his question, now feeling very despondent.

"Andrew," Stavros began looking at his watch again, he continued, "I think you have done enough recalling for one day, now my friend it is time for bed." His words spoken in that firm old manner, he could see that the day had caught up with me.

"I'll make up the bed in the spare room," I said to Stavros as I got up from my comfortable chair, only for him to interrupt me.

"My friend I'm more than capable of making a bed, I remember from staying with you some years ago where all of the necessary materials are," he said at the same time placing his hand on my shoulder, he went on, "you go on up and I'll make sure everything is secure down here, yes!"

I agreed and made my way up to the bedroom I had shared with Louise on more than one occasion, as I prepared myself for bed my thoughts went to her and of course the children, if only I could remember what had happened in the past few days then I might be able to put my life into some sort of order, I'd need to if I was going to carry on alone, but for the moment I had the company of my old and trusted friend Stavros, and I'd taken his advice and not that of my counsellor and not taken my medication that Stuart seemed to put so much emphasis on. I returned from the bathroom after using the toilet then cleaning my teeth, as I looked down the stairs towards the hall I noticed that some of the lights were still on, I thought that Stavros must still be clearing things away so I continued on my route to my bedroom, once under the cover of the duvet and my head resting on the pillow I wriggled my body to in an effort to make myself more comfortable, my head still felt a little tender on the back and I found it more resting to lie on my side, lying here in this big bed I thought I could hear a voice, it was that of Stavros, but I couldn't make out what he was saying, the more I tried the less I could hear and it was the day that caught up with me and I fell asleep thinking I would ask him in the morning.

Chapter Seven

A new day

It was that firm knock on the bedroom door that awoke me from my slumbers the following morning, for a moment my mind raced, who could be at the door I thought to myself? Then slowly last night came back to me, the thump came again and this time I answered for it could only be one person.

"Come in," I called as I stretched in my bed.

"My friend you slept well, yes!" it was Stavros now standing in the bedroom, the door slightly open, and a mug of tea in his hand.

"I did Stavros," I replied as I began to push myself up in the bed.

"I know, I looked in on you at six and you were sleeping like a baby," he said, that half smile to his features.

"What's the time now Stavros?" I asked as I reached out for my glasses.

"Andrew, time is of no importance at the moment, your body needed the rest," he paused and passed me the mug of steaming tea, then continued, "but as you ask, it is now eight forty five."

"Is it?" I said in something of a startled questioning manner, then two things occurred to me, firstly I hadn't awoken feeling as if I'd lost something, that something was thoughts I'd been blocking out of my mind, most mornings when I was sat in bed trying to recall the events of the previous day I'd found myself crying, sobbing uncontrollably for my lost loves, Louise and the children, but now sat here with a mug of hot tea in my hand something else occurred to me, so I continued, "Stavros I have an appointment with my counsellor at eight thirty!"

"There my friend, you are able to recall the past!" was Stavros's instant reply, and he continued, "well, when I came back from collecting the morning papers," he paused looked down at me and went on, "yes I remember where the newsagent's is, anyway as I was saying, when I came back I noticed that your answer machine was flashing, I hadn't spotted it before I went out."

"I don't remember leaving any calls on the machine," I replied as I placed the mug of tea on the bedside cabinet and rubbed my eyes.

"Tell you what Andrew," Stavros started to say as I finished my tea, at the same time extending his hand to take the mug, he went on, "why don't you get up and have a shower, and while you're doing that I'll fix us some breakfast, you think that's a good idea, yes!" he finished with just the slightest of laughter in his voice.

"I will," I said as I pushed the bedding back and swung my legs out of the bed, and I went on, "first I need to check the phone,"

"You go on to the bathroom Andrew and if your counsellor turns up, then I shall keep him entertained," Stavros replied a half chuckle in his voice as he made his way out of the bedroom.

"OK," I called as I made my way into the bathroom, Stavros was well on his way down the stairs and I only heard a muffled reply.

I had a quick shower, then a shave, dressed in some casual chinos and an open neck shirt, I half expected to see Stuart in the kitchen with Stavros, but other than the aroma of cooking bacon some spitting sausages under the grill and the smiling Stavros there was no one.

"Now you look better Andrew!" Stavros said as he made his way to the fridge, adding, "this is where you keep your eggs?"

"It is Stavros," I replied, at the same time I looked at the cooker, he had everything under control, and then he spoke again this time with a question.

"Your counsellor hasn't arrived Andrew, do you think he may have forgotten?"

"He may have," I started to say, then I began to wonder, maybe I'd got the days wrong, last night I was having difficulty remembering anything, "maybe it is tomorrow that he is coming," I casually added.

That comment was sufficient for Stavros to look at me, his reply had a question attached to it, "maybe, but you remember us talking last night, and upstairs you said that you were going to check your answering machine, yes!"

"I did Stavros, and I clearly remember us talking last night," I said as I made my way to the telephone, sure enough the light indicating that I had a new message was flashing, I pressed the small red button that was repeatedly blinking to receive the message, at the same time I turned my head so that my right ear was nearer to the speaker, within a split second a voice was resounding around the kitchen.

"Andrew, it's Stuart," his voice had that awful telephone answering machine echo to it, as if he was speaking into an empty baked bean tin, along with a distance to it, he continued, "I'm awfully sorry but I can't make the appointment today, something of an emergency has occurred, I'll see you tomorrow as we agreed yesterday, any problems you can give me a call later," he paused and it sounded as if he spoke to someone else, there was also a ruffling noise then he went on, "Andrew don't forget to take your medication!" That request had something of a firmness to it, another slight pause in the background a soft 'yes OK' and he finished with "see you in the morning about eight Andrew." Then as he replaced the receiver I could hear a woman's voice, it seemed recognisable, but I couldn't place it and in an instant I thought it was lost from my mind, but would come back to me later.

"There my friend, you could have stayed in bed all day, and you wouldn't have got the message," Stavros said at the same time he laughed in that raucous manner that I was so accustomed to, but the message was playing on my mind, I was sure that I could hear the voice of someone else so I played it again, my action prompted Stavros to come a little closer and question me, "what is it my friend?"

"I'm sure there is another voice in the recording," I said as the message neared the end.

I looked at Stavros as he listened intently, his eyes slightly closed, his right hand came up to his chin, the message ended and he spoke.

"Maybe Andrew but," he was about to reveal some knowledge unknown to myself, "there always sounds like a lot of feedback, its something to do with these digital telephone exchanges they have these days."

I just stood and looked at Stavros, I must say somewhat bemused, and that puzzlement must have shown in my expression.

"I saw a program on the television a few weeks ago," he started to say, his manner reassuring and he gave me a little more of an insight into the program and its reasons, "it was a history of the telecom industry in this country," he paused once more maybe expecting me to ask a question relating to his new found knowledge on the communications business, but I was still digesting this information when he carried on, "on the other hand Andrew he may have been speaking to someone else in the office, yes!"

"Yes of course that hadn't entered my head," I said as I took the body of the phone and looked at the display, pressing the button I could see that it was a mobile telephone number that appeared on the read-out, "it's Stuart's mobile number," I started to tell Stavros only for him to stop me again.

"Come Andrew; let us eat our breakfast, it will get cold very quickly," his words now had a fatherly tone to them, and in truth I was glad to be told of things I needed to do, in particular eat, since returning to my Bristol home I hadn't eaten very much, my appetite taken away by the events I was trying so very hard to recall.

We made our way into the dining room; Stavros had taken care of laying the table in readiness of breakfast, I sat opposite him, his back towards the door, I for some reason needed to see the open door, I didn't know why, and it was to be some considerable time before I was to discover the reason.

"Andrew!" Stavros started to say as he made a start on his breakfast, he continued once he had cleared his mouth, "can you remember why you came back here to live?"

Now here was my old and trusted friend doing what Stuart should have been doing with me, asking me questions about the recent past, but because I knew Stavros and we were relaxing over a fried breakfast together I felt at ease, it didn't take me long to respond to his request, so I set about telling him what I'd been doing since being released from hospital.

Well Stavros, I stayed with Trevor and Diane for a few days, unable to get about very well I was more than glad of every assistance they gave me, but sadly they'd had little time to grieve for the loss of their daughter and grandchildren and my presence in the house only brought them more pain, I'd stayed in Louise's old bedroom, the very one I had slept in with her upon our return from Scotland almost two years previously, my own grief was all consuming, I don't mind admitting to crying myself to sleep during the nights I spent alone in the bed.

One night Trevor came to me, he sat on the edge of the bed, unable to offer any words of comfort to ease my physical and emotional pain, indeed, when I looked him in the eyes I could clearly see that he was crying himself, his own grief overwhelming him.

It was the following morning that I told the two of them that I was going to return to Chillingston Manor, little did I know at the time of making that decision that I wouldn't even be able to spend the night there, Diane was wonderful, she treated me as if I were her son, and if the terrible accident had never taken place then I would have been her son-in-law, I would have had no problem in referring to her as mother, for she would have been a replacement if I'd had to choose one, I already referred to Trevor, as Dad, and he was more than happy with the arrangement.

It was Trevor who called the taxi to take me to the Manor, the words of Diane still in my ears as the cab headed off down the drive and out onto the road and the direction of the home I'd shared with Louise and the children.

"If you need anything, please call," she told me as she openly cried on the doorstep of their home, Trevor re-iterated the words as I clumsily got into the cab, a few bags at my feet, and one holdall next to me on the seat.

It was only a short drive to this magnificent building, the gates at the head of the drive were still closed, and as the car pulled up in front of them something flashed through my mind and a uneasy feeling came over me, it was to last for some time, almost gripping me once I was in the house itself, I was unable to get out and open the gates, it was the taxi driver who took care of that, and it took him a considerable time to open them, he also gave me a great deal of assistance to get into the house; in fact it was he who opened the large front doors for me, leaving my cases at the bottom of the stairs. I hobbled my way to the alarm panel and took care of disabling the system.

I passed him a ten pound note, the cost of the journey didn't even come to five pounds, and I was surprised and at the same time warmed by his reaction.

"This one's on me Mr Jackson!" he told me declining to take the note, nodding his head at the same time.

"You have to take it!" I said pushing the note into his hand again, a forcefulness in my tone, but he just closed his hand and turned and headed for the door, there he stopped, looked back at me, his facial expressions told me his thoughts long before he opened his mouth to explain his reasons.

"I can't imagine what you're going through Mr Jackson!" he said, a wavering tone in his voice. This man felt emotion for what had happened to me, then he continued as he stepped back and passed me a card, "if you need a lift at any time, just give me a call," these words had a genuine sincerity to them, looking into his eyes I could clearly see them glazing over. Then he turned and headed out of the double doors.

I watched him as he made his way out to his car, the big doors still open, I hobbled to the doors as best I could my lower right leg was still bandaged from the knee down to my ankle, I was told I'd received a knock to this part of my leg and it would heal quicker if it remained in a support for a few days.

I stood resting my body against the doorframe as the taxi drove off up the long sweeping driveway and back towards the main road, dust whirling behind it as it made its way towards the gates. Now I was alone.

I was alone in this big empty grand house and abandoned with my thoughts. To the side of the stairs was a small unit, an occasional table, a pile of post sat on it, the housekeeper had evidently been in and placed it there, after removing it from the post box in the pillars at the top of the drive, carefully I made my way across to the stairs, my intention was to try and negotiate them, but first my attention was drawn to the collection of letters and cards along with some other documents on the unit in the hall, I lifted them up, and shuffled them through my hands, they were mostly letters regarding the business, the hotel business at that, addressed to both Louise and myself, or just addressed to the owners, that was of course the both of us, there were also many cards, condolence cards, I didn't have it in my grieving heart to open them.

But then it crossed my mind that the hotel chain was still functioning with me being out of the way, but I wasn't the driving force behind the venture, no that was Louise, sure it was my money that had purchased the chain in the beginning, but it was her astute business approach that had got the whole affair running smoothly and into a very healthy profitable state.

And now looking at the collection of accumulated post I wondered if I wanted to continue with the business. I made up my mind that I would rather take the post into the part of the house we referred to as the office suite, an area of the house we'd had converted so we could spend as much time as possible at home working, sure we had a fully equipped office in the centre of Bristol, but this at home was so we could be with the children, minimizing the time we spent away from Chillingston Manor.

The suite was at the rear of the house, slowly I made my way to it, but I noticed on my way that the house had an emptiness to it, for one thing there was no noise at all, not even the sound of the breeze, the last time I'd been in the house, it was fully occupied, Louise, Sarah, James and of course the nanny and necessary staff to clean and take care of things, but now, nothing.

Once in the suite I made myself comfortable in the seat behind my desk, Louise had her own and that was on the opposite side of the room to mine, looking across it looked even emptier now, now I knew she wouldn't be coming back.

I placed the post on my desk, I'd always been in the habit of opening the mail with a letter opener, but looking around on my desk I couldn't find it, perhaps, I thought to myself, it's on Louise's desk, slowly I managed to get to the other side of the room, I sat in her seat, gradually I leant back in the chair, the essence of her perfume was still in the room, I inhaled deeply and closing my eyes I could smell the full concentration of that lasting fragrance, but she wasn't here and wouldn't be coming back, and I didn't feel any inkling of her, unlike when my sister Rachel died, her spirit had come to me, telling me she was alright, reassuring, encouraging me to carry on with my life.

I opened my eyes and looked around this tidy and orderly desk, everything was where it should be, the out-tray was empty, as was the in-tray, her lap-top computer was closed and carefully positioned to the side, so that Louise was able to sign or hand-write any letters or documents without any obstructions getting in her way, my desk on the other hand was as I'd left it on the day we went out, a clutter of bits and pieces, the computer still open.

But still I couldn't remember what we had gone out for, and I couldn't find the letter opener, I put my hand down to the handle of the drawer on my right hand side, pulling it open, it revealed a large diary, I took it out and opened it, this was the business diary, it contained information about appointments we had attended and forthcoming events, looking at today's date it was blank, as it was for the continuation of the diary, the preceding weeks were also blank, had I really lost that much time I asked myself as I closed the large A4 book.

I was just about to return it to the drawer I had taken it out of when my eyes caught sight of a smaller A5 diary, I looked longingly at it, I myself used that size to record my own personal daily events in, but this wasn't mine, it can only belong to Louise I thought as I removed it from the back of the drawer. I placed it on the desk in front of me, I felt nervous about opening it, could it contain information about the days leading up to the accident? There could be facts that may well be able to bring my memory back, on the other hand this was in all probability a record of many private events Louise had transferred to paper, I felt a need come over me to return this item of privacy to its place of safe keeping, but the need to know about the past got the better of me, and rather than put it back I opened it at the start of the year.

'Well this is something different for me to do,' it started, and with those few words I was compelled to carry on reading Louise's style of writing, her hand perfect, every letter and word flawlessly formed, she continued. 'This is something that is normally left to Andrew to do, yet it was his prompting that has brought about a need in me to do as he so often does, put my thoughts and feelings down onto paper, and where do I start? Well to give myself a brief recap of what has gone on in the past few years, I met Andrew on a cold and miserable Friday in December, miserable on my part, and only days before I'd received a beating from Gary, for what? The car not starting! Then seeing Andrew again after all those years, well it brought back so many memories, the times we'd shared in the office together, mostly happy, but occasionally unpleasant, I thought he'd continued to lead a normal happy life as he used to ring me and tell me what he'd been up to, but that was when I was expecting Sarah, he hadn't changed, he looked a little older, but don't we all! The memory of the old phone calls came flooding back and I found myself almost begging him to ring me, not expecting that he would, but he did and the time we spent on the phone discussing the past was so wonderful, it breathed new life into me, even on the end of a phone he showed he cared, I remember the day before Andrew called, Gary said I had something on my mind, it wasn't something, it was someone. Every Wednesday when Andrew phoned I would hold my breath, hoping it would be him, but also fearing it might be Gary and I would give the game away by being so jovial upon answering the phone.

'Then as the weeks passed I longed for him to ask me out, at the same time I was frightened, would I be able to get away? And what if I were seen out with this man? Then he asked, I held onto his words, it wasn't to keep him on tenterhooks! No it was as if the whole situation wasn't real, but it was. I said yes knowing I was to be in for the treat of a lifetime, I remember telling Jill, she said I deserved some happiness, for she was the only one who knew of the beatings Gary would inflict upon me for no apparent reason, she lent me some of her own clothes to wear, reassuring me that everything would be fine. How right she was.

'When he walked across the car park at the station my heart skipped a beat, a small posy of flowers in his hand for me, everything he did for me he did with style, he opened the door of his car for me to get in, and carefully closed it once I was seated, the door of the restaurant he held for me, and the bunch of flowers he passed me after I'd given him a welcoming kiss, it was wonderful and I wished the night could have gone on forever, I think I told him that the following day, when as regular as clockwork at ten thirty he rang me, but temporarily any dreams we had were to be shattered. Gary came home early and gave me the most ferocious beating I'd ever had, Andrew received much the same, at the time he thought it was for taking me out, but neither of us knew what was driving Gary on, and to this day I guess I never will, that beating was the final straw, so after seeing Andrew at his home a few days later, I made up my mind I wasn't going to take any more senseless, inane poundings at the hands of my husband.

'Then I recalled Andrew saying he was going to some apartments he owned in Cornwall, I wasn't aware of his vast fortune at that particular time, all I did know for certain was, I enjoyed his company, and he mine, so I asked him if I could go with him, and it was he that now held his breath.

'Well, we went away together, he showed me the same warmth and courtesy as he had when we were out for dinner, he was polite and kind, again opening the doors for me, he paid for everything, took care of me in a way I could never have dreamed of, just the way he looked at me from across the room, made me feel secure, the way I never had with Gary, then on that Good Friday evening when the policeman and his useless assistant came to see us,

Andrew didn't get angry, no, he stayed calm, I was the one upset, but he remained in control of his feelings.

'I remembered many years ago that he told me he was fond of me, so by way of clearing up a few things, I asked about his money, and what he meant when he'd said he was fond of me. As he started to explain and the conversation moved on he went on to tell me that he loved me, words I hadn't really been expecting, but something deep inside of me was relieved to hear them, it cleared up so much of the past, put it into order, he'd held onto his love for me, hoping that one day he would be able to tell me, he explained his love in the most beautiful of ways, simple but full of tenderness, his feelings for me were to leave me speechless for a few days, but after meeting his trusted and rugged old friend Stavros I knew what my feelings were, I loved Andrew.

'When the time was right he made love to me, it was like something I'd only ever dreamt of, so affectionately, so gentle, his delicate touch, his kisses on my body, in my most intimate of places, I felt as if I was in heaven, as I have on every occasion since, just the thought of him next to me and I begin to get excited and aroused, I can feel it now and I'm only thinking of him, but he is sat on the other side of the room to me.'

Those words made me stop and look across at my own empty desk, so Louise had sat and written these words with me only feet from her, she must have known the effect she had upon me, I wiped my face and found I'd been crying, my tears had fallen and until now I'd been completely unaware, the events of the past weeks have robbed me of so much. But I continued to read on.

'That extended Easter weekend away together made me feel as if I wanted to be with him forever, and if Gary's unpleasant past hadn't caught up with him and us then things would have been considerably smoother. Gary as expected went completely ballistic when he found out that Andrew and I had been away, but he only found out with the help of his old accomplice Rimes, he paid for his mistake in dealing in filth and pornography, with his life, and Gary also paid for taking me to hell and back.

'Unknown to either Andrew or myself, Nana was, and to the best of my knowledge, is still working for the Special Protection Team, and she had been given orders not to let anything happen to Andrew or myself, with the help of her father she had complete control of the situation, and Gary made the ultimate sacrifice for his dealings in drugs, his life was ended.

'At the time I was relieved, I was still alive and so was Andrew, but it all seemed too vague, the entire event began to become too much for me to take in, and by mid-day of the following day I'd started what is best described as a breakdown. A need came over me to be with mummy and daddy, and that's where I went, and I'm so sorry to write that I left Andrew alone, I remember hearing him crying on the drive of Stavros's home.

'After weeks of being alone, I slowly began to see the light; daddy was, as always strong and supportive, but still wouldn't interfere. Mummy was wonderful, and it was her who told me to go after my dream and follow it to the end. They had been to see Andrew and were aware that he was going to Scotland, she helped me get my clothes ready, and she filled me with a confidence of what I was doing was right. Daddy to this day doesn't know, and off I went.

'When I was on the other side of that massive lawn at the rear of his house at Ullapool I could see his anger in his eyes, anger at being left alone, I didn't mean to break him, but I felt as if I did when I asked him what he thought was best for himself, I wanted to know that his feelings and love were the same, and they were, they weren't just the same, they were now even stronger, and better.'

"My friend," Stavros said stopping me in mid-flow.

"What is it?" I asked now snapped out of my recalling state.

"Well, it seems to me that Louise had the ability to remember the past better than yourself," he said as he placed his knife and fork on his empty plate.

"She did Stavros, she did!" I replied emphatically, and I continued after clearing my plate, "I have to admit that I didn't read much more of her diary," I paused to get my thoughts clear in my head, "I found some of her writing enlightening, as you've said she was better at recalling the past than I am, but after the recap well most of the days were taken over by appointments we had to keep in connection with the business, along with other forthcoming events." I finished, referring to our wedding.

"But you still haven't told me what made you come back here to your house in Bristol," Stavros said almost hanging on my reply.

"Stavros," I began, my emotions starting to get the better of me, I swallowed hard sat up straight in my chair and went on, "Chillingston Manor was full of the children's laughter, but I felt as if Louise's smile and warmth were evading me in every room, I looked everywhere hoping that I may have been having a bad dream, but as I sat alone on the big wide staircase I realised that all of my happiness was lost, gone for ever, and as a result I couldn't stay, I had to come back to my old home, for here I only have the faded ghosts and memories of my sister and parents."

"I understand my friend," Stavros said as he looked at me from across the big table in the dining room, then taking me by complete surprise he went on, "Andrew what would you say if I said I wanted to go to Chillingston Manor, I'm sure Louise would have wanted you to carry on, I will help you face your recent past," he paused and his big rugged old hand came across to take mine he continued, "you know as I have told you many times before I share your pain, for you are one of my own, I also have a pain in my heart for Louise, I loved her in the same way as I love my Nana." He finished at the same time squeezed my hand.

"Only if you are sure Stavros," I replied, after some careful thought.

"I am, come let us clear these things away, and then we can make our way to the Manor," he paused then had a question, "where is your Porsche?"

"I think it's still at the Manor, but why do you ask?" I enquired of Stavros.

"You need to have some transport, regain your independence, as I've already said return to normality," he paused, looked me long and hard in the eyes before continuing, "it won't be easy Andrew, but you must make the effort, you understand, yes!"

"I do," I replied, as I recalled something from a conversation I'd had with Stuart the day before, we'd been exploring mine and Louise's time together, she'd asked me what I would want her to do if anything happened to me, she'd replied saying that I was to carry on, my thoughts were interrupted by the telephone ringing, and the voice of Stavros.

"Andrew, the telephone!" he said making me almost jump from my seat, and he went on, "you answer that and I'll clear the table."

I made my way into the study, even though the kitchen phone was nearer I felt a need to sit and talk on the phone, "I expect it's Stuart!" I said as I got to the study door.

Now the telephone in the study doesn't have a caller display on it, so I was completely unaware of who may be calling me, and it was a voice that I didn't know that greeted me after I'd said hello.

"Mr Jackson?" a man's voice with what I would best describe as an authoritarian tone to it.

"It is," I replied giving no more information to the caller.

"Mr Andrew Jackson," the man asked again.

"Yes it is, but who is that?" I asked giving a question in return to the answer.

"This is Detective Inspector Braithwaite from the Wiltshire Constabulary," he paused after passing this information to me, maybe giving me time to digest it fully, for myself I was unaware of the police doing anything other than a routine investigation into the accident, and I couldn't understand why a detective should have been assigned to the case, and a detective inspector at that, but before I had the opportunity to ask him a question he continued to speak, "I've been asked to look into your rather tragic accident," again he paused as if to pick his words carefully, he went on, "I understand that this must be a very difficult time for you, but I do need to ask you a few questions." He stopped again giving me the chance to put a question to him.

"Inspector would you like me to come to the station?" I asked; as I did Stavros appeared at the door.

"Is everything alright Andrew?" he mouthed rather than asked, in reply I gave him a thumbs up signal.

"For the moment Mr Jackson I don't think that will be necessary," the inspector began to reply, and he went on, "I understand from my colleagues that you can't remember anything about the collision or the events that took place before the accident."

"That is correct," I said in response to his question, recalling that I had been interviewed in hospital; it was the doctor who intervened informing the police officers that I was as he put it, suffering from 'traumatic amnesia' and it would be some considerable time before I would be able to recall what had happened to me, if I ever would be able to. It was also the doctor, or so I thought, who had put me in contact with the counsellor, Stuart, or rather Stuart in touch with me. I was about to continue when the inspector spoke again.

"Do the events seem any clearer now Mr Jackson?" his tone a little less formal.

"I've been having some counselling," I paused wondering just how much I should tell this man, but before I had a chance to continue he asked me another question.

"And has it helped?" Well he was certainly forthright in his style of questioning.

"Some of the past is beginning to come back to me, but it's a bit of a struggle," I told him, and I went on, "I still don't know what happened to me or how the accident occurred."

"That's fine Mr Jackson, we're satisfied that the incident was caused by joy-riders," he paused maybe giving me the chance to recall what I'd been told by the other officers.

"I was told that another car was found burnt-out," I replied.

"That car was stolen some time last month; we think it had been involved in a robbery on the other side of Chillingston, but we can't be sure at the moment, we need to check some CCTV footage, that may give us a lead on the driver and other occupants of the car," he stopped and I thought he had finished but I heard some papers being ruffled, then he went on, "I think, Mr Jackson, that you and your family were in the wrong place at the wrong time."

"Yes," was all that I could say in reply to his statement of facts as he'd put them to me, but as in any film you may see on the television the inspector had one more enquiry.

"Mr Jackson there is one other thing I need to ask you," he said as once again I heard papers being moved around.

"Yes inspector what is it?" I asked a little puzzled that there was more I could help him with.

"Well it's a little difficult, but did Mrs Shaw wear a lot of jewellery?" he enquired.

I thought about his question, but not his reasons for asking it, of course Louise wore jewellery, she always had, since choosing the engagement ring she had worn it, that together with an eternity ring her mother and father had given her, also her Omega watch that I'd bought her in Scotland and a fine selection of other rings, also earrings, and necklaces so my answer was quite simple.

"Yes she did," I told the waiting inspector, and I had a question of my own, "but why do you ask?"

"Mr Jackson the pathologist who examined the remains found in the burnt out BMW has said in his report that he couldn't find any jewellery, or evidence of any," the inspector told me.

"Could it have melted in the heat?" I enquired at the same time hoping that there would be a logical explanation to the question.

"He concluded that the fire was indeed intense, but," he paused again and I could hear papers being turned. "Ah, here it is Mr Jackson, I'll read this part to you, no evidence of jewellery was found on the remains of the bodies discovered in the car, but I also noted that there were no signs of gold or any other precious metals on the floor of the car, I would have expected to find some melted metals or remains of, i.e. diamonds or other valuable stones. This indicates that the occupants either weren't wearing any jewellery, or they may have had these items removed prior to the fire." He finished.

I felt numbed by his statement, and concluded the worst from his words, I didn't know what had happened to my precious Louise and the two children that I loved, and now to think that someone had stolen Louise's belongings as she and the children lay dying filled me with rage. And that anger came across in my next question to the inspector.

"Do you think that some bastard could have crashed into our car and then stole my Louise's valuables?" I angrily asked my voice raised enough for Stavros to reappear to the door, concern on his face at my sudden outburst.

"Mr Jackson please don't jump to any hasty conclusions," the inspector replied, his tone calming and soft, he went on, "there may well be a logical explanation for why these articles can't be found, maybe Mrs Shaw didn't wear any jewellery on the evening in question."

"She always wore something," I started to reply adding, "from the first time we went out to dinner she had jewellery on."

"As I've said Mr Jackson there is in all probability a rational explanation," was the reply I received from the inspector, then a thought came into my mind, the fact that Stavros and I were going to Chillingston Manor this morning meant I would be able to check Louise's many jewellery boxes and perhaps discover which items were missing, so I put these thoughts to the inspector.

"Inspector," I began picking my words carefully I continued, "I intend to visit the Manor this morning, and whist I'm there I will look to see what jewellery of Mrs Shaw's is missing."

"You don't have to go on our account..." the inspector started to reply, I cut him a little short.

"I need to go and sort some other things out inspector, there are some very important pieces of the past I may be able to resolve whilst I'm at the Manor,"

I said, the need in me to revisit the home I'd shared with Louise and the children even greater now.

"Well if you're sure Mr Jackson, perhaps you could give me a call this afternoon, or tomorrow morning," he paused, there was a silence, no paper ruffling, just his faint breathing in the background, he went on, and "whatever is convenient with yourself."

"I will ring you as soon as I can," I replied forgetting one very important thing, and that was his telephone number, I was just about to replace the receiver when the inspector spoke again.

"In that case Mr Jackson you'll require my telephone number," the inspector said.

"Of course," I said as I frantically looked for a pen and piece of paper, once I'd located both I continued, "carry on inspector, what's your number?"

I wrote down his office telephone number together with his mobile number, we said our goodbyes, and then I looked around the study for my trusted old friend.

Stavros looked at me from the other side of the room, a question in his eyes, one I was able to read a long time before he asked me, and then it would be in the quietness of the Manor.

I relayed to Stavros the unheard inspector's side of the conversation, the reply I received from him was exactly what I was expecting.

"In that case we need to make this visit, it is after all of the most importance, yes!" he told me, a broad smile on his face, but still concern in his eyes.

I made my way to the bathroom, cleaned my teeth, into my bedroom, there I grabbed a jacket, and for the first time in what seemed like ages took an interest in the weather, I glanced out of the bedroom window, a bright sunny day.

"My friend, you won't need that!" Stavros told me as I neared the bottom of the stairs, and he went on, "I was able to remove my jacket when I walked to the newsagent's earlier." He finished and there was laughter in his voice.

I placed my light jacket over the bottom of the stair rail, and with a feeling of a little more confidence in myself looked for my house keys, they were in the study resting on top of the bureau, together with the keys for Chillingston Manor, I slipped the keys for my house here in Bristol into my trouser pocket, the bunch for the Manor I held in my hand for a few seconds, just looking at them, now I had a purpose in going to the family home I shared with Louise and the children, but I also wondered what other secrets might be revealed to me upon this visit. It was Stavros who snapped me out of my trance-like state, making me jump at the same time.

"Andrew, you are ready? Yes!" he said as he rested his large right hand on my shoulder.

"I am Stavros, I was just day dreaming," I replied as I turned to look at him.

"Then let us get a move on, it is now ten o'clock," Stavros told me forcing me to make a move towards the front doors, there I stopped and looked at the control panel for the burglar alarm, instinctively my fingers danced their way around the keypad, I glanced at my own watch as the control panel started bleeping its exit warning, it was indeed ten o'clock, we made our way outside pulling the front door hard as we vacated the building and after sliding the outer doors and locking them I looked at Stavros.

"There didn't seem to be much wrong with your memory then Andrew," he said as we stood on the steps outside of my house.

"But Stavros some things you do by instinct, it's locked away deep in the back of your mind, never to be forgotten," I replied, at that very time I'd forgotten something that Stuart had told me to do, and the effect of this particular lapse of memory was to have some beneficial results. Looking down the drive I could see that Stavros had a new car, the very latest Mercedes-Benz.

"That's very nice Stavros," I said as we approached this very stylish-looking car.

"Thank you Andrew, you know I've always had a love for them, and," he paused pressed the key fob, a flash of the indicators and the locks made that dull thud as they unlocked the doors, he looked across at me and continued, "I had a business venture come to fruition so, I spoilt myself." He finished saying light-heartedly.

"And why not," I agreed as I neared the passenger's door, as I gripped the door handle Stavros spoke again.

"Would you like to drive Andrew?" he asked, holding the key out in front of him.

"No thank you Stavros," I hesitantly replied, somewhat nervous at the thought of getting behind the steering wheel of a car, Stavros was to pick up on my cautious reply once I was seated in the car.

"My friend you have the keys to your Porsche, yes!" he asked as he started the engine, initially the engine seemed to rattle, almost a clatter, instantly Stavros had something to say, "Yes Andrew, it's a diesel." He said looking at the surprised expression on my face, and then he continued as we started to reverse out of the drive. "You'll be alright to drive that powerful car of yours home!"

"Yes I think I will," I replied somewhat cautiously, for in truth I couldn't remember the last time I'd driven a car, and it was that which Stavros picked up on.

"Have the police said who was driving Louise's car at the time of the accident?" he asked glancing sideways at me as we headed up the road.

"Well they seem to think that I had been driving," I began my reply, I stopped because other thoughts were beginning to come back to me, so I continued, "the police told me when I was in hospital that she was found in the front passenger seat, indicating, Stavros that I must have been driving."

"But why were you found in the woods?" Stavros asked.

"That I can't explain," I replied still trying to puzzle the missing pieces of the past into some sort of order.

"Tell you what Andrew," Stavros started to say pausing as we stopped at a set of traffic lights he went on, "why don't we drive to where the accident occurred, maybe it will jog your memory a little more."

"I'm not sure it will do any good Stavros," was my frightened response, frightened I say, for in truth I didn't know what I would feel, but would it do me any good to go over the ground where Louise and the children had died? But I wasn't given the chance to argue.

"I can see you are nervous Andrew, but old Stavros will be with you, I will share your pain," he said placing his hand on mine as he said the words.

So we drove to the very place where the accident had taken place, I was able to give directions, the police had informed me of the exact details of the location, it was a little easier to detect due to the fact that someone had tied a bunch of flowers to one of the trees. Stavros pulled his car into a small clearing about ten metres down the road, together we walked in the direction of the accident spot, the charred and burnt tarmac was clearly visible as we got nearer, but it was the bunch of flowers that took my attention as we got closer.

Before giving the area of the crash my attention I looked at the card that was attached to the flowers, it had Louise's name and the children's, but the words written on the back of the card stuck in my mind, but it was to be some time before their significance was to be revealed to me, they were, 'The reward of time'. Stavros was stood at my side reading the card at the same time as I was.

"No name Andrew!" he said as he took hold of the small card and attempted to turn it over maybe looking for a signature, then he went on giving his own kind of reasoning for the flowers being there in the first place. "Sadly Andrew there is always some kind of eccentric person about."

"But what does that mean?" I asked the powerful man stood at my side.

"I'm afraid I don't know Andrew," he paused looked once more at the card and added, "Like I say some sort of crank or a do-gooder."

I looked around the scene paying particular attention to the burnt tarmac; on the edge of the road was some broken plastic, red and orange, also pieces of clear glass, mixed with dried leaves and twigs, possibly the clear glass was from the headlights from the other vehicle, the coloured particles were clearly the indicators and stop lights from Louise's BMW I thought. I bent down and picked up a rather large piece of red plastic. I turned it over and over in my hands, when I stopped I studied the item closely, I could see the year stamp along with an arrow pointing towards the month of the year it was manufactured, something really puzzled me about this large colourful object I had in my hands.

"What is it?" Stavros asked just as a car went by, I'm not sure if it was Stavros speaking or the car rushing by that startled me the most.

"Well this is from the rear of a car," I paused not wishing to sound foolish I wasn't sure if I should continue.

"And Andrew what are you trying to tell me?" Stavros enquired still looking at the piece of bright red plastic in my hand.

"Stavros, it's not from Louise's BMW," I said once again turning the plastic over.

"How can you be so sure Andrew?" Stavros asked at the same time taking it from me.

"Louise's car had all of the windows and lights etched with the same number as is on the personal number plate," I paused, this was one thing I did remember, due in part to the cost, and the time it took for the plates to be made so I continued, "Stavros we had to wait several weeks for the original owner to sell us the number plate, then we had to have some new ones made for the car," again I stopped, taking the rear light lens from Stavros I looked at it again, "there's something else Stavros," I said pointing to the year of manufacture identification, "this was made almost two years before we had the car."

"Andrew are you sure, you know that you haven't been well!" Stavros replied, but not in a patronising manner, no his voice was full of concern and he went on, "maybe they used some older parts on the car when it was built."

"If that's the case, then where's the registration number?" I asked as I studied the item even closer just a little frustration in my voice.

"I understand Andrew," Stavros said at the same time placing his large right hand on my shoulder, he went on, "there could have been other accidents in this location."

"But it does show the BMW identification logo," I said as I pointed to the plastic.

"Andrew it shows the BM, the W is missing, anyway my friend, there are millions of BMW's on the British roads," Stavros told me as I looked him in the eyes.

"I know you're right Stavros, I just wanted my nightmare to be over, and all of this to be a big mistake," I said, feeling very despondent.

"Come, come Andrew, standing here is doing you no good at all!" Stavros firmly told me, at the same time his left hand was leading me back towards his own car. Just as we started to make our way an enormous articulated lorry roared past throwing leaves and dust into the air, making both Stavros and I jump, also prompting Stavros to pass another comment. "This road is so dangerous; I'm surprised that there aren't more accidents."

His remark made me think, and that was of the past, I stood still so as to gather my thoughts, I watched as the lorry continued on its noisy route though the woods, it occurred to me that I'd been along this particular road many times, it was considered to be a short cut between Chillingston and the main road that leads to Bath, but at both ends were signs prohibiting its use by heavy goods vehicles, so maybe it was just a case of being in the wrong place at the wrong time as the police had said, and it was just joy-riders that ploughed into the back of the BMW, but then another thought occurred to me, where had Louise, the children and myself been to end up in this location on that fateful night? The answer may well lie in Louise's diary, that prompted a new urgency in me to go to the Manor.

"Yes you are right Stavros, we didn't come here to dwell on the past," I paused looked once more at the burnt tarmac, and as I started to walk again in the direction of Stavros's car continued, "hanging about here won't bring Louise, Sarah or James back."

"Now Andrew you are thinking a little more like your old self," Stavros replied as he opened the passenger's door for me to get in. Once he had installed himself in the driver's seat he had a question for me, taking me by surprise somewhat.

"Andrew, do you remember what you were telling me last night?" he asked as he started the engine of the car.

"Yes," I instantly replied not realising that this was a test of Stavros's making.

"And what did you tell me?" he enquired as we began to pull away.

"Well you know Stavros, surely I don't have to go over it all again, after all it's me that has the problem recalling what has happened in the past," I jovially replied still not understanding his need to ask such a question.

"Go on then, the best you can," his words had urgency to them and were spoken in the style of an order.

"Stavros," I started, as I sat in this luxury car I was able to recall all of what I'd told Stavros the evening before, I concluded with, "I spent several days in hospital before being discharged and returning to Louise's parents home," I paused and looked at Stavros, he was nodding his head, we were just approaching the junction that leads back to Chillingston village, "turn right here Stavros!" I quickly said as we slowed sharply in order to negotiate the turning.

"I don't understand Andrew," was the start of Stavros's reply and he continued as we headed in the direction of the Manor, "you have repeated almost word for word what you told me last night, and yet you can't remember what happened to you a little over a week ago." He finished as we neared the big, black wrought iron entrance gates that lead to the Manor house.

"I can't explain the reasons for my memory loss either Stavros," I replied somewhat exasperatedly, as we pulled up at the chained gates and I rummaged in my jacket pocket for the keys to the padlock and the electronic gate opener.

"What is so strange to me Andrew, is that once you have recovered part of the past you are able to hang on to it," he said, I looked at him a little puzzled not fully understanding what he was saying, he went on to explain, "Andrew, let me simplify things, it's like we are peeling an onion, each layer we remove reveals another, but we aren't going back from yesterday, no we are trying to come forward to the present, and as each day is uncovered you are able to remember what has happened and have no problem holding on to those memories."

I sat mesmerised by what Stavros had just revealed to me, and of course he was right, I wasn't going backwards to a particular day, I was trying to remember what had happened the day of the accident and afterwards. Just as I was digesting what I'd been told when a secondary thought crossed my mind and I felt it was important enough to tell Stavros about.

"Stavros, I didn't take my medication this morning, and I haven't brought it with me!" I told Stavros, my manner somewhat distressed.

"Calm yourself Andrew," Stavros began and looking at me he continued, "as I told you last night, one or two doses missed won't make that much difference, anyway," he paused and I wondered just what he was going to say, he went on maybe after gathering his own thoughts, "in my opinion you seem much better for not taking the drugs."

And of course he was right, I felt a little better in myself, but I'd put that down to having Stavros with me to keep me company, his spirit and enthusiasm driving me on, and it was Stavros who was to get me out of the car and on with the necessary task of going into Chillingston Manor.

"Andrew, we won't get into the house unless you unchain those gates!" his voice once again firm but at the same time considerate.

"Sure!" I promptly replied as I unfastened my seatbelt, pulling on the door lever with my left hand, in my right I had the bunch of keys and control pad, similar to a remote locking device for a car.

I got out of Stavros's car, walked the few yards to the gates, I lifted the padlock and inserted the long shafted key into the lock, it turned with ease, then my memory flashed back to the last time I was here, on that occasion I'd been locking the gates together. I retrieved the lock from the chain and at the same time caught the chain before it had chance to fall to the ground, stood there with the padlock in my right hand and the chain in my left something else flashed through my mind, the gates had been extremely stiff on the day that I had closed them and chained them together, but it was to be a little while before the reason would be revealed to me. After placing the chain and padlock on the ground, I found I had to lean against both gates to start the opening operation, at the same time I pressed the button on the key fob, the right hand gate seemed to have a rather large twist in one of the vertical metal upright bars, glancing up at the top I could see that was also out of shape and the base was out of its guide, in fact the whole gate was distorted, for the moment I couldn't remember how they had become disfigured.

But what I did remember was to collect the accumulated post from the letter box that was built into the right hand pillar, there was in fact several days worth, all of the bundles tightly secured with light red elastic bands, normally the post van would drive down to the house and deposit the mail through the letter box in the main entrance doors, with them in my hands I walked ahead of Stavros's car as he drove through the now open gates; no sooner was he through them than the gates started their automatic return to the closed position, the right hand gate was quicker than the left, the closer on that gate was making an awful noise, that in itself prompted Stavros to wind down the passenger's window and ask me a question.

"What is that terrible noise Andrew?" I heard him ask. Before replying I had to go and assist by pushing the dragging gate closed.

"It's the gates Stavros," I said as I made my way towards his car, and as I got into his car I continued, "the one on the left, as you look at them when leaving has been twisted..." I stopped suddenly as we started to move along the gravel drive in the direction of the big house.

"What is it?" Stavros asked, concern in his voice.

"I can't remember how they became bent," I replied holding my head in my hands.

"Maybe Louise will have written something in her diary," Stavros said and in so doing reminded me of the purpose of our visit.

Slowly we made our way down the long driveway to the house, I could faintly hear the gates creaking as they made the painful effort to close, despite feeling somewhat apprehensive about returning to the place it still held a magic over me, and also Stavros and he began to tell me.

"This is a very impressive building Andrew, you agree, yes!" he said as he looked across at me a huge smile on his lips.

"Yes," I began my reply I cast my mind back to the very first time I saw the house, that was of course in the company of Louise and the estate agent, it seemed like a lifetime ago now as Stavros and I cruised slowly towards the front of the house, as we slowed in readiness to stop I continued, "you can see now Stavros why I fell in love with the Manor."

"I can indeed Andrew, and you must hold on to that love," he paused himself as he turned off the engine, and after applying the handbrake he continued, "as you must hold onto the love you have for Louise, her love for you, that you shared will be with you forever."

For a few moments I sat just looking out of the window of the car and onto the Manor, it was the same as when I'd left it a few days ago, I slipped my hand into my inner jacket pocket and removed my wallet.

"What do you need that for Andrew?" Stavros asked a puzzled expression on his face.

"I keep an electronic entrance card in here," I said, at the same time I showed Stavros the credit card sized devise.

"Is that all you have to get into this fine house?" Stavros enquired, still looking a little bemused by my response.

"No, not just this," I replied pulling the bunch of keys from my outer jacket pocket, then I went on, "this card is inserted into the control panel, once that code has been input," I paused amazed that I could once again recall such information.

"It all seems very complicated to me Andrew," was all Stavros would say in reply to the details I had just passed onto him, at the same time he pulled on the door handle and started to get out of the car.

"I'll show you how it works," I said as I got out of the car and headed towards the steps leading to the front door, the keys in my right hand. Stavros and I made our way to the top of the steps; there I started to explain the method that was required to get into the house.

"First Stavros I have to unlock the doors," I told him as I inserted the large key into the mortise lock.

"That part even I could manage," he light-heartedly replied laughter in his voice.

"Then once we go inside of the building you will hear the bleeping coming from the alarm panel, that means we have thirty seconds to disable the system," I said just as I turned the key in the lock.

"But Andrew, where does the need for that card come into it?" Stavros asked.

"Tell you what Stavros, I'll explain once we are inside," I replied as I pushed on the door, it was as the door opened that I was in for a surprise, I stepped over the threshold and waited, not a sound, nothing, it was Stavros who broke the relative silence as I placed the large pile of post on the occasional table to the left of the open door.

"Andrew, no bleeping," he said as I looked across at him.

"No there isn't!" was all I could say.

"Maybe you didn't alarm the place when you left it a few days ago," Stavros said.

"No, no," I quickly replied and continued, "I always put it on, Stavros, always!" I paused, for I was sure I'd alarmed the house, in fact it was the taxi driver who had reminded me to put it on, so I relayed this to Stavros, "as I was leaving the taxi driver told me to put it on."

"But are you sure it has been working properly?" Stavros once again questioned.

"Look Stavros, this is how the system works," I said as we made our way in the direction of the control panel, once stood in front of it I went on, "each of us has a card, that is Louise, Susan the nanny, and myself, there are some spare cards, but we keep them in the safe, anyway, you have to input your own personal code, then the tone changes and you have to insert the card into the side of the unit," I said as I indicated where the card was to be inserted.

"Then maybe Susan has been in the house!" Stavros said looking as much as I was for an explanation for the system being disabled.

"No Stavros, she has gone to stay with her mother," I replied remembering precisely what Susan had said to me during a telephone conversation, she was extremely trustworthy and would not divulge any information to anyone, she was also very upset, then as I stood looking at the control panel something else from the past came into my head, first the reasons for having such a high tech system installed and secondly something that had been explained to me when the installation was completed. I went on to inform Stavros of these facts. "Stavros, this system was installed after I was kidnapped, just to give us peace of mind, and in part something to do with the warning you had given us, coupled with word of warning from Alex, its connected the police station, so in the event of anyone trying to break-in they will be informed instantly, as well as the alarm sounding outside," I paused as I recalled when the system was tested it couldn't be heard very far away, but never the less it was something of a deterrent, but then the other piece of information came back into my mind, so I went on, "it is possible to tell who enabled the system, and disabled the system last."

"And is that an easy thing to do?" Stavros asked a renewed interest in his voice.

"I think," I began as I once again had the card in my hand and started to insert it into the side of the unit, I went on, "if I recall, I have to put the card in, enter my code and then go into the system to interrogate it." I did as I'd just told Stavros, the code to get into the system was quite simple 999, after entering that the display panel changed, some buttons above it indicated that they had become up arrows and the buttons beneath were arrows pointing down, two other buttons were designated enter and cancel, but as you progressed so did their purpose change.

I scrolled through the menu ignoring many of the displays, then I came to the one I'd been looking for, 'system last alarmed by' I looked at Stavros before I prepared to press the enter key, he had a question.

"And what will his show us Andrew?" he asked.

"Exactly what it says there," I replied, my finger poised over the tiny button. I pressed it and the display changed again, this time reading, 'system alarmed by card key number 1' "There, that's my card, when I alarmed the system as I left the day I went home."

"And now you can check when it was disabled, yes!" was Stavros's enthusiastic response.

"I can," I replied as I scrolled though the menu once again, but when I pressed the enter button I was in for a shock. My silence and no doubt startled expression troubled my good old friend.

"What s it Andrew?" his tone as questioning as the enquiry, he continued after coming closer and placing his hand on my shoulder, "I can see the colour has drained from you."

"Stavros," I began not wishing to sound foolish, I may well be suffering from some form of amnesia but the display was perfectly clear in what it was indicating to me, "it says the last person to disable the alarm was Louise!"

"There must be some confusion Andrew," Stavros began to say, and as he looked himself at the display he went on, "surely Andrew you can check the time of the entry."

"No Stavros I can't," I replied and struggling to think what to do next I continued, "there is a way of checking the date and time but I can't remember the codes required to go past the customer entry level."

"Andrew my friend," Stavros said, the way he started to speak to me indicated that he was now having his own doubts about what he could see on the display.

"Yes, what is it Stavros?" I asked looking him straight in the eyes trying as hard as I could to read his inner thoughts, just momentarily I thought I could.

"You haven't been well, maybe you did have a bump on the head," he paused as he noticed my facial expression change, all the same he continued, "perhaps you've got the days muddled up."

"No Stavros, I haven't got that confused," I paused as I was now feeling angry, now with my old friend, no I had a certainty in my mind, so I went on, " I put the alarm on, that I am sure of."

"But Andrew a lot has gone on in the past week…" Stavros started to say only for me to cut him short.

"I put the bloody thing on Stavros, I put it on!" my anger now in my voice at the thought of being doubted.

"OK, Andrew there must be another reason for this, yes!" Stavros replied, his tone now calmer, maybe trying to reassure me.

"Then we had better start to find out what it is," I said still with a little frustration in my voice.

"Perhaps you should start by ringing the company that installed the alarm system, maybe they could get an engineer out to check the system thoroughly," Stavros suggested, and he went on, "and I will find the kettle and make us some coffee." He finished as he headed off in the direction of the kitchen, he was familiar with the Manor, he and Marie had spent a few weekends with us, so it was something of a second home to him.

For my part, I rummaged in the unit next to the telephone, the paperwork associated with the high-tech system was kept there, sure enough I found the telephone number to be used in the event of an emergency, but upon dialling the number all I received was a tone informing me that the number was unobtainable.

"Bugger," I said out loud, frustration and disappointment in my voice. I must have said the word quite vociferously for I heard Stavros reply.

"What's the problem?" he called as he made his way back in the direction of the hall.

"I can't get a reply on the telephone number I have," I said to Stavros as he stood at my side again, I continued, "the number is unobtainable."

"Well let's think of how anyone could have got in," Stavros started to ask, and he continued, "perhaps someone stole Louise's bag, after all the gates were locked."

"Stavros, there is another gate," I started to tell my friend and suddenly something else came back to me, "and we should be able to check who came in using the video cameras that are situated around the grounds."

"That's better Andrew, now I can see that you haven't permanently lost your memory!" Stavros excitedly replied.

We made our way into the room at the back of Chillingston Manor that we'd had converted into an office, in a small cupboard the closed circuit monitors and associated equipment is housed.

"Perhaps we can get to the bottom of this mystery now!" Stavros said as I bent down to activate the system, it was switched on, or so I thought, but the monitors needed to be powered up.

"Yes, let's hope so," I replied as I sat down in front of the screen, for some reason perhaps it was instinct, I'm not sure, but my fingers ran over the control keyboard, but there was nothing, the screen remained blank, I looked up at Stavros, he was standing at my side, "it hasn't recorded a thing!" I said once again despondently, I flicked a few more of the control keys, and an image appeared on the monitor, slowly the picture changed as one by one the different cameras exposed the views of the estate.

"Andrew, do you think it is broken?" Stavros asked as he looked a little more intently at the screen.

"I don't think it's broken Stavros," I began and looking down at the equipment I went on, "the bloody thing has been turned off; well at least the cameras were disabled!"

"In that case whoever came into the house must have switched it off, yes!" Stavros observed.

"Or maybe," I began for now something else Stavros had said came back into my mind, perhaps like the alarm, I'd never turned it on, so it was best that I shared these thoughts with him, "it could be Stavros that you are right," he looked down at me a little puzzled by the start of my statement, I continued, "you said that I may have forgotten to switch the alarm on, the same could be said for this system, perhaps I disabled it and didn't set it up when I was here last."

"Tell you what Andrew," Stavros began, "that may be the case, but as you are here now, perhaps you should set it up," he paused again, and then added, "just so you don't forget."

I did as Stavros suggested, enabled the monitoring system, checked it was functioning properly, before I left the cupboard I checked that the memory on the computer wasn't full, it was completely empty, as if someone had been in and erased it's contents, perhaps it was me, I knew it had the capacity to store up to three weeks of images, that should be plenty of time I thought to myself if I didn't get back to the Manor, then as long as I ensured that the alarm was enabled the house should be safe.

As I came out of the small room Stavros called to me that he was going to make that cup of coffee, but as I stood and looked around the room the purpose of our visit came back into my mind, it was to check in Louise's diary, not to pry into her private thoughts and details, no, it was to try and recall where we had been on that fateful night. But as I made my way in the direction of her desk I noticed that the telephone answering machine was flashing that it had some stored calls, looking a little closer at the display I could see that there were seven unanswered messages. I pressed the button to retrieve them just as Stavros came back into the room with two mugs of coffee in his hands.

'Mr Jackson, Mrs Shaw,' the message began, I couldn't place the voice or the accent, only that it was a woman's voice, but as I listened I was to be informed of who it was who had called, it continued, 'its Mrs Walbridge here, the dressmaker, I'm so sorry to call you so soon after your visit, but I can't seem to find any of the details we discussed last night,' she paused and it gave me the opportunity to look at Stavros, he looked a little puzzled by what he had just heard, but also had an expression of anticipation on his face, the message continued, 'I seem to have mislaid the notes I took down, and to be honest can't remember what we talked about, I wonder if you could call me at your earliest convenience.' There seemed to be another pause, then she must have added, 'I'm sure you have my number, but just in case you've mislaid it' and she proceeded to leave her contact details.

I looked again at Stavros, and I was sure he was about to say something when the answer machine told us the date and time the message was left, it was the morning after the dreadful accident, no sooner had that internal voice finished speaking when the second message began to be relayed around the room, it was again from Mrs Walbridge, only now the message was left for myself, we could clearly hear her voice straining as she struggled to control her emotions, she had called to offer her condolences, she closed by saying that she would be in touch later. The machine informed us that the message had been left some two days after the first. I let the rest of the messages play, not taking a great deal of notice of them; they were from other close business acquaintances, also offering sympathy. Saying that I ignored them wouldn't be strictly true, the last but one caught mine and Stavros's attention, but it was very difficult to make out what was being said, or for that matter the voice, in a muffled and somewhat broken way it sounded as if someone said 'not so easy now' but no matter how many times Stavros and I listened to it we could not make it seem any clearer, the last message sounded like someone coughing down the phone, no words, nothing else, just a cough.

I made my way across to Louise's desk once I'd taken my coffee from Stavros, after placing it on the desk I opened the drawer containing the diary I'd been reading a few days earlier.

"I understand this must be very difficult for you Andrew," Stavros said as he pulled my own chair across from the other side of the room and sat down, then he went on, "if you like Andrew I shall go for a walk, I don't want to pry into Louise's private thoughts."

"Stavros you won't," I replied as I retrieved the diary from the drawer, I continued, "I'm just going to check that there was an appointment for that evening with Mrs Walbridge, no more looking at the distant past."

"Only if you are sure Andrew," Stavros said, at the same time he placed his large hand on my shoulder.

"I am," I said as I opened the diary on the page in question, then upon confirming the date I went on, "Yes, Stavros the appointment was for seven in the evening." I sat looking down at the open page, other notes had been made, but they were of little significance to what was going on in my head at that very moment. For looking at this arranged appointment was beginning to bring other recollections back into my mind, and these thoughts I had to share with Stavros, but before doing so we moved across the room to my desk.

"Stavros you remember last night me telling you about Sarah answering the telephone," I started to say to Stavros, he nodded that I had his attention, so I continued, "well as I said, that was the night of the accident, Sarah and I were waiting for Louise to come down with James," I paused for those thoughts were now correct and accurate in my mind, but now something else had come back to me, so I went on, "we all got in the car, I was in the front with Louise as you would expect, she was driving, Sarah was sat behind me and James was in his child seat obviously behind Louise, well James was a little tired, and really didn't want to go out, but Louise thought it was best if he come with us, keep him involved if you know what I mean," I looked again at Stavros, he understood and nodded indicating so, after taking a sip from my coffee, I went on, "well for some reason Sarah and James started to argue, I remember James saying that he'd just seen a car like ours, you know the BMW, well Sarah said it wasn't, Stavros I don't have to tell you what it's like when two children start to have a go at each other, then," I stopped because James's words came back to me, the last words I remember him saying so clearly, also something Sarah had asked me earlier in the evening, 'would she belong to me when Louise and I were married' anyway I continued, "Sarah must have smacked James, for suddenly he cried out 'daddy tell her to stop it', well, I was in the process of turning to speak to Sarah, I must admit still quite taken aback by James's comment when to my surprise Sarah verbally lashed out again at James, 'he's not our daddy, don't call him that!' her words for the first time spoken with a touch of anger to them, I'm still not sure if they were aimed directly at myself or Sarah was just trying to correct James."

"What did Louise make of this?" Stavros asked as he finished his coffee.

"She told Sarah off instantly, saying that she mustn't ever talk to me like that, as I've explained I was taken completely by surprise by both comments," I said, and added, "she was quite cross with both Sarah and James, neither of them had behaved like that before."

"And you Andrew, what did you think of what the children had said?" Stavros asked now his eyes probing into my inner soul, the same way he had those years ago when he'd first met Louise, there was no point in lying to him, he could see beyond my hidden thoughts.

"Well strangely enough, at first I was pleased when James called me daddy, but Stavros," I said looking at him quite hard I continued, "I'd never set out to be a replacement for his true father, nor that to Sarah," I paused for if it hadn't been for Sarah's intervention in the form of her little drawing during my period of isolation a considerable time ago, then I may never have had any parental feelings towards the children, it also had to be borne in mind that I had a grown up family already.

"But you had taken on Louise, and the children my friend, hadn't you?" Stavros's words were spoken with more than just a little feeling.

"Yes I had Stavros," I paused before continuing, sure I had encompassed my life with Louise and the children, and now I remembered saying that it was the fact that I was financially sound that had helped me to take on a new and growing family, so I passed on these thoughts to my friend, "but it had been made all the easier by me being so rich Stavros."

"My friend," Stavros began, his words only a few but spoken slowly and very accurately, he continued and was to remind me of my past, "oh my friend, I remember only too well that look in your eyes the very first time I met Louise," he paused maybe trying to contain his own emotions, rubbed his face with his right hand then went on, "yes as I've said I can still see that look on your face and in the depth of your eyes, even if you hadn't had all of this wealth then, I know you would have given up everything for this woman," with that comment he looked across to the corner of my desk and the photo of Louise that stood upon it, he went on, "so don't tell this old friend that you couldn't have done it without your money."

Of course he was right, I'd told Louise some time ago that I would have left Kate, my ex-wife for her, and now Stavros's words confirmed my inner recollections, before I had a chance to say any more Stavros spoke again.

"Andrew you never met my first wife Anthelia, did you?" he asked, the question took me a little by surprise, but the answer was quite straightforward.

"No Stavros I didn't," I replied still a little puzzled by his comment or rather the question, as I was still digesting his frank and open comments about myself.

"Well as you know she was Andreas's mother," he paused again to gather his own thoughts and emotions, once in control he went on, "Andrew that was her name, Anthelia, and the moment I saw her I fell in love with her, and I can safely say she was in love with me, I would have done anything for her, and always did, we met in the village where we both grew up, in Greece, well it wasn't long before we married, we stayed in Greece for some considerable time, then one of my many cousins suggested that we come to England with him and his wife, he wanted to set up a business here, both Anthelia and I agreed, at first things were slow to get off the ground, and to be truthful I wondered in the early days if we'd done the right thing, but gradually the business picked up, then for what seemed like no reason my cousin and his wife returned home, well of course by then Anthelia and I had young Andreas," he paused just long enough for me to ask a question.

"But what line of business were you in to in those days Stavros?" I needed to know, yes I knew of some of his rather dodgy dealings from the past, but now here was Stavros explaining his reasons for being in the country in the first place.

"That is rather a strange question for you to ask Andrew!" Stavros replied somewhat startled by my enquiry.

"Well." I began trying to pick my words carefully I continued, "these are subjects about you that I know little, to nothing about."

"You are of course right my friend!" Stavros said and after finishing his coffee he continued, "well in those early days I was involved in what I am doing today, that is antiques."

I looked at him a little puzzled, I didn't realise that his present business, as dubious as it seemed, was where his roots were, and he must have picked up on my puzzled expression for he went on.

"Sure I did diversify over the years, but I was always able to come back to the business I know best," he replied.

"You mean the cars and the diamond smuggling!" I said recalling what I'd been told some time ago.

"Yes I do Andrew," he paused after answering my question, and then he continued, "anyway Andrew that is now firmly in the past, as you are well aware Nana is in the Special Services, I'm sure Alex told you of my connection with that particular arm of the law."

"Yes he did," I replied, for indeed Alex had informed me that Nana was recruited for the special protection team, and at the same time he told me that they were able to persuade Stavros to stop his dealings with stolen cars and the like.

"Well Andrew that brings us to the subject of Nana, and of course Demetri, when I met their mother," he paused and looked at me, his eyes half closed concentration in them, he went on, "you remember Victoria, yes." I nodded in agreement, he continued, "it was what I thought would be a relationship that would last forever and should have, but..." he stopped himself, for now he was rubbing his eyes trying to conceal his emotions.

"Its OK Stavros," I began to say, only for him to put his hand up indicating that he wanted to continue.

"What I haven't told you Andrew, is that Anthelia had gone back to Greece, her mother had been taken very ill, she went back on her own to nurse her, as I was told it was her final days, but Anthelia was killed in a terrible plane crash." Now he stopped and was struggling to control his emotions, he took a handkerchief from his pocket and blew his nose after wiping his eyes, then when he was settled again he continued, "Andrew we had so much planned together, her death really broke my heart, so…" he stopped again and his hand came across the desk and gripped mine very tightly, "so now you can remember what I told you at your house after Louise had left you, I too have seen the pain of a broken heart, I was devastated!"

I didn't know what to say to my dear old friend, for this was information he'd never shared with me before, and now I sat here feeling very helpless, for in all honesty Stavros had been in this very situation himself, albeit many years ago.

"But my friend," Stavros started to say again, and he continued, "I knew that I had to carry on for the welfare of young Andreas, and of course myself, then after a year, or it may have been eighteen months, I met Victoria, she had come to England to work in her uncle's restaurant, in the beginning things went well, and I must say that despite all of our differences, she loved Andreas as if he was her own, and that is the point I am trying to make, she gave each and every one of the children an equal amount of love, and that is what true love is all about," he paused and I could tell he was thinking deeply, his hand came up to his chin before he continued, then he went on, "there is a saying Andrew that when you make babies, then you make the love for them in your heart, that love will be with them forever, well Victoria found extra love in her own heart for Andreas, and to this day she still loves him as if he is her own, and of course he treats her as his natural mother, so there is a great bond between them that we Greeks love so much," he stopped again and now sat upright in his chair, then continued, "but sadly Andrew, Victoria and I used to argue over the simplest of things, but she didn't just walk out on us, no the situation was explained to the children, and they were quite grown-up, not little children, anyway she has stayed in this country, even married again, and we are as it is often said, still good friends."

He finished and now seemed to have a more relaxed composure to himself, this conversation cleared up a lot of the past, I'd never met his first wife, and as a result never asked any questions, and as for Victoria, well I assumed that they had parted for more or less the reasons that he had just given me, I was well aware of her fiery temper, but now I had a better understanding of the person and what sort of relationship they'd had, I'd also been aware of the arguing, as I had witnessed them disagreeing on more than one occasion, but I had taken these incidents to be the exception rather than the normal.

"Andrew," Stavros started, his behaviour now more controlled, and I would say had returned to normal, he went on after a slight pause, "we didn't come to your fine house to discuss my past, we came here to discover what has happened to you."

"You are of course right Stavros," I said, my own manner somewhat respectful, for he had been open and honest with me, and I needed to show that I appreciated his frankness.

"Then Andrew you go up the bedroom and check to see if Louise's jewellery is there, that will be a start on clearing up at least part of this mystery," Stavros started to say, at the same time he got up from his seat, picked up the two coffee mugs and headed for the kitchen, as he got to the doorway he spoke again, "I shall make us a fresh cup of coffee." And he was gone.

I made my way out of the annex, that was also our office, back to the hall, at the bottom of the wide wooden staircase I stopped, gripped the handrail with my right hand and looked up at the landing at the top of the stairs, stood here alone I once again could hear all of the familiar sounds that used to ring around the house, the children's laughter, Louise's voice calling one of us, as she often did, be it for dinner, or to ask a question, then there would be Susan's voice, perhaps telling James and Sarah a story, a feeling of isolation began to engulf me, that was until Stavros's words came back to me, 'I too have shared a broken heart'.

So I had to carry on for myself and also my two adult sons, admittedly they weren't small children, but all the same they needed me. And thinking of them reminded me that I needed to visit the garage, William had told me that the BMW could be released, and disposed of, there seemed to be an eagerness in his words when he told me, maybe he needed the space in the garage, in all probability he was thinking of me, trying the best he could to ease my pain, if the remains of the car were out of the way, then the past couldn't come back to haunt me.

I'd made it to the top of the stairs with these thoughts going round and round in my mind, again I stopped and momentarily listened, nothing that is other than the faintest sound of Stavros moving about in the kitchen and he was a considerable distance away, slowly I made my way along the landing, as I did so I glanced out of one of the windows, the trees in the distance swayed in rhythm to the wind that played with their foliage, I looked down to the gravel bay in front of the house, a cloud of dust ascended into the air as a gust of wind swept across the driveway I could clearly see that it was being deposited on Stavros's new car. On to the master bedroom Louise and I had shared, as I passed each of the children's rooms I paused, hoping for something I would recognise, but there was nothing, no sound of voices, just that faint distant wind.

Once in our bedroom I looked around me, I hadn't had the strength or the will to venture this far on my last visit only as far as the doorway to the bedroom, and I now found the prospect of going through Louise's belongings very daunting. It wasn't that I expected to uncover some dark or hidden secrets, to the best of my knowledge we hadn't any between us, but some of the past was evading me, could it be that I may discover things I thought I'd forgotten, the only way to find out was to set about the task in hand. By now I was stood in front of the dressing table, the mirrors attached to the back reflecting the room that was behind me, I looked at the jewellery box that was placed in the centre of the unit, I open the carved lid and looked at the contents, carefully I moved some of the items of jewellery, but these was no sign of Louise's engagement ring, there was a large brooch, a few earrings, I lifted out the tray expecting to find some other items that I recognised but none of her everyday items of jewellery where there, maybe they are in the safe I thought to myself but I recalled Louise in the past telling me that she didn't require the safe, she was happy to use the jewellery box as a means of storage, I would check all the same when I went downstairs, then quite by chance my senses picked up on something else, just the faintest trace of Louise's perfume, I looked around the dressing table and found the smallest bottle, I lifted it to my nose and inhaled the full strength of the perfume, this act brought many thoughts of Louise rushing back to me, I'd seen her many times sit at this very dressing table and apply the perfume to her neck and wrists but I never knew the name of the scent.

I looked at this small bottle of perfume, Ralph Lauren 'Cool', it was Louise's favourite, I'd already removed the top, and holding the bottle close to my nose inhaled again, this time more deeply, the essence brought back memories of the past, our first meeting in the office so many years ago, the time we went for that secretly arranged dinner. I'd never known the name of the perfume, maybe Louise had told me the name but it hadn't registered in my mind that was until now.

The very action of standing in this bedroom holding this tiny bottle of perfume was like I was re-living the past, Stavros's words came back to me, "not that much wrong with your memory if you can recall that distance past." And of course he was right, yesterday I was very confused, unable to maintain any long term thoughts, but since his arrival I had been able to recover some of the events that had been evading me, but more importantly I'd recovered my ability to think for myself. These thoughts now gave me confidence, a renewed self-belief that I would be able to put the past into some sort of order, there was a possibility that I may never be able to remember exactly what had happened on that fateful evening, it could be one of those events that are better forgotten, how would I cope if I was to be able to hear Louise and the children screaming, crying out for me to help them as they were consumed in fire, the nightmares would surely haunt me forever if that part was to come back to me.

I replaced the cap on the perfume, put the tiny bottle back to its rightful position on the dressing table, once more I checked the jewellery box, but there was no sign of Louise's Omega watch, or her diamond and gold necklace, then I thought to myself that I must look in the safe downstairs, but just as before some form of curiosity took hold of me, maybe I was thinking that some of her jewellery could have fallen in to the top drawer of the dressing table, I placed my hand on the handle and started to pull the drawer open.

As it slid on its runners I was in for something of a surprise, well more like a fright, Louise had always been organised, as I'd told Stavros her desk in the office was in perfect order, but now I was looking in to the top drawer of her dressing table it was a shambles, this particular drawer contained Louise's underwear, now normally every item would be folded and carefully placed in its rightful position, her bras were usually arranged on the left hand side of the drawer, and to the right her panties. I gazed in amazement, it appeared as if the entire contents had been thrown up into the air and caught in the drawer before they'd had chance to land on the floor, nothing was in order, the array I had come to expect, this wasn't right mentally I said to myself, then a previous occurrence re-entered my thoughts, that was the alarm, upon investigation it had revealed that it was Louise's security card that had reset the system, maybe someone had stolen her handbag after the crash, then forced her to reveal her code so they could disable the system, then allowed her and the children to perish in the resulting inferno after the collision, these people may have even deliberately started the fire in an effort to cover their tracks, since then whoever would have had plenty of opportunities to enter the Manor, maybe looking for money, they could have settled for the remaining jewellery, because the items left weren't of any great value.

"This must seem like a terrible dream to you Andrew," Stavros said, making me snap out of my mesmerised state, I turned and nodded my reply, and he continued, "made all the worse because you can't remember, I am right, yes!"

Stavros had come upstairs, his arrival had surprised me, but not to the point of startling me, in his hands two mugs of coffee, he stood in the bedroom doorway

"True!" was all I could say as I fought with my own emotions, my previous thoughts disappeared as he came across the bedroom and to the side of the unit, by now I'd closed the drawer, this was an area of Louise's privacy I didn't want share with anyone, not even my closest of friends.

"Did you find Louise's jewellery?" Stavros asked as he passed me the mug of fresh coffee, he took a sip before I replied, I'm sure sensing what I was about to say.

"There are some items here," I said, then part of my thoughts came back to me, so I continued, "I think someone has used Louise's card to gain access to the Manor, they may well have removed the rest of her jewellery," I paused as I recalled what the pathologist had said in his report, those words made me feel angry, and that anger came out in my words, "you know Stavros, it seems the bastards took her jewellery before she died, they may even have started the fire!"

"Now Andrew I understand your anger, but you mustn't let it consume you," he paused, again rested his hand on my shoulder, then continued, "as I have said time will sort things out." His look told me I had to be patient with myself, along with my emotions.

"I still need to check in the safe, but that is downstairs in the study," I said after taking another sip from my coffee.

"In that case I shall come down with you," Stavros replied and he headed for the door.

I walked a little way behind Stavros, and as I got to the bedroom door I stopped and looked back, something wasn't right, everything was in order, the room wasn't a mess as would be expected if someone had broken in, but then it occurred to me, they hadn't broken in, whoever it was had the necessary equipment to enter the house without causing any damage to the property, then a flash back, the gates, why are they twisted out of shape? Maybe someone had rammed them in an effort to get into the Manor! I was forgetting that the taxi driver had the same problems in opening them when he'd brought me here after leaving Trevor and Diane's.

We were nearing the bottom of the stairs when Stavros's mobile phone began to ring, in an instant his free hand went into his trouser pocket, the whimsical ring tone was echoing around the hall as he pulled out the phone, he held it some way from his body as he looked at the display. "Excuse me Andrew!" he swiftly said as he pressed a button to receive the call. I wasn't to be privy to the conversation, not even Stavros's replies, for whoever the caller was Stavros spoke to them in his native tongue, the words rolled from his mouth with ever increasing speed, he only paused momentarily for a reply and to draw breath, for my part I took his mug of coffee from him as we stood in the hallway he was in danger of spilling its contents on the floor, in doing so it freed his left hand, and that too became involved in the conversation, if only as a measure of signalling his approval or disapproval to what was being said to him. He closed the conversation with his customary Greek farewell that I had heard many times before, and then he returned the phone to his pocket.

"I am sorry Andrew," Stavros began at the same time took his mug of coffee from me, he went on, "it seems that we have problem at home," he paused again took a pull from his coffee, swallowed hard then continued, "I feel as if I'm letting you down, but sadly Andrew I have to go home!"

I was more than a bit surprised by his statement, what could be so wrong that it required the urgent attention of Stavros in person, only last night he'd told me that he would stay, but before I had chance to question his need to go home he spoke again, this time with confidence and assurance in his words.

"Andrew, you must not worry yourself, everything will be alright," he paused giving me the opportunity to think, he was right, I would be able to manage, I had before he'd arrived last night, and today he'd encouraged me to think ahead, for now I had a vague set of plans in my head, things were coming together, sure I would miss Stavros, but as I've said I would be able to manage, I was about to relay these thoughts to him when he spoke again.

"For the moment I can't explain why I have to return to Cornwall, but I can assure you..." he cut himself short so as to finish his coffee. Once he'd finished I asked him to continue.

"Well," he said, hesitancy in the very word, as well as his voice, he seemed for the first time unsure of what to say, almost uncomfortable, and I'd never seen him like this before, but I should have picked up on his manner, by now the start of a smile had formed, just that grin, the edges of his mouth beginning to curl up and his eyes had the slightest hint of a sparkle to them, he went on, "Andrew you have learnt many lessons over the years, yes! And in time this will be one of the toughest you will have learnt," he paused once again, my mind was racing, was he going to tell me something I didn't already know? He went on with a saying that was going to take some understanding, particularly in my present state of mind, "Andrew we have an old Greek saying 'sometimes the lessons are harder to teach rather than learn'" his look now had changed to one of perplexity, as if he'd expected me to understand this phrase instantly, somewhere in the back of my mind I recalled him saying that idiom before, but sadly its location and meaning passed me by, but not wishing to show my lack of perception I nodded in agreement, for my mind was on coping alone, leaving this big house and driving my Porsche back to my house in Bristol.

"Andrew!" Stavros began and regaining my full attention by his strong tone and manner he continued and in doing so stole my thoughts, "I am thinking that you don't think Louise is dead, I am right, yes?"

Now this question made me think again about what I'd discovered upon return to the Manor, certain things could be perceived as indications that Louise herself had been to the house, but on the other hand I had been reliably informed that she along with the children were dead, to answer this question instantly with a positive reply could be a sign to Stavros that I wasn't really ready to be left on my own, but to say that I was sure she was dead seemed also like the wrong thing to say, maybe indicating that I didn't care.

"One thing I am sure of Andrew!" Stavros began again stealing the opportunity for me to reply to his other question, I looked him in the eyes as if I was expecting something to be written in them, but there wasn't a sign, he went on, "I am confident that you will be alright, you are more than capable of looking after yourself, as you've proved to me on other occasions."

That last comment was said in reference to the time when Stavros left me on my own at my house in Bristol after Louise and I had parted, it took me six or seven weeks to recover from that parting but I did, then Louise and I had resumed our relationship, agreed it was under different circumstances but we had been so much together, that is until this recent dreadful event took place.

"Stavros I have plenty of things to occupy myself with until the…" my reply began, but my words all but dried as I was about to say the word funeral.

"I understand!" Stavros replied placing his hand on my shoulder he went on "but when that day arrives you will be a little more prepared for it!"

"I'm sure you are correct," I replied without thinking about my comment, and then I continued thinking more about the immediate future, "for now Stavros we need to go back to my Bristol home so you can collect your belongings before you head off for Cornwall."

"There is no need for you to concern yourself with that Andrew," was his instant response and he went on, "there were only a few bits and pieces, and I can pick them up when I see you again," he paused to pick his words carefully, then continued, "we will be up in a week or so."

"Well if you're sure Stavros," I began my reply for something else had come into my mind, and that was maybe I could pay a visit to Mrs Walbridge rather than go home, it would save going into Bristol and then coming out again, I felt as if I needed to share these thoughts with Stavros, at the same time looking for his approval it could be said, "do you think I should go and see the dressmaker?" I quickly asked my friend.

"Yes Andrew I think that would be good for you, maybe put your mind at rest," he paused and I sensed he understood my need better than I did myself, "you know she may be able to help you clear up some of those doubts you have, and in doing so set your mind at rest, then you will be more focussed on what you have to do in the future. Yes!"

"Then that is what I will do," I replied, for now I was once again believing in myself.

"That is good Andrew! More like the old resourceful Andrew Jackson I remember," Stavros paused before continuing with his reply, for he was about to add a very poignant comment, something that had been said to me before and that time by Stuart and would be said to me again before everything was revealed to me, but at the same time it brought a question from me, "and it is what Louise would have wanted you to do."

"And what is that Stavros?" I instantly asked.

"She would want you to carry on!" Stavros told me, his voice firm and full of determination.

I understood his words perfectly, she had told me that if anything had happened to me she would have got on with her life and that was what I needed to do, but before I was given a chance to reply Stavros had a request for me.

"Andrew, I need to make a phone call!" he said, rather instructed me, I say instructed me for looking into his eyes I could see he needed to be alone to make the phone call, I made my way in the direction of the kitchen with the two coffee mugs in my hand, as I approached the doorway to the kitchen I turned and looked back, not wishing to intrude on Stavros's phone call more so to ensure that he had the privacy he required, he was still dialling the number on the keypad, momentarily he glanced in my direction, but he gave nothing away with his eyes, as I continued into the kitchen I could faintly hear him speaking, fluently, in his native tongue, Greek.

"All is now sorted!" were the words from Stavros that snapped me from my engrossed state as I washed up the coffee mugs at the sink, I spun round to look him in the eyes, and he continued, "I must be on my way Andrew!" his voice had that authoritarian ring to it, but more importantly were the words. For now I was going to be left alone.

"OK." Was all I could reply as I processed what Stavros had just said.

"Well Andrew I will need you to come to the gates with me," he paused as we looked at each other, then he continued, "you know to open them, yes!"

"I don't need to Stavros," I started to say as I came across the kitchen to him, I went on as I got closer, "I can open them from here, there's a button by the front doors next to the intercom."

"Very good Andrew, as I've been saying there seems to be nothing wrong with your memory, well not in my mind," Stavros said as we made our way in the direction of the hall, at the front doors we stopped and I expected Stavros to have some massive words of wisdom for me, something special to keep me going until the next time I would see him, but he just looked harder into my eyes, then his right hand came across to take mine, his grip was as always tight, then he pulled me to him, wrapped his left arm around me, then and only then when I was in his intense grip was he ready to speak and his words were spoken softly and with the greatest of accuracy and for the first time ever he used an unexpected phrase.

"Now Andrew my son, you will need to be strong and very perceptive in the coming days," he paused as I pulled away slightly trying to look into his features but it was no good he held me in a vice like grip, he continued with a few more words, "the future will unfold without any help from ourselves!"

For just a moment I was a little puzzled by his last comment, but then I had been expecting words of a far more poignant nature, so I let the moment pass. I opened the right hand door after Stavros had released his hold on me, together we stood and looked at Stavros's car.

"OK, I must go," he said after giving me one last hug, at the same time he kissed me on both of my cheeks, this was what I had witnessed him do with his sons on many occasions, and then he was on his way down the steps.

"I'll wait until you are at the gates," I started with my reply, then as Stavros climbed into his car I continued, "then I will press the button to open them."

"But I may have to get out and help them open," was the quip I received in reply, for Stavros had remembered that the gates had been playing up when we had entered the grounds.

"You may have to wait a minute or two," I quickly replied as the door of his car closed. I saw his head nod in response to my comment indicating that he'd heard me.

Then, stood on the top step I watched as he started his car and drove the Mercedes up the drive towards the gates, the sun was even hotter now, but the wind had picked up a little, the dust cloud swirled behind the car before being blown out of sight, as Stavros approached the gates the brake lights came on and it was noticeable that the car was slowing down, I stepped inside of the hall, just to the right was the control for the gates, I pressed the button marked 'gates open' I returned to my original position on the top step, I could just make out the gates moving, the right one quite free, but the left hand gate seemed, even from a distance to be struggling, when the gap was big enough between the gates Stavros was through them, his right hand was out of the window, a gesture of farewell as he headed out onto the open road, within seconds he was out of sight.

I remained almost transfixed on the same spot, his car was gone and he was on his way home, but once again Stavros had faith in me to carry on, the conversations we'd had during the time we had been together came flooding back to me as I gazed into the void left by his departure, suddenly the breeze kissed my cheeks, this action reminded me of Louise, the way she would hold my face in her hands before tenderly kissing me, once again my thoughts were stolen from me but at the same time I was reminded of the tasks ahead of me as I recovered from my reminiscent past.

Now firstly I needed to get my car out of the garage, it would be easier to do that now then lock the house up, I would then be in a better position to travel back to my house in Bristol, that would be after I'd paid the visit to the dressmaker, I put my right hand into my trouser pocket, removed the single key that also had a key fob attached to it, I held it in my hands as I inspected it, yet still I couldn't remember the last time I'd driven the Porsche.

Slowly I made my way in the direction of the garages at the back of the Manor, the crunching gravel under my feet the only sound I could hear, there were other noises, the breeze blowing through the trees, the birds singing in the distant woodlands, their song carried on the wind, but in all honesty I was oblivious to any other sound, for now my mind was set on the task I had promised Stavros I would undertake. Once again my hand went into my pocket, this time I removed the keys for the garage, now I was stood in front of one of the double up-and-over doors, yet still I couldn't remember the last time I had been in this very spot, and now my thoughts were becoming complicated by a certain amount of frustration I was feeling with myself, perhaps, I thought if I open one of the doors some of the recent past might come back to me, so I did just that, I turned the handle after unlocking it with the key, the mechanism was free and easy to operate, the difficult part was in actually opening the door with the handle, I pulled hard on the chrome plated lever, very slowly the bottom of the door started to come upwards, I needed to release my grip on the handle and take hold of the bottom edge of the wide door, once in place all that was required was a swift tug, and the door was on its way, the weight and momentum was sufficient for it to carry on along its tracks until it had reached the stops at the end of the runners and stop it did with quite a considerable bump, I stood and let the sound of the thud die away and as I did so the tie that is used to start the reverse operation fell from it's retaining hook, it gave me quite a shock, for in the process it tapped me on the left shoulder making me spin round thinking that someone else was behind me, but it was just the canvas strap swaying in the breeze.

Once I'd recovered from the surprise slap on the back of my shoulder I looked in front of me, the light breeze picked up some dried oak and sycamore leaves and made them dance and skip around the grey painted garage floor, this action drove my attention towards the ground. Where Louise's BMW would normally have been parked was a pile of dirt, not massive in itself, just a scattering of mud and dust surrounding it, before inspecting it in more detail I moved to my right, for some reason I needed more light in the garage, I tugged on the light pull, the fluorescent lights clicked and chattered to themselves before coming to life. The light they emitted only increased my curiosity, for on the workbench were things I couldn't explain, a reel of strong black plastic tape, there was also a hammer, screwdriver along with some other tools. But what were these items doing on the workbench?

I tried hard to remember if I had placed them there, I couldn't recall using them, anyway both of the cars we owned were serviced by the main dealers, and I had no need to tinker with them. Try as much as I did I couldn't account for what had gone on in the garage, I knelt down to inspect the dirt and dust on the garage floor, it looked as if it had come from the wheel arch of a car, a large lump of dried mud, its contents being made up of dirt, dried grass and grit, I picked it up and the mass crumbled in my hand and fell to the floor, then something caught my eye, a small piece of reflective glass, on closer inspection it turned out to be orange plastic, maybe something picked up by the road wheels and compacted into the mud, I thought to myself, but it looked clean, not something that would have been sat encased in mud for weeks under the wheel- arch of a car, still in my crouching position I glanced across at the Porsche, it was as always gleaming, its dazzling lightning blue paintwork reflecting the bright white light from the fluorescent tubes, it was then that I noticed one of the fluorescent lights had a slight hum to it, I glanced up and noticed that the ends of one of the tubes were in fact darker than the rest of the tube, an indication that the light was nearing the end of its life.

After raising myself from the crouching position I moved towards the car, again my hand went into my pocket, I removed the key that was attached to the key-fob, I pressed the button, that dull thud, flash of the indicators, suddenly I remembered some of the times that I'd conducted that very act, but

I couldn't remember the last occasion, by the time I'd made my way round to the driver's door the locking system had activated itself, a pull on the door handle confirmed the car was securely locked, I'd stood so long admiring the car that it had gone into safety mode, still I thought to myself I needed to open the other door to enable me to get the car out of the garage.

This I did, locking the other door before opening the one I needed, the car started as sweetly as always, the initial roar soon died away and the engine ticked over with that familiar clatter of a high performance engine, some things never change, I thought to myself as I opened the driver's door and got into the car, it was then that some of Louise's and my own past caught up with me, suddenly I was engulfed with the essence of Louise's perfume, the very one I smelt in our shared bedroom, I sat struggling with my memory, almost fighting to recall the last time we had been in this car together, but my thoughts were failing me, try as hard as I might I couldn't remember, thinking it best that I get on with the job in hand I reversed the Porsche out of the garage, the gravel crunched and compacted under the wheels as I came out and into the bright daylight, I got out and locked the garage door and at the same time checked that I had secured the other door, just to put my mind at ease before getting into the car and driving round to the front of the Manor.

I made my way back into the house and as I did so I remembered that I needed to check the contents of the safe, that was situated in the study, it was just to satisfy my curiosity as to whether Louise had left any of her jewellery in it, the closer inspection revealed that she hadn't, that confirmed my worst thoughts and fears, someone had stolen her bag at the same time forcing her to reveal her code to open the safe, along with the information required to gain access to the house, I assumed.

I began to once again feel quite despondent, I stood in the emptiness of the big hall after closing and locking the safe, I could hear that light wind brushing itself against the outside of the house, a need now came over me to be away from here, for I was beginning to feel lonely and this was not the place to have these feelings, I made my way towards the big double oak doors, as I approached them I noticed the pile of post I had brought in with me, I'd placed it on a small occasional table, there seemed to be a considerable amount of correspondence, but then I hadn't been to the Manor for a few days, and it was only Stavros's intervention that had brought me here today, for just a moment I stood looking at the mail I was holding in my right hand, I slipped my car key back into my pocket, then I shuffled the post in my hands, in the same way a gambler would with a pack of cards, just allowing them to slip from one hand to the next, I glanced down at the falling letters, some of them had the senders name stamped across the top of the letter, others were just blank, some I could make out to be condolence cards, then one caught my attention, the bright orange logo on the top of the envelope was quite striking, I managed to stop the other letters falling into my left hand and took a closer look at this particular piece of correspondence, as

I've said I noticed it was from the main BMW dealership, the very one that maintained Louise's car, but without bothering to open it I discounted it as either a reminder that the car was due for a service, or it was a sales type letter, no doubt informing me of some special offer that was going on at the moment, thinking it was the latter I placed the rest of the letters in my left hand and proceeded to make my way to the doors, then I recalled that I needed to alarm the building before I vacated it, I alarmed the system in the manner that I had explained to Stavros, after replacing the card in my wallet I quickly made my way to the doors, I pulled them hard as I listened to the faint bleeping sound of the alarm system, I stood on the top step, as the bleeps got quicker, then stopped indicating that the system was armed, in my left hand I still had the post, my right hand held on to the key, slowly I inserted it into the lock, it turned with ease, now I knew that I had left the place secure, I made my way to the car without looking back, once inside I placed the pile of letters in the glove compartment, started the car and headed along the drive, and in the direction of the gates.

I had only travelled a few hundred yards when a feeling of the past came over me, and it was to be quite significant, I slipped my left hand into my jacket pocket to remove the remote control for the gates when I recalled the last time I'd driven in this direction, and that was the evening of the fateful crash, I removed my right foot from the accelerator, the car instantly pulled back as the engine speed died away, suddenly I was just lumbering along under the tick over of this powerful engine, and now I could clearly recall driving the BMW along this sloping part of the drive, but why, I now found I was asking myself, could I remember the children being sat behind us, Sarah had been sitting directly behind Louise and James behind me, and I had only told Stavros a few hours ago, but here I was now wondering how this change had come about, that was for me to be in the passenger seat, as I was trying desperately the gather my thoughts my mobile phone started to ring, this action snapped me out of this momentary mesmerised state, at the same time making me brake quite hard.

I rummaged in my inner jacket pocket and retrieved my phone, this action took away my previous thoughts, I looked intently at the display half expecting it to be Stavros, or even one of my sons, but I didn't recognise the number, anyway William's or Peter's name would have been displayed if it had been either of them, the same would have happened if it had been Stavros, for indeed all of their numbers were programmed into my telephone. The ring tone was beginning to get louder and louder as I sat staring at this modern piece of technology in my hand, the noise it was making was by now drowning out the sound of the engine, as I pressed the answer button on the phone at the same time I switched off the engine, the two actions resulted in a modicum of peace.

"Hello," I said as I placed the phone next to my right ear, the plastic case instantly felt cold against it, I waited a reply, it did come after what seemed like an age.

"Mr Jackson," the voice asked and with those words I recognised who it was.

"Um, inspector," I somewhat hesitantly began to say, almost struggling for words, I hadn't been expecting the inspector to phone me, in fact we had agreed that I would call him after my visit to the Manor, but before I could say anything else the inspector replied.

"I'm well aware that this is still a very difficult time for you Mr Jackson," his tone was questioning, even on the end of phone, and I presumed that a question was indeed on it's way, but the enquiry was to take me even more by surprise, he continued, "Mr Jackson I need to ask you a very sensitive question." He finished and was awaiting confirmation from myself before continuing.

"What is it you need to ask?" I enquired, not giving a thought to what sort of question that was coming.

"Well it's of rather a delicate nature Mr Jackson." The inspector started to say only for me to cut him a little short.

"Please get on with it!" I asked with just a little more than frustration in my voice, but his reply was to set me back somewhat.

"Mr Jackson," a slight pause, I heard him take something of a deep breath, then he continued, "did Mrs Shaw have any dental work done in the last few months?"

The question did indeed take me by surprise, and my reply to the inspector no doubt took him by as much astonishment, "bloody hell man, I can't remember what has happened in the last few weeks and days, now you're asking..." the inspector cut me short.

"I'm sorry Mr Jackson this obviously isn't the best time to be enquiring this sort of information from you." He stopped, giving me the chance to digest his enquiry and come back with a reply, along with a question of my own, together with an apology.

"I am sorry, I didn't mean to bite your head off, but you are right, the past few days have been very trying," I paused, thought of his original question, and then continued, "the answer to your question is a definite no, but why do you ask."

"Mr Jackson, I've been reading some more of the pathologist's report," he stopped and I could clearly hear pages being turned before he continued, there seemed to be a long silence before he went on then he did quite suddenly, "it seems as if Mrs Shaw had had some considerable dental work undertaken within the last few months."

I held on to his words, for now I was scouring my brain, questioning myself as to what had gone on in the last few months, to the best of my knowledge Louise had only undergone her normal routine dental check-up, in fact we would normally all go together, that sort of visit would normally include the children.

"Inspector, I'm sure I would recall if Louise had been to the dentist," I began with my reply, and I went on with a question, "what sort of work do you mean?"
"It would seem from this report that Mrs Shaw underwent some major dental surgery within the last few months." He finished leaving me in just as much of a quandary as when the conversation had started, but I felt that I needed to reply.
"No, I'm absolutely positive that Louise hadn't been to the dentist," I said, my words spoken firmly, then something else crossed my mind, and it was a question regarding the children. "Does the report say anything about the children's teeth?"
"Unfortunately Mr Jackson that part of the report has some more distressing news," the inspector replied. How much more distressing could things get? I asked myself after digesting his initial reply.
"Please continue inspector," I said, at the same time I began to feel extremely hot, a need came over me to open the window, I lowered the driver's window slightly, about two inches, the cool breeze engulfed the car and in the process reduced my temperature.
"Mr Jackson, without going into the technical details of the report, the pathologist says that due to the fact that both Sarah's and James' teeth hadn't developed fully, it would seem that they had disintegrated during the intense heat of the fire." he said.
His words took a time for me to comprehend, I sat in the car numbed, unable to take the facts in, but slowly a question came into my mind, and albeit bizarre I needed to ask it.
"Inspector," I paused, before I could continue a feeling of uneasiness came over me, almost questioning myself about what I was going to ask the officer, and then I went on, "could it be possible that it wasn't Louise and the children in the car?"
"I understand where you are coming from Mr Jackson," the inspector began with his reply as if he was reading my thoughts in much the same way as Louise was able to, as he paused I could hear him flick the pages of the report over, when he'd found the page he wanted he continued to speak, "the pathologist concludes that his findings are accurate and correct, the adult found in the car is Mrs Louise Shaw, as identified by her dental records, even though these records in themselves don't seem to be very accurate, as for the children," the inspector paused, concerned for my silence he asked a question of me, "are you alright Mr Jackson?"
"I'm still here inspector," I softly replied, unable to say if I was alright or not, the reply I gave was sufficient for the inspector to continue.

"The pathologist says and I quote, 'even though it was not possible for me to identify the two children from the given dental records, I have concluded from the evidence in the shell of the car, the height of each of the children that the remains are indeed that of Sarah and James Shaw'." The inspector finished.

That feeling of emptiness once again engulfed me; it was coupled with a feeling of loneliness, my mind flashed back to other occasions when I'd felt this low, and of course it was after my sister Rachel had died, my thoughts were muddled, to the point of rambling you could say, in fact I felt as if I was miles away oblivious to what was going on around me and the fact that I had been talking on my mobile phone, so engrossed was I that I didn't hear the inspector ask me a question until it had been asked three or maybe four times.

"Mr Jackson!" he almost shouted down the phone to me snapping me out of my trance like state.

"Yes," I simply replied.

"How did you get on at the Manor?" he asked.

"The Manor," I responded still in my startled state, unable to put his question and more importantly the answer into any sort of order.

"You told me this morning that you intended to visit the Manor, you said you would check to see if Mrs Shaw's jewellery was there," he paused but hadn't finished, "do you remember now Mr Jackson?"

"Yes inspector I do remember!" I snapped back, feeling now that I had been doubted a little by the inspector.

"And what was the result of your visit?" the inspector sharply asked, sensing my frustration he spoke to me in a similar manner.

"None of Mrs Shaw's jewellery was there," I said at the same time trying to control my feelings a little more.

"Well that kind of confirms my first suspicion," was the inspector's short comment leaving me to ask a question.

"And what is that suspicion?" I asked, but as I did I recalled some of the conversation I had had with the officer this morning.

"Like I told you earlier, I think it was an accident that went terrible wrong, and the perpetrators took advantage of the situation they found themselves in, they saw Mrs Shaw in the car and removed her jewellery before the car caught fire." The inspector told me.

"Bastards," I angrily replied.

"I understand your anger Mr Jackson, and believe me we're doing all we can to find the people who committed this terrible act," the inspector paused and I could hear him place what sounded like the paperwork back in its folder, then he continued, "I have a man checking some CCTV footage as we speak, we will catch the criminals responsible." He finished but his words gave little comfort to the way I was feeling, then for some reason a question came into my mind, just how did the inspector know my mobile telephone number.

"Excuse me inspector, but where did you get my phone number from?" I asked, it was the simplest of questions, but the reply I received was to set me back somewhat.

"Mr Jackson," the detective began, pausing only to gather his words I assumed, and then he continued, "we do have quite an extensive dossier on you and of course the late Mrs Shaw." For a moment I sat in the car completely dumbfounded, just what sort of dossier could the police have compiled on Louise and me? Of course that was the next question I had to ask.

"Inspector, just what does this dossier contain?" I cautiously asked, and awaited the inspector's reply.

"Well let's just say that there are some interesting details about your past contained within the pages of this file," the inspector eventually replied.

His response wasn't quite what I had expected, and to be honest I wasn't of a mind to ask him to elaborate on any of the information he was privy to, but I was to be put out of my curiosity by the inspector.

"I have to say Mr Jackson there are one or two pieces of information that…" he stopped covered the mouthpiece of the phone I could hear him cough, then he came back on the line and his next statement was to come like a bolt out of the blue, "the death of Mr Gary Shaw never did get resolved," a pause again, maybe waiting for some reaction from myself, I kept my thoughts to myself, after what seemed like an age the inspector continued, "it says that he was killed by persons or person unknown, but further into the report it names the chief suspect as…" he stopped again to cough, this time not covering the phone that well, his cough was more like a bark, it reverberated around in my head making me pull my mobile phone away from my ear.

"Sorry Mr Jackson," the officer said as he resumed the one way conversation, "the report names Jan Van-Elderman as the person suspected of killing Mr Shaw," a slight pause, then he continued, "strange that he was never caught!"

Was this a test? I instantly asked myself, clearly I could remember Alex telling both Louise and me that Jan was dead, but was this information the inspector would have access to, come to think about it would he know about Alex, or for that matter Stavros. The question now in my mind was how should I reply to the inspector?

"Are you still there Mr Jackson?" the inspector enquired sensing my silence.

"Yes I am inspector," I started my reply with, then I went on, "I do recall meeting this Jan fellow once," I finished not wishing to reveal that I had indeed seen him twice, the first time was when Gary gave me a beating in the lane, it was in fact Jan who had stopped Gary killing me, the other occasion was at Cathedral View, Stavros's home, but I thought it best that I didn't reveal the details of those meetings that is unless I was asked to, the second meeting was one not to be discussed with anyone.

"Yes Mr Jackson, it says in this report that you met Jan Van-Elderman once, that's in the statement you and Mrs Shaw gave to the police at the time of Mr Shaw's death..." I cut the inspector short.

"Yes that's quite correct inspector," I said.

"It goes on to say that Elderman is dead," he once again paused making me think this was a tactic to unsettle me, I took a deep breath waiting for the inspector to continue, and he did, "says he died under suspicious circumstances."

I didn't recall Alex saying it was suspicious, according to Alex, Jan, had been blown-up, quite straight forward in my mind, brought an old expression back to me, live by the sword, and die by the sword. As these thoughts were going round in my head a question also came to me, completely by surprise and I felt a need to ask the inspector if he thought it could be a possibility, it would also change the subject that I was feeling uncomfortable about.

"Inspector do you think this could have been planned by some villains in the village?" I paused to add one more comment, "you know we are of quite a high profile in Chillingston."

"No Mr Jackson, like I've already explained to you, we know the Range Rover was involved in a ram raid only a few days before this terrible accident took place," the inspector retaliated, in so doing leaving Jan Van-Elderman out of the conversation.

"What I'm saying inspector is, maybe we were targeted..." I started to reply only for the officer to cut me short.

"Just because you and Mrs Shaw have cars with personalised number plates, and own Chillingston Manor doesn't mean that you have been the victim of a vendetta!" was the somewhat angry reply I received. This had the effect of calming me slightly, well more like setting me back somewhat, but I felt as if I wanted to have the last word, so I added another comment.

"Perhaps I was thinking a little ahead of myself," I said to the inspector, adding, "looking for something that isn't there."

"Maybe you are Mr Jackson, like I've said this seems to have been a terrible accident, but that's not to say we aren't treating it as a serious crime." the inspector told me, then he took another change of tack and I wasn't sure if I should reply to his comment, "but if you have any doubts about my ability Mr Jackson to conduct this investigation then you are free to consult with my superiors," he paused and was to add just a few more poignant words, "or perhaps some of your very influential friends."

That very comment signalled that our conversation was coming to an end, just what the inspector knew about me and my late Louise was best left to the pages of the dossier he had in his possession, I once again began to feel uncomfortable, and somewhat foolish, I wasn't trying to tell the officer how to do his job, indeed now I realised that he knew more about my past than I did, and that was certainly true as to the recent past. The inspector informed me that he would be in touch within a matter of days, sooner if he required any more information; he finished adding that his men were doing their utmost to uncover what had gone on in the past few days and bring the culprits to justice.

For a few moments I sat in the car, the breeze soothing my thoughts as it washed over my temple, I was no nearer to putting this in any sort of order, but as I sat there alone I recalled where I was heading before I was interrupted by the phone call from the inspector, I was going to see the dressmaker, Mrs Walbridge, I slipped my phone back into my jacket pocket restarted the car and headed along the drive towards the gates, there I found that my patience got the better of me, I'd pressed the button on the remote control but the right hand gate was slow to open, I had to get out of the car and put my full body weight against it in order to assist it opening.

Chapter Eight

A visit to the past

The drive to the dressmaker's cottage took less than twenty minutes, if that long; I thought to myself that it was strange that I could clearly remember the route to Mrs Walbridge's home, but not what had gone on since the last time I had visited her.

I'd switched the radio on in the car, just as the two o'clock news summary had started; the home news contained the usual items. A major murder trial at the Old Bailey had been halted due to a witness having been threatened.

Police were still baffled after the body of a man was discovered in a domestic freezer in a house in central London, a spokesperson for the police said that investigations were continuing to try to establish the man's identity, the house had been empty for some months, and police have been unable to contact the owners of the property, but a puzzling feature was the fact that all of the services to the house were still connected.

In other news, a leading supermarket has been forced to recall some of its own brand food products, suspecting an outbreak of food contamination from a dye used in the preparation of the foods, the resulting scare had done lasting damage to the company's reputation, and a spokesman said it would take a considerable time to recover; police were not treating the incident as suspicious.

The body found on a remote Cornish beach yesterday, had now been identified as that of the missing retired police sergeant, Desmond Mitchell, he had been reported missing over a week ago, and it had been suggested at the time that the retired sergeant was suffering from depression. Bloody hell, I thought to myself, that name brought back memories, he had been in the room with Inspector Jones, when Louise and I had made our joint statements regarding Gary's death, fancy him dying I thought, but fortunately there was no mention of mine or Louise's name, once again something from the past had come back to haunt me.

When covering some of the foreign events around the world, the newsreader said, a plane crash in America had killed all of the passengers and crew on board, but the breaking news from South Africa said that the Chief of Police in one of the largest cities had been arrested on charges of corruption, and that was after an extensive investigation into irregularities in the handling of some of the country's most notorious drug dealers.

It would appear that some of the culprits had got away with less than minimal prison sentences, while others seemed to have walked free from court with little more than a fine imposed upon them, the investigation centred around claims that the Chief of Police was in fact being paid by one of the country's biggest drug cartels, the report concluded, it was likely that more arrests were expected, as the investigations continued.

It was almost two twenty when I pulled up outside of the dressmaker's cottage, I sat for a few moments in the car, just listening to the engine tick, that being the sound as the exhaust cooled down, I looked through the passenger window of the Porsche, at the stone built dwelling, the tiny wooden windows looked clean, the framework had the appearance of just being painted, the small panes of glass reflecting the strong sunlight back at me, the cottage had a small garden, a little slatted wooden gate painted green, the rest of the boundary being made of a stone wall, there was no pavement. After locking the car with the remote I made my way along the flagstone path that lead to the oak door of the cottage, a gentle tap with the wrought iron knocker and I waited.

I was greeted with a welcome I wasn't expecting, firstly the smiling Mrs Walbridge took both of my hands, I looked into her eyes before she led me into the lounge of her tiny stone built cottage, she seemed not only surprised to see me but also as if she was holding back her tears, she didn't say a word until I was seated on a very large leather settee, she made herself comfortable in a matching winged chair, it was then that she spoke to me.

"Mr Jackson, it's so nice of you to come and see me," she said, her words spoken softly along with genuineness that I hadn't encountered for a long time, she continued after a slight pause, "may I offer my sincerest condolences, this must be the most difficult of times for you," she paused again. I looked at her as she crossed her legs and placed her hands on her lap, she was a woman in her late fifties, maybe sixty, her grey hair held back in a bun style, over her dress she was wearing a brightly coloured patterned tabard, its pockets full of bits and pieces. She went on after this pause, it was as if she was regaining her own composure, "I can't tell you how upset I was to hear of your tragic accident, and I'm told it happened after you had left my cottage." She stopped and it gave me the opportunity to ask a question.

"Do you recall what time it was when we left, Mrs Walbridge?" the enquiry was simple enough, but her reply was to surprise me somewhat.

"No Mr Jackson, I don't," she shifted slightly in her seat, and looked almost distressed by my question, and then she continued with even more of a revelation, "that's where I have a problem, I can't remember what happened after you left me, I seemed to have lost a day."

What did she mean lost a day? I was puzzled by her statement and it must have shown upon my face, for Mrs Walbridge instantly picked up on my bemused expression.

"Let me make a cup of tea and I will try to explain," with those words she was out of her chair and on her way to what I assumed was the kitchen, sat alone I looked around the room.

To the left of the window was an old oak sideboard, the front of it bleached from where it had been exposed to the sun over the years, in the centre of it a large bowl of fruit, the apples appeared fresh, and their skins shiny reflecting the bright light from the window, a few bananas and two oranges, to the left of the fruit bowl was a small selection of drinks. The other side of the sideboard had an array of glasses, I stood up and made my way over to the unit, looking at the selection of accumulated bottles I noticed a full bottle of my favourite malt whisky, I was still studying this collection of bottles when Mrs Walbridge came back into the room, a tray in her hands. On the tray, cups and saucers, a teapot, small milk jug and sugar bowl, the contents chinked and rattled together as she placed the tray on a coffee table that was positioned in the centre of the room. It was then that I noticed a small plate with a selection of biscuits on it. It was Mrs Walbridge who spoke first.

"If you prefer, Mr Jackson, you can have something stronger," she said, as her eyes also focused on the collection of bottles.

"No Mrs Walbridge, tea will be just fine," I replied as I started to return to the settee. As I sat down I continued, "I did notice that you have a bottle of my favourite whisky, and quite a selection of other drinks."

"That's one that I'm particularly fond of as well," Mrs Walbridge said as she poured the milk into the cups, then the tea, as she sat down she resumed the conversation from where we had left off, "I'll try to explain as best I can by what I said, I mean the missing day, well according to my appointment diary you were due here at seven thirty, the fitting didn't take long, at the most an hour, the dresses only needed a few minor alterations, I say dresses because little Sarah had grown quite a bit since the last fitting," she paused and took a sip from her cup, I sensed she could understand my puzzled expression, she went on, "you can't remember much can you Mr Jackson?"

"No I can't," was my simple reply. Mrs Walbridge continued.

"Well by the time I'd finished pinning up Mrs Shaw's dress your little boy, James isn't it? Well he was fast asleep and Sarah was near to falling asleep as well."

"Mrs Walbridge, I really can't remember any of this," I said as I picked up my cup and saucer.

"Do have a biscuit, Mr Jackson," Mrs Walbridge insisted, at the same time she passed me the plate, I took one of the chocolate digestives and she continued to enlighten me as to what else had gone on that evening, "I offered you and Mrs Shaw a drink, the other times that you had been here we always enjoyed a glass of whisky, Mrs Shaw said she would have an orange juice, as she was driving, you had a glass of malt, that very one on the side, I joined you, there wasn't much in the bottle," she paused and I sensed she was now scouring her own memory. After a few seconds she continued, "but I don't think we finished it…" she stopped again as something fell into place, she went on, "in fact Mr Jackson I poured the remains of the bottle away, it seemed to have some white powdery residue in the bottom of the bottle, most unusual I must say."

I looked across at the bottle, but still the evening wouldn't come back to me, but a question did come to me. "Do you recall how long we stayed?"

"To be perfectly honest Mr Jackson no, I can't remember, and that's why I said about the lost day, I can't clearly remember what happened the day after, it was very late in the afternoon when I heard about the awful accident, it really did shock me." she finished and I thought we had come to a close, but Mrs Walbridge was about to say one more thing that would intrigue me. "I thought at first that the accident had taken place the day after your visit to me," she paused and finished her tea then went on, "the reason I say that is I was sure I saw you car in the village, you did have a dark blue BMW, didn't you?"

"Yes," I instantly replied, adding, "well Louise did." I said, and then something else occurred to me, James and Sarah had been disagreeing in the car on our way to Mrs Walbridge, James had said he'd seen a car like ours; maybe it was that car she had seen in the village.

"Your car or rather Mrs Shaw's car was quite distinctive, wasn't it…?" Mrs Walbridge started to reply only to be cut short by the telephone ringing, "excuse me," she added as she got up from her seat again. No sooner had she left the room and my own mobile phone began to ring, I removed it from my jacket pocket, for some unknown reason I was thinking it was the inspector again; I was a little taken aback when I looked at the display to discover it was in fact Trevor, Louise's father, the last conversation I'd had with him was just after returning to my home in Bristol, it was I who was meant to contact him.

"Hello Trevor," I said after pressing one of the buttons to answer the call, he didn't reply so I continued, "I wasn't expecting to hear from you, how are things?"

There seemed to be a long pause before Trevor replied, but he did.

"Well Andrew, you can guess how things are," his words spoken very softly, I felt as if he needed to be prompted to continue the conversation.

"I wasn't expecting you home until nearer the funeral," my own words died away as I realised what I had just said.

"Diane and I came home, just in case you needed us," was Trevor's hesitant response, I guessed he had more to say, and I wasn't mistaken, for he went on, "it isn't just that Andrew," he paused again and I heard him draw breath, "Jackie and Diane had something of a fall-out, Jackie is so much like her grandfather, Henry Peacock, that was Gladys's husband, very much gets on with life, sure Jackie was upset, but she always was more robust than my Louise." He finished but I was sure there was more to be revealed.

"I'm sorry to hear that Trevor," I started to say, then I recalled Louise saying that she had wanted to be more like her sister Jackie, but that was a considerable time ago, and since then Louise had become more confident and a lot stronger in the process.

"Of course I don't take that much notice of Jackie's nature, sometimes it seems a little harsh, but she means well," Trevor began to reply, and he continued with something of revelation, "I know we shouldn't have favourites, but Jackie is our first, she never came to either Diane or myself for advice, always happy to stand on her own two feet, too hell with the consequences if she had made the wrong decision." He stopped and I guessed that this was something of an out-pouring of his own grief, as much as explaining the temperament of his eldest daughter. "As you know Andrew," Trevor started again, "Louise had a much softer nature, more gentle, perhaps a deeper individual," how right he was, and how well he knew his daughters.

"How is Diane?" I asked almost interrupting him in mid-flow.

"She's sound, sends her love of course," he paused and I knew a question was on its way, and Trevor didn't fail me, "she asked if you'll come and see us before the funeral."

"Of course I will," I started to reply, and recalling what I had been doing these past few days I thought it best if I give Trevor a recap of events, but sat here in the dressmaker's lounge was not the best place to start that lengthy conversation, "maybe I could give you a call this evening Trevor." I said.

"Yes that would be fine Andrew," Trevor replied and continued, "I must say you sound a little better in yourself."

"Well I'm beginning to put some of the past into some sort of order," I paused and heard Trevor reply with his customary 'sound', I continued, "I'll tell you more this evening."

"Andrew that will be fine," he said and then he was gone from the line.

I looked at the phone before slipping it into my jacket pocket, the display held for a spilt second before returning to the image I had as back-ground wallpaper, that being of the mountains of Scotland, taken from one of the many vantage points on the estate I own in the highlands. As I felt the phone fall into the inner jacket pocket and give that tug on the fabric indicating that it had landed Mrs Walbridge came back into the room.

"I'm so sorry Mr Jackson," she said as she returned to her seat, she continued once she was seated, "now where was I?"

With the conversation I'd just had with Trevor still going round in my head I couldn't recall what we had been talking about before Mrs Walbridge departed the room, and it became evident that the telephone call she had just answered must have had the same effect upon her.

"Do you know Mr Jackson," Mrs Walbridge began again, that was after picking up her cup and saucer, "I've had the most awful trouble remembering what went on over those days after you had been to see me, and to tell you the truth, the events of the days leading up to your visit are very sketchy." She finished talking, and then finished her tea, but now there was something else bothering me, I wasn't the only one who couldn't put the past in order, and to the best of my knowledge Mrs Walbridge hadn't had a bump on the head, not that it had been confirmed that I had received such a blow.

"Mrs Walbridge," I began to ask, noticing that I had her attention I continued. "Have you, by any chance hit your head in the past few days?"

"I don't think so," she replied quite adamantly, at the same time she rubbed the top of her head with her right hand, and then came back with a question, "why do you ask Mr Jackson?"

"Well it seems as if we are both suffering from the same problem, that is, a loss of memory, only mine," I needed to be precise and didn't want to insult the lady, I needed to pick my words carefully, so I continued, "well mine has been diagnosed as traumatic amnesia," I said looking at the waiting Mrs Walbridge.

"That'll be down to the accident," was she straightforward reply, and maybe she was right, I thought to myself, but something was still nagging away at my memory, just what it was I couldn't put my finger on, I was still trying desperately to remember what we had been talking about before our respective telephone calls when Mrs Walbridge stole my thoughts.

"Do you know Mr Jackson," Mrs Walbridge started to say snapping me out of my recollect state, she continued to enlighten me to some of her own past, "this sort of thing has never happened to me before, but I was sure that I had another couple that were meant to be returning for another fitting," she once again paused, looked long and hard at me indicating that she was indeed puzzled, replacing her cup and saucer on the small occasional table that separated us she went on, "I checked in the diary, they were meant to be here two days after your visit, but they never showed up." She finished, at the same time replaced her hands on her lap.

"Perhaps they left a message for you, maybe you deleted it by accident," I told her trying to look for a logical explanation.

"I don't think that can be that case Mr Jackson, I haven't had any messages for days," she stopped and seemed a little disconcerted, after trying to make herself comfortable she went on, "I remember the man so well, he shared our taste in whisky," she said at the same time looking across at the full bottle of malt, she went on, "and his name was also Scottish, yes I can remember that now," with those words she was out of her chair again and headed out of the room, as she entered the hall she called back, "I'll get the diary, then I can check and be sure."

She wasn't gone very long; she came back into the room with a large black diary in her hands, resuming her seated position she opened it on her lap, and then she began to read her notes to me, "Miss Charlotte Evans, dress to be taken in at the waist, arms to be shortened, cuffs, and the hem to be taken up slightly," she paused and looked across at me, then continued, "I'd put in notes, not that Miss Evans knew I had, but the dress was second-hand, I'd done the work in the morning before Mrs Shaw and yourself came for the fitting of her own dress," she stopped and looked up from her diary, perhaps sensing that this information didn't really have much of an effect upon me, it wasn't helping me recall my past at all.

As I looked across at her I noticed that she once again started to study the book in front of her, she went on to speak again.

"Miss Evans partner's name was Stuart," she paused just long enough for me to ask her to repeat the name. "yes I have it written here "Mr Douglas Stuart," she stopped again a surprised look upon her face, then she went on, "I have his mobile telephone number here, I think I'll give him a call, just to see if everything is ok."

"Yes that would be a good idea," I started to say, then realising that I had my own mobile phone in my pocket I continued, "tell you what Mrs Walbridge, I'll use my phone," I said as I retrieved it from my inner jacket pocket. Mrs Walbridge told me the number, and I dialled it for her, holding the phone next to my right ear as it started ring out I passed it to her.

"Hello," she said softly, indicating that someone had answered her, she continued, "hello, it's Mrs Walbridge here," she paused and I got the impression that the person she was speaking to didn't recognise her because she continued, "Mrs Walbridge, the dressmaker from Chillingston, is that Mr Stuart?" I couldn't hear what the reply was, but judging by the expression on her face she must have had the wrong number, she continued, "it's not, I'm so sorry to have bothered you." She finished and passed me the phone, by the time I looked at it the display it had returned to the wallpaper image of Scotland.

"I take it that wasn't the person you were expecting," I said as I returned the phone to the confines of my pocket.

"No it wasn't Mr Jackson. Yet…" she stopped so as to gather her thoughts, after closing her diary she went on, "yet the voice sounded the same but without the accent."

"Accent," I said somewhat confused by her comment.

"Oh yes, he was Scottish, had a very mild accent, he didn't say very much, only a few words," she paused and again was gathering her own thoughts, "while I was in the other room with Miss Evans pinning up the dress he sat in here reading the paper, yes I remember now, I'd given him a whisky, the very one that we enjoy," she paused, something came back to her, she continued, "I said that it was also our favourite, as we'd shared a glass together on the previous occasions that you and Mrs Shaw had been here," her words were spoken very confidently, then I was in for something of a surprise, and her face was to show that surprise before she spoke, her eyes seemed to light up.

"Is there something else Mrs Walbridge?" I asked in an effort to get her to reveal her thoughts.

"Well the two of them said that they had heard that I was making Mrs Shaw's wedding dress," she paused just to study my startled expression, I say startled because I couldn't recall telling anyone that we or rather Louise had chosen Mrs Walbridge to make the dress, I also wondered who these individuals could be, Mrs Walbridge came to my aid with a comment that eased my curiosity, just a little.

"News always travels fast in a tiny village," her words spoken quite firmly, but at the same time softly.

And of course she was right; this wasn't so much a revelation, but a fact of village life, and sat here in Mrs Walbridge's tiny lounge brought back something Louise had said to me on our first outing some considerable time ago, that was the evening we had been for dinner, towards the end of the evening I had offered to take her home, she had told me then, 'the neighbours like to gossip'. I had indeed noticed for a short while after we had moved into the Manor, whenever we were out together that curtains would twitch, I also recalled that it was Louise's friend Jill, who had suggested using the services of Mrs Walbridge, and come to think of it the announcement in the local press had said that we intended to use as many of the local facilities as possible.

"You are of course right Mrs Walbridge," I replied after taking note of these facts, I glanced at my watch, it was now three forty five, recalling that I hadn't taken my medication this morning I felt a need come over me to return to my other house, but I did have one more question to ask the lady sat opposite.

"Mrs Walbridge, you must send me an invoice for the work you carried out on making the wedding dress," I paused and was taken aback by the surprised expression on her face, I quickly continued, "and of course the bridesmaids' dresses."

"But I couldn't!" was her forthright reply, suddenly I felt as if I'd offended the lady, it definitely wasn't my intention, so I quickly tried to reassure her.

"You must accept something for all the hard work you put in," I said.

"Mr Jackson," she began and at the same time sensing I needed to be moving on she stood, I did likewise, she then continued to speak, "I understand from the vicar that a considerable amount of work is required on the church tower, the roof is leaking," she paused again and I knew exactly what she meant.

"I understand completely," I said indicating that I had her drift, she wouldn't take any money herself and would rather it be put to good use.

We walked along the narrow passageway towards the front door; there she carefully opened the heavy oak door, pulling hard on the metal lock, as the door opened the afternoon sunshine burst into the small ante-chamber making my eyes smart in the process, I stood momentarily trying to focus from the doorway into the strong afternoon sunlight. I made my way over the threshold and onto the flagstones that led to the wooden gate at the end of this picture postcard cottage. Suddenly I felt as if I'd had a flash-back, almost to the last time I stood here, for now I imagined that Louise's BMW was parked outside, I closed my eyes tightly hoping that my mind's eye might reveal some distant image from the past.

"Are you alright Mr Jackson?" Mrs Walbridge asked drawing me out of my mesmerised state of mind.

"Yes Mrs Walbridge," I replied in something of a startled state, then as I recovered my senses I continued, "something just flashed through my mind reminding me of the last time I was here, but I can't remember what it was."

"Well you didn't have that car," was her prompt reply.

"No, we came to see you in Louise's BMW," I said, still looking at Mrs Walbridge.

"Yes you did, and that was why I said it was so distinctive," Mrs Walbridge said, at the same time she looked again at the Porsche, I, in turn looked myself, the strong sunlight reflecting off of the bright paintwork made my eyes once again squint. Mrs Walbridge continued, "it's more or less the same colour, but," she paused again and took my left hand, then went on "that is what we were talking about before the phone rang."

"Yes, you'd said then that it was very distinctive…" I started, but she cut me short.

"And I said I'd seen it in the village the day after your terrible accident," she was now what I would call a little excited, suddenly I felt as if I was going to be told something about my past that I didn't know, and Mrs Walbridge continued, "it looked for all the world the same as Mrs Shaw's, but it had a big dent in the front wing, all smashed in." she finished at the same time she was pointing towards the nearside of my Porsche.

"Show me exactly what you mean!" I quickly said leading her towards my car.

"This part," she said, at the same time running her hand over the slick line of the nearside front wing of the Porsche, and she continued to speak, "all of this was dented and smashed in as if the car had been in collision with a tree," she paused and looked me directly in the eyes, she went on, "well something as hard as a tree, I remember it clearly now," she looked down at the wing and something else came into her mind, another recollection from the past, "yes the orange indicator light was held in with black tape."

"Tell me Mrs Walbridge, did Louise's car have this damage on the evening we came to see you?" I asked, for now she had gripped my attention, I needed to know more, what she had just told me indicated what I had seen in the garage had some relevance to what had happened.

"Mr Jackson," Mrs Walbridge began, I looked at her hoping her expression would tell me some instant fact that could bring my memory back, but she was expressionless. I needed to prompt her.

"Go on Mrs Walbridge," I said, adding again, "go on!"

"I don't know Mr Jackson, I don't know!" her own words faded away as my expression changed to one of disbelief.

"What do you mean? You don't know!" I retaliated, frustration in my words and voice, I gave another prompt, "you must have seen the car!"

"Exactly what I said Mr Jackson, I don't know!" was her equally sharp response.

"Is it that you can't remember, Mrs Walbridge, or has something else come into your mind?" I questioned trying desperately to control my feelings, realising that I had come close to losing my temper. But Mrs Walbridge was about to enlighten me, tell me something that was so obvious, I was to feel foolish for not realising it myself.

"The reason I can't tell Mr Jackson is the Mrs Shaw's car was pointing in the opposite direction." I gripped my head as she revealed this plain and palpable fact to me.

"I'm so sorry Mrs Walbridge," I began with my reply, taking her hands I continued, "I should have realised," then something she had told me came back into my mind, "you said the indicator was held in with tape, didn't you?"

"Yes, black insulating tape," was the start of her reply, she continued, "it was as I've told you, the following day in the village I thought I saw Mrs Shaw's car," she paused then added, "but it couldn't have been, not if the car had been involved in the accident the night before." She finished but her words once again brought back thoughts to my mind, when I was stood in the garage at the Manor, on the floor was some dirt, along with pieces of orange reflector, on the workbench, a role of strong black tape, along with an assortment of tools. Mrs Walbridge had a question of her own, "did Mrs Shaw's car have any damage to the wing?"

I wasn't sure, and more importantly didn't want to answer the question until my mind was clear, it was best I thought to myself that I didn't reveal the limited knowledge I had circulating in my head, well not until I had been able to talk the details over with Stuart, he would be in the best position to help me put these facts into some sort of order, I thought to myself.

"Mrs Walbridge, I can't remember," I said, her look was one of understanding, and her words confirmed the look.

"Things don't seem any clearer, do they?" she said, as again she took my hand.

"No, not really," I said, thinking it was best that I return to my home in Bristol I continued, "thank you for your kind words Mrs Walbridge," I paused as I remembered what she had asked me to do in the way of recompense for the work she had undertaken, "I will see that a contribution is made towards the restoration of the church tower,"

"Thank you Mr Jackson," Mrs Walbridge said as I made my way round to the driver's side of the car, a press of the key fob, clunk and the doors unlocked, at the same time the indicators flashed, as I opened the door and got into the car Mrs Walbridge moved back behind the garden gate, closed it and stood watching me as I started the car. As I pulled away it came into my mind that I should have written down all that I had been able to recall, the events that had taken place, if put it down on paper then I would be able to discuss these issues with Stuart, I drove a short way down the road, finding a lay-by I pulled in, turned off the engine, a rummage in the glove box revealed the pile of post I had brought from the Manor, also a notepad, I had a pen in my inner jacket pocket, I hastily made some notes, firstly the alarm system at the Manor, the missing jewellery, the items I'd found in the garage at the Manor, the reported damage to Louise's car, there seemed to be so many things, and even more unanswered questions, I thought to myself as I studied the notes I'd made, but sat there looking at these collective notes still the jigsaw wouldn't come together. I continued my journey home concentrating on where I was going rather than where I had been in the past few days.

Chapter Nine

A question from the law

It was almost five forty five by the time I arrived back at my detached Bristol home, I pulled the Porsche onto the drive, I got out of the car and quickly made my way along the drive, I was in need of the toilet, after letting myself in and disarming the alarm system I visited the cloakroom.

When I came out I looked in the direction of the porch, on the floor was a small pile of post, I bent down and picked it up, nothing of any importance I thought to myself as once again I shuffled the items through my hands, I made my way into the study and placed the letters on the bureau. Glancing around the room I noticed that my medication was neatly placed on the table, two large bottles next to each other, I picked up one of the bottles, looking at the label I couldn't make out what the contents were, it did say that they were to be taken three times a day, with water and preferably after food, the other bottle said the contents should be taken at bedtime and first thing in the morning, again with plenty of water. I studied the labels, then words of Stavros came back to me, 'won't harm to miss a few doses' he was right, I felt better in myself, I still couldn't recall the past but I wasn't troubled by it either.

"Bollocks," I said to myself as I replaced the medication on the table, I mumbled a few more words, "I'm not taking the bloody things." Then I made my way out of the room, I headed in the direction of the kitchen thinking that if Stuart should ask if I'd taken the medication, then I would lie and say that I have been doing as he instructed me.

Now it was six o'clock, I was in need of some food, sure I'd had a fried breakfast with Stavros, but that was some considerable time ago, now my appetite seemed to be returning, maybe that was due to not having taken those pills I thought to myself, I opened the freezer, to my surprise I found a ready meal, a frozen curry at that, in fact on closer inspection I found that the freezer was well stocked, the reason for this was that my youngest son had been staying in the house while his own was being renovated.

Peter wasn't one to spend a lot of time in the kitchen preparing meals, neither was his partner Sophie, it could be said that it was anything for an easy life, 'more time to go partying' they would frequently remind me, I was even more surprised at the selection of ready meals, everything from curries to roast dinners.

Now it wasn't that Peter and Sophie had returned to the house they shared together, quite the opposite, they had moved in with my eldest son, William, and his partner Natasha, all of them realising that I needed some space and privacy so that I could get over my grief.

William, Natasha, along with Peter and Sophie had been at my bedside when I came out of my semi-conscious state, along with Trevor and Diane, all of them being as consumed with grief as I was, but I had to admit that I was feeling slightly better in myself today.

I looked at the rectangular packet I had in my hand, the coldness was now beginning to creep into my fingers, the instructions said to cook from frozen, something I needed to attend to quickly or the ready meal would be a unready meal, I moved across the kitchen and turned on the oven, set the control to 180 degrees, then removed all the packaging, placed the dinner on a baking sheet and put it in the oven, closed the door and retired to the lounge, there I switched on the television, I felt that I needed a drink before my dinner, telling myself that I would enjoy the food all the more if I had a nice glass of wine. In the study I found what I was looking for, a well- aged bottle of Cabernet Sauvignon, I removed the cork and poured a large glass, toasting myself as I brought the glass up to take a sip, I'd got through the day. It was rich and fruity, but also had a chalkiness to the after taste, not unpleasant, on the contrary, a feeling of enjoyment came over me, I returned to the lounge and was about to sit down and watch what remained of the news when the door bell rang, not once, no it was being repeatedly rung.

"OK, OK!" I called as I made my way along the hall and towards the inner door, this was still ajar, but the outer porch doors were firmly closed. I opened the inner door, looking towards the sliding doors I could make out a figure, that of a man, but the outline didn't trigger any thoughts of who it might be, I certainly wasn't expecting any visitors. Looking again I could see that this individual was about six feet tall, of slight build, and I could make out that his jacket was blowing in the early evening breeze. The bell rang again.

"Alright," I somewhat angrily responded, I still had the glass of wine in my right hand, with my left I turned the key and pulled the door back on its runners, before I had chance to even get a closer look at this person on the other side of the threshold I was questioned.

"Mr Andrew David Jackson?" the person asked, he had an authority in his voice and the way he asked me my name indicated that he had done this sort of thing before, suddenly I recognised the voice, and I definitely hadn't been expecting a visit from the detective.

"Yes it is," I began to reply, still wondering what need the inspector had to come visiting at this time of day, so I posed that question to him at the same time saving him from introducing himself, "and what brings Detective Inspector Braithwaite to my house at this time of day," thinking slightly faster than normal I made the wrong conclusion, and I blurted it out, "inspector, you've apprehended the individuals responsible for the crash." His response wasn't what I was expecting; it was to the point and very matter of fact.

"No we haven't, May I come in?" he asked as he proceeded to step over the threshold of my house.

"Of course," I said, still in something of a surprised state, as he continued into the hall I asked a question, "well if you haven't caught the people responsible what need do you have to see me?" His reply was even more shocking.

"Mr Jackson I must caution you…" he began.

"What the bloody hell are you talking about, caution me!" was my immediate reaction to his words of warning, cutting the inspector off less than half way though his well-rehearsed idiom.

"Mr Jackson, we are conducting a murder enquiry," he started again, "and I need to inform you that anything you say may be given in evidence…" he stopped as my left hand went up in the air.

"Inspector, are you saying that I am a suspect?" I asked.

"What I am trying to tell you Mr Jackson is that we are still conducting a murder investigation, I'm not accusing you of anything, I'm just informing you of your rights." The inspector told me.

"Will you be arresting me?" I asked still feeling angry, as if the finger of guilt was being pointed at me.

"That won't be necessary, but I do need to inform you of your rights and ask you some very important questions," the inspector replied, adding, "please try to calm yourself."

"You'd better come into the lounge," I said, at the same time I offered a guiding hand, as we went into the room the news summary on the television was coming to an end, I just picked up on part of the item, it was a little more of an elaborated version of what I'd heard in the car at two o'clock, the news from South Africa, I was still looking at the television when he inspector spoke to me again.

"Could you turn the television off please Mr Jackson?" he seemed a little more polite now he was in my house. I did as he requested missing the remaining information regarding South Africa.

"Please sit inspector," I said as I offered him a seat.

"Thank you Mr Jackson, but before I do will you please confirm who you are?" He asked, at the same time he looked me directly in the eyes, his own were light blue, his hair dark brown and swept back over his head, I would say he was in his late thirties, if that, maybe thirty five, but not much older, I now felt as if I'd put up enough of a fight, he had a job to do, I may not be able to recall all of the past, but I was certain that I hadn't done anything wrong, so it was best that I answer his questions, to the best of my ability.

"I am indeed Andrew David Jackson; my address apart from this house in the suburbs of Bristol is also Chillingston Manor, in the county of Wiltshire." I said as I began to lower myself into a winged chair.

"Thank you Mr Jackson, I see you are preparing to have your dinner Mr Jackson," the inspector said, after glancing at the wine glass I still had in my right hand, the aroma of the ready meal was also wafting into the lounge. There are no flies on you I thought to myself; at the same time I nodded indicating that he was correct, at least he was a little more perceptive than some of the police officers I had encountered over the years.

"How can I help you inspector?" I asked as I reclined slightly in my seat, I took a pull from my glass of wine just as the inspector replied.

"Well Mr Jackson," he paused and looked at me before continuing, having gained my attention he went on, and "can you tell me the last time you went to South Africa?"

"What?" I asked, my words said in total disbelief, my facial expression the must have been the same.

"Perhaps I didn't make myself clear, I need to know when you went to South Africa last," he asked the same question again only now in a different format.

"Inspector," I began, at the same time I was thinking that maybe I hadn't misjudged the local constabulary at all, they still seemed to be fumbling around in the dark, so I continued, "inspector, I have never been to South Africa, and to the best of my knowledge haven't planned to go there."

The inspector looked long and hard at me before continuing, and it wasn't with a comment I was expecting.

"Mr Jackson, perhaps you need to go and have a look at your dinner," he said at the same time looking in the direction of the kitchen.

"Yes of course," I replied as I jumped up from my seat, I put my now nearly empty wine glass on a side unit and made my way into the kitchen, a look in the oven revealed that the ready meal was more than ready, it had gone past that juncture in its development and was now nearing the cremation stage of its life. "Bugger" I shouted out loud, in doing so attracting the attention of the inspector.

"Is everything alright Mr Jackson?" he called from what I assumed was still his seated position in the lounge.

"Yes fine," I half heartedly replied and I continued, "it's just my ready meal has gone past the stage of being ready for me, it's now ready for the bin." I finished and started to make my way back towards the lounge. Now thinking that I may not only have come across as grumpy, but I was also displaying a rudeness that was quite unacceptable.

"Inspector, would you like a drink, maybe tea or something stronger?" I asked as I entered the room, the reply was what I should have expected.

"No thank you sir," he said as I resumed my seated position, this was the first time he had called me sir, it was just a change of tack, he went on, I'm sure he was now trying to catch me out, "now about this visit to South Africa," just a pause not giving me time to reply or long enough to think of a reply without getting angry, "when was it you said you went?"

"I didn't say I'd been," I started to say, only for the inspector to interrupt me again, this time with what could be referred to as a leading question.

"Oh it must have been a planned trip," he said, a half smile to his lips.

"As I have told you, I have never been to, or for that matter planned to go to South Africa," I paused myself, feeling a little frustrated I tried to control my emotions, I went on, "inspector, can you please inform me what a visit to South Africa that hasn't taken place has to do with the death of my fiancée and her children?"

"Mr Jackson, I'm trying my best to understand what has gone on in the past, this is just one part of the jigsaw that I need to fit into place," the inspector started to say, I stopped him from continuing.

"As I see it inspector," I said, at the same time sitting upright in my seat, I went on, "South Africa has no bearing on the death of Louise Shaw whatsoever, all you have succeeded in doing is upsetting me."

"Well that may well be the case," the inspector started to say, and now having gained my attention he went on, "but I do have some rather interesting news from the southern hemisphere." He stopped, for now he could see he had my undivided attention.

"And what news could that be?" I enquired unsure of what was to come next.

"Well it involves one…" he paused again, just to keep me on tenterhooks, or just to see if my expression changed at all, he went on, "it involves Jan Van-Elderman…"

"But he's dead," I blurted out, this time without thinking of the consequences.

"Yes we know he is," the inspector replied, not asking where I had got my information from he went on, "he's been dead a little while now, but what came to the attention of my colleagues in South Africa was a…" the officer stopped, rubbed his face, then asked a different question, "may I have a drink of water Mr Jackson? Please."

"Yes of course," I said, now completely thrown by his manner, quickly I got up and made my way into the kitchen, I found a tumbler and filled it with chilled water from the fridge, upon returning to the lounge I asked the inspector to continue.

"As I was saying, the authorities in Cape Town found a diary in Jan's apartment." He stopped and I sensed he was waiting for me to ask him to continue.

"And," I casually replied, not wishing to disappoint the officer.

"Well Mr Jackson, your name was mentioned several times in this diary," was the inspector's straightforward reply.

"And you're assuming that…" I started to say only to be cut short by the officer.

"I'm not assuming anything Mr Jackson; I'm trying to tie up some loose ends, and ascertain the facts" the inspector reminded me.

"Well, you keep on about these, as you put it, loose ends, but to be honest I don't see any connection between Jan and myself, other than some notes that have been written in his diary," I replied feeling just a little frustrated at the inspector's inference.

"Perhaps we need to look at the question from another angle," the officer said.

"What do you mean?" I asked a little more puzzled by the statement.

"These dates marked in Mr Elderman's diary coincide with dates when he was in this country," the inspector informed me.

"Really," I replied, suddenly two thoughts collided in my brain; firstly, Alex hadn't said a word about Jan having being in England, he'd just informed Louise and I that the Dutch man was dead, secondly I was now in danger of allowing information I was privy to, to become common knowledge, I'd sat in the same room as Jan, in fact on the opposite side of the table to the big man, only a few other people were aware of that, I instantly knew I needed to think fast and say even less. I was also aware that I was renowned for giving facts away with my facial expressions, a trait I hoped the inspector hadn't picked up yet. But he did have a rather unsettling question for me, one that I would have to answer very carefully.

"May I ask how you knew of Mr Van-Elderman's death? Mr Jackson," the inspector enquired at the same time I noticed his eyes probing, looking hard and deep into my inner soul. Let's not beat about the bush I thought to myself, I'll give him part of the answer he requires, worry about the consequences later.

"Well inspector you can indeed ask where I got my information from, shall we say one of my very influential friends!" I said with just a hint of a smile on my lips and a touch of sarcasm in my voice, the reason being that the reply wasn't what the inspector was expecting, I managed to defuse the situation just enough for me think a little longer.

"And when did you hear of his death?" the inspector asked, again a change of style, maybe trying to mislead me. When was it that Alex had told Louise and me of the demise of Jan? It was November, after the failed court case.

"It must have been November," I quickly said, not expecting much of a response, but respond the inspector did.

"Then have you any idea Mr Jackson, what Mr Van-Elderman, was doing in this country in April?" the inspector asked, and now I couldn't remove the startled expression from my face.

"As I've told you, I was informed that he was dead in November, there must be some confusion, Jan Van-Elderman is dead," I replied, but something way in the back of my mind was causing me some concern, I had no reason to doubt Alex, but maybe his information was incorrect, perhaps it was someone else who had died in that car explosion.

"In his diary Mr Jackson, Jan, had a date and time of an appointment with you, clearly marked for April." He finished and could see my confused state, I was thinking that I needed to contact Alex, but then I recalled that I was going to see him tomorrow, then I would be able to confirm some of this information that the inspector had relayed to me. But then the inspector had another change of tack, he really was trying to unnerve me, but all he seemed to do was confuse me all the more, "let's leave your business association with Mr Van-Elderman for the moment…" with those word I cut him short.

"For Christ's sake inspector, I didn't have any financial dealings with Jan Van-Elderman, business or otherwise," I protested to the officer, only for him to remain calm, and fire another question at me.

"I said we would leave that side of things for the moment and concentrate on the other issue, mainly the death of Mrs Louise Shaw and her two children Sarah and James,"

"Look inspector, haven't you and your colleagues spoken to each other?" I asked feeling very frustrated at having to go over the same ground again, or was the inspector trying to catch me out, hoping that I might make a slip, something he could use as evidence against me.

"Mr Jackson, it's not a question of whether I've spoken to my subordinates or not," he paused and took another drink from his glass; I noticed that the condensation on the side of the glass had all but disappeared, as had the water. He continued, "I need to get the facts straight in my mind, you must admit it does seem a little strange that you were found wandering in Chillingston woods, shortly after your fiancée's car was set ablaze on the main road, now Mr Jackson if you heard such a story on the news even you would have some suspicion, wouldn't you?" I suppose he was right, only now it was me that was affected, and from what the inspector had just said it seemed as if I was under suspicion.

"Well from the way you have put it to me then yes I would have my doubts, but this has happened to me!" I replied, and I continued with a question, "then am I under suspicion inspector?" he didn't answer the question directly, just continued to give me more details as to what had happened.

"And the fact that you can't remember what has happened doesn't help matters," he said at the same time he finished his glass of water and proceeded to pass me the empty glass.

"I'm telling you the truth inspector," I paused for now I remembered that some information had come back to me, and the fact that I was seeing a counsellor must add some weight to the issue of me not being able to remember, but the inspector didn't pick up on that, instead he had a question about what I had been doing today.

"Now you told me that you were going to the Manor this morning, did you find anything I need to know about?" he asked.

"Nothing more than I told you when you phoned me," I replied, thinking that might be an end to the matter, I wasn't expecting the officer to come back with anything other than a confirmation of that telephone call.

"Mr Jackson, it seems strange to me that you can recall the events of this morning, but nothing from a few days ago," he said looking again into my eyes.

"I thought you'd read my notes," I began, now feeling as if the inspector was wasting not only the taxpayers' money but also my time, I continued, "you would have seen that I am in fact suffering from traumatic amnesia, I have been told that in time I may regain some, maybe all of my memory, but it can't be guaranteed, it could be that I may never know what happened on that dreadful night."

"Yes I do recall reading that in the report," he began to say, then after a slight pause he continued, "if I remember rightly it said that you had been prescribed some medication."

"I have inspector, I have," I said, somewhat relieved, thinking that now maybe the inspector did believe me, with that I got up and made my way into the lounge, returning after a few seconds with the medication in my hand. As I entered the room the inspector had a question for me.

"Can I have a look please Mr Jackson?" he asked, at the same time his right hand outstretched.

"Of course," I said as I passed him the two bottles, he took them from me and I watched as he studied the labels, they weren't printed as in the normal manner if I had been to the local chemist, no these were hand written, something I assumed Stuart had taken care of, after all I was paying a considerable sum for his consultation services, this man didn't come cheap. The inspector's silence puzzled me a little and forced me to ask a question of him. "Have you studied medicine inspector?"

"No, Mr Jackson," the inspector replied, but at the same time he put his right hand into his jacket, then removed a notepad, and went on to explain his actions to me, "well Mr Jackson, were are given a basic training in drugs, you know so we can recognise what drug someone may have taken in the case of an overdose," he paused giving me a chance to ask another question.

"What about the notepad inspector?" I asked looking at him.

He looked up at me after writing something down in the notepad, and then he spoke.

"Well these I recognise," he said with one of the bottles in his hand, and he continued to enlighten me, "they're a mild anti-depressant, you may also find that they help you to sleep," he paused and picked up the other bottle, then continued, "but I've no idea what these are," he said giving the bottle a shake at the same time, then he added, "that's why I've made a note of the name, I'll look them up when I return to the station."

He did surprise me, a policeman that had a logical understanding of drugs, well that was more than I possessed. I thought he'd finished as he passed the two containers back to me, and had just one more thing to say on the matter of the drugs.

"I shouldn't take any of these tablets with alcoholic drink." He really didn't need to say that to me, for I had already made up my mind that I wasn't going to take any of the medication this evening, I placed the bottles next to the wine glass on the unit, the inspector stood and I felt as if the interview had come to a natural close, but he had one more question that was to send my mind racing, throwing my mental state into complete disarray.

"Well I think that will do for this evening Mr Jackson," the inspector said after returning his notepad to his inner jacket pocket and standing, we made our way towards the hall, it was as we were standing at the front door the inspector dropped his bombshell.

"Tell me Mr Jackson?" the inspector began, this time he was to catch me completely off guard, after a moment's pause he continued, "when did you set up the transportation firm in South Africa?"

"What?" was the only word I could reply with, for my mouth had fallen open with his question, and the inspector continued with something of a satirical response.

"Now I suppose you can't remember that, either," he said, a smug smile had formed on his face, I didn't know what he was talking about, and he wasn't going to inform me either.

"Inspector I don't have any financial interests in South Africa," was all I could muster, for I felt as if I was reeling from a body blow.

"Well Mr Jackson," he paused, "it may be best if you have your solicitor present at our next meeting." I thought he'd finished but he just looked at my dumbfounded expression, then added, "there will be a next time Mr Jackson, I can assure you, and I think it will be at the station, so please don't make any plans to go away." He slid the outer door back himself and stepped over the threshold leaving me in a completely dazed state, as he made progress along my drive he called back, "see you soon Mr Jackson." His features had the appearance of someone who had just won a competition, very smug and self-satisfied; he almost had a skip in his step as he walked along my driveway.

What the bloody hell has been going on I thought to myself, as I stood and watched this arrogant self-centred person get into his police issued motor vehicle, he even had the bloody cheek to wave to me as he pulled away.

I stood alone on the doorstep pondering what I was to do next, it was far too late in the day to try and contact the management firm that operates the business for me, I glanced at my watch, it was gone eight o'clock, Dennis the secretary would also be at home, I desperately needed some help so as to get things in order.

I turned and made my way in the direction of the kitchen, that was after closing and locking the sliding outer door, as I passed the lounge I picked up the wine glass I had been using; momentarily I stood and looked at the medication still on the side unit, should I take it? I mentally asked myself, the reply I gave to my inner thoughts was negative. I arrived in the kitchen and looked at the burnt remains that had been a ready meal, I was still in need of some food, I had another rummage in the freezer and found a similar frozen curry, this time I'll take more care, I said to myself as I placed it in the still hot oven.

Looking at the empty packet in my hand I thought that it wouldn't harm to contact Dennis Bennett, the secretary, it was now eight thirty, I didn't need to discuss the issues with him now, and I could just say that I needed to talk to him in the morning when he would be in the office.

I'd made my way into the study, a refilled glass of wine in my hand when the telephone began to ring, as I lifted the receiver I looked at the display, no one that I recognised, I answered in my usual guarded manner.

"Hello," was all I needed to say, I just had to wait for a reply, this I had done many times over the years.

"Andrew," a pause, it was a woman's voice, not one that I instantly recognised, I didn't have to wait long for the caller to continue, "Andrew, it's Melissa," she paused again, I now knew who it was on the other end of the telephone line, she went on as I drew breath, "Melissa Thorne, I've just heard of your terrible loss." She stopped and was waiting for something of reply.

"Thank you," I said, thinking that she would let me continue, but she didn't.

"How are you?" she asked, but again I didn't have long enough to respond to her question, she went on, "if there is anything I can do to help, then you must give me a call," her tone and offer sounded genuine, I quickly thought if there was anything that I did need, the answer for the moment was nothing, but it would be polite to thank her, even though my mind was still racing over this business I had in South Africa that I knew nothing about.

"Well it's one day at a time for the moment Melissa," I began to say, having now relaxed myself a little I continued, "thank you for the offer of help, but," I paused for now I was feeling some pain, everyone apart from the officialdom of the police force had been so kind, now those acts of kindness were becoming overwhelming, I went on in the best way I could not wishing to offend the young woman, but also not wishing to put upon her, "if there is anything I want, then I'll give you a call." As I said the words a thought crossed my mind, how did this woman get my telephone number, I hadn't seen her for years, other than the brief encounter in April, and that was a short encounter at the main railway station, in the centre of Bristol, we'd only just had enough time to exchange names, nothing more, as if I'd asked the question Melissa had an answer in her next statement.

"I expect you're wondering where I got your number from," she said, and before I had a chance to say anything she was to enlighten me, "I kept a note of it in one of my old handbags," pausing, making me think that it wasn't only Louise who did that sort of thing she continued, "yes from the days when we worked in the office together."

"Oh yes," I replied. Still surprised that she had taken the time to call me, again politeness kicked in, "and are you alright?" I asked.

"Yes fine," she began to say, she stopped and I was sure I could hear a man's voice in the background, almost as if he'd said 'come on', but I couldn't be positive, what I did notice was a change in Melissa's manner.

"Well alright then Andy," her tone had also changed, it now had something of casualness to it, and the genuineness seemed to have disappeared from her words, she continued in what seemed like a hurry to bring the call to an end, "if there's anything you want then give me a call."

"I'd better make a note of your number," I started to say, she cut in.

"Yes you had," she then proceeded to repeat her mobile number to me; I found a pen and a small notepad by the side of the phone, I noticed as I wrote it down that it wasn't the same number that was on the display of my phone.

"It's not the same number you are calling from now," I said after checking both the display and what I'd written down.

"No," was her instant response, then after a moment's pause she continued, "I'm calling from a girlfriend's."

"Fine," was all I could say, I felt in myself that the conversation had come to an end, and it had for the next words Melissa said were her own form of goodbye.

"See you then Andy," and she was gone.

Strange I thought to myself, the call had been completely unexpected, and had started with her sounding sympathetic and understanding, only for her to bring it to a sudden and abrupt end, her words were still circulating in my head when I found myself looking at the notepad I had in my hand, the number I had written down seemed very familiar, but where had I seen it before, if I had at all, these mobile telephone numbers all look the same I said to myself as I replaced the notepad next to the phone, then it occurred to me that I had come into the study with the intention of calling Dennis, his number was programmed into the phone, all I needed to do was scroll through the menu, this I did and in no time I had the phone next to my right ear, but sadly it wasn't Dennis who answered, it was his answering machine. 'Thanks for calling Dennis Bennett, I'm sorry I can't take your call at the moment I'm either doing something I shouldn't be, or doing something I been putting off for long time, or being done by someone and enjoying it, either way please leave a message and I'll get back to you as soon as I can', there seemed to be a pause and he added, 'oh you'd better leave a contact number, thanks'. Then there was the customary tone. His message made me smile, it wasn't what I'd expected to hear Dennis say, he'd always behaved in a very professional manner, and it was reassuring to discover that he had a light-hearted side to him.

"Dennis," I started to say, I glanced at my watch, it was now eight thirty, so, conscious of the time I continued, "Dennis, it's Andrew here, I know it's late but I could do with having a chat with you, in connection with the business," I paused I didn't want to alarm him, so I added, "if you get this message after ten this evening, then leave replying until the morning," I thought I'd completed what I wanted to say but, added, "thank you."

I took a pull from my wine glass, still I wondered to myself what on earth had been going on, and so many things seem to have taken place that I am completely unaware of.

I took the opportunity to phone Trevor, as I had promised him I would, and after giving him a quick résumé of what I'd been doing during the day, I returned to the kitchen Looking in the oven, I could see that the curry was now ready, very carefully I removed it, placed it on a tray, took a knife and fork from the drawer, then made my way into the lounge, turned the television on again, relaxed as best I could as I ate my supper.

Chapter Ten

Morning and a fresh start

I'd stayed awake until ten thirty, watched the remaining program on the television about the methods of interrogation. As used by the Special Services, not only is the evocative process used, often written evidence is offered as an additional suggestive method, the program went on to explain that the success rate was high in comparison with some of the other methods used. My intention was to stay down long enough to watch the news, but sadly I fell asleep at the start and didn't wake up until the end, the program that followed concerned the growing dependency on drugs, and the frustration the police encounter when trying to apprehend the people behind the operations, no sooner is one criminal put behind bars, and another mastermind appears to take over from where the last one left off, the program was somewhat depressing, so I made myself a cup of coffee, then on to bed.

I slept well, not waking during the night, and when I did wake I felt much better in myself, the reason, I put it down to not having taken my medication, I decided that I would not tell Stuart I hadn't been taking it. By the time I came downstairs after having a shower and shave it was seven thirty, I made some tea, and fixed breakfast for myself, and I must say I was feeling a little more positive in myself. Seven fifty five and the phone rang, looking at the display I could see it was Dennis, calling from the office in Bristol.

"Good morning Dennis," I said as I answered the phone, feeling a lot better in myself, this response surprised Dennis somewhat.

"Andrew, good morning," he paused, maybe trying to judge my reaction, or just still in a state of shock, after a few moments he continued, "you sound more like your old self." He paused again just long enough for me to answer him.

"I do feel better Dennis," I paused, not wishing to sound to light-hearted, I'd managed to put some things in order, and now I needed to find out what had been going on in the past few weeks, let alone days, so it was best I continue and with a question, "Dennis, what do you know about a business in South Africa."

"Nothing, Andrew," was his immediate response, and he came back with a question himself, "why do you ask Andrew?" I didn't want to go into lengthy details, those would keep for later, and I just needed to ascertain some facts for the moment.

"Well apparently I've been informed that we have a transportation company there." I finished and awaited Dennis's reply, there was no hesitation.

"Well if you have then it's something you," he did pause and I knew in myself what he was going to say, and he continued, "it's something you or Mrs Shaw set up." This couldn't be the case; there was no way Louise would have set up a business in another part of the world without me or Dennis knowing. Dennis had full authority to take care of almost any of the business needs that might arise, other than him the only other people who had such power was the management company that Louise and I had set up, this we did to save us dealing with the day-to-day running of the hotels, it would be best if I ring them next, I was just thinking when Dennis asked me a question. "Would you like me to phone the management consultants Andrew?" I paused before answering him, but I did.

"I think it might be best if I call them," I said, but having said that I thought I needed to enquire if everything was alright with Dennis, so I went on, "how's things with you Dennis?"

"I'm OK Andrew," he paused and I wasn't sure of what he was going to say next, and he did surprise me, "it's been hard coming to terms with your terrible news Andrew."

His words touched a nerve; Dennis had always been very business-like, professional and very good at keeping his work life separate from his private life, determined to do his job well, and always respectful to both Louise and I, his next question was to be back to that very business-like manner.

"Andrew," Dennis started to say, after a slight pause I knew a question was on its way, and he continued, "do you remember the system going down back in March or April?" I replied that I could remember something about the event, "well I paid the bill from the IT consultants at the time," Dennis reminded me, and then he went on, "Andrew I know it must seem strange but the computers had a hiccup last week, they were down for about an hour."

"They're alright now, are they Dennis?" I asked almost interrupting him.

"Yes everything is fine, it happened the day after your accident." Dennis replied.

"I think it must have been a coincidence Dennis," I said, still trying to recollect fully the first incident.

"You're probably right Andrew, well, it hasn't happened since then," Dennis said, bringing me back into the real world, his comment brought a question from myself, for now I did recall the problem, but couldn't remember what the outcome was.

"Yes I remember the first time it went down," I said, for now I could clearly remember that our entire system went down, this didn't effect the management team as they worked on a different system, but it had created all sorts of problems for Louise, Dennis and myself, I went on, "did they get to the bottom of the problem?" I asked.

"Yes, the engineer who came out said we'd picked up a virus on the main server, and said it could have come in on an e-mail attachment," he paused and I could hear him tapping away on a keyboard, "yes he installed some new software to stop them coming in again." He finished

All this technical talk was a little too much for me, I knew how to turn the computer on and off, that was just about my limit, but I needed to show my gratitude to Dennis.

"Well done Dennis, let's hope that's an end to it," I stopped and heard Dennis say thank you, I continued, "I'll let you get on Dennis, I'll call the management team," I paused and needed to let Dennis know that I would get back to him if I needed to, "I'll try and give you a call later this afternoon."

"That's fine Andrew," he paused and again was going to surprise me, "take care Andrew." He was gone from the line.

My next call was to my management consultants, I was greeted with that usual professionalism I had come to expect, not that I had reason to phone very often, normally Dennis would take care of everything, but this South African business was playing on my mind and I'd made a decision to get to the bottom of what I thought was a simple mistake.

"Jackson Shaw Enterprises, good morning," the young lady paused, then continued to add her name, "Emma Davis speaking, can I help you?" her tone had a formal but at the same time business-like tone to it, I'd dealt with this young lady before, in fact both Louise and I had interviewed her for the post of hotel development administrator, a position she was more than suited to, but she had also taken on other roles within the organisation and hadn't failed in any of the tasks she had undertaken.

"Good morning Emma, it's Andrew Jackson here." I paused after speaking my name and caught Emma draw breath, I allowed her to speak again.

"Mr Jackson, we're all so sorry to hear of your sad news," she said, her tone and manner reminded me why we had been so keen to take her on.

"Thank you Emma," I replied and went on, "please pass on my thanks to the rest of the team in the office, and thank them also for their kind thoughts, and the card."

"I will Mr Jackson, but how can I help you this morning?" she enquired returning to her business approach.

"Well Emma, first I'd like you to call me Andrew, after all I call you by your first name," I paused just long enough for her say that she agreed she would, so I continued, "now this may seem like a strange request, but can you tell me who may have dealt with a business transaction in South Africa." I finished and it wasn't long before Emma started to reply.

"Andrew, I had something to do with the initial set up," she paused, and then had a question of her own; "is there something wrong Andrew?" her request caught me a little by surprise.

"Oh, I'm just trying to piece one or two things together," I replied not wishing to say at this stage that I knew absolutely nothing about the business venture in South Africa. Emma's response was to surprise me even more.

"Well funny as it may seem, this is the first time you've spoken to any of us in the office about the firm Mrs Shaw..." her words died away as she realised what she had just said.

"It's alright Emma, you don't have to be on your guard all of the time," I said, as reassuringly as I could, and I added, "there are a lot of things that I can't remember; I'm still trying to put the past into some sort of order." I stopped and recalled what she had just said about the setting up of the business, "you say Emma that this is the first time I've spoken to you about the new company, did Louise, I mean Mrs Shaw do most of the work behind the setting up?"

"Yes Andrew," was Emma's immediate response, and without any prompting she continued, "Mrs Shaw conducted everything via e-mail on behalf of both of you." She finished and I was left in even more of a puzzled state of mind.

"And did the accountants know of this transaction Emma?" I asked, well more like stumbled for words.

"Yes, it was a brand new business venture, Mrs Shaw had given them full authority to release the money, and it was done in very little time at all." She replied, prompting another question from me.

"Did Dennis know what was going on?" I asked.

"Just a few moments Andrew and I'll check," Emma replied, at the same time I could hear her fingers dancing over her keypad, then she came back to me, "yes he is fully aware of the new business venture," she said, but when I'd asked him he'd said that he knew nothing about the new business in South Africa, now either he was lying, or something far more sinister was going on, in the time we employed Dennis we'd never had any reason to doubt his credentials, and I saw no reason to doubt them now.

"Emma," I began, and continued "what is the name of the company in South Africa?"

"It's called," she paused, then came back with something of a reassuring comment, "I can say it's doing very well, Andrew its called Amender Transport," she stopped again and came back with another question, "are you sure you can't remember?"

"Emma, I can't remember a thing about it," I started to say, and went on, "I don't know a thing about transport in this country, let alone in South Africa, I can't imagine where I got the idea from."

"That's easy Andrew, Mrs Shaw said in her opening e-mail that a friend had suggested the idea to both of you, a bit of diversification, we were quite puzzled in the beginning, but after all Mrs Shaw and you are the bosses, and I think this was to be something of a surprise, Mrs Shaw did respond to every e-mail we sent her." That she was right about, a little more than a surprise, but what sort of owner was I if I couldn't remember being informed of the business and that brought another question from me.

"What was our initial outlay?" I asked, still in a confused state.

"I think you set aside twenty five million but," Emma paused, then continued, "you'd have to check with the accountants to be sure." I couldn't believe what I had just heard; I'd spent twenty five million pounds in setting up another company and never put a signature on a single piece of paper. I went on, "why is it called Amender Transport?"

"The name Mrs Shaw said was suggested to you by your friend!" She replied, by now she was beginning to sound as surprised as I was.

"Just when did Louise set up this business?" I asked, and still wondered who this friend could be, but for now I was gone past the stage of alarming Emma, and she could tell.

"Let me see Andrew," she began with her reply, "well the first e-mail we had was at the beginning of March, things progressed quite quickly, it was all done and dusted and set up by the end of April."

"Thank you Emma," I said, still in a state of puzzlement, Louise had never mentioned a thing to me about setting up a new company, let alone one in South Africa, but judging by the conversation I'd just had everything seemed to be factual and very much in order. Then another thought occurred to me, April, why was that month playing on my mind, did it have any significance? My thoughts were interrupted by the door bell ringing.

"Emma, I'll call the accountants later today," I said as I prepared to go to the door," thank you for all your help," I paused again, just one more thing I needed to add, "and Emma your kind thoughts are very much appreciated."

"That's OK Andrew, I hope everything goes well," she replied and she was gone from the line.

I made my way along the hall towards the front door, again the bell rang, but as I opened the inner door I could make out the figure of Stuart stood the other side of the sliding glass doors, in his left hand I could make out his briefcase.

"Good morning Andrew," was the greeting I received as I pulled the door back along its runners, Stuart was smiling quite profusely.

"Good morning Stuart," I replied, at the same time I glanced at my watch, it was now ten past eight, just a little late, I thought to myself, then I considered what I'd planned to do, I could give the accountants a quick call before we left to meet Alex, I thought, then Stuart spoke again as he stepped over the threshold.

"Andrew you seem a little more relaxed this morning," he paused and turned so as to close the outer door, then he continued, "and I notice that you have your Porsche on the drive."

"Yes, a friend took me to the Manor yesterday," I started to reply, as I did so I looked at Stuart, in his left hand he had his black leather briefcase, his right hand was still resting on the door handle, but now his expression had changed, almost to one of bewilderment, but his reply wasn't what I was expecting.

"You've been taking your medication, haven't you Andrew?" he quite abruptly asked.

"Yes of course," I replied as I turned and headed in the direction of the study, not wishing to look him in the eyes as I spoke, knowing that I may give the game away, I continued to lie as we neared the door in to the study, "I took them this morning, just before you arrived."

"That's good," was all I let Stuart say.

"Would you like some coffee?" I asked almost catching Stuart by surprise.

"Yes that would be fine," Stuart replied, I turned and headed in towards the kitchen, I filled the kettle and noticed that Stuart was stood in the doorway. The phone call I'd just had with Emma from the management team was still fresh in my mind, also the need I felt to ring the accountants, better I do it now I thought to myself.

"Stuart, I need to make a quick phone call, do you mind?" I asked.

"Not at all Andrew," Stuart began to reply, and then he surprised me with a comment, "you definitely seem much more positive this morning."

"I do," was all I needed to say.

"I'll go into the lounge and perhaps we can have an hour session before we go to meet your friend," he paused, and I wasn't sure if he could remember, or if he was testing me, "Stavros isn't it?"

"No it's Alex we're going to meet, at his golf club." I said, and I went on, "I'll make this coffee and bring it into you."

"Yes of course, you did say the other day it was Alex we're going to meet," he paused and chuckled, "it should be me having the therapy," I heard him say as he made his way along the hall towards the lounge.

By now the kettle had boiled, I made the instant coffee, and noticed that I was low on milk, I did have some dried, but its not the same as fresh, I'll need to get some when I'm out today, I said to myself, I made my way into the lounge and placed Stuart's on the small table in front of him, I noticed that he was making some notes, I assumed that they were case notes regarding myself, or perhaps one of his other patients.

"I won't be long," I said as I came out of the lounge, I didn't think to close the door behind me, once in the study I picked up the phone and called the accountants.

The conversation was in much the same vein as the one I'd had with Emma Davis, the young man I spoke to confirmed that I was now the owner of a firm in South Africa, one that specialised in container transportation, they also confirmed that the business had cost me twenty five million pounds. When I enquired as to why I hadn't been informed at the time of purchase I was told that Louise had taken care of everything, even down to the signing of the contracts, I was reminded that I had given her full authority to make any necessary business decisions on our behalf.

What did puzzle me was not only the fact that I couldn't remember any of these goings-on, but I also couldn't remember seeing anything written in her diary when I'd been at the Manor. Then the partner informed me that all of the correspondence had been sent to a different address, when I enquired as to what the address was he told me that he didn't know, the reason being was that all of the related paperwork had been packed away, ready to go into storage, and they were also experiencing problems with their computer system, but he did reassure me that he would ask for the necessary documents to be retrieved from the storage department, as soon as he had them in his possession he would contact me. This matter would need further investigation; not only by me but also the police no doubt, at the moment I was in no frame of mind to consider such actions, it could wait a day or two, and this I told myself as I headed in the direction of the lounge and the waiting Stuart.

"Problems, Andrew?" Stuart questioned me as I entered the lounge with my own mug of coffee in my hand.

"Not really, just this dilemma I seem to have recalling things from the past," I replied not instantly realising that he must have been listening to my conversation.

"It was something to do with one of your companies, was it Andrew?" he once again asked, he seemed to be probing, this was the first time he'd mentioned anything to do with my business interests, and I didn't feel a need to confide in him about them, I was more concerned with finding out what had gone on in the past few days. This he must have sensed for his next comment was a change of subject.

"Shall we go back to where we finished off the other day," he paused and added another question, "or would you prefer to start somewhere else?"

"Let me tell you what has happened since I last saw you Stuart," I started to say as I made myself comfortable in one of the chairs, my coffee in my right hand. "I've had a police officer here Stuart; he seems to think that I know more than I'm letting on, and he's uncovered other things that I was unaware of." I stopped, for now I could see I had Stuart's attention.

"Carry on Andrew," he replied relaxing back in his own chair and taking a sip from his coffee.

"Well, he rang and asked if," I paused for now I felt almost uncomfortable, Stuart didn't seem to have that caring edge to him that he'd had the day before yesterday when he was here, no, now he seemed to be waiting, almost as if he was expecting some grisly details, I went on and was to be surprised by his change of expression.

"He asked if Louise had undergone any dental treatment recently." I stopped because of the startled look upon his face, and then he spoke.

"Oh, really Andrew," at the same time his colour changed, he became an ashen white; it prompted me to ask him a question.

"Are you alright Stuart?" I enquired.

"Um, yes, fine Andrew," Stuart stumbled to reply, and slowly he went on to explain himself. "That seems such an unusual question; I'm just a little taken aback as to why they should ask you that."

"I think it was something to do with how badly burnt the bodies were," I replied, as I studied his response, and once again I was to be surprised by Stuart's reaction.

"Good," he suddenly said, and after a second's thought he continued, "well I suppose that you're right, and that explains the question about the teeth." Suddenly he looked at his watch almost spilling his coffee.

"Andrew, we don't want to keep your friend waiting," he paused and now seemed a little more in control of his emotions, "perhaps we should be making a move," he quickly said.

"I thought you wanted to hear more of what I have been doing since I saw you last," I started to say, but Stuart was by now out of his chair, he finished his coffee in one go and was closing his briefcase as I struggled to finish my coffee, I looked at my own watch, it was now nine o'clock.

"We can cover what's been happening since our last meeting next time we have a session," he replied, his manner now seemed to be a little on the impatient side.

This sudden change in Stuart's manner disturbed me somewhat, and it was to be a little while before I was to understand his change in attitude, and it would be too late for Stuart to explain things to me.

"Yes, perhaps we can do some work this afternoon," I began to say, still looking at Stuart I have to say he looked as if he was on edge, not at all as he had been, perhaps a change of subject might help, I thought to myself, "fancy a ride in the Porsche?" I asked, thinking it may relax him and give me the chance to show I hadn't lost any of my driving skills.

"That would be rather nice," Stuart started to say, then he picked up his briefcase, returned his notepad, and continued to speak in what seemed like a more subdued manner, "do you know Andrew, I've never been in a Porsche."

"Well there's a first time for everything Stuart," I said, after finishing my coffee, and I went on, "you can leave your case here, if you like."

"Yes I'll pick it up on my return this afternoon," Stuart said and at the same time placed the case by the side of the chair he'd been sitting on.

The drive to the golf club that Alex frequents took about an hour, and in that time Stuart and I chatted, most of the conversation was from me, but I sensed that he was studying me, more like my reactions, or so I thought, he did say that he was surprised by the awesome power of the Porsche, and on one occasion I was able to put it through its paces, the smooth and effortless acceleration was always a pleasure to behold.

Chapter Eleven

A meeting with Alex

We arrived at Alex's golf club at eleven o'clock; we had stopped on route to refuel the Porsche. Now I have never played golf, and to the best of my knowledge neither had Stuart, but Alex had suggested during our telephone conversation that it would be good for me to get out of the house for a few hours, something Stuart had concurred with, prior to the visit.

As I pulled up in the car park of the club I looked around for Alex's car, his light green Honda was parked in the president's space, I didn't know Alex was that involved in the club, I thought to myself, or was it something else I'd forgotten since the terrible accident?

"This is very nice," Stuart said as his hand went to the door lever, he glanced across at me as he said the words, and then asked a question, "have you been here on many occasions?"

"No!" I instantly replied, but then a question crossed my own mind, had I? I continued "well I can't remember if I have or haven't."

"Andrew I'm sure things will start to fall into place soon enough," Stuart replied, his manner now a little more relaxed, at the same time he pushed the door of the car open and he started to get out, his behaviour and words very calming.

I got out of the car, together we closed the doors, a press of the key-fob and there was the familiar clunk of the locks, followed by the orange flash of the indicators the car was locked. We walked around to the entrance of the clubhouse, but Stuart was, I would say, one or two steps behind me, I looked back at him.

"You seem to know where you're going Andrew," he said as I caught his attention.

"So you think I may have been here before?" I replied as I stood on the first step that led to the doors.

"Either that or it could be instinct!" was his quick response, later I was to ask the same question of Alex.

I stood at the top of the stairs holding the door open waiting for Stuart to catch up, he looked closely into my eyes as he approached me, then as he stepped onto the wooden landing he placed his right hand on my shoulder, I looked up at him, he was about six feet tall hence my reason for looking up at him, his dark brown hair parted on the right hand side, he seemed to have returned to his very composed state of mind, this must be his training, counselling must be a very stressful occupation I thought to myself. After entering the foyer I looked around for a sign for the bar, sure enough I saw it above a set of double doors, we entered together, I looked around for Alex and I spotted him.

I found Alex installed in the bar, as I expected, a gin and tonic positioned in front of him, his paper, The Guardian open wide and occupying the rest of the bar area, he must have been waiting for me, for as soon as I approached him he was off his stool his arms outstretched as he came towards me.
"Andrew my boy!" his words carried forward before he got to me.
On other occasions he'd taken my hand, with just the occasional embrace, but now here I was stood in the middle of the bar of this exclusive golf club with a man's arms wrapped around me, it took a few moments for me to compose myself and reply to Alex's greeting, and it was something of a whispered response.
"Alex, it's so good to see you," I softly said, my own arms wrapped around him, this was a feeling of security I'd missed so much.
Slowly we released our grip on each other; it was then that I observed Alex looking at Stuart.
"Oh, excuse me Stuart," I said as I stepped towards him, my right arm out in front of me almost offering guidance, but as I looked at Stuart I could see his facial expression had changed, still I continued thinking that he may not be used to seeing two men greet each other in this intimate manner, "Stuart, please forgive me, this is Alex, you remember me talking about him!" I finished and Stuart came forward and extended his right hand, taking Alex's he spoke before Alex had a chance to say anything.
"It's very nice to meet you Alex," he said but his tone now had hesitancy to it, the words softly spoken and he continued, "Andrew has told me a great deal about you."
Had I? I thought to myself as their hands made contact, I was having awful problems remembering the events of a few weeks ago, and now I couldn't recall if I'd said anything to Stuart about Alex during the last couple of days.
"And you Stuart, I understand you've been helping Andrew through this most difficult of times," Alex replied still gripping Stuart's hand.
I stood and watched as these two men completed their greetings to each other, but now Stuart looked a little uncomfortable, he was not so at ease, his manner that I had become accustomed to, then I recalled the reason for our visit, to relax so I wondered if it would be possible for me to have a drink with the approval of Stuart, even though I'd had a few last night with Stavros, but I thought it best if I didn't reveal these facts to Stuart.
"Stuart," I began, then looking at Alex I continued, "Alex would you like a drink?" I asked regaining their attention as I enquired, and I continued with another question, "would it be alright for me to have a drink Stuart?"

"I don't see why not Andrew," he replied looking in my direction as he spoke, I noticed Alex look at the same time his expression somewhat puzzled, but it was Stuart who spoke, "a few beers or glass or two of wine won't harm with the medication you're on."

"What medication?" Alex asked looking again at me, then Stuart, and he replied.

"Oh, just some mild sedatives," Stuart said as we began to make our way to the bar and Alex's reclusive spot.

"Helps me manage the day," I said as I positioned myself on a bar stool, and I added "and something to help me sleep." I was going to mention that the police officer had looked at them, but Alex spoke and took my mind off the subject.

"Well whatever it takes Andrew," Alex said as he picked up his glass, just the remains of a gin and tonic and some small pieces of ice still in the glass.

"Same again is it Alex?" I asked reaching for my wallet from my inner jacket pocket; I looked at Stuart and as I did Alex asked a question of him and instantly Stuart's expression changed.

"Where did you study Stuart?" Alex enquired, adding, "oh yes please Andrew, a G and T will be fine." as he finished talking I noticed two men walking in our direction from the far end of the room, one was about five feet eight, of slight build, casually dressed I would say he was about sixty, his companion, and I say that with some confidence due the fact that they were having quite a conversation, he would have been about six feet, a full head of dark brown hair, unlike the first man, who was bald, as they got nearer the first man looked at me, a soft smile formed across his lips, but it was Alex he spoke to, at the same time placing his right hand on Alex's shoulder.

"What's this then Alex, some new members?" his words spoken with a touch of humour in his voice, but also very articulately, Alex spun round before answering the man.

"George, good to see you," he paused, took this man's right hand, looked at myself before continuing, "this George is my very good friend Andrew Jackson." As Alex said my name I extended my right hand.

"Andrew, meet George Clifford," Alex said by way of introducing me, but before I had chance to say a word George spoke to me.

"Nice to meet you Andrew, it's a damn shame about the accident." He said as he squeezed my right hand, then Alex continued to introduce me to the other man.

"And this gentleman, Andrew is," he paused and quipped "I say gentleman in the nicest possible way, is Bertram Hardcore," this man now took my hand and again tried to crush every finger in my right hand.

"Andrew you have a lot to put up with," Bertram started to say, suddenly I noticed him look at Stuart, he seemed to be glancing in the other direction, I was just about to introduce these two men to him when Bertram spoke again, this time directing his words towards Stuart, "I know you, don't I?" it was a question that brought Stuart's attention to the four of us.

"I don't think so!" he replied at the same time I noticed that he covered his face slightly.

"Aren't you that chap from St Mary's Hospital," Bertram said at the same time he was trying to get a closer look at Stuart.

"Yes I've been there a few times for some of my patients," Stuart softly replied.

"Never forget a face," was Bertram's response, and he had another question, "what department are you attached to?"

"Oh the mental health wing, you know the poor side of the national health family," Stuart said, I looked across at him and he seemed to have coloured up, and was looking quite hot, I was about to ask him if he was alright when George spoke again.

"Come on old man, we'll never get this round of golf in if you stand here chatting all day," he said distracting the conversation away from Stuart.

"Yes I'm coming," Bertram began to reply to his friend, then once again turned and looked at Stuart again, "Douglas, isn't it?"

Douglas, I thought, now where had I heard that name before, and not so long ago, my mind was still racing when Stuart abruptly replied to the question.

No. no!" was Stuart's sharp reply, he now looked very uncomfortable, but it wasn't that that deterred Bertram, it was Alex.

"Go on Bert," he began to say, adding, "we'll catch you back here in a couple of hours." They both nodded their agreement to Alex's statement, I watched as the two men made their way towards the doors that led to the locker room, once I noticed Bertram look back, then they were out of the bar area and gone from sight.

"Now where were we?" Alex started to say trying to pick up the conversation from before the two individuals had come to us and as always Alex could remember what it was we or rather he had been saying. "Where did you say you studied Stuart?"

"Ah!" was the start of his response and suddenly Stuart's right hand slipped into his own jacket pocket, removing his hand I could see he was holding his mobile phone.

"Excuse me," he said as he moved away from Alex and me, his phone now pressed to his right ear, his conversation began as he moved away from us, I could just make out a few words before they became inaudible.

"Strange Andrew, I didn't hear his phone ring," Alex said as he slid his empty glass forward on the bar.

"No, neither did I Alex." I remarked just as the barman came to take my order, I continued, "I'll have a gin and tonic for…" I was cut a little short by the steward.

"Usual is it Mr Collins?" he said taking a clean glass from under the bar.

"Yes please," Alex said and added, "I wonder what Stuart will have to drink?"

With those words I looked round to see Stuart on his way back to us, it gave me the opportunity to ask him what his preferred drink was and I was somewhat surprised by his reply.

"And what can I get for you?" I asked him as he got nearer.

"I'm afraid I can't stop Andrew," was his instant and sharp reply, so sudden that even Alex looked round at him, Stuart turned away so he was looking directly at me and he continued to speak, "I need to order a taxi, if that's OK Andrew!" and he went on, "that was my office, it seems as if I'm needed urgently, one of my other clients," he paused, glanced at Alex before continuing, "someone near to suicide!"

"That sounds awful!" was my immediate response, I glanced at Alex, and a puzzled expression was now on his face and it was Alex who spoke taking me a little by surprise, and Stuart.

"I didn't hear your phone ring Stuart!" he said his comment to the point as was his gaze and he continued, "you never said where you studied either."

"I'm sorry," Stuart began, he was still looking directly at me, but was about to answer Alex's question, "always have the mobile on vibrate," and he finished just as the barman returned saving him from continuing.

"And what can I get you sir?" he asked me, at the same time leaning forward on the bar a little, having passed Alex his drink.

"Well I think I'll have a pint of bitter," I replied looking directly into his eyes.

"Oh go on then, Andrew I'll have a half with you," Stuart suddenly interjected taking me a little by surprise and the barman as well, and he had a question for the barman, "could you order me a taxi to take me to Bristol?"

"Yes sir, that won't be a problem." The barman replied.

I sat and watched as he pulled first the half of bitter then the pint, before he'd finished pulling the pint Stuart had almost consumed his half, gone in two swift movements, not giving any of us a chance to comment on his rapidity at drinking, and the barman was to speak first.

"The taxi will be outside in five minutes, sir" he said looking at Stuart as he did so.

"There, I said it would have to be a quick half," he said as he placed his empty glass back on the bar, I hadn't even had time to take a sip from mine and Stuart was ready to leave, he continued to speak, "if you will excuse me I really must be going."

With those words he was heading for the door taking myself and Alex by complete surprise, there seemed to be a greater urgency in his departure than when he'd taken his phone call, this was the most unexpected behaviour, as he neared the door he turned only slightly to look at myself and he spoke again, "see you tomorrow Andrew, say ten o'clock?"

"Yes," was all I could say, and he was gone, I looked at Alex, his face reflected my thoughts and it was he who spoke first.

"What a strange way to behave, Andrew, I must say!" sternness in his words and his voice.

"Well I've only known him a few days Alex, perhaps he takes his work very seriously," I replied to Alex who by now had moved his stool closer to me.

"I didn't mean just his sudden departure Andrew!" Alex began, then picked up his glass, twirled it in his hand making the ice chink against the side of the glass, he took a long sip from it then went on, "he seemed very nervous, almost uneasy," again he stopped and looked hard into my eyes, I was just about to pick up my pint of beer but his actions made me feel very uncomfortable, Alex then continued with a question, "what did you say his name was?"

"Stuart," I replied still with that cold uncomfortable feeling running through my body.

"Stuart?" Alex enquired, I knew what he required, and that was Stuart's surname.

"Stuart Thomas," I could clearly recall his name, but as I said the words I had the most unusual feeling come over me, something from the not so distant past flashed through my mind, but it was only momentary and I couldn't hold the thought, Alex must have sensed this condition, for something inside of me made me ask a question of him, "why do you ask Alex?"

"No particular reason my boy," he replied with a strange casualness to his tone, but there was a reason for him asking, yet it was to be some time before I was to receive the answer to the enquiry I'd made.

Then something came back to me, it was something Stuart had said to me as we made our way into the golf club, and that was to do with the number of times I had been here, "Alex have I been to this club before?" I asked looking again at Alex as he finished his drink.

"Well not with me Andrew," was his positive reply and he continued with a question of his own, "why do you ask?"

"It's just something Stuart said as we came into the clubhouse, he said it appeared as if I'd been here on other occasions," I paused trying to recall his exact words, "maybe by the way I made myself to the bar!" I finished not sure in my own mind if that was what Stuart had said.

"Well I must say Andrew when you appeared at the bar it did seem as if you were a regular visitor." Alex said and at the same time looked at his empty glass, then he went on, "but I may well have told you a lot about the place," he paused and must have recalled my reason for the visit in the first place, "are we going to have this round of golf, or sit at the bar all afternoon?" he finished and at the same time slipped off the stool he'd been perched on.

"Yes of course," I replied after taking a pull from my pint, then I continued, "that was, after all, the purpose of my visit," I said as I remembered Alex's original request from the day before. Then something came into my mind as I recalled a program I'd watched on the television the previous night. "Do you mind if I ask you an awkward question Alex?"

"As long as it's nothing to do with money Andrew, fire away my boy," was his now light-hearted response.

I drew a little closer, the question wasn't of a personal nature but I was unsure if any other members of the club were aware of Alex's occupation and I didn't want to place Alex in an embarrassing situation.

"Do you know anything about brainwashing Alex?" I almost whispered in his ear, his reaction was as I should have expected.

"I've never actually taken part in any of this so called 'brainwashing' but why do you ask my boy," Alex replied his look intense.

"It was a two part program I saw on the television last night and the previous evening," I started to reply and sensing I had Alex's full attention I went on, "well they showed some methods employed by various military agencies…" I was cut short by Alex.

"You're referring to the injecting of drugs and sleep deprivation," was his instant reply.

"Yes, so you do know about some of the methods that are used," I said as I looked at the glass I was still holding.

"Andrew I'm not sure why this has come into your head, but let me assure you that there are hundreds of other ways that are used to brainwash people," he paused, placed his hand on my shoulder, then continued, "I understand one of the most successful and preferred methods is by suggestion."

"I'm not sure I understand you Alex," I said just a little confused by his reply.

"What I mean is this Andrew, if we think we have the person we want, and that they are holding back the information we require, then we tell them that we know all that they do, but not just once, no repeatedly, keeping them awake to remind them, and that we know more than them, all the time dropping little hints, most of them being wrong, but then the person gets so fed up of hearing the inaccuracies that they start to tell us the truth." Alex told me and had something to add, "but Andrew, you're suffering from loss of memory, not the other way about."

"I know that Alex but," I paused sensing that what I was about to say could seem ridiculous, "but could I have been brainwashed into forgetting the past."

"Not at all Andrew, you mustn't even think that, firstly you've had a terrible shock, and there was evidence that you'd had a bump on the head…" I didn't give Alex time to complete his answer.

"But is there another way of making people forget the past?" I said interrupting him.

"Yes, and you're holding one of the methods in your hand," Alex replied at the same time looking at the pint glass I was still holding, and he continued, "of course drugs are sometimes used." He stopped and now his eyes were peering into my own. "No." he added somewhat abruptly.

By now I had almost finished my drink just a small amount left in the glass, but I was now feeling just a little agitated, I reached into my outer jacket pocket and removed my medication.

"Can I have a look please Andrew?" Alex asked as he looked at the small container in my right hand.

"Of course you can Alex," I said as I passed it to him, and I continued, "they're meant to help me get through the day Alex, you understand, when I get a little pent-up, I also have some different ones I take at night, I think they're sleeping pills, but to be honest I haven't taken either of them for a few days," I paused and concluded with an admission, "not that I've told Stuart that."

"If that's what it takes Andrew," Alex casually replied passing the bottle back to me, I unscrewed the cap and removed one of the tablets, I was about to pop it into my mouth, and then wash it down with the remaining beer I had in the glass, I looked at Alex and I spoke, "they kick in very quickly."

"I'm sure they do Andrew, I'm sure they do, but to be honest, I don't think you need to take any more tablets Andrew," he said, in an uncomplicated manner, his eyes not giving away any more of his thoughts. Then he was to spring a surprise question on me bringing me back to reality instantly, "have any plans been formalised for the funeral of Louise and the children?"

Suddenly I felt myself come out in a cold sweat, this was the first time this had been mentioned since my conversation with Stuart and that had only been talking about the death of Louise, Sarah and James, I'd put off thinking about any funeral arrangements, Alex wasn't prying, no, I could sense his concern for me.

"To tell you the truth Alex, I can't make any firm arrangements until the bodies have been identified," I paused to recall what the inspector had told me, once in my mind I went on, "as they were burnt then they have to be identified by dental records and DNA, I think we're looking at the end of next week, at the earliest."

"I know this must be the most difficult of times for you Andrew," Alex started to reply, before continuing he placed his right hand on my left shoulder, "if there is anything I can do to help, you only have to ask."

"If you could find the bastards who rammed the car..." I started to say with anger in my voice, but his hand going up in the air stopped me along with his words.

"I'm sure the police are working on something!" was his straightforward reply, and it was to be a little while before I was to discover the importance in his words.

For some reason I felt a change of subject was in order, "my son William rang yesterday." I said regaining Alex's attention, "well he phones most days."

"How is he Andrew?" Alex asked in reply.

"He's fine, so is Peter, William wants me to go to the garage," I paused again to recall his conversation, "he says the police have finished with the BMW and we, or rather he can dispose of it."

"How does that make you feel?" he enquired, a probing to his words, maybe looking for an emotional reaction.

"I'm not sure Alex, I haven't seen it since before the accident," I said as I desperately tried to remember the incident.

"I don't suppose you have," Alex said as he began to lead me in the direction of the door at the back of the golf club, this was with the intention of going out to play the round of golf. Suddenly another phone call came back into my mind and I felt a need to share it with Alex.

"I also had a call from a woman I used to work with," I started to tell Alex as we approached the kit room where the golf clubs and other paraphernalia were kept, I went on once Alex had sorted some irons for me and a caddy for me to put them in, "she offered her condolences."

"Did she offer any other help?" Alex enquired.

"No." I stopped not sure of what Alex would think.

"Well you could have asked if she would have liked to have a drink with you, some female company will do you good, it may help you to unwind," was his instant response.

"Don't you think it's disrespectful, Alex?" I asked still feeling a little uncomfortable about the thought of going out with another woman.

"Andrew, if it bothers you that much don't ask, that is if she should phone again," he paused himself, thought for a moment then continued with just the slightest smile on his face, "of course you could always take Christine with you."

"Talking of Christine," I started to reply, "she came to my house one evening at the beginning of the week; you know just after I'd left hospital, Alex, she was so upset, yet at the same time strong for me, in fact she stayed over the night, she was a great comfort."

"I know she did Andrew, the following day she rang me, that was why I called you," he replied.

"It seems, Alex, that so much has been going on without my knowledge," I said to Alex as we approached the first hole on the green.

"Yes Andrew and I expect a lot more will be going on before you have recovered from these terrible events and they are behind you." Alex told me.

"Are you working at the moment Alex?" I asked unsure of what he was doing, other than relaxing during some spare time.

"Well I'm sure you're aware Andrew, something could come up at any time, and I may well be called upon to deal," he paused as he prepared to place his ball on the tee, looking up at me from his crouching position he went on but I didn't take in the significance of his reply, "I'll have a few things to occupy my time in the coming days."

I stood and watched as Alex prepared himself to take a swing at the golf ball he had so carefully positioned on the tee, with just one powerful stroke he propelled the ball into the distance, I could clearly hear the sound of the ball as it flew through the air, after the ringing sound of the iron had died away.

"Good shot," I remarked as we watched the ball land close to the green, two bounces and it was only a matter of feet away from the hole.

"You may have guessed Andrew," he paused before enlightening me on one of his favourite pastimes, "I have played the game once or twice."

"That I sensed," I said as I tried to copy his style as I pushed the tee into the ground, after placing the ball on it I stood up, it was then that Alex was to surprise me.

"I do have some news that I can share with you Andrew," he started to say, just as I took the golf club and practiced my swing away from the golf ball.

"Go on then Alex," I replied looking at him, totally unprepared for what he was about to say.

"Well Andrew, Delphine is dead!" his words had a calmness that I'd heard before, but the comment took me by complete surprise.

"What did you say?" I asked looking him in the eyes and lowering the golf club to the ground.

"I said Andrew, that Delphine is dead," he replied still holding my attention.

"I heard what you said Alex, but it was the way you told me," I said, still trying to comprehend what I'd just been told, and I continued with a question of my own, "how did she die?, I thought she was going to be watched for the rest of her life, you told Louise and I."

"These things happen, Andrew," Alex started to say and after placing his iron back in his caddy he continued, "from what I've been told Andrew, it was a hit and run."

"And don't they have anyone?" I started to ask.

"I said, it was a hit and run Andrew," he paused and could see I was uneasy about what he had just told me, Alex continued, his manner now one of trying to reassure me, "the police are looking at some closed circuit television tapes to see if they can identify the vehicle."

I felt drained at this news, in the past two days I'd received information about the death of two people I'd had some form of contact with, yesterday it had been the retired police sergeant, Mitchell was his name and now Alex was telling me that Delphine was dead, she had been on the other side of the law, that coupled with the interview I'd had with the inspector really did set me back, and Alex picked up on my expression.

"Andrew, are you alright?" Alex asked.

"Well to tell you the truth Alex, no I'm not alright," I replied and at the same time looked down at the white ball resting on the tee.

"What is it? You don't look at all well Andrew," Alex said as he came closer to me.

"Well Alex, yesterday I heard on the radio that Sergeant Mitchell was dead, found on a beach in Cornwall, and now you tell me that Delphine is also dead." I told him and after pausing for a moment I continued, "Alex less than a week ago the woman I was going to marry, along with her children were killed in a car crash, and you wonder why I don't look well."

"I understand what you're saying Andrew," he paused and came closer, placed his right hand on my shoulder and continued, "sometimes it seems as if life has these unpleasantries stored up, I'm sure they are just a coincidence."

"I expect you're right Alex," I began as once again I made an effort to swing the club at the small white ball resting on its tee, Alex stepped back as I took the proper shot at the ball, hit it I did, but it veered off at quite an acute angle, gazing in the direction it had taken I continued to speak, "it's not only the deaths that have been bothering me, I've also had the police at my house."

"Come on Andrew," Alex started to say as his hand went to the caddy and we started to walk in the direction of my ball, after a few yards he continued, "what did the police want Andrew?"

"Well amongst other things, the officer kind of inferred that he wasn't sure about my explanation of what had gone on leading up to the accident and of course afterwards, but I still can't remember Alex," I told him as we neared my nearly lost ball, it was in some thick grass.

"Go on Andrew take a swing to get it towards the green," Alex said, at the same time suggesting that I use a different iron; I took his advice and made the ball fly out of the rough and on towards the green. It was as we were heading in that direction that he had a question for me, but firstly a sort of justification for the officer's initial enquiry. "He has to cover every angle Andrew, what were the other things you mentioned?"

"Well Alex I clearly remember you telling Louise and I that Jan Van-Elderman was dead," I looked at Alex as we were close to his golf ball, he'd stopped and I sensed I had his attention.

"Go on Andrew," Alex said, indicating with his hand for me to continue.

"Alex the officer said that Jan had been to England in April, apparently some police officers in South Africa had found a diary in his flat," I paused for now Alex looked as puzzled as I had felt when I was told the news, he nodded, I went on, "well my name was in there, it seems as if he'd planned a meeting with me."

"That can't be right Andrew, I was told on good authority that Jan is dead, this officer, what did you say his name is?" Alex started to reply.

"Inspector Braithwaite," I said looking hard at Alex.

"He's just fishing for information, perhaps trying to unnerve you." Alex said.

"Well if that is the case then he may well have succeeded," I replied as I recalled the other things he'd told me.

"What do you mean Andrew?" Alex asked, his eyes slightly closed but still focused on me.

"It seems, Alex. that I now have a business venture in South Africa, as well as in this country," I told the waiting Alex, his expression changed to one of bewilderment, and I concluded, "I know nothing about this new business other than what the inspector has told me, and what I've been able to ascertain from my management team."

"Have you any idea when this company was set up?" Alex asked at the same time scratching his head.

"I've been informed that it was started up in April, this year," I replied to Alex's question, and I continued, "I've been told that it was Louise who took care of all of the arrangements, but I still can't believe she would have done such a big transaction without informing me."

We continued to make our way around the golf course, I was displaying my incapability at playing golf, as well as my inability to understand Alex, all the time we discussed the new business venture, along with some of the other issues I'd talked to Stuart about, and all the time Alex was absorbing the information I was feeding him. By the time we'd reached the eighth hole we had caught up with the two men who had been in the bar.

"Just the two of you," George asked as we neared them, but it was his companion who continued with the conversation, catching me out with his words.

"I remember that other chap now Alex," Bertram started to tell Alex but at the same time his look was in my direction.

"Go on then Bert, put me out of my misery," Alex quipped in response, he obviously knew this individual very well for as he spoke he leant back against his caddy.

"He doesn't work at St Mary's, it's the infirmary I've seen him at," he paused and I knew he was going to carry on without any prompting from Alex or myself, "his name is Douglas Evans."

I looked long and hard at Alex, and then Bertram, now this was not only the Christian name I'd heard before but also the surname was the same as Mrs Walbridge had said the young woman had.

"Are you sure?" I asked before Alex had a chance to say anything.

"I would say ninety nine per-cent," was Bert's reply, I looked again at Alex, hoping his eyes would say that his friend couldn't be mistaken, I could see nothing, but Bert had a question of his own, "is there a problem?" It was then that I noticed Alex's eyes give me a clue, and that was to say nothing, well not get involved in a lengthy conversation.

"No, probably my mistake," I said as I made my way towards the green. As I stepped nearer to my ball George spoke to his companion, Bert.

"Are we going to call it quits after this shot," he paused and I noticed him look at Bert, and he went on, "I do have an appointment at two o'clock Bert."

"Yes, that'll mean we have time for a quick one in the bar before you shoot off," Bert replied, he spoke in a manner similar to Trevor, positive and to the point; all he lacked was Trevor's little phrase 'sound'.

Alex and I stood and watched as these two men completed their round of golf, short it may have been, Bert did mention that he would see the two of us in the bar later, Alex nodded his agreement, I on the other hand was becoming even more mystified, just who is this Douglas Evans, or is it Douglas Stuart, my confusion must have shown on my face, and Alex was to pick up on it. We completed our own game, I lost by a considerable margin, Alex had tried to reassure me as we continued around the rest of the course, that Bert could possibly be wrong, his final words on the subject as we came away from the eighteenth hole were that 'he would ask some questions in the right places'

By the time we had returned to the club house I didn't really feel much like having a drink, in fact what I was in need of was a cup of tea, this I explained to Alex, he did say that he could arrange to have a pot made freshly for me, I took him up on the offer, I sat at one of the small tables and Alex brought the tray over himself, his friend Bert had left, so Alex joined me, all the time we made small talk, after half an hour I had drained the tea pot dry, and I said I was ready to leave remembering that I'd promised William that I would visit the garage, I made up my mind that was what I was going to do, Alex accompanied me to the car park, it was there that he gave me my customary farewell hug, also reminding me that he would see me very soon, and if I needed anything then I was to call him. I agreed that I would.

Chapter Twelve

The garage

"Go home Andrew," Alex started to tell me as I headed towards my car, his words were spoken in a way I hadn't heard before, and he continued, "try and relax, things will sort themselves out," they hung in the still afternoon air as I got into my car, and were to play on my mind sometime after they were spoken.

But relax was the last thing I was going to do. I got into my Porsche, started the engine and could only have gone half a mile along the road when my mobile phone began to ring, I thought it might be the inspector, or possibly one of my sons phoning me, namely William, I'd said I would call at the garage, Louise's BMW had been released from the police enquires, and William was keen to have it removed, in so doing giving up valuable space in the garage that he needed, but to my surprise it wasn't, in fact I didn't recognise the number at all.

"Mr Jackson?" the male voice asked a very polite but at the same time a diplomatic tone to his words.

"It is," I replied, awaiting something of a lengthy conversation, I started pull the car to the side of the road in anticipation.

"Mr Jackson, it's Benjamin Wilcox, of Wilcox, Sumner and Richards here," he paused and I felt as if I needed to prompt him but he did continue, "the funeral directors." His words now brought a sudden coldness with them, this was a call I had been dreading.

"Carry on Mr Wilcox," I said as the car came to a stop at the side of the road.

"We have finalised all of the arrangements Mr Jackson, the funerals are set to take place next Wednesday," he paused as he had no doubt heard me draw breath at the same time as I brought the car to a halt, a feeling came over me of being unable to speak, coupled with a wish for a very strong drink, before I had a chance to say anything Mr Wilcox continued, in the politest of manners, "the plot has been marked out at St Mary's church, Chillingston, as to yours, and Mrs Shaw's parents' wishes, and the service is scheduled to take place at twelve noon."

He stopped as I managed to mumble a 'thank you.'

I thought I needed to make a note of what I had just been told, I reached across to the glove box in the car, upon opening it the small pile of letters I'd placed in there yesterday tumbled out, on top the letter from the BMW dealership, I picked it up and turned it over, the back was clear, removing a pen from my jacket pocket I carefully noted what I had just been told. My silence prompted a question from Mr Wilcox.

"Are you alright Mr Jackson?" he asked very softly.

"Yes," I started to reply; I needed to continue as this gentleman had shown some concern for me, I went on, "I'm just making a note of the details you have just explained to me."

"That's fine Mr Jackson, take as long as you need," he paused and I listened, nothing, no other sound at all, not even Mr Wilcox breathing, this was so unlike all of the other phone calls I'd received and made during the past few days, having given me this time of privacy he continued to speak, "if you wish Mr Jackson, we can make an announcement in the local press, and of course the national papers if you require us to."

"Well, if you wouldn't mind," I said, accepting his offer and realising that it would save me along with Trevor and Diane a considerable amount of time and trauma, I added, "I'll need to confirm the announcement with Louise's parents in the mean time, thank you Mr Wilcox."

"Indeed sir, it's all part of the service, Mr Jackson," the gentleman replied, and went on, "I shall personally contact you the day before the service to confirm the details, in the mean time, Mr Jackson, if you have any questions then, please don't hesitate to contact myself."

"Thank you Mr Wilcox, you're very kind," I said, grateful that the world still had some very understanding people left in it; I finished with, "thank you I'll be in touch."

"Mr Jackson, at your service," And with those words he was gone from the line.

I sat in the car, the engine still ticking over, just for a few moments, digesting the words of Mr Wilcox, he was the perfect gentleman, a thought crossed my mind as I sat alone, I was only fifteen minutes away from St Mary's church, now for some reason I felt a need to go and look at the plot that had been prepared. I drove as if I was on autopilot, carefully but at the same time not taking any immediate notice of my surroundings, when I arrived at the church I pulled up in more or less the same place I'd seen Len and Mark stop at, and that was the day of Gary's funeral, albeit they were late.

I got out of the car, and call it instinct or something else, perhaps another sense leading me, I made my way directly to where the new grave was to be dug, sure enough it was marked out on the ground, a large square, about ten feet by ten feet, a wooden peg hammered into the ground at each corner, some white tape marking out the area, tied between the pegs, a start had been made in excavating some of the earth. I stood looking at the shallow hole in the ground, at least the future is clear, I thought, but I still couldn't remember what had gone on in the past.

Standing here I now had the most unusual of feelings come over me, knowing what was going to happen next week brought a sense of peace and quiet over me, calmness descended upon me, I felt as if I could do no more, the past was soon to be laid to rest.

I looked across the graveyard, and at the grave of Louise's ex-husband Gary, as I looked I noticed a woman at the grave, she was dressed in black, Gary's grave had over the past few years blended in, it looked similar to the rest, the headstone was cleaner, and the grass around it wasn't as long and rugged as the surrounding graves, but it didn't look new and out of place, I glanced down again at the ground in front of me, my intention was to have a large stone erected, and when the time came and I passed away I would also be buried in the same plot.

I didn't notice the woman in black come across the churchyard, I almost jumped, somewhat startled by her presence by my side, and it was she who spoke breaking me out of my trance-like state.

"She would have been happy with you," the woman said.

"Sorry," I replied in my surprised state, I continued with a question of my own, "and you are?"

"Never you mind," the woman replied, I looked at her, she was about fifty, maybe fifty five, her medium length dark hair caught by the light breeze blew away from her eyes, I thought I recognised a resemblance but as I looked at her she turned away slightly, then she spoke again, "she was too good for him," a pause and softly she said, "he was just like his father."

"You knew Gary?" I enquired, trying to gain some information from her.

"Yes I knew him alright," she replied, instantly her connection fell into place, this was Gary's mother, but as I was about to ask her to confirm her identity my mobile phone began to ring, I took it from my pocket, looking at the display I could see it was William, my eldest son.

"Excuse me," I said to the woman, I walked a few feet towards my car, so that I could take the call with a little privacy.

He asked where I was, what I'd been doing, apparently he had been trying to contact me on my home telephone number, and had left a message for me, but as I hadn't been home since leaving with Stuart earlier this morning I hadn't picked up any of the messages left for me, I went on to explain where I was, the reason for my visit, that being the call I'd received from the funeral directors. He seemed quiet at my response, but also had a request of his own.

"Are you coming to the garage dad?" he softly asked, his words as always said with care and consideration.

"Yes son, I'll be on my way in a few minutes," I replied, at the same time I looked back in the direction of the marked-out grave, the woman, Gary's mother, was gone.

"OK dad, see you in…" I stopped him in his tracks, at the same time I scoured the church yard looking for the lady dressed in black.

"I'll see you in three quarters of an hour son," I said realising I couldn't see this woman any more, and that I now needed to move on.

"Fine," William said in response, then he was gone from the line, I looked at the phone as the display and his number died away.

For some reason I continued to look at the mobile phone, William had said he'd been trying to contact me; this phone hadn't rung until the funeral director had called me, and now, with William's call, so I thought I'd check the call register. No missed calls today, I said to myself, then the display moved onto the day before, I mentally remembered the numbers, the times that the calls had taken place were displayed by the side of the number, the inspector's call was displayed, and quite lengthy, then I noticed Stuart's number, that too was in the afternoon, I couldn't remember calling him, but stood here in the churchyard I put it down to the absent mindedness I'd been suffering from for some time now.

The drive to the garage took less time than I had estimated, forty minutes and I was pulling up on the driveway to the workshop, William was at the garage doors in a flash having heard the roar of the Porsche engine.

"Come on in dad," he said as he approached me, his arms open wide, I have to say that he was unusually clean. I put my arms around him and pulled him close to me, again I felt secure, father and son, something that is hard to explain, and even harder to find with anyone else. "Good to see you." He said as we relaxed our grip on each other.

"And you my boy," I said in response to his greeting, and then I had a question for him, "Peter not about?"

"He's just popped out with Liam to recover a broken-down car," William said as we made our way into the workshop, in the far corner I noticed what resembled a car, but it was covered by grey a tarpaulin, I assumed it to be Louise's BMW. William continued to speak, "yes one of our regular customers, a window cleaner, has broken down in the middle of the high street." I nodded my reply, but my attention was still drawn to the covered car at the end of the garage, William picked up on my distraction, and taking my right hand he lead me in the direction of the covered object.

"We'd best get this over and done with dad," he said as we neared the somewhat darkened end of the garage.

"Go on," I told him as he took the corner of the tarpaulin, I continued as he lifted it in readiness to remove it, "then we can lay some more of the past to rest."

As William pulled on the tarpaulin so as to uncover the car, dust started to fly in the air, I waved my hands in an effort to try and clear the view. William pulled the cover towards him and began to role it up in the process. I stood, mesmerised, looking at this burnt and now rusty shell of an estate car, as I got nearer, I put my head through one of the rear door windows, there was no glass in the door, I assumed it had been broken during the heat of the fire, the frame of the door was bent and twisted, looking inside of the shell, I could see the wire and rusty metal frames of the seats, front and rear, every part of the car had been charred, I moved in the direction of the rear end of the car, evidence was there, the size of the impact on the back end, the back door of the estate was smashed in, the crumple zones having folded on impact, perhaps jamming the rear doors shut, slowly I moved around the car, all of the paint work was destroyed, no evidence of any of the blue metallic finish, I started to study certain parts of the burnt out shell, no marks on the doors, no runs of melted plastic where the door handles had been, I glanced down at the wheels, the blackened alloys had started to melt, wrapped around them the rusty wire remains of the tyres, as I got closer to the front nearside of the car something struck me, and the words of Mrs Walbridge came back to me. I stood frozen in my tracks.

"What is it dad?" William asked as he joined me by the front passenger's door.

"It's this," I said pointing towards the front of the shell.

"I'm not with you dad," William questioned me, I glanced at him, his eyes followed mine towards the front of the car, "I don't understand."

"This isn't Louise's car," I said, not in an excited manner, for I wasn't, because I couldn't fully remember what Mrs Walbridge had said, looking again at William I could see he was puzzled, but for me, something was slowly returning.

"Dad," William started to say, at the same time he placed his hand on my shoulder, I more or less knew what he was going to continue with, "you've had the most stressful of times, perhaps you're still confused."

"No William, I remember the dressmaker telling me something!" I began to almost protest at my son, I continued, "I'm not that confused, the dressmaker told me that she had seen Louise's car, she said the day after the accident, she recognised it because the nearside front wing was damaged," I stopped and looked again at the wing in question, it was intact, albeit burnt and now rusty.

"Well, this is how the car came to us dad," William said moving forward to take a closer look.

Then I recalled that Mrs Walbridge hadn't been able to see the nearside of the car on the evening we had been to her cottage for the fitting, the very evening the accident had taken place, this cast some doubt in my mind, and William was to confirm that doubt with his next comment.

"But dad, there are hundreds, if not thousands of BMWs similar to this model," his words had a touch of frustration to them, I'd almost expected his response, still deep inside I hoped that this could all be a terrible dream, a nightmare I would soon wake up from, I felt that I had to argue my case with him, albeit futile in my son's eyes.

"William, Mrs Walbridge told me, and I clearly remember her saying that she had seen the car in the village the following day," by now my voice was raised, not shouting, but loud enough for me to put my case across.

"If you like dad I'll take you out and onto the high street now, we'll see plenty of BMWs" his own temper was now beginning to edge its way into the conversation, it was enough to break my spirit, along with showing my own doubts as to what Mrs Walbridge had told me.

"I know, I know my son," I began, at the same time I was struggling to control my emotions, William's reaction was to open his arms, he moved forward, and I more or less fell into them.

"I understand dad," he said as he tightened his grip on me, it was all I could do to stop myself from crying, he continued softly and gently "I can't imagine what you are going through, we all loved Louise and the children, Natasha is devastated, as are Sophie and Peter."

"I just want this to be over," I began to tell my son, his attention was on me, he'd released his grip on me, I could see that in fact he did understand, for his own eyes had started to water.

"I know you do dad, we all do," he replied, then after wiping his eyes with the backs of his hands he continued with another question, "what else have you been doing for the past few days, you said the other day that the counsellor has been spending quite a lot of time with you."

"Yes he has," I said as I regained my own composure, and I went on, "we went to Alex's golf club today, but..." then I recalled that Stuart didn't stay, and just how strange that was, I was stopped from continuing by William.

"You've been playing golf dad," he started, a surprised note in his voice, and he quipped, "why spoil a good walk dad?" now he had laughter in his words.

I chuckled myself, not at the joke, more so for seeing him laugh.

"I also had a visit from Stavros," I said, this brought William back to his serious nature, he enquired as to everyone's wellbeing in Truro, "I've also been interviewed by the police," I added.

"What for dad?" William asked as he started to replace to cover over the BMW.

"Son, I wish I knew, Alex seems to think that the officer was digging, just trying to make a name for himself." I said as I too pulled on one side of the cover, I had something I needed to add, "you'd best let the car go William."

"I'll arrange for the scrap man to collect it in the morning," he replied as we started to walk back towards the office at the other end of the garage.

"I've also been informed of the arrangements for the funerals," I said, as I did we both stopped in our tracks.

"When are they taking place dad?" William asked looking me directly in the eyes.

"Oh, next week," I said, and I went on, "Wednesday I think the funeral director said, I made a note, so that I wouldn't forget, I've got it in the car."

"Go and get it dad, I'll put the kettle on and we can have a cup of tea," he paused and added as I neared the Porsche, "I'll make a note myself, so that I can close the garage for the day."

I walked on to my car, making my way round to the passenger's side, I hadn't locked it, I opened the door, the envelope I'd written on was still on the passengers seat, I picked it up, I was going to shout the details to William, but he was in the goldfish bowl of an office and wouldn't have heard me, so I closed the car door and walked back to the garage and on into the office.

"Right we'll have a nice cup of tea in a few minutes," William said as I went in, and he continued as he looked at the envelope I was holding in my hand, "can I have a look dad, I'll note the details down in the diary."

I passed him the letter and watched as he turned it over and looked at the addressed side of the envelope, "were you thinking of changing the car dad?" he asked as he studied the address window.

"I can't remember William," I started to say, and I went on, "I expect it's just a sales brochure, you know trying to drum up some business and get me to part with some more money."

"You haven't opened it Dad," William said as he now looked at the back of the envelope, and he went on as he placed the letter on the desk, "I'll just write down these details."

I watched as he did so and very quickly he had completed the task.

"Here you are dad," he said as he passed the letter back to me, as he did so the kettle stopped boiling and switched itself off, I took the envelope from him and studied the address window myself, the name and address was typed, 'A D Jackson Esq.' now with this article in my hand I realised it wasn't a brochure, it was a proper letter addressed to myself, curiosity got the better of me, I looked around William's cluttered desk for a letter opener, he glanced back at me as he was pouring the boiling water into the teapot, "what are you looking for dad?" he asked.

"A letter opener," I replied.

"Under that pile of post to your right," he said, at the same time he pointed with his left hand.

Sure enough I found a wooden handled letter opener, holding the envelope in my left hand I carefully slid the pointed end into the gap at the top of the envelope, William spoke again, "probably one of those sales circulars dad," I pulled the opener that seemed a sharp as a knife, it sliced the paper with considerable ease, William asked me a question as I started to retrieve the folded letter from the envelope, "fancy a biscuit dad?"

"Yes please," I began to reply as I started to unfold the letter, then my words must have become inaudible because the next thing I remember was William asking me to repeat myself, rather than do that I said, "I think you'd better read the letter yourself William."

I sank into a seat after passing him the piece of paper, placed my head in my hands, I fought with my emotions, I was near to crying, and suddenly some of the past came back to me. I looked up at William from my seated position, he was still studying the paperwork, but now his own expression had changed, I awaited his comment; it wasn't quite what I was expecting.

"Well dad," he began and at the same time came across to me, then he continued to speak to me, "this estimate for some repairs to the BMW seems to cast a new light on things, I'm sorry that I doubted you Dad," he paused again and I felt his hand grip my shoulder tightly, I looked into his eyes, they were focused on my own, then as I expected, a question. "This car, according to the estimate, requires some extensive repairs, it mentions a new wing, bumper, and several other parts, plus the re-spray of the front of the car, have you any idea of how the damage could have occurred?"

That question was sufficient for part of the past to kick in, not a flash of something happening, no a full blown mind recalling event came back to me.

"Yes William, I remember clearly how the damage occurred," I said as my mind went back to the event in question, I continued, "we had an accident about a fortnight ago, Louise and I had been out, we'd left the Manor in the morning, as we approached the main gates at the top of the drive I pressed the button on the remote to open them, they did, but as we drove through them the right hand gate suddenly started to close of its own accord, Louise had to accelerate quite quickly to avoid it hitting the car, but it was on our return that I had the problem, I was driving, it opened but I'd forgotten about the way it had behaved in the morning when we were going out," I paused and could see I had William's attention, he'd made his way over to where the kettle and teapot were, and had just poured the tea, I continued, as he made his way back to me, a mug in each of his hands, "I didn't drive through the gates fast enough, the gate sprang back very sharply, it hit the front of the car, breaking the indicator, and also smashing the headlight, along with the damage it did to the wing, the following day I took the car to the main BMW dealer to have it looked at," then something else came back to me, I'd had to make a temporary repair, I went on, "I remember now fixing the indicator back in place with some tape, that was still on the workbench at the Manor."

"And how long have you had this letter?" William asked, now he was as intrigued about the past, as much as I was, for this was the first main event that I had been able to remember, for the past few days to a week I'd felt as if I'd been on drugs.

"I picked it up yesterday when I was at the Manor," I replied to his question, "Stavros was with me." I added.

William looked again at the letter, he'd placed it on the table when he'd gone to pour the tea, "well this was posted five days ago," he said as he pointed at the post mark.

"That was after we'd been to the dressmakers, for the fitting." I said.

"Look," William began after taking a sip from his mug of tea, he went on, "I'll hold on to the car for a few more days, I think you need to contact the police," he paused and was to add some very poignant words, they reflected my own thoughts, "there's something not right about this dad."

I looked at my watch, it was now five forty five, the afternoon had disappeared, I felt as if I'd been all over the place, and in reality I had, but a feeling of some satisfaction was beginning to form, my memory was starting to come back, maybe only small events, but I recalled yesterday I'd stood at the gates of the Manor, I'd studied the bent and twisted gate, but couldn't recall how it had got into that shape, now I could.

"Why don't you come and have dinner with us this evening?" William asked.

"That would be very nice," I began to reply, and I added, "I'd like to go home first, you know, so that I can have a shower and change."

"Sure, let's say we'll see you about seven thirty," William said, that was after looking at his own watch, and he continued, "Natasha will be pleased to see you dad."

Then I remembered that I was in need of some milk, something I'd noticed this morning when I was making coffee for Stuart and myself.

"William, is there a small shop on the High Street, where I can get some milk?" I asked my son, he was in the process of refolding the letter and was about to put it back in the envelope.

"I think it's still there," he began with his reply at the same time he passed me the letter, I folded it and put it in the inner jacket pocket, and that was to be the next part of the conversation, "you'll probably need to show this to the police, what was it that you said you wanted dad?"

"Oh, I'm nearly out of milk," I said, at the same time I stood, then I went on, "I look forward to seeing all of you later, it's a shame I've missed Peter and Liam."

"Well, you'll see Peter at my house, and next time you're here you'll see Liam," William said.

He walked with me to my car, there he gave me a hug, and reminded me of the time I needed to be at his house for dinner, before I started the car I watched him walk back towards the garage, it was then that I thought I may be recovering my memory, important items of the past had returned to me, things I thought I'd lost forever. I started the car and slowly reversed out of the garage, then I headed in the direction of the High Street, what I didn't remember was the difficultly in parking on the High Street, the corner shop was at the far end of the street, the very one where Smiths, and the bank were situated, and of course my accountants, I had to park some considerable distance from the shop, in fact in a side street, about fifty metres away. I made my way to the shop after locking the car, there seemed to be a steady stream of people emerging from it, and what looked like a long queue of people waiting to be served, for myself I didn't mind the wait, five minutes, if that and I was back on the street, I walked slowly back to my Porsche, the usual press of the key-fob and the doors unlocked, as I was about to get in my mobile phone began to ring, I fumbled trying to take it out of my inner pocket, in the process I dropped the milk, 'bugger' I said as I struggled to pick it up and at the same time answer the phone.

"Andrew," the voice said as I held the mobile next to my right ear, in my left hand I was holding the plastic container of milk, instantly I recognised the voice.

"Alex," I replied, and unthinking I continued, "I've some news for you."

"And I have some for you my boy," he replied, and thinking that mine would keep I let him continue, that was after a little prompting.

"Go on Alex," I said as I got into the car and placed the milk in the passenger footwell.

"I understand that the car involved in the hit and run that killed Delphine was a black Range Rover, apparently the local police are still looking for it," he paused, maybe thinking I hadn't heard what he'd just told me, he came back with a question, "did you hear me Andrew?"

"I heard what you said Alex," I replied in something of a dazed state, and I continued, "that is the same colour as the car that is supposed to have hit Louise's BMW..." I was cut short by another question from Alex.

"What do you mean, supposed?" he asked his words had that probing menacing style that I knew Alex possessed, he was looking for the truth, I couldn't escape from this even on the end of the phone, even if I'd wanted too.

"Alex, the car William has in his garage isn't Louise's," I started to tell him, the line went dead as I explained to him the conversation and time I had spent with my son, his reply wasn't what I was expecting.

"Right Andrew," he began, I sensed something serious was about to be said, and Alex didn't fail me, "don't take anymore of those bloody tablets Andrew," he paused and I could hear him fiddle with something, then he continued, "I'll be in touch with you soon my boy."

"Alright Alex," was all I could say, I didn't feel alarmed by what he had just said, maybe a bit confused, what I did feel was a need for a strong drink, and I wanted it now, I didn't want to go back to my house in the suburbs of Bristol and drink on my own, I was in desperate need of a drink now.

'What on earth has been going on?' I asked myself as I got out of my car, 'I need a drink' I thought as I headed in the direction of the High Street, if I had one before going home, then I could order a taxi to take me to William's for dinner.

The nearest pub was about two hundred yards along the street; I walked quite quickly towards the Black Horse public house, only stopping to check that I had sufficient money in my wallet for a quick pint. For this time of the evening the pub was quite full, at the bar were three young men, it seemed as if they were involved in quite a deep and meaningful conversation, one banging his fist on the bar at the same time denouncing what his friend was saying, the other man, sat to his right was leaning against the bar a smile across his face, at the far end of the pub was a group of five or six, somewhat scantily clad females, they appeared to be laughing and joking, almost at every word one of them spoke.

After ordering my pint I managed to find a small table, it was under a window that would have looked out on to the street, if it hadn't been of the frosted sort, I sat down with my pint of bitter and was about to reflect on my day when I was to be surprised, no, I would say stunned.

"Hello Andrew," a female voice said.

I looked up in what must have seemed like complete amazement, for standing by the table and directly in front of me was Melissa Thorne, the woman I had spoken to only the day before.

"Oh hello," I said, in something of a surprised manner, at the same time I stood and offered her a place to sit, but Melissa chose to sit opposite me.

"I thought I saw you come in," she started to say, then she looked towards the far end of the pub and went on, "I was down there," she pointed with her right hand, at the young ladies as they started to laugh again, none of them looked in the direction Melissa had pointed, and then she had a question for me, "what sort of day have you had Andrew?"

"A little better," I began to say, but was cut short by another question, one that would make me look directly at Melissa.

"What have you been up to Andrew?" she asked, I looked at her trying to study some of her details, her hazel hair was immaculate, as was the make-up she was wearing, as for her clothes, what I could see fitted perfectly, her appearance indicated that she was out for the evening, her low cut light brown top revealing her cleavage, I noticed when she was standing that she was wearing a short suede skirt, a small evening bag in her hand, her question prompted a question from myself, that was after answering hers.

"Well you know, trying to put some of the past into order, while still coming to terms with what has happened," I said in response to her initial question, then I followed on with my own question, "and you, out for the evening?"

"Oh something like that," was her hesitant reply, suddenly she glanced around the rest of the bar, then another question, and "did you manage to sort things out in your mind?"

"Yes I did," I said in reply to her question, but I didn't want to go into details, I was trying to put the day into some sort of order, hence the reason for coming in for a drink, then a thought crossed my mind, more like a question, it was one I didn't want to ask, and would keep to myself, 'how did she know about my confused state?' I thought a change of subject might be in order, so I asked another question, "you and your friends in here for the evening, or moving on?"

"Oh, I expect we'll go on to a nightclub a little later," she replied, as she did so she shifted on the seat, and came back with another question of her own, and it was very much to the point, "are the police any nearer to catching the people who did that to Mrs Shaw and the kids?"

What a strange question to ask, not that much information had been revealed to the public, and fancy Melissa referring to Louise by her married name.

"Well to tell you the truth," I started to reply, suddenly I didn't feel at all comfortable sitting here with this woman, she seemed to be fishing for information, I looked again into her eyes, instantly she looked away, across the bar at the three young men, it was as if she was trying to avoid direct eye contact, I went on, "I'm not sure if they are any further forward now than they were a few days ago." I said as I lifted my pint and took a pull from it, in doing so my line of vision took in the frosted glass window, still holding the glass to my mouth I noticed a large framed person pass by the other side of the window, very slowly, I could make out that this individual was about six feet tall, maybe six feet six, the one thing I was sure of as the silhouette passed by was that the person was black. For a moment I sat waiting, expecting this person to come into the bar, they didn't, I looked toward the next window and watched as the outline passed that one, then Melissa was to spring another question on me.

"And what brings you in here Andrew?" she asked as I replaced my beer on the table.

"I'm going to my son's house for dinner, and I fancied a beer before I went home to change," I replied, it brought a very strange response from Melissa.

"Not the way I would expect a man who has lost his fiancée and her children to behave," she said quite abruptly, the comment provoked an instant response from me.

"If I knew how I should be behaving then I would!" I replied in something of an angry manner.

"Sorry Andrew," Melissa started to say, and she went on, "I didn't mean to infer that you don't care," she stopped as I put my hand up.

"I didn't mean to snap at you," I said, and I went on, "it's just that I can't remember that much about the last few weeks, let alone days, but slowly…" I was cut short by her reply.

"Good!" she stopped, and then continued after moving again, her gaze was in the direction of the bar once more, she went on, "I mean it's good that you are feeling better." Her words stopped as suddenly her handbag started to sing; well I mean her mobile phone in her bag. "Excuse me," she said as she removed the phone after rummaging for a few moments. I watched as she pressed a button to answer the call, then pressing the phone close to her right ear after flicking her hair out of the way she spoke.

"Hello," she said, and waited the reply from the caller, I tried to look away, assuming that would give her some privacy, but still I could hear Melissa speaking, "what?" her voice was somewhat raised, and she went on with another question, "and when did this happen?" she paused to take the reply, "half an hour ago and its taken until now for you to inform me," she paused again and I could faintly make out the other voice, a man, "well you had better start to look for her," again she stopped and now as I looked at her I could see she had coloured up, quite red, I rightly sensed she was angry, "I'll see you outside in ten, no five minutes," she said as she glanced in my direction, she closed the conversation with a sharp, "right!"

"Problems," I asked looking at the somewhat frustrated Melissa.

"Oh, it's just," she paused and finished her drink in one movement, then continued, "my mother, she suffers with dementia of one sort or another, and it would seem that she has gone on a walk-about," she stopped again, I thought to gather her thoughts, but she went on, "that was my brother, he's coming to pick me up so we can go and look for her."

"Is there anything I can do to help?" I asked politely, but really in my mind I knew there was little I could do to help.

"No, you stay here and enjoy your drink," was Melissa's quick response, at the same time she was on her feet, one more comment and she was on her way to the door, "'bye Andrew," she said as she opened the door, and stepped out onto the street.

I sat here for a few moments puzzling her actions, the last time I recalled seeing Melissa was at the station, and that was in April, then she had almost demanded that I give her a kiss to greet her, but this evening she came up to me, no hassle tonight, I took another pull from my remaining beer, then something else occurred to me, she had gone out of the pub without saying goodbye to her friends, this brought a question to my mind, but I couldn't be bothered to go to the end of the pub to ask it, 'had she been with those other young women?' I looked at my watch, it was six fifteen, I was only a five minute drive away from my home, I still had plenty of time to have a shower, get changed and arrange for a taxi to pick me up, I finished my pint, stood and walked to the bar with the empty glass, "thanks," I called to the barman as I placed the glass on the counter, "cheers mate," was the response, I made my way to the door, upon opening it I noticed that the evening was descending quite rapidly, as I stepped out of the bar and onto the pavement something caught my eye, a child ran across the road, about a hundred yards away, not just any child, no this one looked like Sarah.

I looked again, but now with more intensity, as this little girl ran into an alleyway, her auburn hair tumbling down her back as she did so, this can't be, I thought to myself as I tried to comprehend what I had just seen, I'd only had a pint, so this couldn't be an illusion I told myself, as I walked in the direction of the alleyway the little girl had taken shelter in, as I walked along the high street I noticed the sodium lights come on, they faintly glowed red to start with, the intensity getting brighter and changing to orange as I moved along, I passed several side turnings, as I did so I looked down them, they seemed to be bathed in darkness, the night had come early to the back streets of the town. I stopped quite abruptly as a car went by, the driver blowing his horn, this gesture was aimed at a group of young girls about to go into the pub I had just vacated, their response was to wave their hands in return, what I missed as I turned to witness this event was a car pulling up by the lane way that the little girl, who I assumed to be Sarah, had taken refuge in, I just caught sight of someone else running into the alley, I could clearly see it was a man, and a man I knew.

Chapter Thirteen

Time and people, closing in!

Very carefully I entered the alleyway, I looked closely at the floor not wishing to disturb any of the items of accumulated rubbish that were scattered around the ground, I was paying more attention to where I was stepping when suddenly I was amazed at what I could see.

Stuart was stood in the shadows, some ten feet in front of me holding the little girl I had seen run into the alleyway, it was indeed Sarah, she was pulled tight to his big body, her soft sobbing muffled by his hand over her mouth; I could just make out the glint of her eyes as they caught the poor light coming from the tall street lights behind me as their orange glow began to replace the darkness. A strange silence had engulfed the entire area, I was aware of the traffic on the High Street behind me, but all of my senses were concentrating on little Sarah. And as I looked at Stuart things started to fall into place, information that hadn't registered when it had been said the first time suddenly became clear.
"You harm her Stuart!" I paused; this little girl meant so much to me, her looks that of her mother, grandmother and of course great grandmother, along with an innocence of my late sister, Rachel.
"Yea, and what the fuck will you do?" he replied, his tone full of anger, he continued, "you haven't got any of your fancy friends here to help you now, have you?" he paused again, I felt his eyes looking hard at me, then he added, "you certainly filled me in on the details of some of your acquaintances."
I wasn't sure what or who he was referring to, but it didn't stop me replying.
"You harm her and I'll track you down" I paused not wishing to sound over dramatic, gathering my thoughts I continued, "and I'll kill you myself, I won't need any help, believe me, I will see you to the end!" I said, my tone calm and still.
"Never, you won't get a second chance, this is the only one you've got, and I recall something Jan told me, it was about the time Gary gave you a good kicking, I know more about you, remember you've been telling me all about your weaknesses, so in truth you don't stand a chance against me!" he said, just then Sarah struggled to break free from his grip.
"Don't let him hurt me Andrew!" Sarah called. Her voice begging and harrowing, the hackles on the back of my neck reacted, tightening my cheek

muscles, before his hand covered her mouth again, silencing her for the moment.

This gave me the opportunity to ask a question, trying to stall Stuart, maybe long enough that I would be able to strike in the darkness, take him by surprise, even though the chances were slim I had to look at every possibility.

"What do you plan to do with her?" I asked as I made one step closer to him.

"Well, she'll do very nicely in one of the establishment Jan's brother set up!" he replied, cold and very much to the point, and he continued, "that was before his brother was killed, that is as I understand it."

"But Jan Van-Elderman is dead as well…" I began to say, my words drifted away as suddenly something else fell into place, information passed on to me from the inspector, to do with a meeting which I was supposed to have had with Jan in April, and then I recalled the habit the Dutchman had for disappearing, and other incidents from the not so distant past began to fall into a new sort of order.

"Well let's say that's what we wanted you to think," Stuart paused, Sarah wriggled a little, he tightened his grip, and continued, "and it would have worked if you'd done as you were told."

"So after all this time Stuart, I now find that you work for Jan Van-Elderman," I said trying to defuse the situation a little, and giving myself a little more time to think.

"Well you've taken your time in coming to that conclusion," Stuart started to say, he paused and I noticed him pull Sarah even tighter, then he continued, "judging by your remarkable recovery from the amnesia you were suffering from I can firmly assume that you haven't been taking your medication."

Alex's words came back to me, along with those of the inspector, Alex had only an hour ago told me not to take any more of those tablets, and the inspector had been unable to identify one particular tablet, so it was now with a little more sternness that I spoke to Stuart again.

"So that was how you did it, fed me full of drugs, keeping me in the dark," I paused and noticed his hand pull Sarah's head in tighter, I went on with a warning, "I'm telling you again, if you harm her, I'll track you down and personally kill you." I guessed what he might say with regard to Gary killing Jan's brother, I didn't want Sarah to know those facts yet, but my voice was now straining with the anger that I was feeling building inside of me.

"Oh Andrew," he mockingly started to reply, and he continued in the same vein, "she won't feel much pain, once the first time has passed, and then she'll soon get used to it!" was Stuart's reply to my threat of death upon him, an unpleasant casualness to his manner, and now with slight laughter in his tone, and he continued to speak knowing he had my full attention, "we have gone to such painstaking detail to get all of your new family into this situation, there's no chance of you messing it up now."

"What do you mean?" I asked stalling for time.

"We've been watching you for months, putting everything into place," he paused, coughed to clear his throat, then went on, "mind you nearly rumbled me yesterday."

"Sorry," I asked as I now felt that I'd missed a very important point.

"When you phoned me from the dressmakers house yesterday afternoon, I nearly answered with 'hello Andrew'," was his smart smug answer, he continued, "I guessed then that you weren't taking the medication I'd left with you, yes Andrew we even planned to have Mrs Walbridge make a wedding dress for my bride-to-be."

"And I can assume from what you have just told me that it was there that you laced the whisky, you really have gone to such a lot of trouble," I paused for now I was indeed far more informed than I had been, the planning had taken a lot of time and effort, Stuart and Jan Van-Elderman required a certain amount of admiration, but it didn't detract from what they had planned for Sarah and the immediate danger I found she was confronted with, so I issued my threat again, but now in a different style.

"You know Stuart, if you let her go we can bring this to an end now, and no more needs to be said," I told him, I noticed his head turn slightly, I continued, "or I'll carry out my threat, I'll find you and kill you."

"You don't stand a chance, she goes with me," he said as Sarah tried to move away from him.

"I don't think you heard what Mr Jackson said!" a dark sounding voice came from the equally murky shadows, a voice I knew, but what the hell was he doing here? I mentally asked myself.

"I smell a Kaffir!" was Stuart's reply, to the words of wisdom from the black man, in as much blackness as the night's darkness, and judging by that comment it proved Stuart must have spent a considerable time in South Africa.

"Now that's Mr Kaffir to you!" the voice from the depths of darkness replied, just a hint of sarcasm in his tone, adding, "white boy!"

I was taken aback, where the hell had E J come from, and just what was he capable of doing, I couldn't see him in the darkness, but his voice indicated that he was somewhere to the right hand side of the alleyway, possibly behind Stuart and Sarah, it gave me the chance to take one more step in the direction of Stuart, thinking he wouldn't try and make a move on me, for he was as equally unaware of the whereabouts of the owner of this voice from the night, as I was, but once I'd taken that step nearer I was to be reminded chillingly who was in charge.

"That's far enough Andrew!" that coldness back in his voice, then he went on, "you see I have an accomplice with a gun trained on your head, so as I've said you can't win, if you, or that nigger try anything I'll have you killed!"

I stood frozen to the ground, what the hell was I going to do, now not only did I feel for the little girl I loved as my own, but I feared for my own life, for now I was aware that I was in the position Gary had unknowingly found himself in some years ago.

"Oh!" the voice exclaimed again from the darkness, and he continued, as what seemed like a rolled up carpet landed about six feet in front of me, and a few feet in front of Stuart and Sarah, she let out a somewhat muffled scream, and E J continued "you must mean her! Now let me tell you white boy, she won't be doing any shooting!"

I looked hard into the darkness, in front of Stuart, there lay a body, completely motionless, it prompted him to speak.

"You, nigger will regret making an enemy of me, I'm going to kill the two of you, and then!" he paused, anger and frustration now strong in his voice, he still had the upper hand in this situation. I sensed he was about to say something that I would find revolting and hugely offensive, I struggled to make eye contact in the poor sodium orange street light, little Sarah continued to sob. "Yes, then I can have the pleasure of having her!" he said pulling her tight to his body again, his anger now replaced with a tone of superiority.

I felt sick, the adrenalin began to pump through my veins, my hands formed into fists, and I prepared to launch what I thought was to be a single handed attack on this man who I now felt nothing more than hatred for, I didn't give a thought for my own safety, I needed to get Sarah free, if I was to be injured or worse, killed it didn't matter, her safety was paramount in my mind, I had no idea of where E J was in the shadows, or how long it would take for him to come to my aid, I had to do something, but as I lurched forward, my hands now out in front of me, E J was to reveal his presence and his enormity to me, along with his agility.

For as suddenly as I moved forward a dark mass sprang from my right, he was now behind Stuart and Sarah, clearly I could see his outstretched hands as he gripped Stuart around his neck, the surprise of the vice-like grip forced Stuart to release his hold on Sarah, she took the opportunity to leap from his grasp and into my waiting outstretched arms, I pulled her in tight to my legs, then resumed my gaze at Stuart, slowly he began to sink to the ground as E J tightened his hold around Stuart's neck, his hands came up to take hold of E J's wrists in an effort to free himself, for now he couldn't breathe, the grip of E J's hands was so powerful.

Now Stuart was indeed a big man, but E J dwarfed him, I watched as the struggling began to lessen, Stuart's body became lifeless as he couldn't even draw air, but then the three of us were in for a surprise. But that wasn't before he had chance to speak, and pass on some very important information to me, along with one of his old phrases.

"We've been looking for this dude for some considerable time now Mr Jackson," E J said as Stuart made another feeble attempt to release E J's powerful hands, "Mr Jackson have I ever told you about the time..." he was cut short by another voice I recognised, and so did E J.

"Let him go E J!" someone said from behind me, the voice I knew of old, a voice that represented safety, along with authority, and the owner who had introduced E J to me in that hotel suite over a year ago, and I had been spending the afternoon with this individual, but it was E J who replied to the voice.

"But Mr A!" E J started to say, only to be cut short again by Alex.

"He won't be any use to me if you kill him, please let him go E J!" Alex said, even firmer now.

"I just want to teach him some respect, Mr A!" he said, I could clearly make out E J shake Stuart as he said the words.

"Now, I told you E J!" Alex said his voice now slightly higher, with even more authority

E J did as he was told, at the same time as releasing his grip he cast Stuart's body to the ground, I heard a thud as he hit the floor next to his dead accomplice, then another dull thump as I think E J projected his foot into Stuart's side, it would be some time before he would recover, but slowly I could make out Stuart as he started to regain his breath, he also started to cough.

Now I felt a presence at my side, Sarah was still holding on tightly to me, her crying had stopped, I ran my hand through her hair, the softness reminded me of her mother, I bent down and picked her up, her arms wrapped themselves tightly round my neck, then that other family trait, the kiss on the side of my cheek, my right hand around her tiny body I pulled her in close to me.

"I knew you wouldn't let anything happen to me Andrew," she told me softly, then words that would take my breath away in the same way as that little box had done all that time ago, "I love you Andrew."

This statement made my heart pound, tears formed in my eyes, my left hand came up to cradle her head, and she pressed it into my neck as I spoke.

"And I love you Sarah," I softly replied, I didn't need to say anymore, I knew she did, I never thought that I could love someone else's child, but all the time I'd spent with her was as rewarding as when my own children were small, they now were men, but this little girl had depended upon me to save her, I'd only played a part in that rescue, but it was me that she was clinging too.

"Are you alright Andrew?" it was the voice of Alex that asked the question as he got closer to us.

"Yes, I'm fine Alex," I replied as I turned to look at him, even in this dim light I could make out his smiling face, I looked him up and down, he was wearing his faithful old gabardine coat, open, the breeze just caught it, in his right hand an object of death.

"Is Sarah OK?" he asked, now his tone soft and warm, genuineness and concern in his voice as he looked again in our direction, then he asked, "would you like her to see a doctor?"

"I think she'll be alright Alex," I said, at the same time Sarah nodded her head in approval of my words, her arms pulled tightly around my neck.

I looked at Alex again; I watched as he put something inside his inner jacket, then he re-fastened his coat.

"Yes, you're right, even I had to be prepared," he told me as his now empty right hand came up to my shoulder and he read my thoughts.

Then he looked at the ground in front of him, I watched as his eyes scanned the entire area, and then he seemed to relax, just a little.

"E J what happened to her?" Alex asked, just as Stuart started to make more progress towards a recovery.

"Well Mr A, she put up a bit of resistance, that along with her having a gun!" E J replied, just then Stuart started to role over, I looked down at him, his own hands came up to his neck, and he began to rub the sides just below his cheeks.

"OK, I'll have to let you have this one!" was Alex's reply as he looked at the dead body on the ground, and he continued to ask E J a question, "is it that woman?"

"Yes Mr A, Melissa Thorne," E J replied, a feeling of sickness came over me, less than an hour ago I'd been sat opposite her in the bar down the street, and now I found she was an accomplice in some deadly deal.

Then Alex bent down to the side of Stuart, he was trying to get himself up, I watched, shielding little Sarah as best I could, as Alex removed the gun he had only just returned to the holster under his coat, E J stood towering over the two of them as Alex started to talk to Stuart.

"Now let me tell you one thing, and I'm only going to say it once, either you help me, or I'll let E J finish you off now, do I make myself perfectly clear?" Alex's words had coldness to them that I'd never heard before, a forthright clinical sound to every phrase, it was as if he was chastising a child who had done something wrong, and even I felt a shiver run down my spine.

In the time since discovering that Alex worked for the Special Forces, I'd learnt that he wasn't a man to be crossed, but neither was he an unnecessarily brutal man, this was business to him, he was a man of his word, if he said he would help then he would, so when he told Stuart that he could get E J to finish the job off he meant exactly what he said.

Stuart sat himself on the floor, I watched as he looked into Alex's eyes, it was the same look he'd given me when he was getting me to reveal my past, and in all probability he'd already known about what had gone on, but it was Alex who was speak again.

"Now," Alex began, pausing only momentarily he went on, "I'm not sure who I'm addressing, is it Stuart Thomas, or Thomas Douglas, you do seem to have a number of nom de plumes, don't you?" Alex said, he glanced up at

Sarah and me, then went on, "or perhaps you'd prefer me to call you by your Dutch name, Carl Heiger."

I noticed even in the dim light Stuart's facial expression change, not surprised, more startled; he was still rubbing his neck, and then had a reply for Alex.

"My, my, you have been busy since I saw you at the golf club this morning," he began to say, in something of a sneering manner, then looking up at me he went on, "but you never guessed Andrew."

"But it was *you* who planted the uncertainty in my mind," Alex started to reply, looking hard at Stuart, or whatever his name was, at the same time stopping me from saying anything, he went on, "if you'd replied when I'd asked where you had studied then it may never have come to this, but then, my friend Bert watered the seed of doubt that had been sown, and then once Andrew had shown me those tablets, well I had a nasty feeling something was not quite right, fancy feeding someone with Rohypnol." Alex looked at me as he spoke, I'd never heard of it before, but I was soon to be informed of what effect it has.

"It's more commonly known as one of the 'date rape drugs', mixed with alcohol the recipient can't remember a thing that has happened to them, and until Stavros turned up at your house Andrew, you had been taking them daily," Alex told me.

I felt angry that I'd been fooled so easily, but my mind was taken off the anger by Sarah moving in my arms, Alex spoke again.

"So you see, Stuart, Thomas, Carl, well, whatever you want to call yourself, we seem to know a great deal more about you than you think," he paused and I was unable to sense what tack Stuart would take, he just looked blank, Alex reminded him of the previous conversation.

"So either you help me, or," Alex stopped and looked up at the waiting E J, "I let this man finish the job." Alex's manner was calm and very much in control of the situation, and he had one more comment to add, and it was aimed at me. "Its best if you take Sarah home, and do as I told you this afternoon, relax, we'll deal with this from here." But I had a question for Stuart before leaving.

"So how did you manage to fool the authorities at the hospital?" I asked Stuart, still looking down at him on the ground.

"He's only a helper on the mental health wing Andrew," Alex informed me before Stuart had a chance to reply, but he did manage to squeeze in a comment.

"Your case notes were left lying around," he smugly said, and he added, "the National Health Service is in such a mess, but that private hospital was even worse."

"OK Alex," I replied recalling what he had previously told me with regard to going home, and kind of satisfied with the reply Stuart had given me, I looked into Sarah's eyes, they were saying something far more than any words could say, and it was as if she approved of what Alex had just told us to do.

So thinking that maybe those words of authority, tinged with a slight kindness in his tone had an effect on Stuart, I turned to walk away, now my eyes smarting from the brightness of the strong orange lights I was walking towards, still with Sarah in my arms, it was then that I heard Stuart's muffled reply to Alex's offer.

"You won't kill me; you're all fucking cowards, you English!" Stuart said, his reply was directed at Alex that I could make out, even though I was nearing the entrance to the alleyway, I just heard Alex speak, and that was telling me to carry on.
Once out on the High Street I put Sarah down, she took my hand.
"Thank you Andrew," she said as she looked up into my eyes, we walked along this now not so busy thoroughfare her tiny right hand gripping my left hand tightly, our pace quickened as we neared the side street where I had parked the Porsche, a press of the button and the doors were unlocked, along with a flash of the indicators, I opened the passenger's door, Sarah jumped into the seat, I was conscious that we may have been followed, and almost ran around the car to the driver's side, by the time I'd got into the car Sarah had fastened her seat belt and was looking directly at me, it was then that she was to surprise me.

"I know where mummy and James are Andrew," Sarah told me after I settled myself in the driver's seat of the Porsche.
"What?" I questioned as I pressed the buckle of the seatbelt into its clasp, then I inserted the key into the ignition lock, a turn and the engine started.
"I do, it's not far away," she replied still having gained my attention; she continued to speak as I began to manoeuvre the car out of the tight parking position, "but I think you'll need some help." She said as I pulled away.

"But Sarah I don't even know where we should start!" I said, thinking that maybe for safety sake we should go back and inform Alex that Sarah knew where her mother and brother were, and they would be able to take care of the situation.
"As I said Andrew, you'll need some help, and if you don't mind me saying so the best people to help you now are," she stopped as I pulled the car over to the side of the road, amazed at what this little girl was telling me, some one travelling behind me blew their horn, taken by surprise by the suddenness of my action.
"Just a minute Sarah, where do you think I'm going to get help from at this time of night?" I asked still digesting what she had just said, I was to be even more surprised by her next comment.

"Maybe William and Peter will help us!" was her reply, her face alight with childlike enthusiasm.

Only a few days ago William had almost convinced me that Louise, Sarah and James were dead, thoughts that were almost confirmed as I stood at the new grave site in the village church this afternoon, but things had taken a dramatic turn after William and I had discovered that letter. And to add credence to the situation I now had a very much alive Sarah in the car, and she was talking to me in the same manner as her mother would, forthright and to the point.

I was going to William's for dinner anyway, so if I turned up with Sarah, then perhaps they would help me, that was if we could draw up some sort of plan, my mind was racing, struggling to digest the information Sarah had just imparted to me, but then Sarah was to surprise me again with her next comment.

"Andrew, mummy says this car will go very fast," Sarah said looking across at me from the passenger's seat.

"Yes it will" I replied somewhat subdued, my mind still full of what I had just heard her say.

"Then Andrew, I suggest you put your foot down if we're going to help mummy and James!" she had the same forthright manner her mother had, and possessed the style and poise of Louise, for an eight year old girl her demeanour was very powerful.

"OK," I started to say, at the same time I checked in the mirror to see if it was clear to pull out into the flow of faster moving traffic; it was and I pressed the throttle hard, as always the response was instant, the engine growled back to me as we took off in the direction of my eldest son's house. As we progressed along the ring road I had a question of my own for this astute little girl.

"How did you manage to escape, Sarah?" I asked briefly looking at her as I did so.

"That was easy Andrew, I squeezed myself through the transom window in the bathroom," she paused, I glanced at her as she wriggled in the seat, then she continued, "the bathroom was between the two main bedrooms at the top of the stairs, at the back of the house, well the main window in the bathroom was locked, and before when I needed to go the toilet, that woman, Melissa would come with me, but once we were sure she was out of the way, I knew I could get through the window at the top, from there I was able to jump down onto a little roof, then I got down a drain pipe and into the garden." She finished, now with laughter in her voice, as if it had been an adventure to her.

"Well done," I started to reply, then a thought crossed my mind, well more of a question, "does mummy know that you planned to escape?"

"Oh yes Andrew," she started to reply, still with that excited tone in her voice, she went on, "mummy said I had to go to the police station, but I was spotted by that Stuart," she paused again, and added, "well whatever his name is."

"It was lucky I was going along the High Street when I saw you running into the alleyway," I started to say, only for Sarah to interrupt me.

"The house where mummy and James are being held isn't far away, well just across the road," she paused as I slowed down so as to negotiate a roundabout, as I pulled off onto the road that leads to William's house she continued.

"Andrew, you know where the car park is behind the bank on the High Street?" Sarah asked.

"Yes I know where you mean," I replied and surely I did, that is the car park linked to the High Street by the lane that I received a beating from Sarah's father, as Jan stood and watched, she continued as these thoughts continued to circulate in my head.

"Well the back of the house looks out over the car park, the front of the house has a large overgrown garden, with a big turning bay in front of it," she finished, and I knew exactly where she was talking about, the road to the house ran parallel with the High Street, then Sarah was to add one more detail, "it has a blue front door."

"OK," I replied as I neared William's house, I could see the lights on in the lounge as I pulled the Porsche on to the drive. William's car was parked in front of the garage doors. Parked with its front close to the dividing hedge was a light blue estate car, a set of ladders tied to the roof-rack, I assumed it to be the window cleaner's car that Peter and Liam had been called out to this afternoon, I didn't pay much attention to what make of car it was, I think it was a Ford. I turned off the engine, it stopped with its customary clatter, looking towards the house I noticed someone moving in the bay window of the lounge, and as I glanced across towards the front door, I saw a figure move past the frosted glass door, that I could clearly make out as William.

"Andrew," Sarah started to ask as I unfastened my seat belt, at the same time she did likewise, and then she continued with a question, "do you think we should surprise them?"

"Sarah," I began to say as I pulled on the door handle, "I don't think we'll have to arrange another surprise, seeing you will be enough." I watched as she too pulled on the passenger door handle, a push of the door and she was out of the car, seconds later and she'd skipped her way round to my side instinctively taking my hand as she neared me.

We walked to the front door, one press of the bell push, and only a moments wait for the figure I'd seen silhouetted against the frosted glass front door when we had pulled up, to turn and head for the door, it was indeed William, now somehow Sarah had, unknowingly to myself, slipped behind me, and as William opened the door he didn't instantly notice her.

"Hello dad," he started to say as he opened the oak framed opaque glass panelled door, he continued as he opened it further, "you're early," a startled look to his features.

"Yes I know I am," I replied, and was about to continue when Sarah stepped out from behind me, the look of surprise on William's face was amazing, as was his next comment.

"Christ dad, where did you find Sarah?" his mouth wide open with complete astonishment and almost disbelief.

"William, it's a long and very complicated story," I started to say, at the same time I looked down at Sarah, her face was one of beaming pleasure, her eyes sparkling as her mother's do when she is excited, and it was Sarah who spoke next, her manner exactly the same as Louise.

"Andrew is right William, and we need yours and Peter's help to rescue mummy and James," she said, her style, straight to the point, it was as she said those words that I noticed Natasha at the far end of the hall, she at the same time noticed me, instantly she headed in the direction of the open door and William.

"Andrew," she softly said, concern in the word, as she neared us and could see Sarah now standing at my side, she went on with a question, "Sarah darling where have you been?"

Natasha bent down and Sarah almost jumped into her waiting arms, I looked down at them, Sarah's back was towards me, Natasha's eyes were watering with delight at seeing this little girl, then Natasha spoke and at the same time she stood.

"William, bring your father indoors, don't keep him on the doorstep," she said as she headed along the hall with Sarah in her arms.

"Yes, come on in dad," William started to say as I stepped over the threshold, once in the hall he continued, "this has come as such a shock, it's left me completely speechless."

"That I can tell," I said as I neared the doorway leading into the lounge.

"What can you tell, dad," Peter asked as he also entered the room, that was followed by another question, his voice as surprised as the enquiry "where did Sarah come from?"

"It's a long story Peter, and I'm not sure of all of the details," I started to reply to my youngest son, and I continued, "but I could do with some…" I was cut short by Sarah.

"We need your help to rescue mummy and James," she said as Natasha and she entered the lounge, Sarah still in Natasha's arms.

"What's going on, I thought I heard Sarah's voice…" it was Sophie who spoke as she entered the lounge, then looking at Natasha she continued, "oh my god, where have you come from?" at the same time she ran her right hand over Sarah's head, then instantly she put her arms around both Sarah and Natasha gripping them tightly she continued albeit in somewhat softer and less alarmed tones, "Sarah, we thought you were dead, I'm sorry if I alarmed you."

"That's OK, as you can see I'm not dead," Sarah replied and at the same time she reached out from the arms of Natasha and kissed Sophie, then turned her attention to Natasha, a long kiss for her as well, then more words, "but we do need the help of William and Peter if we are going to save mummy and James."

"What sort of help do you mean?" William asked as he looked into Sarah's eyes, and added another question, "how do you mean save your mother and James?"

"That man, Jan, I think his name is," Sarah paused, maybe to confirm she had our full attention, then she continued, "well he said he was going to take us all to Holland, he even said he would kill mummy if she didn't do as she was told..." I cut Sarah short, I felt as if I and the others had heard enough, there was no point in her reliving any more of the details of her confinement, along with that of Louise and James.

"Sarah told me that she was being held at the old place in Bank Road," I quickly said.

"What, the old witch's place?" Peter asked, this comment was something of reference to both his and William's childhood, the house having been a place all children seem to give a wide berth too, probably having something to do with the occupant, a wizened old woman who had the appearance of a witch, and the accompanying stories that seem to circulate around such people.

"But the place has been empty for ages," Sophie said, joining in with the conversation.

"I noticed it had been sold," Natasha said, she paused and we could see she was trying to recall some details, "yes I saw the sold sign in the garden back in May, mind you not much has been done to it since then."

"Sarah said she needed our help," Peter said breaking the topic of the house the witch used to occupy, and he went on, "well if it is just a case of going up there and finding them, then I'm up for it, what about you Will?"

"I think it might be a little more complicated than just knocking on the door," I interjected noticing Peter's enthusiasm to get on and do the job, I continued with a question to Sarah, "do you know how many men there are at the house?"

"Well," she began and looking hard into my eyes she continued after a moments thought, "there was that man that you saw in the lane, his name was Carl, there is also that Jan, and I think another two in the house all the time."

"Carl, or as I knew him Stuart is well and truly out of the way," I started to say, I noticed a puzzled look on William's face and felt that I needed to enlighten him, "Alex took Carl away, so that leaves at least three in the house." I didn't feel a need to enlighten William as to why Alex was involved, that would keep for later.

"Not a problem," Peter emphatically replied at the same time smashed his right fist into the palm of his left hand.

"But we don't know what these people may be capable of," I questioned, not wishing to dampen his enthusiasm, but at the same time not wanting to be foolhardy.

"Dad the best form of attack is always surprise," William said, he'd picked up on Peter's willingness to get on and do the job, and he continued, "they won't be expecting us, if we leave it to the police then it could be too late."

I looked at Sarah, she shared the boy's fervour, her eyes telling me to get on with the job in hand, after all, it was Sarah who had said that my sons would be able to help, to say no now would not only show a lack of confidence in them, but also a lack of faith in her judgement.

"OK, but we need to be very clear on what we are going to do," I said and as I did I noticed Sarah's eyes light up, her arms came out in front of her and I took her from Natasha.

"You'll be OK," she whispered in my ear as I held her tight.

"We'll take my car so that we can get in and out fast," I said, but as soon as I'd made the statement Peter had a comment of his own.

"No we won't, it makes too much bloody noise," he paused and we all waited his next offering, "I've got just the car outside."

"That'll do nicely," William said confirming his brother's idea.

"What if it breaks down again?" I asked with just the slightest concern in my voice.

"Do have some faith dad," Peter replied.

I looked again at Sarah, her head was slightly tilted, her eyes probing, the same look her mother possessed, I couldn't escape from her intense gaze, and I couldn't let her and the rest of the family down.

"Let's do it then," I said, at the same time I kissed Sarah on her brow. Softly she said "good" in reply. It was then that Natasha stepped in, once again her arms outstretched in readiness to take Sarah from me.

"Tell you what, while William, Peter and Andrew go and fetch mummy and James, why don't I give you a nice bath," she paused long enough for Sarah to nod her head in approval, and then Natasha continued, "I'm sure we can find something nice and clean for you to put on by the time mummy and James get back, and perhaps you can have some supper as well."

"OK, but let me see the boys go first," Sarah replied, by now there was tiredness in her voice, I'd no idea of how long we had been standing around talking, or for that matter how long Sarah had been awake, and it must have seemed obvious to Natasha that she would need some food.

"I promise that we won't be long," I said at the same time I took her hands, I could now see fear, or it may have just been the tiredness, I felt a hand on my back, turning slightly I could see it was William.

"Come on then dad, let's go and do the business," he said as he also directed me in the direction of the hall.

Now for some reason as we stood at the front door, I turned and kissed both Sophie and Natasha, when it came to Sarah, I held her face in both of my hands and kissed her tenderly on the forehead.

"Take care," she said, as Peter opened the driver's door of the estate car that was parked on the drive.

"I will," I replied as I made my way out on to the top step, momentarily I stood still, just taking in the night air and the stillness that accompanied it, faintly in the distance the sound of traffic on the ring-road, I looked down at the window cleaner's car as Peter started the engine, it started with a clatter, and a cloud of smoke was issued from the exhaust, William was stood by the open passenger rear door, as I made my way down the few steps to the driveway Sarah called to William, his response was to return up the steps, it was as I got into the car that I thought I heard Sarah say something to William.

"William," Sarah began, she paused, then having gained his attention she continued, "take care of daddy," her words were spoken softly, and I wasn't sure if I was meant to hear them, I faintly heard William's reply.

"I will darling, I will." He softly said, and at the same time leant forward and kissed the little girl on her cheek.

Natasha pulled Sarah close to her as William returned to the car, he jumped into the front passenger's seat with the ease of a twenty-something-year-old, and we pulled our doors closed in unison. As we pulled away I watched Sarah's hand go up and wave, I did likewise, but I didn't turn my head to look back.

Chapter Fourteen

A house and its captives!

As we pulled out of William's drive and onto the main road Sarah's words to William came back to me, they lingered in my head as we sped of in the direction of the main road that only a little while I had come from.

Sarah's request to William became more poignant as we drove along the ring-road heading for the town centre, it seemed as if the past was now rushing back into my mind, it was as we were on our way to the dressmaker's that Sarah and James had had a dispute, and that was caused by James referring to me as daddy, now here I was still with Sarah's words going round and round in my head, I was to be snapped out of this trance-like state by my eldest son asking me a question.

"You alright dad?" he asked, I looked up and into his eyes, there was no point in not replying to his question, just as I was about to, and tell him my thoughts we drove over what seemed like a massive pothole, the whole of the car rocked and that included us three occupants, that together with the clatter of the ladders on the roof of the car almost deafened us, and for one moment I thought they were about to join us in the car.

"I'm fine," I replied but in reality I was anything but fine, for now I was beginning to feel somewhat nervous, but I didn't want William or Peter to know that fact, so I continued in a light-hearted vein. "Peter you said my car was noisy."

I heard him laugh a response as we clattered over another pothole.

"Dad the ladders may come in handy," William said as we approached the one-way system that encircles the town centre. We weren't very far away from the garage, and I did wonder why Peter had the car anyway, so I put that question to William.

"What made you bring this car home?" I asked, at the same time trying to make out in the darkness exactly where we were.

"It was late when Liam and I got back to the garage, I couldn't be bothered to move my car, so I dropped Liam off at his home and went back to Will's in this," Peter replied half turning his head with his response, kind of directing his conversation in my direction. I didn't get a chance to say anything else because William informed us that we were in fact outside of the 'witch's old place'.

Very slowly Peter turned the car into the drive, the privet hedges at the entrance were indeed very overgrown, they brushed against both sides of the car as we entered, they obscured any view of the old stone pillars that had once supported some fine wrought iron gates. Carefully Peter drove along the drive, and as the house came into view we could see some of the lights were on, light shining out through the gaps in the curtains where they hadn't been pulled together very well.

As we got nearer I could make out the full details of this house, it was of a double bay villa- type construction, the blue, partly glazed front door being in the centre of the building, and above this entrance was a tiled roof that went from one bay to the other, two or three steps led to the door, the area in front of it being quite large. I looked up towards the first floor windows, the curtains weren't drawn, and the rooms appeared to be in darkness. And that darkness seemed to surround the building, as my eyes adjusted to the poor light I could make out a van parked to the right hand side of the house, and as I studied it I could see it was a camper van, a Volkswagen at that.

"Let's just suss the place out first," Peter said as we neared the steps and the car came to a halt.

"Perhaps they've moved Louise and James," I said, not really thinking, I suppose I'd been expecting to see someone outside, and to all intents and purposes it looked as if there was no one here.

"Tell you what, I'll give them a knock," Peter said after switching off the engine, next he pulled on the door handle, in what seemed like a flash he was out of the car and up the steps, his right hand banging on the half-glazed front door.

"Get your head down dad!" William instantly told me, I did without thinking what he had told me, and as I struggled to make out what was going on he informed me as to his reasons. "If that Jan bloke comes to the door, he might recognise you, then we won't have a chance, I'll tell you when it's safe for you to look."

I felt as if my head was pressed between my knees, all the time I was struggling to hear what was being said, after what seemed like an age my son spoke again.

"Look now dad, is that Jan?" William asked.

Very carefully I lifted my head, looked towards the steps and the now open half glazed door, dim light was emitting from it. I could see a man stood facing Peter, he was about the same height as my son, but his hair was light, I would say blond, he wasn't as broad as Peter, he was gesturing with his hands, but it seemed as if the person he was talking to couldn't understand what was being said to him, out of curiosity I began to wind down the car window.

"No, that's not Jan," I quietly replied to William, and then I was able to pick up on what Peter was saying.

"We are vision technicians," Peter said very slowly, and at the same time looked in the direction of the car.

"What are you talking about?" the man asked, his accent being one of Scandinavian descent and his words were broken, not being formed fully.

Peter lowered both of his arms to his side, shrugged his shoulders, and then made another comment as he once again looked this man in the eyes.

"We will be working in the area tomorrow, and wondered if you could do with your…" he was cut short by the man standing opposite him.

"Why don't you fuck off and leave me alone," he said, at the same time gesturing with his hands, but this time the words were clear, and his accent stronger.

"What did you say?" Peter asked a touch of anger and frustration in his own voice. It wasn't long before he got another abrupt reply.

"You heard, go, fuck off," the foreigner repeated his original request; he too was now looking at the car, adding, "and take that with you!"

Peter took one step towards the steps that led down onto the bay in front of the house, I thought he was going to come back to the car, but he stopped dead in his track, quick as a flash he spun on his left foot, at the same time I watched as his right hand came up, his speed and aim were perfect, his fist made contact with the left side of the man's jaw, his head went back as he absorbed the blow, it was one hell of a punch and he was on his way to the floor, Peter did grab his body before he hit the ground, he was out cold, Peter's action saved this man having a bump on the back of his head as well.

"I only wanted to know if he wanted his windows cleaned," Peter called to us as we looked on, and he continued, "no one tells me to fuck off, and certainly not twice," he paused again, and then had a request for us, "see if you can find some rope in the back of the car. William and I jumped out of the car, as Peter began to pick up the man, I sent William to help his brother as I began to rummage in the back of the car, I found a plastic bucket and placed it by the side of the car, and then to my surprise I discovered a coil of rope.

"Is this any good?" I called to the boys as they neared me with this person between them, Peter had hold of his arms and William his feet.

"Bloody right it will," Peter replied as they got closer.

I stood speechless as Peter first placed the bucket over the man's head, then proceeded to tie the rope to the handle, he continued to secure the man's hands behind his back, pulling the rope quite tightly, and then onto his feet, he did resemble a poorly trussed chicken, well, slightly. Between them they placed the individual in the bushes at the front of the dwelling.

"Well being in the scouts did have some advantages dad," he light-heartedly said as he looked at me, then his brother, rubbing his hands together at the same time as if he was dusting the dirt from them.

"Right," William began to say looking towards the open doorway, he continued, "I think we need to get into the house, there are at least two others in there."

"Well maybe it would be best if I go indoors," I replied, by now after watching the actions of my younger son the adrenalin was pumping through my veins, the fear I had earlier experienced was subsiding. I could feel the eyes of both of my sons looking at me, maybe questioning my statement, even my judgement at such a comment.

"And what, dad, are we going to do?" Peter asked testing my reason for the statement I'd just issued.

"Perhaps you could take these ladders and have a look through the windows at the back of the house, maybe you'll locate Louise and James in the back bedroom," I swiftly replied.

"First I'll take care of that van," William said as he made his way in the direction of the camper van, Peter began to remove the ladders from the top of the car, I carefully made my way up the steps of the house, it was poorly lit, and was also in need of renovation, from where I was stood I could see the walls were yellow, the paper old, and in places it was beginning to peel from the walls. The odd thing I noticed was the lack of sound, I would have expected to hear voices, or maybe a television or radio, as I stepped over the threshold I could see that all of the interior doors were closed, the paintwork faded over the years of neglect, dirty smudge marks were evident around the door handles.

"I've sorted the van dad," William said, and now he was at my side, his words spoken softly so that no one else could hear, he placed his hand on my shoulder, and spoke again, "Pete's got the ladder off the car and is going to have a look through the side window upstairs, I'm going round the back to take a look," he paused as he started to turn, we were only a few yards into the hall, both of us noticed an alcove, he added, "stay there until I come back."

I did as he told me, stepped into the dark and cobweb-strewn hideaway, I had to brush the thick dirty webs off of my face, I felt very uncomfortable, not fear, just a feeling of being useless, then without warning I heard a noise come from behind one of the closed doors, followed by a man's voice calling another man. A rattle of cutlery indicated the owner of the voice was in the kitchen, strangely it was a voice I recognised, it belonged to a local person, and someone that had been in the Manor not so long ago. The individual called out again with the same question.

"Carl, Hans is that you?" he paused maybe expecting a reply, then continued in an abusive manner, "you got that fucking kid yet Carl ?" he once again stopped, sensing the lack of response he called the two names in a questioning style again, but now with what I would describe a nervousness in the words, "Hans, Carl, you there?"

Now I knew who Carl was, even though I had referred to him as Stuart, and Hans I assumed to be the individual Peter had taken care of, but getting no reply didn't stop this man from continuing.

"Jan is planning to move on in the morning, it can't have been that difficult to have caught her," his words now had a more worrying tone to them.

I stepped out from the confines of this dark and dinghy alcove just as the door that I assumed led into the kitchen opened, the light that was emitted was quite strong, it made me squint, the door opened into the hall and I managed to dodge behind it without being noticed, my eyes still smarting from the shock of the light. I watched as the individual came into view, his gaze was on the open front door, instantly he sensed that something was wrong, and he began to back track into the kitchen, what was I to do? I asked myself, I was completely alone in the hall; I made up my mind to go into the kitchen and confront this person. I pulled the door fully open and was instantly in eye contact with the owner of the voice, he was one of the engineers who had fitted the alarm and security system at the Manor.

"Mr Jackson, what the f...." he started to ask, his manner very startled, I placed my index finger of my right hand over my lips, and I could see that his left hand was behind his back.

"I could ask you the same thing," I started to reply, and feeling that I required an answer I continued, "just what are you doing here?"

"He paid me well," he paused then went on, "now get out of my way." His words were spoken firmly, almost an urgency to them, then to my horror he produced a long-bladed kitchen knife from behind his back, the black handle gripped tightly in his left hand, the blade glinted in the light from the fluorescent tube attached to the kitchen ceiling, and then he issued more words, "you'd better let me go by."

As he spoke, I noticed William at the kitchen window, he was nodding his head from side to side, I would say perhaps, indicating for me to let this individual pass, I made up my mind that I wouldn't. I stepped out of the doorway backwards, but my left hand was still on the door itself.

"OK," I said as this person neared me, I went on as he got closer, "have it your way, but if you're looking for Hans, I'm afraid you won't find him."

"Shut the fuck up Jackson," was all he could respond with, now with anger in his voice, the knife was held out in front of him still in his left hand.

Suddenly his name came back to me, so I thought it maybe best if I played it in a different style.

"It's Mike, isn't it, why don't we have a chat?" I said stopping him in his tracks.

"My name is Nick, not Mike," he replied angrily, then after pausing he went on, "you can't buy me off."

"Whatever made you think I would try and buy you off, as you put it," I said, at the same time I noticed his left arm relax slightly, he was still standing in the kitchen, his hand with the kitchen implement still out in front of him, it was now or never, I thought, I couldn't risk looking in the direction of the kitchen window to see if William was there or not.

With my left hand I pulled the door as hard as I could, the action caught Nick by complete surprise, and my speed was most impressive, I managed to jam his hand between the door and the door frame, momentarily I released it slightly, and then I resumed the pressure of the door on his wrist, placing my left foot against the bottom of the door, the pain must have been excruciating,

I could hear him cry out in agony, but he had more pain to come, but he released the object in his hand.

The knife fell to the ground, the pointed end embedded itself in the floor, I bent down to pick it up as I did so released the pressure on the door, as it opened I noticed Nick was looking at his left wrist, massaging it frantically with his right hand, I looked for William through the window at the rear of the kitchen, but he was gone, I assumed he was on his way to the front of the house, by now Nick was beginning to recover, he was still rubbing the wrist of his left arm, before he had chance to say anything, I smashed him in the face with my clenched right fist, the shock of the impact making my elbow hurt in the process, he went back, now with both of his hands clutching his face, the blow was enough to make him fall backwards, before he landed on the floor, I rushed into the kitchen, placing the knife on the work surface by the door as I entered, then I leapt over his body, now both of my hands gripping him by his throat, I held him to the ground, then I had a question for him.

"Where's Jan?" I demanded, looking into his eyes, I continued, "I'm not alone." He didn't respond, so I lifted his head off the floor and banged it back down, still no response, in fact it was then that I realised Nick was quite lifeless, the blow to the face had completely knocked him out, he was unconscious, and by now there was a steady stream of blood coming from his nose.

"Shit," I said out loud to myself, and continued to think, he's no use now, and he wasn't, but he could present a danger very shortly, I looked around the kitchen, I needed to tie Nick up, just to make things safer for myself, the first thing I spotted was the electric lead for the kettle, after taking it off the side I rolled him over, tied both of his hands behind his back, I realised that I needed to immobilise him completely, so after taking the microwave oven off the work surface next to the sink, I secured his feet with the flex, still attached to the device, it was as I was moving Nick to the side of the kitchen that he started to regain consciousness, his eyes were still rolling as I started to ask him again where his master was.

"Where's Jan?" I asked, now safe in the knowledge that Nick couldn't retaliate.

"Upstairs," he paused and tried to move his body.

"Tell me where?" I enquired again, now there was no point in threatening Nick again, he was helpless that was apart from his mouth.

"In the back bedroom on the left at the top of the stairs," Nick began to say, he paused as he recalled more of his own recent past, then he continued, "he had a migraine come on, just after that kid got away, so he went for a lie down." Nick told me, I stopped him by putting my finger over my lips, as he'd spoken I realised the reason for the house being in relative darkness, I also remembered Sarah saying that Louise and James were being held in one of the rear bedrooms, that being on the right at the top of the stairs.

I looked down at Nick, he didn't struggle, he must have realised he was beat, a pool of blood was now beginning to form on the floor, I rolled him back on to his stomach, and grabbing hold of his belt and the top of his shirt I forced his head between two units, my reasoning being that any vocal noise he made would be deafened as he would be calling into the floor, not only that, but William and Peter would soon be in the house and may well take him outside.

All of these events had taken place very quickly, I hadn't given a lot of thought for my own safety, but now as I looked at the back of my right hand, I could see the skin was grazed and had been bleeding, just a little, I still felt no pain, that I put down to the rush of adrenalin, it was still pumping though my veins, driving me on, making me think and react quickly.

I looked in the direction of the open door, and then I recalled that Nick had made a considerable bump when he hit the floor, it could have been enough to disturb Jan, I grabbed the knife off the unit as I started to head for the hall, and ultimately the stairs.

The front door was still open, the thought did cross my mind that the boys should be on their way by now, but I also knew that I had to get on with the job in hand, and single handed I was.

Carefully I made my way up the stairs, each tread seemed to creak and groan no matter how lightly I progressed, the knife in my right hand, my left gripping the loose and rickety banister, as I reached the top I turned and looked around me, in front, a large landing, to my right a door, leading I assumed to one of the front bedrooms, as I turned back I could see directly in front of me three doors, the middle one being the bathroom door, on the left side the bedroom that Jan was in, the one to the right, where Louise and James were being held, as I studied the door I noticed a padlock just above the old china door handle, that confirmed my thoughts that they were in there, I stopped myself from calling their names, I wanted to be sure that Jan was disabled, slowly I walked across the dry timber boards, they seemed to softly screech with every step I took.

I placed my right hand on the door handle, the knife now in my left hand, I thought it best if I entered the room slowly, as I began to twist the handle I heard a noise downstairs, I assumed it to be William or Peter, but by now had committed myself to going into the room, it was too late to call to them, slowly I opened the door, in the dim light I could see a double bed on the far side of the room, as I looked harder I could make out a figure laying under the covers, the curtains were drawn, and it was a struggle to see anything more than an outline, I moved closer, so far it was the only part of the house that hadn't announced my imminent arrival before I'd got to my intended destination.

As I neared the bed and my eyes became accustomed to what light there was, I could see it was Jan on the bed, I took the knife in my right hand, I didn't want to use it, but I was being driven by fear and adrenalin, I moved closer to the side of the bed, the side where Jan was laying, looking down at the big man he seemed so still, completely motionless, I prepared to wake him, I lowered the knife to only inches away from his throat, then suddenly his eyes opened, I didn't move backwards, but wished I had, his sudden awakening was such a shock, and he was to catch me out again, his agility and strength was beyond control, and certainly mine, his right hand came up from the bed with lightning speed, at the same time he rolled over onto his back, his fist caught me squarely on the chin, sending me backwards, in the process loosing my balance, I began to fall, in an effort to steady myself I dropped the knife, Jan was out of bed in a shot, I swung my right fist, hoping that I might catch him a glancing blow, he moved his body, and I failed to connect with the target, then much to my surprise he grabbed hold of me by my shirt, saving me from falling to the floor.

"I've been waiting to meet you again Jackson," he said as he steadied me. I was lost for words, still trying to recover from the blow to my chin, my right hand came up to rub the injured area. Slowly I began to regain my senses, still holding me upright Jan bent down and picked up the knife, holding it in his left hand he spoke again, "and what the fuck were you going to do with this?" he asked as he held it close to my throat, a wisecrack now was not the best thing I thought, I knew Jan had a reputation for being ruthless, I didn't want to become a victim, well not just yet, so I began thinking it best if I pick my words carefully.

"I don't understand what difference you have with me," I asked as I steadied myself, to my surprise Jan let go of me, not only had he been maintaining my balance, he also kept my full body weight from being on my feet, I wobbled a little as he lowered his powerful right hand.

"Don't you recall the last time we met?" Jan asked, I would say in something of a relaxed manner, oh yes I remembered our last encounter all too well, but before I had chance to answer, Jan continued, "it was with your Greek friends." There seemed to be a coldness to his words now, and I was to be given the reason for his frosty tone.

"Well they had me packed off to South Africa," he paused, his words were spoken perfectly, the last time I'd seen Jan he was full of anger, an unwillingness to co-operate, but now apart from his Dutch accent his words were precise, and he was very articulate, he spoke very softly, "that wasn't such a hardship, I met up with some old acquaintances, we, how you English say, 'rubbed along together' quite well, plenty of opportunities in South Africa," he stopped so as to look at me a little closer in the dim light, then he went on. "Well one day I was reading a newspaper, and guess what?" I didn't need to guess, I had a damn good idea what was coming next just by looking in Jan's eyes.

"Your face was plastered across the front pages," he said, with just a little anger back in his voice, but at the same time the slightest of smiles to his features.

"Was it?" was all I could respond, but at the same time a gut instinct told me there was more to come, Jan didn't fail me.

"It was when you had been kidnapped, I followed the news with interest, but the thing that really did piss me off was seeing the picture of the real Mrs Shaw in the newspaper," he stopped and I thought I might have the chance to explain the reasons for substituting Louise with Nana, but he didn't allow me to, he went on. "You and the rest of the Greeks made me feel like a fool, I vowed I would take my revenge, and I'm going to."

Now not only were his words spoken with controlled anger, but as I looked into his eyes I could see they were full of rage, if after taking care of Louise, James and me, would Jan take his anger out on our adoptive family? It prompted a question from me.

"What do you plan to do with us?" I asked.

"That Andrew," Jan sneeringly began to reply, calling me by my forename for the first time, and he went on, "is my business," but then he had a question of his own, "how did you get past Nick and Hans?" his eyes as puzzled as the enquiry.

"Just a bit of luck," I began with my reply, in something of a casual manner; I didn't want him to know that William and Peter were in the building, as I thought.

"OK," he said, accepting my reply, Jan went on, "I shall re-unite you loved ones and then go and kick their asses," with those words he instantly spun me round one hundred and eighty degrees I was still in a dazed state from the blow to my chin, I wobbled on my feet, Jan's reaction was to grab me around the neck with his left arm, in the process pulling me close to him, my back against his front, he lifted me with his arm, he'd taken the knife in his right hand, as he brought it to my throat he spoke, "you try anything, and I'll kill you first."

So his intentions were to kill me, Louise and James at some time or another, it was just a matter of waiting, he had just told me that he intended going downstairs to remind his accomplices of their duties, then it came to me that the boys may well take care of him, it settled my mind a little, he was a big man, but I felt sure that William and Peter could handle him.

Jan marched me out of his bedroom, holding me tight by my neck, as we approached the other bedroom I noticed him stab the knife into the doorframe, next he pushed a light switch to the on position, then he proceeded to remove a bunch of keys out of his right hand trouser pocket, a flick of his wrist and the padlock was undone, he pushed the door open and at the same time tossed me into the room, I fell to the floor in something of a heap, as Jan pulled the door shut he spoke, "I'll leave the light on." I heard him replace the lock in the clasp, and also as he made his way down the stairs, they seemed to creak all the more, but then Jan was a big heavy man.

Now, as I lay on the bare floor, the light was my biggest problem, I pushed my glasses up onto my head in an effort to massage my eyes, I looked around the room, my eyes trying to focus, as my glasses slipped back down and onto my nose I could see Louise standing in the corner of the room, James was in her arms, two small beds also occupied part of the room, the rest of the bedroom was dank and bare, the grubby walls indicated the place hadn't been cleaned or decorated for years. I looked up at Louise from the floorboards where I had landed, she looked frightened, drawn and a little bewildered but at the same time resolute, as I began to stand I noticed her pull James closer to her but it was James who was to break the silence between us.

"Daddy," he said, and his arms came out in readiness for me to take him from Louise, she seemed to maintain her cautious look at me.

"Everything is OK," I said softly as I rose to my feet, and I went on, "William and Peter are downstairs, we'll be out of here in no time at all." I told Louise and James as confidently as I could, in my own mind unsure of what the boys were doing, at the same time hoping that they would have taken care of Jan. I began to approach Louise and the waiting James, I looked at her, she seemed now dazed, I put it down to having been in the dark, as I got closer she spoke.

"I knew you'd come!" Louise said as her arms released James for me to take him, and take him I did in my left arm, and at the same time I took Louise in my right arm, but to my surprise Louise didn't respond, she almost pulled away, forcing me to ask a question.

"What is it?" I asked knowing full well that she and the children had had the most awful of times; I added sensing something was deeply wrong, "but *you* don't seem that pleased to see me."

"Jan said you would show up sooner or later," Louise replied as she moved away from me slightly.

"I don't understand," I began to say, then realising that more had gone on than just the three of them being kidnapped, I continued with another question, "what has Jan told you darling?"

"Just, that you have been in charge of this whole affair, since you had Gary killed, right up to having the children and me kidnapped," she replied.

I looked at her astonished, I couldn't believe what I had just been told, but then I remembered what I had been through in the past few days to a week; perhaps someone had been applying a similar process to Louise, attempting to brainwash her into believing almost anything.

"But *you* know that isn't true," I said in response to what she had just told me, my tone quite firm, all the time wondering if I would be able to convince her otherwise, I looked her hard in the eyes, she had always been able to hide any emotions, unlike myself, my thoughts and feeling were always given away by my eyes, Louise had the ability to look deep into my inner self and in the process reveal those hidden secrets, now stood only a few feet from her I was worried, concerned that it may require professional help to release her from the mentally trapped state of mind she was in, then there was that trick, the knack of surprise that the female line of the family processed, as I continued to look at Louise her eyes just glinted, sparkled a little, the smallest of smiles began to form, my confidence returned, it was a confidence I had in Louise, and it proved she was more resilient, much stronger, and capable of handling anything that Jan and his accomplices could throw at her, it was confirmed with her words.

"Of course I do darling," she said at the same time her face beamed, a full smile had formed, and this reinforced my earlier feelings, she continued as she saw my reaction, "come here!" Her arms opened wide, I fell into them still holding James. After what seemed like a few moments we released our grip on each other, it was then that I needed to ask another question.

"Has he hurt you?" I enquired, as I began to study the room Louise and the children had been kept in.

"No Andrew," Louise started to reply, and she continued, "he started to ask some awkward questions, that was when I began to feign my replies, letting them believe what they wanted to," she paused and then went on, "it bought us some time, but I think Jan had been busy long before he got to us." I was about to reply when we both heard a noise on the stairs, sensing it was Jan on his way back up them I went over to the window, there I pulled the curtains back, but there was no outlook, it was black, I pressed my face to the glass, it was then that Louise spoke.

"I think they have been painted black on the outside," she said, I rubbed the glass with my hand.

"Yes I'm sure you're right," I replied as I couldn't see a thing through them. It was as I spoke that we heard the lock being undone, then the door opened, Jan was silhouetted against the darkness of the landing, the knife still in his right hand, and he had a question, one that would take me by surprise, for it wasn't what I expected him to ask.

"Why is the microwave on the floor in the kitchen?" he asked his eyes scanning the room, checking that the three of us were still in the room, strange I thought to myself, why didn't he ask, why was Nick tied to the microwave? But before I had chance to answer his first question he fired another at me.

"Just tell me, where are Nick and Hans?" he didn't mention Carl, or Sarah, I assumed he must have known they wouldn't be coming back, but the rage was now beginning to show in his voice. What could I say? I didn't know where Nick was, I'd left him on the floor of the kitchen, attached by his feet to the microwave, hands tied behind his back, and his head wedged between two kitchen units, as for Hans, to the best of my knowledge he was inspecting an overgrown bush at front of the house. At the same time I was unsure of what the boys were up to, I felt sure it would only be a matter of time and they would come to our aid, best I play it cool I thought to myself, but Louise was to come to my rescue with a complete change of subject.

"Andrew, tell Jan how the police sergeant managed to shoot Gary!" she quickly interjected, perhaps sensing my uncomfortable feeling.

"You don't have to," Jan began to reply almost cutting Louise short, before I had my chance to say a word; he continued quite freely, "yes I've taken care of him." Shit I thought to myself, I wished I had a tape recorder with me now, that was a full blown confession, and he then continued, "anyway, I don't think it was him, he was never sober enough to hold a pint, let alone a gun," he paused and could tell he had our attention, he continued with some grisly details, "he told me that he didn't even know who killed your husband, that was as I was strangling him," his reply once again a disclosure of his brutality.

"Then who was it?" I quickly asked, at the same time trying to sound surprised at Jan's confession of guilt, I looked at Louise, she indicated for me to cover James's ears, even though we didn't refer to Gary as the children's father we had always been aware that they may have been able to connect the name to him.

"That is something I intend to find out," Jan began with his reply, I have to say in the most chilling of ways, and he continued, "then I'm going to kill them."

"Jan. What about Andrew, James and me?" Louise asked, her tone soft and relaxed, maybe she figured that there was no point in antagonising Jan; after all she had spent longer with him.

"What about you three?" Jan started to say, and just relaxing a little he went on, "I intend to kill you..." he paused again, and then continued, "well, sooner or later."

"Why?" I asked, still trying to fathom this individual out, I'd already realised there was no point in trying to buy him off, to offer would only offend and could possibly irritate the situation all the more.

"As I've told you Andrew, you really did piss me off, taking me for a fool," Jan replied, and he hadn't finished, now with real anger in his voice he continued, "seeing the two of you in the papers made me angry, no one makes me to be their fall guy, this has taken so much planning, I'm really going to make you pay, then kill you!"

I was completely puzzled by his statement, what reason did he have for kidnapping Louise and the children? But then another question came to me, and that was with regard to making me pay, was it something to do with the South African venture, so I asked him, but in a roundabout manner.

"But Jan, I can only assume you've already had twenty five million pounds out of me, do you want all of my money?" I said and looked carefully at his expression, momentarily I glanced at Louise, James wriggled in my arms a little, he was very sleepy.

"Oh, you've guessed," he replied with something of a smile to his features, although his tone was tinged with a touch of anger, he went on, "a nice move, and you never had a clue," he paused, and I looked at Louise, she looked as bemused as I had felt when I first heard the news that I, or rather we, had a business venture in South Africa, Jan continued to reveal the secrets behind the setting up of the operation, "well that part was relatively easy, I managed to send a virus to your main computer and that slowed it down to the point of standstill, then, when your man Dennis sent for the man to repair the system, I had a little piece of software installed so that I could receive and send e-mails in Louise's name, good, don't you think? I also managed to download all of your business telephone numbers, including the one for the Manor," he paused to add one more comment, "I even phoned you on the night of the kidnap, I spoke to Sarah if I remember rightly." Now he had a degree of smugness in his voice.

"Oh, that was brilliant," I said, and to some degree it was a very clever move, and I had a small amount of admiration for him, but standing here in this cold room other parts of this conundrum began to challenge my mind, forcing me to ask even more questions, and they involved Delphine and the use of Stuart, or rather Carl.

"Jan did you have anything to do with the death of Delphine?" I bluntly asked, if I was going to be one of his victims then I thought I had the right to ask.

"Yes," he calmly replied, then went on, "well I managed to persuade her into turning, how you say 'queen's evidence', we made an agreement before the trial, she gave me the names of all of her contacts, plus some she didn't give to the police, and I said I would help her get out of the country as soon as she had a new identity," he paused and scratched his blond bearded chin, then continued, "but then I thought if she was to give in so easily to my requirements, then she couldn't be trusted, and I had to kill her, she put a nasty dent in the Range Rover, still we smashed that up when we drove it into the back of that old BMW."

"So you must have had quite a team working with you," I said in response to his free enlightenment.

"Yes, Carl and I go back a long way, and Hans is my cousin," Jan told Louise and I, then he had a question of his own, one that he seemed eager to answer himself, almost as soon as he'd asked it, "aren't you going to ask about the people in the car?" my startled expression prompted him to continue, "now, I'm no seafaring man, and it did take quite a bit of doing, Carl took care of getting the bodies off the boat, but then we had the trouble of disposing of the man, we only wanted the woman and the children." His words seemed to have an even colder ring to them now, and he had something to add, "we even used your harbour in Cornwall, nice move, yes." His reply prompted a question from me, and I was sure that the police would ask at some stage if we were to survive this incident.

"But what happened to the man?" I enquired recalling the article Louise and I had read in the paper when we were on the train returning from London.

"Oh, that was easy, we'd rented a house in the capital, the man, well he was of no use to us, and so we left him in the freezer." That statement brought back another news item that had recently been reported, Jan was more than ruthless, he'd stop at nothing to get his vengeance, then something else occurred to me, and that was the main reason for me finding out what had gone on, and it related to the damage to Louise's car.

"But it was the car that let you down," I said as I looked at the equally surprised Louise, I continued with a question, "would you mind if I lay James down?" for now he was fast asleep in my arms and I was beginning to tire.

"Yes, that will be OK," he replied, and continued, in something of a derogatory manner, "she," he said, looking at Louise, and went on, "said she needed some personal items from your house, the Manor, as you call it, so I sent Nick, he said he could remember all of the codes..." he was interrupted by Louise.

"I'd said that you would notice the car was damaged, Andrew," she said as if trying to stop Jan from stealing the moment.

"She's right," he paused, "you know, I've got to like her these past few days, a very smart woman, she told us about the fact that you had taken the car to the dealers for the repair work to be assessed, I thought that there may be a letter, and told Nick to look for it, but he came back saying he couldn't find anything."

"He didn't look in the right place," I somewhat smugly replied, that haughtiness was to be an error on my part; Jan didn't want to be made a fool of again, no matter how small his audience was, but I had some other piece of information to add, "he may not have found the letter, but he must have helped himself to Louise's jewellery." I finished and looked at Louise; her expression was one of complete surprise.

"He just made a mistake," was Jan's somewhat irritated reply, adding angrily, "alright! I shall deal with him with regard to stealing."

That was a bit rich coming from a man who would kill without asking any questions, and Nick could well answer for his actions with his life, if Jan's dealings so far were anything to go by, it prompted another comment from me.

"So Jan, how long have you been planning this take-over of my life?" I asked trying to defuse the situation slightly thinking a change of the immediate subject might help.

"Over a year, remember I told you I saw your photos in the newspaper in South Africa, first it was reported that you were dead, then once they found you, yours and the real Mrs Shaw's photographs were everywhere," he paused, I would say relieved that he could now tell the two of us about his master plan, he even seemed relaxed, and he went on, "I set about the operation straight away, had myself blown-up," he stopped again, now with a half smile to his face, that worried me slightly, "you know the South African police are even worse than the English, and as for your friend Alex Collins, well I passed him on the High Street the other day and he didn't even notice me…"

"That doesn't mean that he hadn't taken note Jan," I foolishly interrupted him, I say foolish because Jan started to make his way across the room to me, the knife in his right hand, there was no way I could tackle this man, he was enormous, but him coming towards me did leave the door open, making me think that if I could disable him, Louise and I might be able to grab James and make a dash for freedom, but then another thought crossed my mind, where were William and Peter? I looked at Louise, nodded my head, she picked up on my intentions, reading my thoughts perfectly, she moved towards James, and that was also closer to myself.

"You aren't going anywhere," Jan said as if we had told him of our joint intentions.

"What are you going to do?" I asked, just the slightest sound of fear in my voice, Louise took my hand as I spoke sensing my trepidation I have to say it didn't calm me.

"We are moving on tomorrow, I'll keep the three of you here until my friends arrive from Holland, then we can get you out of the country." He replied, very cool in his words and actions, for now he was within touching distance, and he had more words of caution for me, making me feel very unsettled, "don't try anything stupid Andrew, remember I could have killed you any time since you've been in the house." And he was correct, from the moment that I'd disturbed him in his bed, to this very moment I'd been in great danger, as had Louise and the children all the time they had been held.

"But you must realise that you can't get away, Sarah is well aware of where you are holding us," I said and added another cautionary warning, "it won't be long before the authorities are here."

"What you mean the wonderful British police force; they'll still be fumbling in the dark long after I've killed the three of you," Jan sharply responded, it was as he spoke that I, along with Louise and Jan heard a noise the other side of the door, a floor board creaked out on the landing, that'll be one of the boys I thought to myself, I looked at Louise, then back at Jan, the groan of the flooring unnerved him, I just caught sight of him from the corner of my eye as he leaped in my direction, he grabbed me by my throat with his left hand pulling my head back as he did so, and the knife came up to my windpipe, I couldn't move, all I could feel was the edge of the blade pressing against my larynx, it was difficult even to breath. Louise let out a shallow scream, I just managed to turn my eyes to look at her, and she looked petrified.

"I don't know what's going on Andrew, but if I have to, I'll kill you now." Jan said as I felt the blade dig in a little more, I didn't know what was going on, now Jan turned me so that we were able to look at the doorway, I half expected William or Peter to appear, but there seemed to be nothing but darkness, then very slowly a figure dressed in black came into view from the open frame side of the doorway. Not only was this person dressed in black, but their head was covered, as if they were wearing some form of gas-mask, but even more frightening was what they were holding in their hands.

The laser guide from the high velocity rifle was so bright it made my eyes smart, forcing me to squint; clearly it was aimed at Jan, as were the words that were to follow.

"Jan, let go of Andrew!" the individual said, every word clear, but at the same time muffled, spoken through the protective face mask, as I studied this person I could now see that it was someone from the Special Forces, full black combats, pockets stuffed with items of death along with no doubt many other pieces of necessary equipment. Jan's reaction was that of a man who meant business, his own business, he released the knife from my throat; the release gave me the opportunity to take a sharp intake of breath, but it wasn't going to give me the chance to resume normal breathing, I saw the blade glint in the light from the single bulb hanging from the ceiling, Jan spun the knife so that the point was now digging into my throat, he increased the pressure as the person the other side of the door spoke again.

"I told you to release him Jan." the stern voice demanded again, Jan began to press the tip of the blade even harder into the side of my throat next to my windpipe, now I could feel the steady warm flow of blood as it began to trickle down my neck, there didn't seem to be any pain, but to even try and turn my head would surely result in even more injury to myself, Jan's left arm tightened it's grip, at the same time lifting my head back. I could still see the marker light, a pin prick of red, ready to guide the bullet. Jan didn't fear the situation he now found himself in, and had a request of his own, and it was to be aimed at myself.

"Andrew, I want to know who killed Gary," he paused then added, "I'm sure you know." The knife dug in a little more, I couldn't speak, so I was unable to tell him, I shifted my eyesight in the direction of Louise, gently she shook her head from side to side, and mouthed 'no' I looked back at the person holding the weapon, the aim of the gun dropped, and to my total astonishment and no doubt Louise's, a hand went up to the protective mask, in a flash the person was revealed, along with more words.

"It was me!" and as I, and I'm sure Louise looked at her, Nana's long hair began to tumble down her back, her eyes were peering at Jan, the look intense, I could only imagine the surprised expression on Jan's face, and it wouldn't have lasted long, for suddenly there was another voice from the darkness.

"Now!" was all that was said, I looked towards where I thought the voice had come from, it was from floor level on the other side of the door, then I could see another fine red light.

The next thing I remember was closing my eyes as the flash of the rifle went off, I'm sure I felt the warmth of the bullet as it passed by my right cheek, then momentarily the knife dug in a little deeper, only for it to be withdrawn quickly, then the sensation of being sprayed on the back of my head with what seemed like warm water, but it wasn't!

There was a tremendous thud as Jan hit the floor, before he made contact Louise grabbed at my left arm and pulled me away from the falling entity, she didn't scream, no just the softest of sighs, then her other arm came around me, embracing me, holding me tight, then the voice that had uttered the death warning spoke again, almost in machine gun style, but it wasn't directed at Louise and myself.

"Nana, you're dismissed I'll see you after debriefing," both Louise and I watched as Nana picked up her weapon with one hand, her face mask still in the other, and she moved away into the darkness of the landing, then there were words for us.

"Mrs Shaw, are you and James alright?" the person asked, before she had a chance to answer an order was issued to me and instructions called to the other members of the team downstairs. "Andrew you need to see the medic, that injury looks nasty," I was told, and then this character turned and looked out onto the dark landing, "I'll need an ambulance for Louise and James." This individual called in the direction of the stairs.

No sooner had these commands been issued and we were I would say engulfed with other military staff, one person came into the room and picked up the sleeping James off the bed, then two more came to escort Louise and myself out of the bedroom, as we got to the door Louise and I looked back, instinctively we linked arms and held hands, Jan lay in a heap, blood still pouring from the deadly wound to his throat, the accuracy of the shoot was only evident by the instantaneousness of his death, as with Gary the bullet had entered just below the chin, exiting at the back of his neck, he had been in very close range and had taken the full power of the shot, make no mistake, Jan was dead.

"It's over Louise, Andrew," a slight pause, then more words, "let's get you out of here." And get us out they did.

Outside in the dull, dingy and very overgrown courtyard, I was having my lesion dressed, I watched as Louise and James were whisked away in an ambulance, it would be a few days before we would be reunited as a family, back at the Manor.

"Andrew, my boy," A familiar voice called from the entrance of the driveway, I looked around and could make out Alex as he appeared from the shadows, and as he came into full view I noticed his right hand was out in front of him, I took it as he got closer to me, then I had a question for him.

"Have you been here long?" I asked almost expecting his positive reply.

"Yes," he paused and for some reason clicked his fingers, then continued to speak, "we took a leaf out of yours, or rather Louise's captor's book, the team followed you and the boys," he paused again, then a change of tack, "smart lads you have there, I have to say Andrew, they handled themselves very well." No sooner had he said the words than William and Peter came out of the semi-darkness, but Alex had something else to add, "Louise and James will be fine, just need to have them checked over." I'm sure he was going to continue, but was distracted by the arrival of my sons.

"Are you all right dad?" William asked as his and Peter's arms went around me, as always concern in his voice.

"I've survived," I began to reply, just as a member of the team appeared from the house, he had some comments, and they were directed at us three family members.

"You did very well in there Andrew, and your sons were a great help," he said as he got closer to us, then he had another request, this time directed at Alex, "can I have a word with you please, Mr Collins?"

"Certainly," Alex began to reply, then to mine and no doubt the boys' surprise he went on, "anything you need to say can be said in front of these people."

"Well Mr Collins, we've cleared up things in there, Jan is dead, and we have the other two members of the gang ready to be handed over to the police," he paused and then added, "do you need us for anything else?"

"No, that will be fine captain," Alex replied, almost as soon as he'd spoken we noticed a police officer walk along the drive in our direction, within seconds more police cars arrived their blue lights flashing, but no sirens.

I looked at Alex, at the same time placed my right hand over the treated wound on my throat, my sons were stood either side of me, and Alex spoke again.

"I think I can relieve you of this," he paused and came a little closer, with his right hand he reached across to the lapel of my jacket, with flick of his wrist he removed something from behind it, then continued to speak, "we won't be needing this anymore," I thought he'd finished, but as he placed the item in his pocket he went on, "Andrew, we needed to be sure that Jan would confess, it wasn't expected that he would try and kill you."

I stood and looked somewhat amazed at Alex, the whole affair had been recorded, but then in my mind I should have expected something of this sort to have taken place, I was still digesting these thoughts when he issued another statement, and one myself and the boys would be in favour of.

"Right, we're finished here, let's go and have a drink." That was all that needed to be said, until a much later date.

Chapter Fifteen

Louise's doubt

As I pulled up outside of Chillingston Manor I noticed the hall lights were on, glancing at the clock in the car I could see it was only seven thirty, maybe someone had forgotten to turn them off, I thought to myself as I vacated the Porsche, but then the wind caught me, it was mid- September but it had a chill to it that reminded me of a winter's night, it made me shiver, just slightly, at the same time making me think I may be coming down with something.

I had spent the day in our office in Bristol, together with Dennis, our secretary, we had been sorting out the South African affair, trying to put this new acquisition into some sort of order, also discussing ways of preventing this sort of thing from happening again, that along with undoing some of the other less comfortable plans, the pre-arranged funerals, amongst other things, had taken up most of my day.

Louise hadn't ventured outside of Chillingston Manor since her return from hospital, and that had been less than a week ago, Susan our nanny had returned to our employment, and her help was greatly appreciated, not only by Louise, but also myself, the children were delighted to see her as well.

The traumatic experience over the past few weeks had taken Louise to the utmost breaking point, I had been warned that her mental and physical state could take a long time to return to normal, but day by day she seemed to be improving, her spirit returning to it's old ways, when I'd left her in the morning she was preparing the children in readiness for returning to school, again with the help of the nanny. But as I stood at the front doors of the Manor something didn't feel right. As I closed the oak door after entering the hall, I looked around me, I could see Sarah sat on the small settee to the left of the doorway, in her hands a book, very slowly she looked in my direction, her face appeared sullen and withdrawn, no expression to her features, yet she had been the one to recover from the nightmare the best, her strong nature, her ability to understand, restored to its former past very quickly, but now as she looked at me she seemed unhappy, that chill wind caught me again, but now I was inside of the house and the doors were closed.

"What is it Sarah darling?" I asked as I approached her, the book she had been reading fell to the floor.

"Mummy is in the study..." she paused and as I looked closer I could see Sarah had in fact been crying, still she continued, "she says that she needs to talk to you Andrew." Her tears started to flow.

I instantly bent down to comfort her, my arms wrapped around her, holding this precious child tight.

"I do want you to be my daddy!" she said through her tears, the way she spoke indicated to me that something was wrong, Louise had been badly affected by the events of a few weeks ago, still she hadn't recovered from me coming so near to death.

"I know you do darling," I replied as I comforted this little girl that I treated as my own, and I continued, "sometimes we have to wait for the things we want in life." But in my heart I knew that I was about to be hit by a bombshell, I also knew that I would have to be strong, and I would need to explain that reasoning to this child.

"I need you to be a very big girl," I paused so as to let Sarah know it wasn't just for me she needed to be resilient, "mummy is going to need your help, and she'll need you to be very strong!"

"I will be Andrew," Sarah replied and after blowing her nose she continued with just a few simple words, "I love you!"

"I know you do darling, and I love you," I told her as I stood in readiness to make my way to the study.

As I reached the door of the study I looked back, Sarah was again wiping her eyes, a half smile to her face, her eyes looked sore now, as if she had been crying for a considerable amount of time, I smiled myself, her response was to manage a little more of a smile.

"Hello," I said as I entered the study, Louise was sat at the table, she still looked tired and somewhat drawn.

"Andrew, please come to me!" her words spoken softy but very positively.

I did as she requested all the time knowing that the news she was going to impart to me wasn't going to be that easy to digest, why I knew this I couldn't understand, I just had a feeling that things hadn't recovered to the way it had been before she and the children had been abducted, and finally released, but that had also brought about the death of Jan Van-Elderman and a female accomplice, along with the arrest of three of his male partners in crime, they were now safely behind bars, awaiting trial.

"Darling," she began again her voice sounding as if it was full of remorse, she went on, "please come and sit next to me."

I did as she asked and pulled my chair close to her, Louise took my hand before she began to talk to me. "Andrew darling," I looked into her eyes as she spoke, nodding, indicating that she had my attention she continued, "these past few weeks have been probably some of the worst of my life," she paused and added "not that I'm in any way blaming you, but things have taken their toll on myself and of course the children." She stopped so as to retrieve a tissue from her cardigan sleeve; I felt once again that I knew what was to come, so I prompted her.

"Go on," I softly said as I took her hand and gently squeezed it, looking into her eyes once more I noticed they were beginning to glaze over slightly.

"I love you with all my heart," she said, at the same time she began to sob and lowered her head, then she went on, albeit her words were somewhat muffled, "this is one of the most difficult things I have ever had to ask you," lifting her head so as to look me in the eyes she went on, "I know you love me and of course the children, but I'm afraid I can't marry you!" she cut herself short with her own tears.

"I understand," I said very softly, and of course I did, I'd been half expecting this statement, Louise and the children had been through hell in the past few days to a week, her and of course myself, along with James escaping death only by the intervention of the Special Forces, but she beat me with her next statement.

"I'm going to live back at my old home, please forgive me Andrew!" she said as her tears began to flow, her sorrow engulfing her and beginning to affect me.

"I told you once, a long time ago," I paused so as to pick the correct words, not wishing to offend her, but so as to reassure her, to let her know that I would always be there for her, I went on, "I told you that I would forgive you for anything, I do know how difficult things have been, but this time you have explained your feelings to me, you don't need to move out, I'll go back to my old home."

"No, no you mustn't, this is your house," she replied wiping her weeping eyes at the same time.

"I bought this house for you, you and the children can stay as long as you want, I do understand," I said as once again I squeezed her tiny hand.

"But what will you do?" she asked.

"Oh, I've still got my place in Bristol, as you know," I began to reply, but then I thought, I've been cheated, not by Louise, no, by the circumstances we had found ourselves in, and my statement about buying the Manor for Louise and the children, it wasn't just for them, it was so we could live together as a family as we had been until the dreadful events of just over a few weeks ago, I didn't want Louise to move out, and I didn't want to resume my life alone, in 'my detached house in the suburbs of Bristol' I needed to put up a fight, show Louise that I was strong, prove that I loved the children as much as I loved her, I wasn't going to give up and let her leave me.

"Now, this may seem a little unkind," I began to say, after a moment's thought, I went on, "if we part now, then although this time you have spoken to me about your feelings, and I fully understand the way that you must feel, but it will be like leaving me the way you did in Cornwall those years ago," I stopped, I noticed I had her attention, she turned her head and wiped her eyes again, looking directly at me, I continued.

"I too, have been to hell my darling," I began to tell Louise, and taking her hands I squeezed them as I continued, "and this time I didn't give in, I never broke down wondering what I was to do with my life, I carried on, I kept the business running, albeit only after a fashion," I paused as I recalled the past week, "I did that for your memory, I'm not prepared to let you go without a fight, in the time that we have been together, we have been so good, we have achieved so much, and there is so much more for us to do, I will always be here for you," I stopped and felt as if I needed to add just one more request, "please don't give up now." I almost begged her.

"But how can we be sure that things will work?" Louise asked, it was evident by the question that she was still thinking in the way she had before the incident.

"We can't be sure about anything Louise," I began to reply, and not wishing to be too forceful, but at the same time not wishing to give in to her doubts, I continued, "but if we don't try then we'll never know, we have to do what we have done so far…" I paused again, looked her directly in the eyes, there was a spark of a challenge in them, something I had seen so many times before, so I continued, "we must look to the future, and keep on going!"

Chapter Sixteen

The Reward of Time

"Louise, that went very well, or should I say Mrs Jackson?" I heard a voice call as the owner of it approached Louise and I from behind us, and he had something to add to his comment, "I must say you look stunning in that dress," he paused again just to include, "and you don't look too bad my boy either."

"Alex!" Louise replied her voice full of excitement, along with being slightly startled, she spun round, and taking Alex's hands as she did so, then pulled him close for a kiss to each of his cheeks.

"I'm so glad you could come, Alex," I said as I took his right hand, his grip tight and the shake of his hand reminded me of our long-lasting friendship.

"I wouldn't have missed your wedding for the world," he replied, I noticed as he spoke that Alex seemed to be looking for someone, and I wasn't mistaken, he continued, "now, I know Sonia is here somewhere." But before he had a chance to say another word, both Louise and I were distracted by our adoptive father.

"My children, you don't know how happy we all are for you," Stavros said as he too joined us on the terrace at the rear of the Manor. His arms went out so as to embrace the two of us, once he had us in his grasp he whispered in our ears, "this is the way it should be. Yes?"

"Of course," we both replied, then Louise and I released our hold on Stavros; he went off with Alex, the two of them full of conversation, strangely enough both of them speaking Greek, Alex quite fluently. Together we looked around us, mentally noting all of the guests who had attended our wedding, I looked into Louise's eyes, the blueness seemed even more prominent now, the makeup as always applied to perfection, her smile engulfed me with happiness, the wedding veil she was wearing had been pulled back, and the ringlets of her auburn hair tumbled over her bare shoulders and rested upon the delicately scalloped top of her revealing cream wedding dress. 'This is what was meant to be!' I mentally told myself.

We mingled with our guests, taking compliments from all of them, the afternoon sun was warm, even though it was late September, there also seemed to be a heavy scent that lingered in the air, it was in fact the last of the summer roses, some of the larger flowers had begun to drop their petals, but the Manor seemed to be festooned with bouquets of flowers of all sorts and descriptions. On one of the largest lawns at the rear of the Manor a large marquee had been erected, and it was as Louise and I were heading in its direction that we were met by two other members of the new Jackson family.

Mummy, daddy!" both Sarah and James called as they ran towards us, together we jointly bent down and picked up the children, we each received a kiss from them.

"Sarah and James, why don't you both go and find your seats in the marquee," Louise suggested as she prepared to lower James back down to the ground, I did likewise.

"Yes, yes," James called as he ran off in the direction of the white marquee.

"Wait for me," Sarah said, as I placed her on the ground, but momentarily she stopped running and looked back at both her mother and I, but her gaze was upon myself, her smile spoke volumes. Once again I looked into Louise's eyes, but didn't have to say a word, then another voice, this time an adult's, and a female from our adoptive family.

"Louise, you look beautiful," Nana said as she came closer to us, her hands out in front of her in readiness to take my wife's.

"Thank you Nana," Louise replied as she began to embrace Nana, this was the first time we'd seen Nana since the night that had seen the three of us released from the very house Louise and the children had been held in, after releasing her hold on Louise, Nana turned her attention to me.

"Andrew," she began and after giving me a hug and a kiss on each of my cheeks she went on, "you look like the happiest man in the world." Her words hung in the air, for they were true, I was, in return I looked into her eyes, they seemed to say she was relaxed, more so than on any other occasion that I had seen her in, and it prompted a question from me.

"You're looking very well, aren't you?" I asked, as I still held her hands, her reply was aimed at both Louise and me.

"Yes I am," she began to say, and as she continued her smile broadened, "I've resigned my commission from the Special Services," Nana told the two of us.

"What do you have planned?" Louise asked as she once again took Nana's hands.

"I'm going to work in the family business; you know father will find plenty for me to do." Nana replied, this time with laughter in her voice, it sounded as if she was happy to be released from her former duties, and then she had a question for Louise and me, "and what have the two of you planned to do?"

"Oh," Louise began to reply, then looking into my eyes she continued, "Nana, we have the future to look forward to."

Andrew and Louise's future will continue to unfold.

Printed in the United Kingdom
by Lightning Source UK Ltd.
119211UK00001B/418